Praise for beloved romance author Betty Neels

"Neels is especially good at painting her scenes with choice words, and this adds to the charm of the story."
—USATODAY.com's *Happy Ever After* blog on *Tulips for Augusta*

"Betty Neels surpasses herself with an excellent story line, a hearty conflict and pleasing characters."
—*RT Book Reviews* on *The Right Kind of Girl*

"Once again Betty Neels delights readers with a sweet tale in which love conquers all."
—*RT Book Reviews* on *Fate Takes a Hand*

"One of the first Harlequin authors I remember reading. I was completely enthralled by the exotic locales...her books will always be some of my favorites to reread."
—*Goodreads* on *A Valentine for Daisy*

"I just love Betty Neels! If you like a good old-fashioned romance...you can't go wrong with this author."
—*Goodreads* on *Caroline's Waterloo*

BETTY NEELS

The Girl with Green Eyes
& The Moon for Lavinia

HARLEQUIN® SPECIAL RELEASE

ISBN-13: 978-1-335-04503-4

The Girl with Green Eyes & The Moon for Lavinia

CONTENTS

Romance readers around the world were sad to note the passing of **Betty Neels** in June 2001. Her career spanned thirty years, and she continued to write into her ninetieth year. To her millions of fans, Betty epitomized the romance writer, and yet she began writing almost by accident. She had retired from nursing, but her inquiring mind still sought stimulation. Her new career was born when she heard a lady in her local library bemoaning the lack of good romance novels. Betty's first book, *Sister Peters in Amsterdam*, was published in 1969, and she eventually completed 134 books. Her novels offer a reassuring warmth that was very much a part of her own personality. She was a wonderful writer, and she is greatly missed. Her spirit and genuine talent live on in all her stories.

THE GIRL WITH GREEN EYES

Chapter 1

The vast waiting room, despite the cheerful yellow paint on its Victorian walls, its bright posters and even a picture or two, its small counter for tea and coffee and the playthings all scattered around, was still a depressing place. It was also a noisy one, its benches filled by mothers, babies and toddlers awaiting their turn to be seen by the consultant paediatrician. From time to time a name would be called by a plump middle-aged sister and another small patient with an evidently anxious mother would be borne away while those who were waiting rearranged themselves hopefully.

The dark, wet day of early February was already dwindling into dusk, although it was barely four o'clock. The waiting room was damp and chilly despite the heating, and as the rows of patients gradually lessened it seemed to become even chillier.

Presently there was only one patient left, a small fair-haired toddler, asleep curled up in the arms of the girl who held her. A pretty girl with a tip-tilted nose, a gentle mouth and large green eyes. Her abundant pale brown hair was scraped back fiercely into a top knot and she looked tired. She watched the two registrars who had been dealing with the less urgent cases come from their offices and walk away, and thought longingly of her tea. If this specialist didn't get a move on, she reflected, the child she was holding would wake and demand hers.

A door opened and the sister came through. 'I'm sorry, dear, that you've had to wait for so long; Dr Thurloe got held up. He'll see you now.'

The girl got up and went past her into the room beyond, hesitating inside the door. The man sitting at the desk glanced up and got to his feet, a large man and tall, with fair hair heavily sprinkled with silver and the kind of good looks to make any woman look at him twice, with a commanding nose, a wide, firm mouth and heavily lidded eyes. He smiled at her now. 'Do sit down—' his voice was slow and deep '—I am so sorry that you've had to wait for such a long time.' He sat down again and picked up the notes and doctor's letter before him; halfway through he glanced up. 'You aren't this little girl's mother?'

She had been waiting and watching him, aware of a peculiar sensation in her insides.

'Me? Oh, no. I work at the orphanage. Miranda's not very easy, but I mostly look after her; she's a darling, but she does get—well, disturbed.'

He nodded and went on reading, and she stared at his downbent head. She had frequently wondered what it would be like to fall in love, but she had never imagined that it would be quite like this—and could one fall in love with someone at first glance? Heroines in romantic novels often did, but a romantic novel was one thing, real life was something quite different, or so she had always thought. He looked up and smiled at her and her heart turned over—perhaps after all real life wasn't all that different from a romantic novel. She smiled with delight and his eyebrows rose and his glance became questioning, but since she said nothing—she was too short of breath to do that—he sat back in his chair. 'Well, now, shall we see what can be done for Miranda, Miss…?'

'Lockitt—Lucy Lockitt.'

His firm mouth quivered. '"Lost her pocket, Kitty Fisher found it…"'

'Everyone says that,' she told him seriously.

'Tiresome for you, but I suppose we all learnt nursery rhymes when we were small.' With an abrupt change of manner he went on, 'If you could put her on to the couch, I'll take a look.'

Lucy laid the still sleeping child down and the doctor came over to the couch and stood looking down at her. 'I wonder why nothing was done when hydrocephalus was first diagnosed. I see in her notes that her skull was abnormally enlarged at birth. You don't happen to know why her notes are so sparse?'

'They've been lost—that is, Matron thinks so. You see, she was abandoned when she was a few weeks old, no one knows who her parents are; they left her with the landlady of the rooms they were living in. They left some money too, so I suppose she didn't bother to see a doctor—perhaps she didn't know that Miranda wasn't quite normal. A week or two ago the landlady had to go to hospital and Miranda was taken in by neighbours who thought that there was something wrong, so they brought her to the orphanage and Dr Watts arranged for you to see her.'

Dr Thurloe bent over the toddler, who woke then and burst into tears. 'Perhaps you could undress her?' he suggested. 'Would you like Sister or one of the nurses to help you?'

'Strange faces frighten her,' said Lucy matter-of-factly, 'and I can manage, thank you.'

He was very gentle, and when he had made his general examination he said in a quiet voice, 'Take her on your lap, will you? I need to examine her head.'

It took a considerable time and he had to sit very close. A pity, thought Lucy, that for all he cares I could be one of the hospital chairs. It occurred to her then that he was probably married, with children of his own; he wasn't young, but he wasn't old either—just right, in fact. She began to puzzle out ways and means of getting to know something about him, so deeply engrossed that he had to ask her twice if she was a nurse.

'Me? Oh, no. I just go each day from nine in the morning until five o'clock in the afternoon. I do odd jobs, feeding the babies and changing them and making up cots—that sort of thing.'

He was running a gentle hand over the distended

little skull. 'Was there no nurse to accompany Miranda here?'

'Well, no. You see, it's hard to get trained nurses in an orphanage—it's not very exciting, just routine. There's Matron and a deputy matron and three state enrolled nurses, and then four of us to help.'

The doctor already knew how many children there were; all the same, he asked that too.

'Between forty and fifty,' she replied, then added, 'I've been there for four years.'

He was measuring the small head with callipers, his large, well-tended hands feather-light. 'And you have never wished to train as a nurse?'

'Oh, yes, but it hasn't been possible.'

He said smoothly, 'The training does tie one down for several years. You understand what is wrong with Miranda?'

'Not precisely, only that there is too much fluid inside her skull.'

'It is a fairly rare condition—the several parts of the skull don't unite and the cerebrospinal fluid increases so that the child's head swells. There are sometimes mental symptoms, already apparent in Miranda. I should like her to be admitted here and insert a catheter in a ventricle which will drain off some of the surplus fluid.'

'Where to?'

'Possibly a pleural cavity via the jugular vein with a valve to prevent a flow-back.'

'It won't hurt her?' she asked urgently.

'No. It will need skilled attention when necessary, though.'

He straightened to his full height, towering over her. 'Will you set her to rights? I'll write to Dr Watts and arrange for her to be admitted as soon as possible.'

Lucy, arranging a nappy, just so, said thickly round the safety-pin between her teeth, 'You can cure her?'

'At least we can make life more comfortable for her. Take that pin out of your mouth, it could do a great deal of damage if you swallowed it. What transport do you have?' He glanced at the notes before him. 'Sparrow Street, isn't it? You came by ambulance?'

She shook her head, busy putting reluctant little arms into a woolly jacket. 'Taxi. I'm to get one to take us back.'

'My dear girl, it is now five o'clock and the rush hour, you might have to wait for some time. I'll arrange an ambulance,' he stretched out an arm to the telephone, 'or better still, I'll take you on my way home.'

'That's very kind of you,' said Lucy politely, 'but it wouldn't do at all, you know. For one thing the orphanage is in Willoughby Street and that's even more East End than here, and for another, I'm sure consultants don't make a habit of giving lifts to their patients—though perhaps you do if they're private...'

The doctor sat back in his chair and looked her

over. 'I am aware of where the orphanage is and I give lifts to anyone I wish to. You have a poor opinion of consultants... We are, I should suppose, exactly like anyone else.'

'Oh, I'm sure you are,' said Lucy kindly, 'only much cleverer, of course.'

His heavy eyelids lifted, revealing a pair of very blue eyes. 'A debatable point,' he observed. 'And now if you will go to the front entrance I will meet you there in a few minutes.'

He spoke quietly and she did as he asked, because she had to admit to herself that he had that kind of voice and she was tired. Miranda had gone to sleep again, but once she woke she would want her tea and her cot and would fly into a storm of tears; to be driven back to the orphanage would be a relief. She was already late and it would be another half-hour or more before she was home. She sat on a bench facing the door so that she would see the doctor when he came, but he came unnoticed from one of the corridors at the back of the entrance hall. He paused before he reached her and gave her a long look; she was pretty enough to warrant it, and seen in profile her nose had a most appealing tilt... He spoke as he reached her. 'The car's just outside. It will be better if you carry her, I think; it wouldn't do to wake her.'

They crossed the hall and he held the door for her and went ahead to open the door of the dark grey Rolls-Royce outside. She got in carefully and he fastened her safety-belt without disturbing the child, and then got in beside her, drove out of the forecourt and joined the stream of traffic in the street.

Lucy waited until they stopped in a traffic jam. 'You said Sparrow Street, and it is, of course, only the staff and children use the Willoughby Street entrance.'

'I see—and who uses the Sparrow Street door?' He edged the car forward a few yards and turned to look at her.

'Oh, the committee and visiting doctors and the governors—you know, important people.'

'I should have thought that in an orphanage the orphans were the important people.'

'They are. They're awfully well looked after.' She lapsed into silence as the big car slid smoothly ahead and presently stopped in Willoughby Street. The doctor got out and opened her door for her and she got out carefully. 'Thank you very much for the lift, it was kind of you.' She smiled up into his impassive face.

'I'm coming in with you, I want to see the matron. Where do you live?'

'Me? In Chelsea.'

'I pass it on my way home. I'll drop you off.'

'I'll be at least fifteen minutes…'

'So shall I.' They had gone inside and he indicated the row of chairs lined up against the wall of the small reception room. 'Wait here, will you?'

He nodded to the nurse who came to meet them and walked off, leaving Lucy to follow her to the back of the building where the toddlers had their cots and where the sister-in-charge was waiting. It was all of fifteen minutes by the time Lucy had explained everything, handed over the now wakeful Miranda, and said goodnight.

'Thanks for staying on over your time,' Sister said. 'I'll make it up to you some time.' She smiled nicely because Lucy was a good worker and didn't grumble at the unending task of keeping the toddlers clean and fed and happy. We could do with a few more like her, she thought, watching Lucy's slender shape disappearing down the corridor.

There was no sign of the doctor when Lucy got back to the reception-room. Perhaps she had been too long and he had gone without her, and she could hardly blame him for that—he had probably had a long and tiring day and was just as anxious to get home as she was. All the same, she sat down on one of the hard wooden chairs; there was no one else there, or she could have asked...

He came five minutes later, calm and unhurried, smiling genially, and accompanied by the matron. Lucy got to her feet and, rather to her surprise, was thanked for her afternoon's duties; it was by no means an uncommon thing for her to take children to hospital to be examined, and she was surprised that anyone had found it necessary to thank her. She muttered politely, added a goodnight and followed the doctor out to his car.

'Exactly where do you live?' he enquired of her as he settled himself beside her.

She mentioned a quiet road, one of those leading away from the Embankment, and added, 'It is very kind of you. I hope it's not taking you out of your way?'

'I live in Chiswick. Do you share a flat?' The question was casual.

'Me? No. I live with my parents…'

'Of course, now I remember—is your father an archaeologist, *the* Gregory Lockitt?' And when she murmured that he was, 'I met your parents some time ago at a dinner party. They were just back from the Andes.'

'That's right,' she agreed composedly, 'they travel a good deal.'

'But you prefer your orphanage?' His voice was kindly impersonal.

'Yes.' She didn't add to that, to explain that it was a job she had found for herself and taken on with the good humoured tolerance of her parents. She had been a disappointment to them, she knew that, although they had never actually said so; her elder sister, with a university degree and distinguished good looks, was personal assistant to the director of a City firm, and her younger sister, equally good-looking and chic with it, worked in one of the art galleries—moreover she was engaged to a young executive who was rising through his financial world with the ruthless intention of reaching the top before anyone else. Only Lucy, the middle sister and overshadowed by them both, had failed to be a success. There was no question but that they all loved her with an easygoing tolerance, but there was also no question that she had failed to live up to the family's high standards. She was capable, sensible and practical and not in the least clever, and despite her gentle prettiness she was a shy girl. At twenty-five, she knew that her mother was beginning to despair of her marrying.

Dr Thurloe stopped the car before her home and got out to open her door, and she thanked him again. Pauline and Imogen would have known exactly what to say to make him interested enough to suggest meeting again, but she had no idea; the only thought in her head was that she wasn't likely to see him again, and that almost broke her heart. She stared up into his face, learning it by heart, knowing that she would never forget it, still bemused by the surprise of loving him.

His quiet, 'A pleasure, enjoy your evening, Miss Lockitt,' brought her to her senses again, and she bade him a hasty goodnight and thumped the door knocker. He waited by his car until Alice, the housekeeper, opened the door, and then he got into the car and drove away. Perhaps I should have asked him in, reflected Lucy uneasily as she said hello to Alice.

'And who was that now?' asked Alice. 'Nice car too. Got yourself a young man, love?'

Lucy shook her head. 'Just a lift home. Is everyone in, Alice?'

'In the drawing-room and 'is nibs with them.' She gave Lucy a motherly pat. 'Best go and tidy yerself, love—they're having drinks...'

Lucy went slowly upstairs to her room, show-

ered and got into a wool dress, brushed out her hair
and did her face. She knew her mother disliked her
wearing the clothes she had worn at the orphanage,
even though they were covered by an overall and
a plastic apron. She didn't hurry—there would just
be time for a drink before dinner, and that meant
that she wouldn't have to listen to Cyril, Pauline's
fiancé, prosing about stocks and shares for too long.
She went slowly downstairs, wondering if her sister
really loved him or whether she was merely carried
away at the prospect of being the wife of a successful businessman, with a flat in town, a nice little
cottage in the country, two cars and enough money
to allow her to dress well and entertain lavishly. In
Lucy's opinion, none of these was a good reason
for marrying him.

She found them all sitting round the fire in the
drawing-room and her mother looked round to say,
'There you are, darling. Have the orphans been trying? You're so late...'

Lucy took the drink her father had handed her
and she sat down beside him. 'I took one of them
to be seen by a specialist at the City Royal; it took
rather a long time.' She didn't say any more, for they
weren't interested—although they always asked her
about her day, they didn't listen to her reply. And
indeed, she admitted to herself, it made dull listening compared with Pauline's witty accounts of
the people who had called in to the art gallery, and
Imogen's amusing little titbits of news about the
important people she met so often. She sipped her

sherry and listened to Cyril clearing his throat preparatory to addressing them. He never just talked, she thought; he either gave a potted lecture, or gave them his opinion about some matter with the air of a man who believed that no one else was clever enough to do so. She swallowed her sherry in a gulp and listened to his diatribe about the National Health Service. She didn't hear a word; she was thinking about Dr Thurloe.

Later, as Lucy said goodnight to her mother, that lady observed lightly, 'You were very quiet this evening, darling—quieter than usual. Is this little job of yours too much for you, do you suppose?'

Lucy wondered if her mother had any idea of what her little job entailed, but she didn't say so. 'Oh, no, Mother.' She spoke briskly. 'It's really easy...'

'Oh, good—it doesn't bore you?'

'Not in the least.' How could she ever explain to her mother that the orphans were never boring? Tiresome, infuriating, lovable and exhausting, but never boring. 'I only help around, you know.'

Her mother offered a cheek for a goodnight kiss. 'Well, as long as you're happy, darling. I do wish you could meet some nice man...'

But I have, thought Lucy, and a lot of good it's done me. She said, 'Goodnight, Mother dear...'

'Goodnight, Lucy. Don't forget we are all going to the Walters' for dinner tomorrow evening, so don't be late home, and wear something pretty.'

Lucy went to bed and forgot all about the dinner

party; she was going over, syllable by syllable, every word which Dr Thurloe had uttered.

She got home in good time the next evening. The day had been busy and she felt the worse for wear, so it was a relief to find that her sisters were in their rooms dressing and her parents were still out. She drank the tea Alice had just made, gobbled a slice of toast and went to her room to get ready for the party.

The Walters were old friends of her parents, recently retired from the diplomatic service, and Lucy and her sisters had known them since they were small girls; the friendship was close enough for frequent invitations to their dinner parties. Lucy burrowed through her wardrobe, deciding what to wear. She had a nice taste in dress, although she wasn't a slavish follower of fashion, and the green dress she finally hauled out was simple in style with a long, full skirt, long, tight sleeves and a round, low neckline. She ran a bath and then lay in it, daydreaming about Dr Thurloe, quite forgetting the time, so that she had to dress in a tearing hurry, brush out her hair and dash on powder and lipstick without much thought to her appearance. Everyone was in the hall waiting for her as she ran downstairs and her mother said tolerantly, 'Darling, you're wearing that green dress again. Surely it's time you had something new?'

'You'd better come with me on your next free day,' said Imogen. 'I know just the shop for you— there was a gorgeous pink suit in the window, just right for you.'

Lucy forbore from saying that she didn't look nice in pink, only if it were very pale pink like almond blossom. 'Sorry if I've kept you all waiting. Pauline, you and Imogen look stunning enough for the lot of us.'

Pauline patted her on the shoulder. 'You could look stunning too,' she pointed out, 'if you took the trouble.'

It was pointless to remind her sister that the orphans didn't mind whether she looked stunning or not. She followed her father out to the car and squashed into the back with her sisters.

The Walters gave rather grand dinner parties; they had many friends and they enjoyed entertaining. The Lockitts found that there were half a dozen guests already there, and Mrs Walter, welcoming them warmly, observed that there were only two more expected. 'That charming Mrs Seymour,' she observed, 'so handsome, and I dare say very lonely now that she is widowed, and I don't know if you've met—' She broke off, smiling towards the door, 'Here he is, anyway. William, how delightful that you could come! I was just saying...perhaps you know Mrs Lockitt?'

Imogen and Pauline had gone to speak to Mr Walter; only Lucy was with her mother. She watched Dr Thurloe, the very epitome of the well-dressed man, walk towards his hostess, her gentle mouth slightly open, her cheeks pinkening with surprise and delight. Here he was again, fallen as it were into her lap, and on his own too, so perhaps he wasn't married or even engaged.

He greeted his hostess, shook hands with Lucy's mother, and when Mrs Walter would have introduced Lucy he forestalled her with a pleasant, 'Oh, but we have already met—during working hours...'

He smiled down at Lucy, who beamed back at him, regretting at the same time that she had worn the green, by no means her prettiest dress. She regretted it even more as the door was opened again and Mrs Seymour swept in. A splendid blonde, exquisitely dressed and possessed of a haughty manner and good looks, she greeted Mrs Walter with a kiss on one cheek, bade Mrs Lockitt a charming good evening, smiled perfunctorily at Lucy, and turned to the doctor. 'William!' she exclaimed. 'I had no idea that you would be here—I had to take a taxi. If I'd known you could have picked me up.' She smiled sweetly and Lucy ground silent teeth. 'But you shall drive me home—you will, won't you?'

'Delighted, Fiona.'

She put a hand on his sleeve and said brightly, 'Oh, there is Tim Wetherby, I must speak to him—you know him, of course...'

It seemed that Dr Thurloe did. The pair of them strolled away and, since Mrs Walter had turned aside to talk to one of the guests, Lucy was left standing by her mother.

Mrs Lockitt gave her an exasperated glance. 'I want to talk to Mr Walter before we go into dinner.

Do exert yourself, darling, and go and chat with someone—it is such a pity that you're so shy...'

A remark which made Lucy even more so. But, obedient to her mother's suggestion, she joined a group of people she knew and made the kind of conversation expected of her while managing to keep an eye on the doctor. That he and Fiona Seymour knew each other well was obvious, but Lucy had already decided that Fiona was not at all the kind of girl he should marry—he needed a wife who would listen to him when he got back from his work each day, someone who liked children, someone who understood how tiresome they could be and how lovable and how ill... Lucy nodded her head gently, seeing herself as that wife. She wasn't sure how she was going to set about it, but she would find a way.

'You're not listening to a word I'm saying,' remarked the young man who had been talking for a few minutes. When she apologised, everyone laughed—nicely, because they liked her—and someone said, 'Lucy's thinking about her orphans.' Her job was a mild joke among those she knew and there was no malice in the remark. She smiled at the speaker as they went in to dinner.

She sat between the Walters' rather solemn elder son and a young man attached to one of the foreign embassies, now home on leave, and she dutifully lent an attentive ear first to Joe Walter's explaining rather prosily about computers, and then to her neighbour on the other side, who was anxious to tell her what a splendid time he was having in his far-flung post. With an effort she smiled and nodded and said all the right things, and the doctor, from the other side of the table, thought how restful she was and how very pretty. She looked different, of course, dressed in that green thing and with her hair curling almost to her shoulders. She was sensible too, when it came to handling small children. He bent a bland listening face towards his dinner companion while he allowed the nucleus of a plan to take shape in his sagacious mind.

People sat around talking after dinner, and beyond a few passing remarks Lucy saw nothing of the doctor. Since she left with her family before he did, she had no chance to see him and Fiona Seymour leave together. She told herself stoutly that it didn't matter one bit, one day she would marry him, only she couldn't leave it too long, for she was twenty-five already. She was immensely cheered by the thought that Mrs Seymour, however well made-up she was, couldn't disguise the fact that she wouldn't see thirty again.

Back home, all of them in the kitchen, drinking hot milk before bed, her mother remarked, 'What a nice man William Thurloe is, so good-looking and clever and not an ounce of conceit in him.'

'We had quite a long chat,' said Imogen complacently.

'But Fiona Seymour has got her talons into him,' said Pauline. She added, 'He must be all of thirty-five—she'd make him a very suitable wife.'

'Why?' asked Lucy quietly.

Both sisters turned to look at her. 'She's what is known as a handsome woman, intelligent and always well dressed,' they chorused kindly, 'and she would look just right sitting opposite him at the dinner table. A splendid hostess…'

'But she can't be a hostess all the time—I mean, what about looking after the children, and seeing that he gets a good meal when he comes home late, and gets enough sleep…?'

Her family stared at her. 'Why, Lucy,' said her mother, 'you sound,' she paused, seeking a word, 'concerned.'

Lucy finished her milk and put the mug in the sink. 'I just think that Fiona Seymour isn't the wife for him. He was the specialist I took Miranda to see yesterday; he likes children and somehow I don't think she does.' She kissed her mother and father, nodded goodnight to her sisters and went up to her room. She had said more than she had intended to say, which had been silly of her. The doctor's future was nothing to her; she would probably meet him from time to time at some mutual friend's house, and he would greet her politely and go and talk to someone else, forgetting her at once.

It was raining dismally when she left home the next morning. The orphanage looked bleaker than ever as she got off her bus, although once inside it became more cheerful with its bright painted walls and colourful curtains. All the same, the morning dragged with its unending round of chores. She was ministering to a vomiting four-year-old when Sister came to find her. 'Matron wants you in the office, Lucy. You'd better go at once.'

Lucy handed over the small child, took off her apron and made her way to the office on the first floor.

Matron was quite young and well liked. 'Sit down, Lucy,' she invited. 'I've a favour to ask of you. Miranda has to go off into hospital in two days' time. Dr Thurloe has asked if you would be allowed to go with her—it's important that she is not too disturbed, and she responds to you. You would have to live at the City Royal for a few days—she would be in a room off the children's ward and you would have a room next to hers. You would be relieved for meals and off-duty, but it might be necessary for you to get up at night if she is very disturbed.' She smiled. 'And we both know what that's like.'

'Yes, of course I'll go, Matron.' Lucy smiled too; she would see Dr Thurloe again after all, and perhaps she would be able to say something witty or clever and get his attention—not just polite attention, but real interest... 'When exactly are we to go?'

'Have a day off tomorrow and report here at eight o'clock on the day after. I believe Dr Thurloe means to insert the tube later in the day, and I must warn you that you may have a difficult night afterwards. It depends on her reactions as to how long she stays there. You'll be free?'

'Oh, yes, Matron—for as long as you want me to be with Miranda.'

'Good, that's settled, then. I won't keep you longer.'

The day had suddenly become perfect; the children were little angels, and the hours sped away in a flurry of tasks which were no longer boring or tiresome. Lucy changed nappies, cleaned up messes, fed protesting toddlers and dreamt of the days ahead, days in which she would become the object of admiration—Dr Thurloe's admiration—because of some skilful act on her part—saving Miranda's life by her quick thinking, rescuing a ward full of children by her bravery in case of fire...a bomb outrage...burst pipes...? It didn't really matter what it was as long as it caused him to notice her and then fall in love with her.

She finished at last and went off duty and home. It was still raining, and as she hurried from the bus-stop the steady downpour brought her to her usual senses. She laughed out loud so that an elderly couple passing looked at her with suspicion. 'No more useless daydreaming,' she told herself briskly. 'You're too old for that anyway, but that doesn't mean that you aren't going to marry him some day.'

It was nice to be home for a day. She pottered around, helping her mother with the flowers, sorting out the sheets of scrawled writing which flowed from her father's pen as he worked at the lengthy task of putting together notes for the book he intended to write. At the end of the day she packed the bag that she would need while she was in hospital, washed her hair, did her nails and inspected her pretty face for the first wrinkles and lines. She couldn't find any.

She and Miranda were fetched from the orphanage by ambulance the next morning, and to everyone's relief the child slept quietly in Lucy's arms. It wasn't until they were in the room where she was to stay that she woke and, sensing something out of the ordinary, began to cry.

Lucy sat down, still in her outdoor things, and set about the task of quieting Miranda. She had just succeeded when Dr Thurloe came in.

His 'Good morning, Lucy,' was quietly spoken and uttered with impersonal courtesy before he began giving the ward sister his instructions, and presently Miranda, still snivelling a bit, was given an injection and carried away to Theatre, leaving Lucy free to unpack her bag in the adjoining room and envelop her nicely curved person in the voluminous overall she had been told that she must wear. Her duties, as far as she could make out, were light enough—certainly no worse than they were at the orphanage. The only difference was that they would extend for a much longer period each day, and quite possibly each night too. A small price to pay for seeing the doctor from time to time, and on his own ground too.

She drank the coffee that one of the nurses brought her; the nurse was a nice girl, but faintly condescending. 'Why don't you train as a nurse?' she asked.

'I'm not clever,' observed Lucy, 'but I like children.' She might have added that she had no need to earn her living, and that her mother and father found it difficult to understand as well as faintly amusing that she should spend her days feeding babies and toddlers and everlastingly clearing up their mess, only it didn't enter her head to do so.

'How long will it take?' she wanted to know, and was treated to a lengthy description of exactly what Dr Thurloe was doing. She didn't understand half of it, but it was nice to talk about him. 'I thought he was a physician,' she ventured.

The nurse gave her an impatient look. 'Well, of course he is, but he does this kind of surgery too. He's a paediatrician—that's a children's doctor.'

Lucy, who had looked all that up in her father's study, already knew that, but she expressed suitable gratitude for being told, and when her companion said importantly that she must return to the ward and continue what sounded like a mountain of tasks, she thanked her for her company and settled herself down to wait. It wouldn't be too long.

Miranda returned ten minutes later, borne in the arms of Theatre Sister and already rousing from the anaesthetic. There was just time for her to be settled in Lucy's arms before she opened her eyes, and then her small mouth was ready to let out an enraged yell.

'Hello, love,' said Lucy in her gentle voice, and Miranda smiled instead.

'Lucy,' she mumbled contentedly, and closed her eyes and her mouth too.

Dr Thurloe, standing silently behind her, nodded his handsome head. He had been right to follow his instinctive wish to have Lucy there; it would make things a good deal easier on the ward, and besides, she looked nice sitting there in that oversized overall. He had a sudden jumble of ridiculous thoughts run through his clever head; nurseries, rice pudding, children shouting and laughing, and small figures pattering to and fro…

He frowned. Fiona had told him laughingly only the other day that he saw enough children without needing any of his own. 'What you need,' she had told him in her charming way, 'is a quiet house to come home to, pleasant evenings with friends, and someone to talk to at the end of the day without any interruptions.' She had made it sound very inviting and, because he had been very tired then, he had more or less agreed with her, but now he realised that that wasn't what he wanted. He wasn't sure what he did want, and anyway, it was hardly the time to worry about it now. He went to bend over his small patient, taking no notice of Lucy, then he gave more instructions to his ward sister and went away.

Chapter 2

The day seemed very long to Lucy. She was relieved for her meals, but Miranda, now fully awake, became restless towards the evening, and the only way to placate her was for Lucy to take her on her lap and murmur the moppet's favourite nursery rhymes over and over again in her gentle voice. But eventually Miranda slept, and Lucy was able to tuck her into her cot and, with a nurse in her place, go to the canteen for her supper. The nurses there were casually kind, showing her where to get her meal and where she might sit, but beyond a few smiles and hellos she was ignored while they discussed their work on the wards, their boyfriends and their lack of money. She ate her supper quickly and slipped away unnoticed, back to the austere little room where Miranda was. The ward sister was there conning the chart.

'Had your supper? Good. Night Sister will be along in about an hour. I think it might be a good idea if you had a bath and got ready for bed while I can spare a nurse to sit here—that will mean that if Miranda wakes up later and is difficult you'll be available. Go to bed once Sister's been—but you do know you may have to get up in the night? I don't think there will be a nurse to spare to attend the child; we're rather busy...'

She nodded and smiled and went away, and Lucy set about getting ready for bed in her own small room, leaving the door open in case Miranda woke and the nurse couldn't placate her.

But the child slept on and Lucy bathed in peace, brushed her hair, got into a dressing-gown and padded back to take the nurse's place.

The nurse yawned. 'She hasn't moved,' she told Lucy. 'She looks like a cherub, doesn't she? If it weren't for that outsized head...' She glanced at her watch. 'I'm off duty, thank heaven; it's been a long day. See you in the morning.'

Lucy sat down. Miranda was sleeping peacefully, and her pulse, which Lucy had been shown how to take and record, was exactly as it should be. Lucy studied the chart and started to read up the notes behind it. The small operation had been written up in red ink in an almost unreadable scrawl and initialled W.T., and she puzzled it out with patience. Dr Thurloe might be an excellent paediatrician, but his writing appeared to be appalling. She smiled, pleased that she knew something about him, and then she sat quietly thinking about him until Night Sister, a small brisk woman, came into the room. She checked the valve, looked at the chart and asked, 'You know what you're looking for, Miss Lockitt? Slow pulse, vomiting, headache—not that Miranda

will be able to tell you that... But if you're worried,
or even doubtful, ring the bell at once. I'll be back
later on, and if I can't come then my junior night sister will. I should go to bed if I were you. Her pulse
is steady and she's sleeping, but I depend on you to
see to her during the night.'

She went away as quietly as she had come, and
Lucy did as she had been told and got into the narrow, cold bed in the adjoining room. She got up
again in a few minutes and put on her dressing-
gown again, and then tucked her cold feet into its
cosy folds and rolled into a tight ball, and dozed off.

It was only a little after an hour later when Miranda's first restless whimpers woke her. She was
out of bed in a flash and bending over the cot. Miranda was awake and cross, but her pulse seemed
all right. Lucy picked her up carefully and sat down
with her on her lap, gave her a drink and began the
one-sided conversation which the toddler seemed
to enjoy. Miranda stopped grizzling and presently
began a conversation of her own, although when
Lucy stopped talking her small face creased into
infantile rage again, so that Lucy hurried into the
Three Bears, growling gently so that Miranda
chuckled. 'And Father Bear blew on his porridge
to cool it,' said Lucy, and blew, to stop and draw
a quick breath because Dr Thurloe had come silently into the room and was watching her. He had
someone with him, a pretty, dark girl in sister's
uniform, and it was to her that he spoke. 'You see,
Marian, how well my plan has worked? With Miss

Lucy Lockitt's co-operation we shall have Miranda greatly improved in no time.'

He nodded, smiling faintly at Lucy. 'Has she been very restless?'

'No, only for the last twenty minutes or so. She began to cry, but I think she'll settle down again.' She went red at his look; she had no business telling a specialist something he must already know for himself.

'I'll take a look while I'm here. Can you sit her up a little on your knee?'

He bent over her to examine Miranda and Lucy studied the top of his head; he had a lot of hair, a pleasing mixture of fairness and silver cut short by a master hand.

He straightened up and spoke to the sister. 'I think something to settle her, don't you, Marian?' He glanced at the thin gold watch on his wrist. 'Let's see, it's getting on for eleven o'clock.' He glanced at Lucy. 'A few hours of sleep will do you both good...' He took the chart from the sister's hand and wrote. 'That should see to it.' He walked to the door. 'Go to bed, Miss Lockitt; Sister will see that someone wakes you before Miranda rouses. Goodnight.'

He had gone before she could reply. She waited until the sister came back with an injection and then sat soothing Miranda until she dozed off and she was able to tuck her up in her cot once more. She wasn't very happy about going back to bed, but she was sure that Dr Thurloe wouldn't have suggested it if he hadn't been quite convinced that Miranda would sleep quietly for a few hours. So she got back into bed again and presently fell asleep, to wake very early in the morning and go and take a look at Miranda, who was still sleeping peacefully. Lucy took her pulse and was relieved to find that it was just what it was supposed to be. She was dressed and tied into her ample overall long before a nurse poked her head round the door. 'Oh, good, you're up already. I'll bring you a cup of tea just as soon as I've got the time. If she wakes can you wash her and pot her?'

Lucy nodded. 'Oh, yes. I expect I'll need clean sheets and another nightie.'

'In that cupboard in the corner, and there's a plastic bag where you can put the stuff that needs washing...'

The nurse's head disappeared to be replaced almost at once by the bulk of Dr Thurloe, immaculate and looking as though he had had ten hours' sleep. He was alone this time and his 'good morning' was friendly, so that Lucy regretted that she hadn't bothered to powder her nose or put on lipstick.

'Had a good night? You're up early.'

'So are you,' observed Lucy, and wished she hadn't said it; she must remember that they weren't at a dinner party but in hospital, where he was someone important and she wasn't of any account, especially in the bunchy garment she was wearing. And she felt worse because he didn't answer her, only bent over the cot.

'We'll have a look,' he said with impersonal politeness, and waited expectantly.

Lucy took down the cot side. She said in her sensible way, 'She's wet—I didn't like to change her until I'd seen Sister. Do you mind?'

The look he gave her was amused and kind too. 'I dare say I've dealt with more wet infants than you've had hot dinners. No, I don't mind! I'm glad she's had a good night. I don't intend to give her anything today though, and you may have your work cut out keeping her happy.'

He was halfway through his examination when the junior night sister came in. She said sharply, 'I'm sorry, sir, I didn't know you were here.' And then to Lucy. 'You should have rung the bell, Miss Lockitt.'

'My fault,' said the doctor smoothly, 'I told her not to bother.' Which was kind of him, reflected Lucy, listening to him giving the night sister his instructions. 'And I'll be in some time during the day. I think Miranda will be all right, but we must look out for mental disturbance—there may be a deficiency...'

Lucy couldn't understand everything he was saying, but she presumed it wasn't necessary; she was there to keep Miranda quiet and happy until she was deemed fit to return to the orphanage. She supposed that would be in a couple of days' time and that she would be told in due course. The doctor strolled to the door with the junior night sister beside him. As he went out of the room, he said over his shoulder, 'Thank you, Miss Lockitt. Be sure and let someone know if you're anxious about anything, never mind how trivial it may seem.'

Lucy watched him go, wishing with her whole heart that she were the junior night sister, not only on good terms with him, but able to understand what he was talking about and give the right answers. Not for the first time she wished fervently that she were clever and not just practical and sensible.

There was no point in dwelling upon that; Miranda was showing signs of waking up, and she fetched clean linen from the cupboard and ran warm water into the deep sink in one corner of the room. She was very grateful when the nurse brought her a cup of tea, for the next half-hour was busy and noisy: Miranda was fretful and screamed her annoyance at the top of her voice. It was nothing new, and Lucy did all that was necessary, talking in her quiet voice all the while. When the ward sister came on duty and poked her head round the door with a 'Can you cope alone?' Lucy said placidly that she was quite all right, thank you, and the head disappeared without another word. She had Miranda tucked up in bed by the time a nurse came with the toddler's breakfast. 'Ring when she's had it,' she advised, 'and someone will relieve you while you go to the canteen.' She grinned widely. 'I bet you're ready for breakfast. Did you get a cup of tea?'

'Yes, thanks. Are you very busy?'

The nurse cast her eyes to heaven. 'You can say that again.' She darted off leaving Lucy to feed Miranda, who, clean and smiling again, was more than pleased to eat her breakfast.

The same nurse came back when Lucy rang the bell. 'Half an hour,' she warned. 'We've got theatre cases this morning, so it's all go. Someone will bring you coffee, though, and you'll get time for your dinner. I don't know about off-duty, I expect that Sister will tell you.'

Lucy went thankfully to the canteen; she was hungry, and besides, it was nice to have a change of scene. She was fond of Miranda and she saw a lot of her at the orphanage, but all the same she could see that her patience and good temper were going to be tried for the next day or two.

There weren't many people in the canteen. She took her tray to a table by a window and ate with her eye on the clock, and then hurried back to find Miranda sobbing and refusing to be comforted. It took a little while to soothe her again, but presently the little girl fell asleep and Lucy was free to walk round the little room and look out of the window. The hospital forecourt was below. She watched Dr Thurloe's car come to a dignified halt in the consultants' car park, and then studied him as he got out and crossed to the hospital entrance. He walked fast, but halfway there he paused and looked up to the window where she stood. There wasn't time to draw back; she stood there while he looked and presently went on his way.

She was in the canteen having her dinner when he came to see Miranda again, and that evening it was his registrar who paid a visit. And in the morning when he came with the ward sister his good morning to Lucy was pleasant but cool, and anything he had to say was said to the sister.

Miranda was to go back to the orphanage the next day; everything was going well and the matron there would know how to deal with any emergency. Miranda was to come to his next out-patients' clinic in two weeks' time. He paused to thank Lucy as he went away. She was watching him go with regret; at the same time her wish to marry him had never been so strong.

She took Miranda back the next day without having seen him again. He was in the hospital; his car was parked in the forecourt. She glimpsed it as she got into the ambulance which was to take them to the orphanage. She consoled herself with the thought that she would be taking Miranda to his clinic in two weeks' time. In the meantime she might be able to think of something to attract his attention. A different hairstyle? Different make-up? A striking outfit? Better still, a few amusing, witty remarks... She occupied her brief ride trying to think of them.

It was early afternoon by the time she had handed over Miranda and reported to Matron, to be told that, since she had had almost no time off in the hospital, she was to go home at once and not return to the orphanage until the day following the next.

'You enjoyed your stay at the City Royal?'

'Yes, thank you. I didn't have anything much to

do, just keep Miranda happy and see that she ate her food. She was very good.'

'She slept?'

'Oh, quite a bit. I got up once or twice during the night, but she soon settled.'

'Good. Dr Thurloe seemed to be pleased with the arrangement; it took a good deal of the work off the nurses' shoulders. Miranda seems to need a lot of attention, but he thinks that she will improve fairly rapidly.'

'That's good. What will happen to her, Matron? I mean when she's older and more—more normal?'

'Well, as to that, we must wait and see. But she will always have a home here, you know. Now do go home, you must be tired.'

It was still early afternoon and only Alice was at home when Lucy let herself in. 'A nice cup of tea and a sandwich or two,' said Alice comfortably. 'You look tired, love. Your mother and father are at the Victoria and Albert. Someone there wanted your pa to see some old rocks that someone had sent from Africa—or was it the Andes? One of those foreign places, anyway. They won't be back until after tea. Imogen's working late and Pauline's going out to dinner with her fiancé.' She sniffed. 'You go and change and I'll have a snack for you in ten minutes.'

So Lucy went to her room, unpacked her few things, had a shower, washed her hair and wandered downstairs with her head in a towel and wearing a dressing-gown. Her mother wouldn't have approved, but since the house was empty except for herself and Alice she couldn't see that it mattered. Alice had made a pot of tea and cut a plateful of sandwiches and Lucy sat down at the kitchen table to eat them. Somehow she had missed dinner at the hospital, what with feeding Miranda and getting her ready to go back to the orphanage, and the nurses on the ward being in short supply since they took it in turns to go to the canteen. She lifted the edge of a sandwich and saw with satisfaction that it was generously filled with chopped egg and cress. She wolfed it down delicately, poured tea and invited Alice to have a cup.

'Not me, love,' said Alice. "Ad me lunch not an hour back. You eat that lot and have a nice rest before your mother and father come home.'

Lucy polished off the egg and cress and started on the ham. The kitchen was pleasantly warm and cheerful. It was a semi-basement room, for the house had been built at the turn of the century, a late Victorian gentleman's residence with ornate brickwork and large rooms. It had been Lucy's home for as long as she could remember, and although her mother often expressed a wish for a house in the country nothing ever came of it, for the Chelsea house was convenient for her father's headquarters; he still travelled widely, taking her mother with him, and when they were at home he worked for various museums and he lectured a good deal. Lucy, a sensible girl not given to wanting things she couldn't have, accepted her life cheerfully, aware that she didn't quite fit in with her family and that she was a source of mild disappointment, to her mother at least, even though she was loved. Until now she had been quite prepared to go on working at the orphanage with the hope at the back of her mind that one day she would meet a man who might want to marry her. So far she hadn't met anyone whom she would want to marry—that was, until she'd met Dr Thurloe. An event which incited her to do something about it. She took another sandwich and bit into it. Clothes, she thought, new clothes—she had plenty, but a few more might help—and then she might try and discover mutual friends—the Walters, of course, for a start, and there must be others. Her parents knew any number of people, it would be a process of elimination. But first the new clothes, so that if and when they met again she would be able to compete with Fiona Seymour.

The front door bell, one of a row of old-fashioned bells along the kitchen wall, jangled and Alice put down the plates that she was stacking.

'Postman?' asked Lucy. 'He's late...'

'I'd best go, I suppose,' grumbled Alice, and went out of the kitchen, shutting the door after her as she went up the short flight of stairs to the hall.

Lucy sat back, a second cup of tea in her hand. There was one sandwich left; it was a pity to leave it. She took it off the plate and bit into it. The door behind her opened and she said, 'Was it the postman?' and turned round as she took another bite.

Alice had returned, but not alone. Dr Thurloe

was with her, looking completely at home, elegant as always and smiling faintly.

'Gracious heavens!' Lucy spoke rather thickly because of the sandwich. 'Whatever are you doing here?' She put an agitated hand up to the towel. 'I've just washed my hair...'

She frowned heavily, all her plans knocked edge-ways; instead of sporting an elegant outfit and a tidy head of hair, here she was looking just about as awful as she possibly could. She turned the frown on Alice and the doctor spoke.

'Don't be annoyed with your housekeeper, I told her that you wouldn't mind. You don't, do you? After all, I've seen you in a dressing-gown at the hospital.' He sounded kind and friendly and the smile held charm.

Lucy smiled back. 'Is it something important? Would you like a cup of tea?'

'Indeed I would.'

Alice gave a small sound which might have been a chuckle and pulled out a chair. 'The kettle's on the boil,' she informed him, 'and I've as nice a bit of Madeira cake as you'll taste anywhere, though I says it that oughtn't, being me own baking.'

'I'm partial to Madeira cake, and what a pleasant kitchen you have.'

He sat down opposite Lucy and eyed the towel. 'Do you know, all the girls I know go to the hair-dresser every few days; I can't remember when I last saw a young woman washing her own hair.' He studied Lucy thoughtfully. 'Will it take long to dry?'

'No. It's almost dry now.' She poured him a cup of tea from the fresh pot Alice had put on the table. 'Is it something to do with Miranda? She's not ill...?'

'No, she's doing nicely. I wondered if we might go somewhere this evening and have dinner; I'm sure you would like to know the details of her treatment, and there really was no time at the City Royal to say much.'

He ate some cake and watched her, amused at her hesitation.

'Well,' said Lucy, 'Mother and Father—' She was interrupted by the telephone's ringing, and Alice answered it. She listened for a moment, said, 'Yes, ma'am' twice and then hung up. 'Yer ma and pa,' she told Lucy. 'They're going on to Professor Schinkel's house for dinner.' She added, 'I expect your ma thought you weren't home today.'

The look on Lucy's face made the doctor say quickly, 'Now isn't that providential, you will be free to dine with me, then?' That settled, he took another piece of cake and passed his cup for more tea. 'Your sisters won't mind?'

'They're both out too.'

'Then may I call for you this evening? Half-past seven or thereabouts? Somewhere fairly quiet? Boulestin's, perhaps?'

'That sounds very nice,' said Lucy, 'but only if you can spare the time...'

He looked as though he was going to laugh, but said gravely, 'As far as I know there will be no calls upon me until tomorrow morning at nine o'clock.'

He got to his feet. 'Until half-past seven. I look forward to it.'

Alice showed him out and came bustling back. 'There now, what a nice gentleman, to be sure. Take that towel off and I'll dry that hair. What will you wear?' She began to rub vigorously. 'That's a posh restaurant...'

'Those sandals I got from Rayne's and haven't worn—and I'll leave my hair loose...'

'All right as far as it goes, but what about a dress? Sandals and hair aren't enough.'

'That silver-grey satin, you know, the one with the calf-length skirt and the wide lace collar and cuffs.' Lucy's voice, muffled by the towel, sounded pleased. It was a very pretty dress, so simple that it stood out among other more striking dresses, and the colour, she hoped, would make her look the kind of girl a man might like to marry, elegant but demure.

She left a note for her mother on the hall table, collected an enormous cashmere shawl in which to wrap herself, and her little grey handbag, and eased her feet into her new sandals. They were a little tight, but they were exactly right with the dress, and what was a little discomfort compared with that?

The drawing-room looked charming with its soft lighting and the fire blazing. She arranged herself to the very best advantage on a small balloon-backed chair covered in old-rose velvet, and waited for the doorbell.

The doctor was punctual to the minute, and Alice ushered him into the drawing-room, opening the door wide so that he had a splendid view of Lucy, delightfully pretty and at great pains to appear cool.

She got up as he came in, and said in her best hostess voice, 'Oh, hello again. Would you like a drink before we go?'

'Hello, Lucy. How very elegant you look, and so punctual. Almost unheard of and quite refreshing.'

She should have stayed in her room until he had arrived and kept him waiting, she thought crossly.

She said haughtily, 'I have to be punctual at the orphanage, it's a habit.'

'Of course. I booked a table for half-past eight; I thought we might have a drink there first. Shall we go?'

She smiled at him, she couldn't help herself; he looked so large and handsome and so assured. She wondered fleetingly if he ever lost his temper.

Southampton Street wasn't all that far away, but the evening traffic was heavy and slow moving, so it was well past eight o'clock by the time Lucy found herself at a table opposite the doctor. It was a good table too, she noticed, and he was known at the restaurant. Perhaps he took Fiona Seymour there... She wasn't going to waste thought about that; here she was doing exactly what she had dreamed of doing, being alone with the doctor, nicely dressed, looking her best, and hopefully at her best when it came to conversation.

It was a pity that no witty remarks filled her head; indeed, it was regrettably empty. She sipped her sherry and thankfully bowed her head over the menu card. She was hungry and he said encouragingly, 'I dare say you had a very scanty lunch. I know I did. How about the terrine of leeks with prawns for a start, and if you like fish the red mullet is delicious—or roast pigeon?'

'I couldn't eat a pigeon,' said Lucy. 'I feed them on the way to work every morning.' She was reassured by his understanding smile. 'I'd like the red mullet.'

It wasn't until these delicacies had been eaten, followed by a dessert of puff pastry, piled with a hazelnut mousse and topped with caramel, that the doctor switched smoothly from the gentle conversation, calculated to put his companion at her ease, to the more serious subject of Miranda.

'Do you see a great deal of her at the orphanage?' he wanted to know.

'Well, yes—not all the time, of course, but always each morning, bathing her and getting her to walk and that kind of thing.'

He nodded. 'You do realise that she will probably be backward—mentally retarded—but this operation that I have just done should give her a better chance. One would wish to do everything possible for her—she is such a pretty child, and if only she had been brought to our attention while she was still a baby we could have done so much more.'

'But isn't there any special treatment? She talks a little, you know, and although she's a bit wobbly when she's walking she does try.'

'I'm going to ask you to do all you can to help her,

and don't be discouraged when she makes almost no progress. I know you have a busy day and there are other children to look after, but Matron tells me that Miranda responds to you much more willingly than to anyone else there. Once the shunt gets into its stride we should take advantage of that and get her little brain stimulated. If all goes well, she will be able to have therapy in a few months.'

'Do you get many children like her?' Lucy poured their coffee and reflected sadly that the only reason he had asked her out was to make sure that she was going to stay at the orphanage and look after Miranda. Well, he need not have gone to so much trouble, wasting an evening with her when he might have been spending it with the glamorous Fiona. It was quite obvious that she had no effect upon him whatsoever, despite the fashionable grey dress and the new sandals. He probably hadn't even noticed them.

He guided their talk into more general channels, and when Lucy said that she should really go back home since she was on duty in the morning he made no objection, but signed the bill and followed her out of the restaurant without one word of persuasion to remain a little longer—or even go dancing. But that was a good thing, for the sandals were pinching horribly and walking in them, even the short distance across the pavement to the car, was crippling.

'Take them off,' suggested the doctor as he started the car.

'Oh, you don't mind? They're killing me. How did you know?'

'You have quite a fierce frown which, I hasten to add, I am quite sure no one noticed except me.' He gave her a sideways glance. 'They're quite delightful though; indeed, the rest of you looks delightful too, Lucy. Demure and malleable. Are you demure and malleable, I wonder?'

She curled her toes in blissful comfort. 'No, I don't think so; I don't think girls are demure nowadays, are they? Anyway, I'm too old…and I'm not sure what malleable means—I thought it meant squashy.'

He gave a growl of laughter. 'I meant it to mean tender and gentle, and I wasn't aware that age had anything to do with being demure. How old are you?'

'Twenty-five. You're thirty-five, aren't you?'

'We might say that we have reached the ages of discretion.'

They had reached her home and he stopped the car gently, and when she made to get out he put out a restraining hand. 'No, wait.'

He got out and opened her door. 'You'll never cram your feet back into those sandals.' He picked them up and put them into her hand, scooped her out of the seat and carried her to the front door, where he asked her to ring the doorbell.

Alice answered the door, flung it wide to allow him to get inside, and said urgently, 'You're not hurt, love? What's the matter? You've not 'ad too much to drink?'

The doctor set Lucy gently on her feet. 'Her feet,'

he explained. 'Her sandals were pinching and, of course, once they were off they wouldn't go on again.'

Alice laughed. 'And there's me wondering what on earth had happened. Your mother and father are in the drawing-room—you go too, sir. I'll bring in a nice tray of coffee and you, Miss Lucy, go and fetch a pair of slippers this minute—what your ma will say I don't know.'

'It could happen to anyone,' remarked the doctor mildly, and gave Alice a nice smile so that she said,

'Oh, well, perhaps it won't be noticed,' and went ahead of them to open the drawing-room door.

Lucy's mother and father were sitting one on each side of the hearth, her father immersed in a sheaf of papers and her mother turning the pages of Harper's. They both looked up as she and the doctor went in and her father got to his feet. 'There you are, Lucy and Dr Thurloe, how delightful. Come and sit down for half an hour—Lucy, run and ask Alice to bring coffee—'

'She's making it now, Father!' Lucy bent to kiss her mother's cheek and wished she knew how to raise a graceful hand to greet the doctor in the same manner as that lady. 'Delighted to see you, Dr Thurloe. Do sit down. How very kind of you to take Lucy out to dinner.'

'It was Lucy who was kind, Mrs Lockitt,' he replied, and paused, smiling, as Mrs Lockitt caught sight of Lucy's feet.

'Lucy, your shoes? You've never lost them? You aren't hurt?'

'They pinched, Mother, so I took them off.'

'Well, really!' She turned her attention to her guest. 'I have been hoping that we might meet again, you really must dine one evening before we go to Turkey.'

'Kayseri, the ancient Hittite city—there have been some interesting finds lately, and I've been asked to go out there and take a look,' Mr Lockitt joined in. 'We plan to fly out at the end of next week.'

The doctor, much to Lucy's surprise, expressed his delight at the invitation, and Mrs Lockitt said, 'Lucy, dear, run up to my room and get my engagement book, will you? And do get some slippers at the same time.'

Lucy went slowly upstairs. Her parents, whom she loved dearly, were spoiling everything for her; she showed up in a bad light in her own home with no chance to outshine their intellectual talk—she had hardly scintillated over dinner, and since she had entered the drawing-room she had uttered only a few words. She found the book, poked her feet into a pair of frivolous satin mules and went back downstairs. Alice had brought in the coffee and Lucy's father had fetched the brandy; the doctor looked as though he had settled for the rest of the evening, already making knowledgeable replies to her father's observations—apparently he knew all about the iron-smelting activities of the Hittites, and he knew too where they had lived in Asia Minor.

As she handed round the coffee-cups he asked pleasantly, 'And do you not wish to go too, Lucy?'

Her mother answered for her. 'Lucy's a home-bird, aren't you, darling? This nice little job at the orphanage gives her something to do while we're away.' Mrs Lockitt went on, not meaning to be unkind, 'She hasn't had a training for anything. Of course, Imogen is the clever one in the family—she has this super job in the City—and Pauline works in an art gallery, and will marry at the end of this year. They are all such capable girls, and of course we have an excellent housekeeper.'

The doctor murmured politely and presently got up to go, and Mr Lockitt went to the door with him, so that beyond a stiff little speech of thanks Lucy had no chance to speak. There was nothing to say anyway. Her fragile dream, never more than a fantasy, had been blown away; he would think of her, if he ever did, as a dull girl not worth a second thought.

She bade her parents goodnight and went to bed. Surprisingly, just before she slept, she decided that somehow or other she would get to know him better, and eventually, in the teeth of all hazards, marry him.

Chapter 3

For several days Lucy had no chance to put her resolve into practice. There was no sign of Dr Thurloe at the orphanage and it had been silly of her to imagine that she might see him there. Very occasionally in an emergency he might be asked to go there, but there weren't any emergencies; Miranda was doing very nicely—she was even showing small signs of improvement.

Mr and Mrs Lockitt, their journey arranged, had decided to invite a few friends as well as the doctor for dinner. 'Rather short notice,' observed Mrs Lockitt, 'but they're all old friends and we don't stand on ceremony. I suppose I'll have to ask Mrs Seymour...'

'Why?' asked Lucy, making a list of guests.

'Well, dear, she and Dr Thurloe seem to be old friends. Indeed, people seem to think that he might marry her—heaven knows she's trying hard enough—but I don't think he will. Mind you're home in good time and wear something pretty the grey, perhaps?'

'Definitely not the grey. There's that rust velvet I've hardly worn...'

'Ah, yes. I'd forgotten that.' Her mother eyed her a little anxiously. 'You'll be all right while we're away, darling? It is such a pity that Pauline will be in Edinburgh at that Art Exhibition for the next two weeks, and Imogen tells me that she has to accompany Sir George to Brussels—for a few weeks, she thought. But you'll have Alice.'

'We'll be quite all right, Mother, dear. How long will you and Father be away?'

'Well, we aren't sure, it rather depends on what they've found. I must say Turkey is as good a place as anywhere to go at this time of year. Of course, we'll phone you, darling.' She smiled at Lucy. 'Now, how many have we got? I thought we might have soup first, so comforting in this weather, and then that nice fish salad and lamb chops with new potatoes and green peas—I'm sure I saw some in Harrods. They cost the earth, but they are so delicious. I'll get Alice to make some of those chocolate mousses, the ones with orange, and cheese of course.'

Lucy wrote it all down tidily and handed it to her mother.

'Thank you, dear; you're such a good daughter. I'm so glad you're not a career girl, Lucy. You must find a nice man and marry him, darling.'

Lucy said, 'Yes, Mother.' It wasn't much use telling her that she had found the nice man. The chances of marrying him, were, as far as she could see, negligible.

She dressed for the dinner party with extra care and viewed the result with some satisfaction. The rust velvet suited her—it made her eyes greener than they were, gave her hair a reflected glint, and showed off her pretty figure to its best advantage. She was even more satisfied when she joined her family in the drawing-room and her mother exclaimed, 'Why, Lucy, how delightfully that dress suits you! There's the doorbell—I've put you between Cyril and Mr Walter...'

So much for her painstaking dressing; Cyril didn't like her, she was beneath his notice, and Mr Walter was a dear, but hard of hearing. She joined in greeting the first of the guests, moving from one to the other, watching the door out of the corner of her eye. Dr Thurloe came in alone and she beamed at him across the room; at least he hadn't given Fiona Seymour a lift. He smiled back as he greeted his hostess and host, but made no effort to join Lucy—probably because she was trapped in a corner by old Mrs Winchell, who was eighty if she was a day and invited to everyone's table although no one really knew why. Lucy, listening with patience to that lady's opinion of the government, watched Fiona Seymour, the last to arrive, make her entrance. She really was good-looking and this evening she was wearing a starkly plain black dress, superbly cut, with her hair swept into an elaborate arrangement of curls on top of her head. She had half a dozen golden bangles on one arm and several gold chains hung around her slender neck. Old Mrs Winchell turned to look at her, using her old-fashioned *lorgnettes* to do so. 'She's wasting her time,' she muttered, and then in her usual rather loud voice, went on to reorganise the government.

The talk at dinner was largely concerned with the forthcoming trip to Turkey, so that Lucy was kept busy listening first to Cyril carrying on about the rate of exchange, and then repeating to Mr Walter what people were saying at the table that he hadn't quite heard. The doctor, to her disappointment, was at the other end of the rectangular table, with Imogen on one side and Fiona on the other.

It wasn't until Mrs Winchell got up to go, forming the spearhead of departure, that he came over to Lucy. His casual observation that Miranda was making splendid progress, and his equally casual hope that she wasn't working too hard, doused any hopes she had had of conversation of a more personal nature. She answered him woodenly and bade him a brisk goodnight.

'Goodnight, Lucy. Your eyes are very green; is that because you are bottling up bad temper? I wish I had the opportunity to find out.'

He smiled with charm and turned at the touch of Mrs Seymour's hand. She smiled too, a quite different smile from the doctor's. 'Such a nice evening, Lucy. William, will you take me home? It's only a little out of your way.'

A dismal failure, decided Lucy, reviewing her

evening as she got into bed. Fiona Seymour out-
shone her in both looks and clothes. What was the
use of just being pretty—there were hundreds of
pretty girls around, but not many Fionas with their
dramatic clothes and subtle make-up. Lucy sighed
heavily and went to sleep to wake the next morning filled with resolve to outshine Mrs Seymour.
She had no idea how to do it, but something would
turn up.

Which it did, but hardly in a manner which she
expected or welcomed.

Her parents left for their journey to Turkey two
days later, followed first by Pauline, who flew to
Edinburgh, and then, the following day, by Imogen, the picture of smart efficiency, on her way to
Brussels with Sir George. They had both taken an
affectionate farewell of Lucy, reiterating all the instructions she had had from her mother and leaving their telephone numbers prominently displayed.
The house seemed empty after they had gone, even
though Alice and the daily cleaner had seized the
opportunity to clean the place from attic to cellar.
Lucy was glad to go to bed early and got up be-
times in the morning, remembering in delight that
today she would take Miranda to the City Royal to
have a check-up by Dr Thurloe. It would be all very
professional, of course, but at least Fiona Seymour
wouldn't be there. The clinic was in the early afternoon; the morning seemed endless, and she had a
few bad moments when Matron couldn't make up
her mind if Lucy should go with Miranda or stay

and take care of the smallest orphans whose usual
attendant had gone off sick.

Lucy, her face serene, her insides churning,
waited for Matron to decide and heaved a sigh of
relief when that lady's eye fell on Miranda working herself into a rage with the girl who was to take
Lucy's place.

'Oh, well—you'd better take her; they'll want her
as quiet as possible at the clinic and she's getting
quite worked up. I'll take over the little ones while
you're gone. Perhaps you won't be away too long.'

So Lucy and Miranda set off together in the ambulance which had been sent for them and arrived
to find the waiting room packed to the doors. Outpatients Sister saw her come in and hurried towards
her. 'There's been a delay,' she explained. 'Dr Thurloe was called away urgently just as we were starting. Luckily you're in the first ten to be seen so it
shouldn't be too long. He'll be here any minute now.'

She bustled away and Lucy sat down, Miranda
on her lap, grizzling a little because she didn't much
like her surroundings. Lucy wasn't too keen either; it
was a chilly blustery day, but the waiting room was
warm and stuffy—moreover, the babies and toddlers were noisy. That was only to be expected, of
course, but after a time it was wearing to the nerves.

It was an hour before it was Miranda's turn and
by then she was cross and whining fretfully despite
Lucy's efforts to keep her amused. Lucy carried the
child into the consulting-room, sat her down on the
couch and wished the doctor a good afternoon. He

said in a detached manner, 'Ah, yes—Miranda. I'll
need to look at that shunt.' He looked tired and she
wasn't surprised—having to deal with dozens of
babies and children, all ill, all in various stages of
peevishness, he must be exhausted. He smiled down
at her suddenly. 'Hello, Lucy,' and then, 'You look
hot and a bit cross…'

'I'm not cross, but I am hot. Half London's sitting out there.'

He nodded. 'If you'll get Miranda's things off
I'll take a look.'

It was at that moment that there was a loud bang
and all the lights went out. And moments later a
voice screamed, 'It's a bomb!'

Lucy, her arms around Miranda, stayed where she
was. The doctor's voice, swearing richly, sounded
reassuring, and a moment later he had turned on a
torch from his desk. 'Don't move,' he commanded.
That was something she wouldn't have dreamed of
doing anyway. 'The auxiliary lighting will come on
in a moment. I'm going into the waiting room…'

The din was fearful, children screaming and
frantic mothers calling and, from the sound of it,
everyone rushing to and fro. She could hear the doctor's voice, raised in a commanding bellow, urging
everyone to stay where they were, but panic had
taken over, for the lights hadn't gone on again and
those people nearest the doors had rushed to open
them, but, because of the press people behind them,
had been unable to do so. The clinic was situated
in the semi-basement of the hospital and depended

entirely upon artificial light, and the dark was Sty-
gian. The door to the waiting room burst wide open
suddenly, and in no time at all the consulting-room
was crammed with people all talking at once while
the children screamed and the babies cried. Lucy
got a good grip of Miranda and took a deep breath.

'Be quiet and stand still!' she shouted urgently,
and, although her lung power was nothing like as
powerful as the doctor's, some of the women around
her heard and there was a moment's lull broken only
by infant wailing. 'Keep still,' she urged, 'you're
safe enough as long as you don't rush around. Do
think of the children. The doors will be opened as
soon as possible and there's auxiliary lighting.'

There was a good deal of murmuring and shuf-
fling, but at least the frantic pushing and shoving
seemed to have stopped. She could hear the noise in
the waiting room and see the flash of torches here
and there; she heard the outpatients sister's calm
voice and then the doctor, his voice loud and calm,
as he made his way towards the doors.

She didn't understand why there was such a long
delay before the doors were at last opened and at the
same time the lights came on again. And then she
knew the reason. They had been blocked by the first
to reach them who, unable to get the doors open,
had been pushed or knocked down by those behind
them, frantic to get out too.

The waiting room was in a state of chaos. Sister and the two nurses who were with her were
already shepherding some of the mothers and chil-

dren towards the further end of the waiting room and out through the door there, while the doctor, head and shoulders above everyone else, waded to and fro through the mass of people, carrying children and babies away from the doors. Sister came back and poked her head round the consulting-room door. 'Everyone all right here? Come with me to the casualty-room and we'll check all of you and the children.'

There were a great many people in the waiting room now, moving the injured away, comforting frightened children and still shaken mothers. Lucy picked up Miranda and followed the trickle of women leaving the clinic. There was no reason to stay—obviously the doctor had his hands full with his helpers, handing back babies and children to their mothers, and checking that no one was seriously hurt. In Casualty a nurse was taking names, making sure that no one was hurt or badly shocked, and cups of tea were being offered. To Casualty Sister's enquiry as to whether she felt able to get back on her own she answered calmly that she felt fine, but it would be best if she got Miranda back to her familiar surroundings as quickly as possible.

'You look a sensible girl,' said Sister. 'As soon as we can, we'll let Matron at the Orphanage know when you can come back.' She glanced at a restless Miranda. 'Dr Thurloe did a shunt, didn't he? I expect he'll want to see her just as soon as we've cleared up the mess in his clinic.'

There were a great many women sitting about,

drinking their tea and mulling over the excitement of the afternoon; quite a few were to be taken home by ambulance, declaring that they were shaken too badly to get on a bus. Lucy made her way to Casualty entrance and into the street. It had begun to rain, a gentle drizzle which seeped through her clothes as she waited for a taxi. Miranda was well wrapped up, but she hated the rain and began to wail; it was a relief when a taxi stopped and Lucy got thankfully inside. Miranda was heavy, and she had to be held carefully.

By the time they reached the orphanage, the toddler was crying in earnest. Lucy paid off the cabby and hurried inside, to get Miranda's clothes off as quickly as possible and ask one of the girls to tell Matron that they were back.

That excellent woman took in the situation at a glance; she sent someone for a cup of tea for Lucy, milk and biscuits for Miranda and then got her into her cot, all the while listening to Lucy's succinct account of the mishap at the clinic.

'It would have been all right if someone hadn't shouted that it was a bomb,' she remarked, 'but of course it was very dark, and once everyone started rushing around it was impossible to stop them, although Dr Thurloe was roaring like a bull. He had a torch, and so, after a few minutes, did Sister, but the clinic is a big place and it was packed with people.'

'And where were you?'

'In the consulting-room. Dr Thurloe was just about to examine Miranda. Sister said she'd let you know when we could go back to the clinic. It was hopeless to go on this afternoon, I think there were several people hurt when they got knocked over by the doors.'

'A mercy it was no worse. You're wet, aren't you. Get that coat off and drink your tea. When you've fed Miranda, go home, Lucy; it's already almost five and you'll be here as usual in the morning?'

'Of course, Matron. I'm sorry that Miranda has to go again, she does so hate it there. I think the noise bothers her.'

'Poor scrap. But we can't ask someone as important as Dr Thurloe to visit here unless it is an emergency or something serious. I might ask one of his registrars to come and see her here.'

It was six o'clock by the time Lucy got home; Miranda hadn't wanted her tea and it had taken time and patience to coax her to eat it, and when Lucy had at last left the orphanage it was to find the bus queue stretching for yards along the pavement. When she finally got home Alice came into the hall at the sound of her key in the lock.

'I was getting worried!' she exclaimed. 'You not home at your usual time—what 'appened?' She bustled Lucy out of her coat. 'All wet you are, and looking as though you could do with a nice cuppa.'

'Oh, Alice, I could. Look, I'll have a shower and change and then come down to the kitchen and tell you all about it.'

'Righto, love. And put on something warm, you look fair chilled.'

Fifteen minutes later Lucy went back downstairs. She had left her hair loose and had got into a thick green sweater and a tweed skirt and she felt a good deal better; a pot of tea would be heaven. She hoped that Alice had been inspired to make a plate of toast too. She opened the kitchen door and danced in. 'Alice…'

Alice was standing there all right, but so was Dr Thurloe, standing at the window, watching the feet of passers-by. He turned round as she came to a surprised standstill. 'Forgive me for calling at this unreasonable hour, but I wanted to make sure that you were all right after this afternoon's incident. I've seen Miranda, she's none the worse luckily. But you? You were all right? You stayed where you were?'

She nodded, trying to think of something to say and failing.

'Good. It could have been much worse, but several women were injured in the rush to get away and I've had to admit four children.' He frowned and she saw that he was concerned as well as angry.

'Well, you did all you could,' she said. 'I could hear you telling everyone to stay in their seats. It must have been impossible to move out there.'

'Yes. Panic is a terrifying thing. I'll make sure that it never happens again. It just so happened that the auxiliary lighting was being checked when the electricity failed—some workman accidentally severed a cable.'

'Oh, was that the bang?' She had a strong wish to put her arms around him and tell him that it wasn't his fault, although she knew that he felt responsible. 'Alice has made a pot of tea; would you like to have a cup?'

She didn't wait for him to answer, but fetched the teapot and put it on the tray Alice had set on the table, collected another cup and saucer from the dresser and sat down at the table while Alice fetched the plate of buttered toast from the Aga.

'Now just you sit there and enjoy your tea,' she advised them, 'while I pop up to your ma and pa's room and get it straight now it's been cleaned.'

She took herself off, looking pleased because the doctor had held the kitchen door open for her. He closed it and came and sat down opposite Lucy.

'I'm sorry you had to find your own way back,' he told her. 'Sister told me that you were going to get a taxi. Did you have to wait?'

'Only for a few minutes.' She passed the toast. 'Do you like strawberry jam? Alice made a batch last summer...' She got up and fetched a pot from a cupboard, found a spoon and handed it across the table.

They sat munching their toast thickly layered with jam, and since there was nothing more to be said about the afternoon's happening their talk became rather more personal. At least, the questions the doctor put were gently probing—so gentle, in fact, that Lucy didn't realise how much she was telling him. For her part she would have dearly loved to have asked him any number of questions, but she wasn't quite sure how to begin. He wasn't married, that she did know, but what about Mrs Seymour? And did he have any family? A mother, a father, brothers and sisters? She wished very much that she had either of her sisters' self-assurance; she was sure that neither of them would have hesitated.

The doctor's quiet voice broke into her thoughts. 'How long will your mother and father be away?' he wanted to know.

'It depends—if it's something interesting I expect they'll be in Turkey for some time.'

'You are not lonely? Your mother told me that your sisters would be away too.'

'Only for a week or two and I've got Alice, and Mrs Simpkins.'

His raised eyebrows looked a question. 'Our cat. She's in the airing cupboard with her kittens. I suppose you wouldn't like a kitten? Not yet, of course, they're only a few weeks old.'

'Er—my housekeeper has an elderly cat, a matron christened, through some misunderstanding—Thomas—I dare say she might like to have a kitten to mother.'

Here was a crumb of information, better than nothing. 'Have you a dog?'

'Two—Robinson and Friday; they like cats.'

Lucy laughed. 'Did you rescue them off a desert island?'

'In a manner of speaking.'

She poured more tea for them both. 'What breed are they?'

'A little bit of everything, I should imagine. You like dogs?'

She nodded. 'Only we can't have one; Father and Mother are away so much, Imogen and Pauline wouldn't have the time and I'm away all day too.'

'You don't need to work,' he suggested gently.

'Oh, no, but you see I had to do something; I can't just be at home. I—I found this job, I wanted to do something useful; I'm not clever, you see, and it's difficult to have a career unless you're clever.'

'Would you not rather prefer to marry?' He spoke with a casual kindness which prompted her to reply.

'Oh, yes, only no one's asked me.'

'You surprise me, you must know that you're a pretty girl.'

It didn't enter her head to be coy about it. 'Yes, but I'm hopelessly shy and I don't know how to talk to people,' and at his quizzical look, 'I can talk to you.'

He agreed gravely, although there was a gleam of amusement in his eyes. 'I have enjoyed our talk and my tea.' He glanced at his watch. 'I am only sorry that I have to go out this evening.' He watched Lucy's face assume a wooden politeness. Her eyes, he noted with interest, were quite blindingly green.

'Of course. It was kind of you to call. I hope no one was badly hurt this afternoon.'

'Fortunately not. I should like to get my hands on whoever it was who screamed that it was a bomb.' He smiled at her. 'Thank you for my tea, Lucy.'

She went to the door with him and ushered him

out, and then closed and locked the door behind him. Well, she knew a little more about him now, but she doubted very much if she would learn much more; she wasn't likely to see anything of him other than at the clinic, and probably Miranda wouldn't need to go again for a long time. Still, there was today's visit to be repeated, although he wouldn't have anything to say to her other than instructions to convey to Matron.

She cleared away the tea things and Alice came back into the kitchen, 'Gorn, 'as 'e?' Mostly she was careful with her aitches, but if she was disturbed or excited she tended to overlook them. 'I could 'ave cooked him a bite of supper.'

'He's going out,' Lucy was putting away the jam, 'he told me so.'

'That Mrs Seymour—the cook at number eleven knows 'er maid, says she's after 'im, ringing 'im up at all hours and cross as two sticks when 'e's not there or got something better to do. The cook told me that this maid says 'e's wedded to his work.'

Which cheered Lucy up. One could always marry a man who was wedded to his work, but not one who was wedded to Mrs Seymour. But all she said was, 'Well, he's old enough to make up his own mind, I expect, don't you, Alice?' She said it in a bright voice and Alice took a look at her.

'Men,' said Alice, and clashed a saucepan. Lucy had always been her favourite and she had seen the look on her face.

Lucy took Miranda to the clinic two days later, and

although Dr Thurloe was there there was no chance to speak to him other than to say good afternoon and goodbye. This time there was a staff nurse there who whisked Miranda away for X-ray and tests and Lucy was politely asked to wait in the waiting room. Miranda bawled to high heaven and on their return from X-ray and Path Lab the staff nurse handed her over to Lucy with a sigh of relief. 'My goodness, she's a handful,' she observed. 'Dr Thurloe wants her back in the consulting-room for a minute or two. Will you take her?'

Miranda, scarlet with rage still, sniffed and snuffled into Lucy's shoulder, but she had stopped screaming and allowed the doctor to examine her head; she even, after a few doubtful glances, smiled at him. He smiled back. Lucy was the only one with an expressionless face, all at sea as to how to behave. One minute the man was eating toast and jam in her mother's kitchen and the next sitting there as remote and grave as a judge. She played safe and said nothing at all.

He finished at length and by then the staff nurse was back again.

'I'll write to her doctor and let your matron have a copy. Miranda's progress is very satisfactory—I'll see her again in a month.' His smile was pleasant and detached. 'Goodbye, Lucy.'

She bade him goodbye gravely, then took Miranda back to the orphanage and got on with the rest of her day's chores. She was disappointed, but she wasn't downcast; she wasn't sure how to beat Fiona

Seymour at her own game, but she was certain that she would get a chance to try. She was quite sure that she would make the doctor a splendid wife, just as she was equally certain that Mrs Seymour would ruin his life for him. When she got home she got out the telephone directory and found his name and address—a house by the river in Chiswick, one of a row of charming old houses with a frontage on the Thames and as peaceful a spot as one could wish for in London. She put the directory away thoughtfully; he had two dogs who would have to be exercised. Richmond Park or Kew Gardens seemed the obvious places for their run; he could take the car easily enough to either—probably not every day, she decided, as there must be quiet streets near his home where he could walk them, but at the weekends...

Her sisters were still away, and Alice saw nothing strange in her announcement that she intended having a nice long walk on the following Sunday. 'And I'll not be back for lunch, Alice,' said Lucy. 'If it's a nice day I could do with some fresh air.'

'I'll cut you a sandwich or two,' said Alice. 'Where are you going?'

'Richmond Park or Kew, I haven't quite decided.'

'Well, be careful, love, don't go off down any lonely paths. I'm not sure that your ma...'

'I'll stay on the main walks, Alice, and I'll be back for tea. Do you want to go to church?'

'In the evening—I'll have something in the Aga for supper.'

Lucy considered it a good omen that Sunday

morning should be all sunshine and blue sky even though it was cooled by a March wind. She wore a new mohair sweater in shades of green to match her eyes, and a pleated tweed skirt; she tucked a scarf into her shoulder-bag, and, after a splendid breakfast and five minutes' listening to Alice's warnings, caught a bus. The temptation to take a look at the doctor's house was great, but she prudently skirted it and started to walk in the direction of Richmond Park. It had been silly of her to get off the bus on an impulse; now she got on the bus once more and stayed on it until it reached the park. She had had to choose between Richmond Park and Kew Gardens, she couldn't be in both at once, and really, she reflected as she began to walk along one of the main paths, she was being childish in the extreme. She had had no idea that falling in love with someone entailed so much planning and plotting which was more than likely to no avail.

There were quite a few people about, most of them with dogs and children, and presently she began to enjoy herself. It was lovely to get away from the streets and houses, and as she walked she allowed herself to daydream: a cottage in the country, just for weekends, where the children could play while she and William gardened and Robinson and Friday roamed at will. A large garden, she decided, full of old-fashioned flowers and roses and with a large lawn where they could all play croquet. She wandered off the path a little way and sat down on a fallen log. Four children, she decided, two of each;

the boys would be doctors like their father, and the girls would be pretty and clever besides. And she and William would grow old gracefully together—he would make a handsome old man... She looked up and saw him coming towards her, still fortunately on the right side of forty and certainly handsome.

He had the dogs with him; a small, nondescript dog with a curly black coat and a whiskered face who pranced up to her and offered his head for a scratch, and a shaggy-coated dog with a mild face and a splendid tail. He was very large and lumbered up to Lucy and bent over her, breathing gently on her face, and she pulled at his ear, glad of something to do for the doctor was standing in front of her, looking down at her heightened colour with amused interest.

'You're a long way from home,' he said, and he sat down beside her.

Lucy tickled the little dog under his chin and didn't look at him. 'It is a lovely day, and it's nice to get away from the streets and just walk.'

He nodded gravely. 'I come here every Sunday when I'm free, and quite often after breakfast for half an hour, once the mornings get light. Until then we have to make do with a brisk walk round the houses.'

'They're nice dogs,' said Lucy, 'and quite different.' She ventured a look at her companion. 'Did you get them from Battersea Dogs' Home?'

'No—Robinson,' he patted the large dog on a massive shoulder, 'was thrown out of a car on a

motorway, and I happened to be behind the car, and
Friday was left in a cardboard box on the side of
the road.'

'How utterly beastly,' said Lucy fiercely, 'to do
a thing like that to an animal! I'm so glad you were
there—they must love you…'

'They're great company and they make a nice
change from babies and children.'

Lucy turned an alarmed face to his. 'Oh, don't
you like babies and children?'

'Of course I do—I wouldn't be a paediatrician
otherwise, would I?'

'Oh, sorry, that was a silly thing to say.'

They sat in silence for a minute or so while she
searched wildly for something to talk about; if he
didn't speak soon she would have to get up and go.
He stayed silent and she sighed soundlessly with her
disappointment and said cheerfully, 'Well, I must
be on my way. It was nice meeting Robinson and
Friday.' She started to get up and put on her scarf,
and he put out a large gentle hand and pulled her
down again.

'Do you have to be home for lunch? Or are you
meeting someone?' he asked.

She shook her head.

'Good, then let us walk together for a while. I've
got the car here, I'll drive you back when you want
to go.' He glanced at his watch. 'It's still early—if
we take the next path on the left there's a coffee
kiosk there.'

She didn't have to worry about something to talk

about, for the doctor embarked on a meandering
conversation which needed few or no replies. By
the time they had reached the kiosk she felt quite at
ease, so much so that she only just stopped herself
in time from telling him that she had come to the
park in the hope of meeting him. She went bright
red at the thought and the doctor eyed her thoughtfully, wondering why she looked quite guilty—it
could be nothing he had said, he was sure of that;
maybe something she had thought…?

He said easily, 'You'll have coffee? Why not sit
down on that bench and I'll fetch it?'

He wandered off, and the dogs, having drunk
noisily from the bowl of water by the kiosk, followed him. They all came back very shortly, and,
while the dogs roamed round close by, they drank
their coffee. It was strong and hot and Lucy remembered the sandwiches Alice had packed for her. She
offered them shyly and the doctor took one. 'Your
Alice must be a treasure. My housekeeper runs her
pretty close, she's a marvellous cook too. Which re-
minds me that I have to be back for lunch. Sunday
is the one day when I can have people in.'

The bright morning lost its brightness; Lucy
brushed crumbs from her gentle mouth and stood
up at once. 'I don't suppose you have a great deal of
time to meet your friends,' she remarked politely.
'Do you go to the hospital every day?'

'No, twice a week for rounds and outpatients,
and one theatre day; I have a private practice too,
and I'm consultant to a couple of other hospitals.'

'My goodness, don't you ever get tired?'

'Oh, yes.' They were walking back to the main path once more, and presently they were at the gates and a few minutes later in the Rolls with the dogs sitting primly side by side in the back.

The journey back was far too short, but not so short that Lucy didn't have the leisure to reflect upon the abject failure of her plan. She had been most successful in meeting him, true enough, but it had got her nowhere.

Chapter 4

D_r Thurloe got out when they reached Lucy's home, went with her to the door and waited until she had gone inside, declining her invitation to come in for a drink, as she had known he would. She hadn't wanted to ask him, but the social niceties had to be observed. She remarked suitably on the pleasures of her morning walk with him and bade him a cheerful goodbye. In the hall, with the closed door between them, she allowed herself a long sigh. All the same she had got to know him just a little more. The dogs, his housekeeper, guests for Sunday lunch—Fiona, of course. Lucy ground her perfect teeth at the thought.

'Back already?' asked Alice, putting her head round the kitchen door. She added innocently, 'Thought I heard a car.'

'You did. I met Dr Thurloe walking his dogs and he drove me back.'

'Didn't he want to come in for coffee?' asked Alice sharply.

'Well, no. We had some in Richmond Park, he's got guests for lunch.'

Alice made a tutting sound. 'A day in the fresh

air would do 'im more good, and 'im stuck in that 'ospital all day and every day.'

'He doesn't go every day, he goes to other hospitals too, and he's got a private practice.'

'That's as may be, 'e still 'as to treat patients, doesn't 'e? From morn till night, and know what 'e's talking about too, and stuck in a stuffy room with germs being breathed all over 'im.'

She sounded indignant and Lucy made haste to agree; put like that the doctor merited sympathy, although he hadn't looked as though he needed it that morning.

'He needs a good wife,' declared Alice, and Lucy agreed in a suitably casual voice.

Pauline came back from Edinburgh the following week and was instantly plunged into a new exhibition at the art gallery. 'There's a preview on Saturday,' she told Lucy, and, 'You're coming, I've got a ticket for you.'

'I'm working on Saturday morning...'

'I know that, darling—the exhibition is in the afternoon. Three o'clock, you'll have plenty time to dress up and get a taxi. I'll be on the look-out for you. Have you bought any new clothes yet?'

'No. I've not had any time.'

'It'll be a dressy affair. Wear that brown velvet suit and the Liberty scarf I gave you for Christmas.'

'All right. What kind of pictures are they?'

'Abstract.'

'Lines and squiggles? I can't make head or tail of them.'

'You don't have to, Lucy—just look interested.'
Pauline added fretfully, 'I thought you'd enjoy it.'

'Oh, but I shall,' said Lucy quickly, 'and it's sweet
of you to ask me.'

And indeed it was nice to have something to look
forward to. The orphans took up most of her days,
but there was still too much time in which to brood
over Dr Thurloe. An outing might take him off her
mind for a time at least. There had been no sign of
him, but then why should there be? Miranda was settling down nicely and her next appointment wasn't
for more than two weeks, and since Lucy's parents
were away there was no chance of meeting him at
a dinner party or drinks, for no one had thought of
inviting her without them.

Her mother telephoned when she could, but, as
she pointed out, they were sometimes in remote
regions and it wasn't always possible. Her father
was full of enthusiasm, she had told Lucy; excava-
tions had uncovered evidence of a high level of ci-
vilisation more than a thousand years B.C. There
was no question of their coming home for several
weeks at least. Each time she asked, 'You're well,
darling?' and without waiting for an answer said,
'That's good. Have a lovely time—I'll ring again
when I can.'

A letter would have been more satisfactory, but
Lucy doubted if her mother would have much chance
to sit down and write letters, and she had been told
not to write to them since they were moving around
so much.

Lucy had plenty of time to dress on Saturday.
The exhibition opened at three o'clock, and if she
took a taxi she didn't need to leave home until ten
minutes or so before the hour; she didn't want to be
the first to arrive. Pauline wasn't coming home for
lunch—she would have it with Cyril, who would,
of course, be at the exhibition too. Lucy got into the
brown suit and draped the lovely scarf around her
shoulders and, after due thought, got into her high-
heeled brown kid shoes. She wasn't keen on very
high heels, but they looked good with the suit.

There were a great many people already at the art
gallery when she got there. She took the proffered
brochure and edged her way through the first room
looking for Pauline. It was Cyril whom she first met.

He greeted her pompously. 'Pauline is besieged
by eager viewers,' he told her. 'As soon as she is free
she will come to you. I would offer my services in
accompanying you round the room, but I feel that I
should be at Pauline's side.'

'Oh, of course you must,' said Lucy, and wondered how her sister could bear him—and for the
rest of her life too. 'I'll start in this room and work
my way round. Do let Pauline know and tell her not
to worry about me.'

Cyril allowed himself to be swept away by a
surge of people and she was left to examine the
exhibits.

She went slowly from one to the other, glad that
she had the brochure, for otherwise she wouldn't
have had the least idea what they were. She had

reached the end of one wall and was starting on the next, contemplating a large square upon which were a series of lines and a few dots, when Dr Thurloe's voice, low in her ear, murmured, 'Noughts and crosses? Enlighten me, Lucy.'

She chuckled. 'It's called *Maiden with a Bucket...*'

'You astound me, any one of your orphans could do better.'

'Why are you—that is, do you like modern art?'

'No.' He sounded quite certain about it. 'Your sister very kindly sent me a ticket and it seemed churlish not to come. Do people actually buy these—these scribbles?'

'Oh, yes. Pauline works here, you know; she says it's a most successful and lucrative aspect of the art world.'

'Do you like them?' He looked down at her and thought how pretty she looked in that brown thing and how ridiculous her high heels were.

'Me? No. I have tried to because of Pauline, but I do agree with you that the orphans are better at it. There's Pauline...'

He took her arm and edged through the crowd and Pauline saw them and came towards them. 'There you are—and Dr Thurloe. How nice! This is so successful. Lucy, I won't be home until late, you'll be all right? I'll go back with Cyril to his flat and have dinner with him.'

She smiled widely at them and turned away with a quick 'bye' as an Arab in flowing robes accosted her.

Lucy had gone very pink. It was tiresome that

Pauline had said all that about coming home late and would she be all right with the doctor standing there. Now he might possibly feel that the least he could do was to see her back home. She said hurriedly, 'Well, I'll say goodbye. I came to please Pauline, and I must fly or I'll be late.' She offered a hand. 'It was nice meeting you again.'

He took her hand, but he didn't let it go. They stood, rather close together because of the squash of people around them, and looked at each other while Lucy's pink face went slowly red and the doctor's firm mouth widened into a smile.

He said quietly, 'Could we escape together, do you think? And will you believe me when I say that I intended asking you to come to tea with me as soon as I saw you here?'

'I'd love a cup of tea,' said Lucy, quite sure that he would never lie to her or anyone else unless it was absolutely necessary.

He took her arm again and they went out of the gallery into the quiet Saturday afternoon street. 'The car's just round the corner.'

When they were in the car she asked, 'Where are we going?'

'My home—Mrs Trump likes the idea of having a kitten, but you ought to have a word with her first, don't you think?'

Which sounded reasonable enough.

She gave a small sigh of pleasure as she got out of the car in front of his house. It was the end one of the row of old houses in Strand on the Green, fac-

ing the river, pristine in its black and white paint-
work and shining brass door knocker. There was a
tub filled with snowdrops at each side of the door,
and staring at them from the window alongside the
door was a very large, fat tabby cat.

'Thomas,' said Lucy happily, and when the doctor
opened his door she went past him into the narrow,
high-ceilinged hall. It smelled of beeswax polish
and very faintly of lavender, and the console-table
and the two chairs on either side of it gleamed with
years of loving care. There was a fine silk rug on
the floor, and the walls were panelled waist-high,
and above that the paper was a soft dim crimson.

The doctor caught her by the arm and swept her
through a half-open door into a room with windows facing the water, and the cat got down off
the window-seat and came to meet them, taking no
notice of the sudden rush and barking of Robinson
and Friday. She offered an elderly head for a rub
and then, with her tail high and ignoring the dogs,
went out of the room, to return almost at once,
walking sedately beside Mrs Trump, a short, stout
lady with a round happy face, a great deal of grey
hair held up by combs and skewered ruthlessly by
hairpins, and faded blue eyes.

'There you are, sir. And you'd like a nice cup
of tea, I've no doubt.' She beamed at Lucy. 'And
the young lady too. Trump will have the tea-tray
in five minutes. Would the young lady like to refresh herself?'

Lucy was conscious of the doctor's amused

glance. She darted a smile at him and said sedately, 'If I might leave my jacket somewhere?'

'This is Miss Lockitt, Mrs Trump; will you see that she has all she wants?'

'Indeed, I will, sir. You come with me, miss, if you would be so kind.'

Lucy followed her into the hall and then into a cloakroom under the gracefully curving staircase at the back of the hall. As she took off her jacket and set the very pale pink blouse to rights, she reflected that her mother wasn't the only one who could boast about her faithful housekeeper—obviously Mrs Trump was a treasure, and presumably the Trump she had mentioned would be her husband and another treasure.

The cloakroom, though small, contained everything needed for the maintainance of cleanliness and beauty. She left it, as Mrs Trump had put it, feeling refreshed and ready to make the most of an hour's company with the doctor.

He got up as she went back into the drawing-room, and the dogs got up with him and fussed around while he settled her in a chair by the fire. She looked around the room, warm, charmingly furnished and softly lit, and then at him sitting opposite her. Dear, darling William, she reflected dreamily, she was getting to know him after all; the gods, or whoever arranged these things, were on her side.

She couldn't stop her delighted smile, and he said kindly, 'You like my home, Lucy?'

'Oh, my goodness, it's perfect—what I've seen of it. It's not like living in London here, is it?'

The door opened before he could answer and a middle-aged, rotund man carrying a tray came in. He bade the doctor a grave good afternoon and repeated his greeting to Lucy when he was introduced. 'Mr and Mrs Trump have been with me for more years than I care to remember. My life would fall apart without them, wouldn't it, Trump?'

'There is that possibility, sir; I trust the occasion may never arise.' He lifted the lid of a silver muffin dish. 'Mrs Trump thought that a muffin might be acceptable, sir—such a chilly afternoon.'

'Muffins will be specially good, Trump. Switch the phone through to this room, will you? And have your own tea in peace.'

'Thank you, sir.' Trump made his stately way out of the room and Lucy was begged to pour the tea.

An hour passed pleasantly. Lucy, comfortably full of muffins and Madeira cake, had lost all count of time; she was far too busy probing delicately for details of the doctor's way of life, an exercise which was affording him a good deal of secret amusement. It was in a brief pause in their conversation that the long case clock by the door chimed a musical six o'clock, and she jumped to her feet like a guilty child. 'Oh, the time—I'm so sorry, I do hope I haven't delayed you. I dare say you're doing something if you're free...'

He didn't deny it. 'Plenty of time and only a few friends coming to dinner. I'll run you home.' He smiled at her very kindly. 'I have enjoyed our afternoon, we must do it again some time.'

Lucy smiled and murmured and her green eyes belied the smile. Nothing, she vowed silently, nothing would induce her to accept any invitation from him again. It was so obvious to her now that he had taken pity on her and sat, probably bored stiff, for two hours listening to her uninspired remarks. She paused in the doorway to say, 'There's really no need to drive me back, there'll be a bus at the end of the street...'

A waste of breath, for he said nothing at all, but summoned Mrs Trump with Lucy's jacket, helped her into it and ushered her out of his front door and into the Rolls-Royce parked there. She was far too cross to listen to his easy flow of talk as he drove her back to Chelsea, and almost before he had stopped in front of her house she had started to open her door.

A large hand came down on hers. 'Stay where you are,' he advised her, and got out of the car to open her door and help her out. He took her key from her and opened the house door, at the same time giving the door knocker a thump so that Alice came from the kitchen.

'There you are,' said Alice. 'I was just wondering where you'd got to.' She beamed at the doctor. 'You'll come in, sir?'

'Thank you, no, Alice.' He glanced at Lucy, standing silent and still cross, feeling like a child brought home from a party and handed over to Nanny.

'Thank you for my tea,' she said frostily. 'Goodbye, Dr Thurloe.'

'Goodbye, Lucy. Shall you be in Richmond Park tomorrow morning?'

'No, I'm going out with a friend.'

She slipped past Alice and she heard him wish the housekeeper goodnight before he got back into his car and drove away.

Alice shut the door. 'Had a nice time, did you, Miss Lucy?'

Lucy heaved a great sigh. 'No, I did not, it was absolutely beastly.' She burst into tears and raced up to her room, and didn't come down until Alice came to tell her that her supper was ready in the dining-room.

'What time will you be going out tomorrow, Miss Lucy?' Alice wanted to know. 'To see these friends of yours?'

'I only said that,' explained Lucy, 'because I was afraid the doctor might take pity on me again…'

'Take pity on you? Whatever do you mean, love? He's the last man to waste 'is time, or I'm a Dutchman. If he wanted to take you out 'e'd 'ave meant it.'

Lucy shook her head. 'Oh, no, Alice dear, he's a kind man, and Pauline asked me if I'd be all right on my own with you, and he was there and he asked me to have tea with him at his house.' She added a little wildly, 'Just as he'd give a stray dog a good meal or feed a lost kitten…' She paused. 'Oh, dear, and that's why I went, because he said his housekeeper would like one of Mrs Simpkins' kittens and I was supposed to talk to her about it.'

'Never mind,' said Alice comfortably. 'You'll be bound to see him again.'

'Not if I can help it,' said Lucy, so fiercely that Alice gave her a sharp look. 'You go and sit by the sitting-room fire,' was all she said, 'and I'll bring you your coffee.'

'I'll help you wash up...'

'That you will not, I've had all day to idle away, and all the other days as well now there's no one here but you. Miss Pauline'll be back tonight?'

'She's going to Cyril's place for dinner, and I think she intends to spend the weekend with his parents and come back tomorrow evening. I'm sure Imogen will be back in a few days—I had a letter.'

When Alice brought the coffee she made the good soul sit down. 'You just stay there,' she ordered nicely and fetched a cup and saucer from the dining-room sideboard. 'Look, Alice, I don't want to do anything tomorrow, only wash my hair and do my nails and loll around with the Sunday papers. Wouldn't you like to take the day off—which you can while you have the chance? You'll be busy enough when Imogen and Pauline and my parents are back.'

'Your lunch—?' began Alice.

'I can cook, you know I can, you taught me. There's food in the fridge?'

'Of course there is,' Alice declared indignantly, 'but it's my place to cook...'

'Oh, Alice, of course it is, you shall cook me a luscious supper when you get back. You know you're dying to see your sister. Go after breakfast and come back after tea. I know Mother would approve.'

'You'll be all right alone? I'm not sure…'

'Oh, go on, Alice,' wheedled Lucy. 'I'm twenty-five, you know, and able to look after myself.'

'Oh, well, it would be nice to go over to Golders Green for an hour or two. But you're to phone me if I'm needed.'

'I promise, Alice.'

The house was quiet once Alice had gone the next morning. Lucy roamed around, played with the kittens, washed her hair and did her nails and then curled up with the Sunday papers. But she didn't read them for long; she went over Saturday's events, almost word for word. 'The trouble is,' she told Mrs Simpkins, who was sitting in her basket with her kittens, 'that I behaved like a silly girl. I'm a grown woman of twenty-five, and that's getting on, but I simply have no idea how to sparkle, though I dare say William wouldn't want that kind of a wife. It's nice to take out someone that looks like that odious Fiona, all gush and black velvet, but she'd be no good at all at the breakfast table if he'd been up half the night slaving over some ill child. I'd do very nicely, you know.'

She wandered into the kitchen and switched on the coffee percolator and found the biscuit tin. The front door bell jangled and she frowned. It could be Pauline and Cyril, or Imogen returned several days early. It could be anyone. She went to the door and opened it, remembering just too late to put up the chain first; it could be a thief.

It was Dr Thurloe and she gaped at him, colour flooding her face. She said idiotically, 'Oh, it's you.'

'Indeed it is I. On my way back for lunch from the park I thought I'd give your housekeeper a message for you about the kitten.' He smiled slowly. 'You changed your mind about spending the day with your friends?'

She said breathlessly, 'Well, yes—no, actually I wasn't going anywhere.'

He said smoothly, 'In that case will you come back with me for lunch? There will be one or two friends—quite informal. Come as you are.'

She gave silent thanks that she had put on a rather nice jersey dress that morning. She said uncertainly, 'Yes, but you weren't expecting me...'

'Another one more or less won't upset Mrs Trump, and I should be delighted if you could come.'

Her resolve not to accept any invitations from him dissolved like jelly in hot water. 'Well, thank you, I'd like to come.'

'In that case may I come in and collect a kitten?'

'Oh, yes, of course, they're in the kitchen. Do you know which one Mrs Trump would like to have?'

'Thomas is a Tabby, so perhaps a contrast? Black and white or ginger.'

She led the way to the kitchen where Mrs Simpkins, bored with her kittens, was stretched out before the Aga. The kittens were charming. They were looked at in turn, and finally the doctor chose the ugliest, if a kitten could ever be called ugly, but she had a large nose and a flat head and very round eyes. Mrs Simpkins merely yawned when Lucy took her to say goodbye, and took no notice when the doctor tucked her under one arm.

'Would you like a cup of coffee?' asked Lucy.

'Why, yes, I would. It will give this little lady time to feel independent.' He sat down at the table and Lucy switched on the percolator and fetched two mugs. The kitten went to sleep in the curve of his arm and when they got up to go Mrs Simpkins took no notice at all. Lucy, a soft-hearted girl, heaved a sigh of relief. 'Do you suppose they'll miss each other?'

'Perhaps, but not with grief; in the wild once a young animal is able to fend for itself it becomes independent. Mrs Simpkins still has three kittens and this young lady will have Thomas and Mrs Trump to spoil her.'

They got into the car and he transferred the kitten to her lap while he drove. At his house he took her straight through the hall and into the kitchen where Mrs Trump was standing at the table beating something in a bowl while Trump sat in a chair by the Aga, reading the paper. Thomas sat at his feet and all three of them looked up as they went in.

Trump got to his feet and Mrs Trump paused in her beating.

'Your kitten, Mrs Trump,' said the doctor, and sat the little creature down beside Thomas, who stared in amazement while the kitten sniffed delicately at her fur and then curled up beside her.

'Well, I never did!' exclaimed Mrs Trump. 'Look at the little darling and my Thomas, taken an instant liking to each other.'

'Highly satisfactory,' said the doctor. 'She'll need feeding four times a day for a week or two, Mrs Trump...'

'You leave that to me, sir, I'll give her just what's needed, and no going outside either.' She smiled at Lucy. 'The young lady will be here for lunch?'

'Yes, Mrs Trump.' He glanced at the kitchen clock. 'We had better go and have a drink in the drawing-room.' He took Lucy's arm and turned her round, whistled to the dogs who had gone to look at the kitten, and walked her through the door into the hall. They were only just in the drawing-room when the front door bell pealed.

Lucy, ushered across the room towards the brightly burning fire, heard Trump's voice mingled with that of a woman. Fiona, she felt sure, and turned to face the door, in time to see that lady make an entry.

'William, darling... I thought I'd get here first so that we could have ten minutes together.' She stopped as her eyes lighted upon Lucy. 'Oh, I had no idea...' She recovered immediately, kissed the doctor's cheek and went on, 'Lucy Lockitt, isn't it? From the orphanage? Has William taken pity upon you? Your parents are away, aren't they?'

'Hello,' said Lucy. 'They're in Turkey. I don't

know if Dr Thurloe has taken pity, but he has invited me to lunch.'

She smiled charmingly. Her eyes, decided the doctor, watching her, looked like emeralds.

He said easily, 'Of course, you two know each other.' The doorbell rang once more and he went on, 'You know the Walters, Lucy…' They came into the room and Lucy was thankfully enveloped in their kindly warmth. She was answering their questions about her parents' plans when the last guest arrived. A colleague of the doctor's, the senior consultant surgeon at City Royal. A man of the doctor's age, already going grey and with a long thin face and a ready smile.

'You know everyone here,' said the doctor, 'but not Lucy Lockitt—her parents—'

'I know of them.' The man shook Lucy's hand as the doctor introduced him as Charles Hyde. 'I'm sorry my wife couldn't make it—you're her stand-in, I expect, and a very charming one, I must say.'

Lucy smiled and murmured. So that was why she had been invited—to make up numbers round the table. It was a pity she loved William so very deeply, otherwise she would have disliked him very much. Men! she thought, and curled a pretty lip.

Lunch, if it hadn't been for Fiona, would have been a delightful meal. The food was superb— lobster tartlets followed by roundels of lamb and finished off with a caramel mousse served with a coulis of raspberries, washed down by a Puligny Montrachet, a wine which Lucy found very pleasant. She knew very little about wines, but Mr Hyde, taking an appreciative sip, pronounced it to be a vintage white burgundy. 'Trust William to keep a good cellar,' he observed. 'Have you known him for long?'

'No,' Lucy replied, then added obscurely, 'Mother and Father are friends of the Walters.'

Mr Hyde glanced sideways at her composed face. 'Oh, quite. I expect you get tired of people asking you how you like working at the orphanage, but I have occasion to go there sometimes. A well-run place, I have always thought.'

'Oh, it is. But sad too—no mothers or fathers, or, if there are any, they don't want to know.'

He nodded. 'Sad indeed. You like children— babies?'

She smiled widely. 'Well, yes, I do, but I can't imagine anyone who didn't being able to work there.'

'We have four children of our own—they seem like an entire orphanage at times! Tell me, did you not wish to go to Turkey with your parents?'

'Well, no. You see, I'd not be of any use. I don't know enough about my father's work.'

Mrs Walter took possession of her after lunch so that she got no opportunity to speak to William even if she had wished to, for Fiona had stayed beside him, not only at the table, but afterwards as they sat around gossiping in the drawing-room. Presently Mrs Walter got up to go and the rest followed her, and when she offered Lucy a lift she accepted at once. It was obvious that Fiona wasn't going to leave with the rest of them, and when the doctor came over to her and offered to drive her home she said cheerfully, 'There's no need for you to bother, but thank you all the same. Mrs Walter will drop me off. Thank you for a delightful lunch.' She smiled too brightly; she wasn't going to concede defeat to the horrible Mrs Seymour, only retreat in good order, more determined than ever to have her dear William. Somehow; she had no idea how.

She refused the Walters' invitation to go back with them and spend the rest of the day, saying, without a grain of truth, that she was expecting a phone call from her mother.

'Isn't that a very long way to phone?' asked Mrs Walter.

'Mother hates writing letters so she rings up once a week instead.'

Lucy said goodbye and let herself into the house. There was the rest of the afternoon to get through, and the evening. She fed Mrs Simpkins and the kittens, switched on the TV and switched it off again, and instead went into the drawing-room, where she sat down at the piano and played all the more sentimental music she could call to mind. She played well and it suited her mood; a mixture of rage, unhappiness and a firm determination to marry William.

She was quite glad to go back to work on the Monday morning. Imogen and Pauline were both back again, and, although they were out most evenings, they slept at home and Lucy saw them briefly

at breakfast most mornings. But she didn't see the doctor at all.

It was at the end of the week, as she got off the bus and started the short walk to her home, that she came face to face with a girl of her own age. 'Francesca!' She gave a small shriek of surprise and delight echoed by the other girl.

'Lucy, how lovely seeing you! You never answered my letter at Christmas—I'm actually on my way to see you.'

'You're here in London, on holiday?'

'Litrik is over here for a seminar. Heavens, isn't this fun?'

Lucy took her arm. 'Come for a quick chat; how long are you here?'

'We're going back in three days' time.'

'The babies? Are they here too?'

'Of course, and Nanny is with us. We're at the Connaught.'

They had reached the house and Lucy let them in and called to Alice, who came hurrying in to see who it was.

'Miss Fran—my goodness, it's years since I'¬ seen you!' She eyed Fran's fashionable outfit real smart young lady too.' She smiled widely bring you both some coffee...'

'Tea, please,' they chorused, and took the into the drawing-room, to curl up on chai change news. They hadn't seen each oth time, although they had been at schoo years, and after that had stayed with e

time to time, but Francesca had begun to train as a nurse and gone to live with her three aunts who had discouraged, in the nicest way possible, too many young visitors to their home, so Fran and Lucy had seen less and less of each other even though they kept up a regular correspondence.

Over cups of tea they made up for not having seen each other for so long and presently Lucy said, 'You're happy, aren't you, Fran?'

'Yes. I can't imagine ever being happier. Lucy, why aren't you married? You're pretty and you must meet any number of men.' She put down her cup. 'There must be someone?'

'Yes, but he's not—not available. At least, I'm pretty sure he's not.'

'You're still at that orphanage you wrote about? Can you get some time off? Will you come and stay with us for a week or so? We'd love to have you. You might find a Dutchman as I did.'

'I've got some holidays due. I think I'd love to come, Fran. Mother and Father are away, and Imogen and Pauline are out a lot. I'd love to see the babies too. Some time in the early summer perhaps?'

'Oh, sooner than that. Look, I must go or Litrik will worry. I'll ring you before we go back and fix a date. Do you work on Saturday?'

'Only in the mornings, I'm home by one o'clock.'

At the door Fran said gently, 'You look sad, Lucy. Do you love him very much?'

'Yes, however, I'll get over it. I'd love to come and ee you, I might even find that Dutchman!'

They laughed together and Lucy stood at the open door and watched Fran walking away down the quiet street in search of a taxi. She looked so happy and content, and was beautifully dressed too—never a pretty girl, she had blossomed into a charming *jolie laide*.

'That's what love does to you,' said Lucy to the empty street.

The seminar was over and the learned gentlemen who had attended it were drifting away or stopping to talk to colleagues or friends. Dr Thurloe wandered unhurriedly towards the entrance, discussing a knotty problem with Litrik van Rijgen. They hadn't seen each other for some months, but ever since they had been at medical school at Edinburgh Royal Infirmary, and later at Cambridge and Leiden, they had kept in touch.

Litrik glanced at his watch. 'Fran's gone to see an old friend, she said she would be back at the hotel about six o'clock—we've time for a drink.'

The pub on the corner was shabby and awfully dark, but almost empty. They settled at a table in a corner and Dr Thurloe said, 'Well, that's over for another year. A pity you can't stay for a few days. Give my love to Fran, she looks marvellous and the babies are enchanting.'

His friend looked faintly smug. 'Fran's a wonderful wife and the children are delightful. Why not come back to the hotel, just for a half an hour, and say goodbye in person?'

Francesca was back by the time they arrived, lying on the floor of their sitting-room playing with the toddler's bricks, but she jumped up as they went in, greeted her husband as though they had been parted for weeks, held up his small son for a kiss and then turned to William, offering a cheek with the simplicity of a child. 'The baby's asleep,' she told them. 'Have you finished your papers?' She smiled at her husband. 'I've had a lovely time with Lucy, it was great to see her again. She's prettier than ever. I've invited her to stay, Litrik, you won't mind? She was getting off the bus and I was just walking up the road to her home. She's still at the orphanage.'

Dr Thurloe had been studying the baby in her carrycot, but he turned round slowly as Fran spoke. 'Not by any chance Lucy Lockitt of nursery rhyme fame?'

'Yes—do you know her? She never said.' Francesca paused, a dozen likely and unlikely ideas in her head. 'We were at school together and we've kept in touch. I said I'd give her a ring before we go back home and settle a date. She said early summer; I'd like her to come before then.'

Dr Thurloe spoke casually. 'Give me a date, will you? I have the ear of the Matron at the orphanage.'

'Oh, splendid. Can you let me know before I phone Lucy, then she can ask—and get it,' she finished hopefully.

'I can't see why not. I'll give you a ring some time in the morning.' He smiled gently. 'I must be going—a dinner date.'

'Who with?' Fran blushed at his look and said, 'Sorry, it's none of my business.'

'A handsome lady of thirty-odd years, widowed, comfortably situated and well versed in the social graces.'

Francesca stretched up to kiss his cheek. 'Then don't let us keep you, she sounds just perfect.'

'What for?'

She gave him an innocent look. 'Why, a doctor's wife, of course. It's time you married, William.'

Chapter 5

Lucy went to the theatre with Pauline and Cyril on Saturday evening. It was something put on by an arts club in one of the smaller theatres and extremely highbrow. She gave up trying to understand what it was about halfway through the first act and allowed her thoughts to wander to William. He would be out, she guessed, dining and dancing probably. Her evening would have been much happier if she had known that he was miles away in the Cotswolds, spending his day with the old professor who had taught him so well in Edinburgh. She was taken to supper after the play ended, and listened to Cyril discussing the dialogue at length. The play had its merits, he informed them gravely, but he then went on to tear it to pieces.

'If you knew it was going to be so bad, why did we go?' asked Lucy.

'I was given tickets,' said Cyril huffily.

It was a pity they disliked each other, she thought, and agreed politely to being taken home before he and Pauline went back to his parents' house for the night.

She tactfully thanked him very nicely before she went indoors, where she kicked off her shoes, drank the cocoa Alice had ready for her, and went to bed. Pauline wouldn't be home until after office hours on Monday, but Imogen came in soon after she did and came along to her room to suggest that they might spend the next day in the country. 'Though I must be back soon after six o'clock—I've got a dinner date. We could drive to Epping—no, we'll go on to Ingatestone and have lunch at that nice place. We haven't had a chance to gossip for ages, have we?'

From which remark Lucy deduced that her sister had something she wanted to tell her. 'It sounds lovely. What time shall we go?'

'Oh, elevenish. Alice could have the day to herself after breakfast.'

It was a bright morning when Lucy got up; March, having come in rather noisily, had now become as quiet as a lamb. She put on a jersey three-piece, with sensible shoes, and went down to breakfast.

Traffic was thin as they drove east through London, and it stayed that way until they reached Epping, although there were cars enough going towards the coast. Imogen parked the car and led the way into the hotel restaurant. 'We might go for a walk after lunch,' she suggested. When she would be told whatever it was that Imogen wanted her to know, decided Lucy, and took care to keep the talk general as they ate lunch.

They had been walking for ten minutes or so,

saying nothing much, when Imogen said abruptly, 'I'm going to be married, Lucy.'

It was a surprise: Imogen, at twenty-eight, had already made her mark in the business world, she had a big salary, she was thought much of by her boss, and her future as an executive was assured. She knew her own worth and had never hesitated to let her family know that, and somehow they had all thought of her as staying single.

'Imogen, what a lovely piece of news! Who is he? Do Mother and Father know?'

'I cabled them yesterday. Of course, we shall wait until they're back home before we marry. You don't know him—he's a Canadian businessman, George Irwell.'

'I hope you'll be very happy,' Lucy said, and meant it. 'You'll be married before Pauline and Cyril.'

'Yes. I'm the eldest anyway…and what about you, Lucy? Haven't you met anyone you would like to marry?' She didn't give Lucy a chance to answer. 'I suppose not, buried at that orphanage of yours. Such a pity, for you're pretty enough, only you don't bother much, do you?' She laughed, and added without meaning to be unkind, 'Mother has always said that you're the home-bird, whatever that means.'

A prospect Lucy didn't care to contemplate. It was a sobering thought which remained with her for the rest of the day, and she was quite glad when Monday morning came round again.

She was halfway through the morning when Matron sent for her.

'I don't want to hassle you, but would you care to take a couple of weeks' holiday in a week or two's time? There will be no one else on holiday and we can cover for you. You have always been very accommodating about fitting in with the rest of us. Any time in March or April will suit me; at a pinch we could manage the first week in May. Will you think it over and let me know?'

Lucy went back to Miranda and set about giving her her midday dinner while she thought about holidays. Fran had asked her to stay, but she remembered that she herself had suggested the early summer, so Fran might not be prepared to have her earlier than that. It was a pity, for if she took two weeks' holiday within the next few weeks she could hardly expect to get more time off before the autumn, especially as the other girls had their plans already made. She finished her day undecided what to do, aware that she would have to make up her mind before she saw Matron again.

As it happened, her mind was made up for her that very evening.

Both her sisters were out, Imogen with her George, Pauline with Cyril. Lucy had eaten her supper in the kitchen with Alice for company, and then wandered away to wash her hair. Only before she could do that the phone rang. It was Francesca.

'Lucy, we're leaving this evening in about an hour. Look, couldn't you manage to come and stay with us before the summer? Surely you could get a couple of weeks off soon?'

'As a matter of fact, Matron asked me this morning if I'd mind taking two weeks either at the end of this month or in April.'

'Oh, good. Then you'll come; when?'

Lucy suddenly felt excited. 'Wait while I get a calendar. How about the last week in March, that's only a week away? You're sure—?'

'Don't be silly, of course I'm sure. Let's see, that will be the twenty-fifth on a Saturday. Litrik'll meet you at Schiphol; let us know the time the flight arrives when you've got everything fixed up. It'll be such fun, Lucy, there are years of gossip to catch up on. I must fly—Litrik's got the car waiting. See you.'

Fran put down the phone and smiled at her husband. 'That's settled. How clever of William to get round that matron. I wonder why he did. Do you suppose he fancies Lucy?'

'My darling, William is a kind man; I dare say he thinks that Lucy needs a holiday and he was able to make things easy for her.'

He smiled at her slowly and crossed the room to kiss her. Fran kissed him back. 'Is that so? They would make a very nice pair.' She frowned in thought. 'Do you suppose William might like to take a week or so's holiday and come and stay with us as well?'

'Matchmaker,' observed Litrik lovingly, and kissed her again. 'We shall miss that hovercraft.'

Lucy gave her holiday dates to Matron the next

day, and when she got home that evening she told her sisters. They smiled at her with affection, remarked that it would be nice for her to have a holiday, and fell to the much more important task of making wedding arrangements. Lucy hadn't expected them to take much interest in such an ordinary happening as a couple of weeks' holiday; she went along to the kitchen and told Alice, who responded with all the warmth her sisters lacked.

'Now that'll be nice,' said Alice, 'and you be sure and take some pretty clothes with you, Miss Lucy; you never know, Mr Right might be waiting for you in Holland. Not that I set much store by foreigners.'

'Francesca married one,' Lucy pointed out, and ate one of the cheese tartlets Alice had just taken from the oven. 'She thinks he's absolutely marvellous.'

'Quite right and proper too,' said Alice, 'since 'e's 'er 'usband.' She whisked the tray of tartlets out of reach. 'You'll have no supper if you eat them now,' she threatened. 'There's grilled sole and spinach and no potatoes—Miss Imogen says she must lose half a stone before the wedding.'

'In that case,' said Lucy, reaching for the tartlets, 'I'd better have another of these, dear Alice.'

She spent the rest of the evening listening to her sisters tossing ideas to and fro; receptions, bridesmaids, which church and the best places for honeymoons were discussed in depth. They paused presently and looked at her. 'You'll be a bridesmaid, Lucy,' said Imogen. 'Pink taffeta and flower wreaths, I think...'

Pauline had other ideas. 'I'll have four attendants, I think—you, of course, Lucy. I don't think Cyril can manage any free time before July. Sea-green, I think, with darker green sashes. The others will be Cyril's little nephew and his two nieces.'

Three tiresome children, reflected Lucy, who loved children, all excepting these three—spoilt, quarrelsome and tending to whine. When she had agreed pleasantly to everything that was suggested she took herself off to bed, to lie awake and think of William Thurloe and wonder where he was and what he was doing. She told herself crossly that she must try not to think about him quite so much; she was still determined to marry him, but when she did think about him it must be positively. Not useless longings which got her nowhere. She rearranged her pillows and began to plan her holiday wardrobe. She would buy some clothes... It was a pity William wouldn't be there to see them. Sleep overtook her before she could feel sad about it.

Her mother, apprised of the forthcoming holiday, said, 'How nice, darling,' and plunged into an enthusiastic account of her father's latest find, the remains of an iron pot—proof, if they had needed it, that the Hittites really had known about smelting. Only when she had passed on this interesting information did she comment happily upon Imogen's forthcoming marriage, adding the rider that Lucy must be looking forward to being a bridesmaid twice over. 'A nice change from those orphans,' she declared with a little laugh, 'and enjoy yourself with

Francesca, dear. Such a nice, quiet girl, and not at all pretty. Yet she has made a splendid marriage from what you tell me. You must see what you can do while you're in Holland, darling.'

Lucy said, 'Yes, Mother.' She had no need to go to Holland; just down the road to Chiswick.

She booked her flight, found her passport, fetched travellers' cheques and embarked on a day's shopping. March so far had been warm and sunny with occasional bouts of pouring rain. Fran had told her to be sure and bring a raincoat with her and a woolly or two, 'And something pretty for the evenings— I've planned a party and we shall go out to dinner and perhaps a concert.' She had sounded quite excited over the phone, and Lucy, immensely cheered at the prospect of some social life, went off and bought two new party dresses as well as a thin woollen suit in which to travel.

Each day she had gone to the orphanage hoping to see Dr Thurloe, but she never did. Miranda was improving by leaps and bounds, but she wasn't due to go to the clinic for another two weeks, when Lucy would be in Holland, so she would miss a chance of seeing him then.

It was on her last day at the orphanage before she started her holiday that she met Fiona Seymour. It had been a busy day and she had hurried home, showered and changed and taken herself for a walk along the Embankment, to meet Fiona coming towards her, strolling along in a stunning outfit.

She stopped and Lucy perforce stopped too. 'My

dear, you are the very last person I would expect to see. I thought you spent your days in the orphanage with those dreary children.'

'I work until five o'clock, and they're not dreary.' Aware that she had sounded snappy, Lucy added, 'It's a gorgeous evening, isn't it?'

'I suppose so, though I'm having to waste some of it. William—Dr Thurloe—was to drive me to Henley, I've a dreary aunt living there, but he phoned to say he has some emergency or other and he won't be able to take me. Luckily I have a number of other friends and no lack of offers to take his place, although I'm having to hang around until I can be called for. I got bored indoors.' She gave Lucy a quick rather malicious glance. 'William's upset, of course; we spend as much time as we possibly can together.'

Lucy racked her brains to find a suitable reply to this. 'He's a busy man,' she observed mildly.

'Of course, I suppose you see him occasionally with those precious orphans. It must be dire working with them, but I suppose if you haven't any prospect of marrying it's better than nothing.' She drew a breath and put up her hand to her mouth. 'Oh, my dear, that sounded awful! Do forgive me, I was only repeating what William said...'

Lucy had gone rather pale, but her voice was quite clear and steady and very quiet. 'It's most interesting, and I like children. I should hate to live the kind of life you do, although I dare say it takes up quite a lot of time, make-up and hair and so on, and dieting...' Her green eyes were like deep green pools, her smile charming. 'I must fly, I've so much to do before I go away. Bye.'

She isn't likely to repeat that to William, decided Lucy, walking home rather fast, and I know I was rude, but she was rude first. And if William really said that about me I'll never speak to him again. She bounced into the house with such vigour that Alice came from the kitchen to see what was the matter.

'There you are, Miss Lucy. A pity you were out, that nice Dr Thurloe phoned to wish you a happy holiday—heard you were going from your matron, he said. I asked him to ring back, but he said he was going out.'

'Oh, he is, is he?' uttered Lucy rather wildly. 'As though I care what he does.'

She pounded upstairs to her room and Alice went back to the kitchen. 'So that's the way the wind blows,' she observed to Mrs Simpkins. 'We'll just have to wait and see, won't we?'

Mrs Simpkins, cleaning her whiskers after her tea, merely stared and yawned.

Right at the back of Lucy's head had been the idea that Dr Thurloe might phone again before she left, but the telephone remained silent and she started on her journey to Heathrow, speeded on her way by Alice and determinedly taking care not to look round in case the doctor, at the very last minute, should appear. Of course, he didn't, and she took herself through the routine at the airport and in due course boarded her plane.

She had met Litrik van Rijgen only twice before, at his wedding to Fran and during a visit they had paid to London just before the first baby had been born. When she saw him waiting for her at Schiphol she thought that he hadn't changed at all. He was a big man with greying fair hair and a handsome face, which in repose looked severe, although, reflected Lucy as she went towards him, it was unlikely that he was, for Francesca adored him and, as far as Lucy could discover from her letters, he made her blissfully happy. He saw her then, and smiled as he strode towards her.

'How very nice to see you again, Lucy.' He bent and kissed her cheek. 'Fran is so looking forward to your visit—so am I. Is this all your luggage?'

He led the way out of the airport and ushered her into the silver-grey Daimler parked close by. 'We shall be home in about half an hour—it is about thirty miles, just the other side of Utrecht. You had a comfortable flight?'

She found him a very likeable man, and they talked comfortably together as he drove until he turned off the motorway and joined a country road, which was very peaceful after the rush of traffic on the motorway. The village they reached was small and dominated by a large church, and a hundred yards further on Litrik swept the car between brick pillars and along a drive bordered by shrubs and trees, rounded a curve and drew up before his home.

It was a solid flat-faced house with orderly rows of windows, each with shutters. The house door was reached by way of circular steps and was solid enough to withstand a siege. It was opened now by a thin elderly man and Francesca flew past him and down the steps, to receive a quick embrace from her husband before she flung herself at Lucy.

'Oh, isn't this fun! Come in...' She flashed a smile at Litrik and took Lucy's arm. 'Are you tired? Did you have a good trip? We'll have lunch in half an hour or so.' She called over her shoulder, 'You won't be long, darling?'

Litrik smiled at her and Lucy, watching them, felt envious of such quiet happiness. 'Five minutes, love.'

'This is Trugg,' said Fran, and waited while Lucy shook hands with him. 'He's our right hand. Come up to your room and I'll leave you for a few minutes to tidy if you want to.'

She led the way up the wide staircase to the gallery above the hall and opened a door. 'Here you are, Lucy; the bathroom's through that door, and if you want anything just ask, won't you?'

She dropped a kiss on Lucy's cheek. 'This is fun, it really is. Come down when you're ready.'

Left to herself, Lucy explored the pretty room, admiring the mahogany furniture and the pretty sprigged chintz at the window and the thick matching bedspread. And the bathroom was quite perfect, pink and white and furnished with a pile of fluffy towels, bowls of soap and bath essences and a wide mirror, well lit. She went back into the bedroom and sat down before the triple mirror on the dressing table. She was a girl who almost always looked immaculate; she powdered her nose, put on more lipstick and brushed her hair, took a quick look at the garden from the window, and went down the staircase.

There were a number of doors in the hall and she paused uncertainly as Litrik flung a half-open door wide. 'We're in here having a drink,' he said and she went past him into the drawing-room.

It was a grand room, furnished most beautifully with antique pieces which gleamed with the patina of years of loving care, but there were great comfortable chairs too, and two enormous sofas, one on each side of the hooded fireplace. French windows opened on to a garden alive with spring flowers and a fire burned brightly. But its grandness was mitigated by all the signs of family living: a teddy bear leaning against a wall cabinet, a pile of knitting cast down on one of the lamp tables, a pile of magazines and newspapers on the sofa table, and before the fire two dogs, a mastiff and a much smaller dog, rather stout and with a long curly coat. They got up and came to sniff her and she put out a hand.

'Thor and Muff,' said Litrik. 'You like dogs?'

'Oh, yes, but we haven't one at home, only Mrs Simpkins the cat and her kittens.'

'Mrs Trugg has a cat—Moses—Litrik fished him out of the canal. There's a donkey too, in the paddock, and horses—Litrik has taught me to ride,' said Fran.

They sat around talking until Fran said, 'Shall

we just peep at the children? Nanny will have fed them—baby has purée twice a day now, though I still feed her.'

The two of them went upstairs to the nursery where a miniature Litrik was perched in a high chair more or less feeding himself, while a young plump woman sat by him with the baby on her lap.

'This is Nanny,' said Fran. 'She was here before we married and I hope she'll never leave us.'

She sat down and took the baby on her lap while they watched little Litrik having the last of his dinner. 'They will rest now,' said Fran, 'and we have them until bathtime—Litrik isn't always home, of course, but he is marvellous with them. Wasn't it nice having a boy and then a girl? We want another pair—four makes a nice family.'

Lucy said wistfully, 'You must be so happy, Fran.' And then, in case she sounded self-pitying, 'They'll have a lovely home; it's so beautiful…'

'The garden's lovely in the summer, and the country around is pretty.' Fran got up and put the baby back in her cot and tucked her in carefully, dropped a kiss on her small son's head, said something to Nanny to make her smile, and suggested that they might go down to their own lunch.

'I say,' said Lucy, 'I suppose you speak Dutch?'

'Yes, but I make lots of mistakes still. Nanny understands some English, and of course Trugg is English, although Mrs Trugg, who cooks and house-keeps, only has a smattering.'

Lunch was a cheerful affair—there was so much

to talk about and Litrik, Lucy decided, really was a very nice man. It was no wonder Fran was so happy. Almost as nice as William, Lucy admitted, a thought which made her ponder about him and, almost as though Fran knew it, she asked casually if Lucy went to the City Royal much and if she knew any of the staff there. She avoided her husband's amused eye as she did so, and appeared very nonchalant.

'Well, yes, I go sometimes to the clinics...' Lucy went a delicate pink. 'Some of the children aren't quite normal and they have to see a—a consultant.'

Such a vivid mental picture of William was imprinted behind her eyelids that for a moment she couldn't go on, and Litrik, apparently unnoticing of that, asked, 'Have they still got that out-of-date Outpatients there? As dark as a cellar, and it always smelled of damp clothes.'

A remark which led the conversation safely back to generalities.

The rest of the day passed pleasantly, Lucy playing with the children, being shown over the house and exploring the garden. In the evening, after one of Mrs Trugg's delicious dinners, they talked again; there was so much to say and, as Fran said, several years to catch up on.

Lucy, getting ready for bed, reflected on her evening. She had enjoyed it very much. Fran hadn't changed; she had beautiful clothes and an elegant hairstyle, but she was still kind-hearted, gentle Fran and Litrik loved her... 'And that is how I wish William would love me,' Lucy said to herself as she jumped into her very comfortable bed.

She woke once in the night, at a time when everything appeared to be at its blackest, convinced that she had no chance at all against the practised charms of Fiona Seymour. Fortunately when she awoke in the morning such a gloomy thought had no chance against daylight's common sense. She had as much chance as any other girl, she told herself stoutly, and sat up in bed to drink the morning tea that a nice cheerful girl had brought.

She was taken to church in the morning after a breakfast of hot rolls, ham and cheese and delicious coffee, and a quick visit to the nursery to see the children. Fran had been up early to feed the baby, and Litrik had been out with the dogs, and there was a pleasant air of bustle about the house.

The family pew was at the front of the church, under the pulpit with its vast sounding-board, and Lucy sat between Fran and Litrik, unable to understand a word, and yet following the service very well—some of the hymns even had tunes she knew. The sermon lasted a very long time, and the *dominee* thundered above her head so that she had the impression that he disliked his congregation, but as they left the church they stopped to speak to him and she discovered him to be a mild man with a splendid command of English and a soft, gentle voice.

He was very pleased to meet her, he said, and if she could spare the time he and his wife would be delighted to see her at his house. She thanked him nicely and Fran said, 'We'll walk down one day; I'm sure you'll have a lot to talk about. Have the children got over their measles?'

She was assured that they had, and they parted on the best of terms, to walk home and spend an hour in the nursery before having drinks and their own lunch. In the afternoon Litrik drove to the Veluwe, this time in a station-wagon with the dogs at the back and Lucy and Fran behind him each with a baby. It was a sunny day, but windy; he found a sheltered spot presently, and they all piled out, poking around the hedges for primroses, walking beside a narrow canal where a duck family was swimming. The hedges petered out very soon and the road ran, narrow and empty, towards the flat horizon, the country between dotted with farmhouses and villages, their church steeples dominating the field around them.

'Just where are we?' asked Lucy, no longer sure of the points of the compass.

'It all looks alike, doesn't it? We have driven through the Veluwe, and now we are on its very edge, back to the fields and flat country. The Veluwe is rather like your New Forest, only very much smaller. It's a great holiday area, and away from the road there are quite a few charming houses. Arnhem is to the south of us,' he waved a large arm, 'over there is Utrecht, and beyond but more to the north is Amsterdam. We'll take you there before you go back.'

They wandered back to the car and went home

to tea round the fire, with Litrik's small son on his knee and the baby asleep in her Moses basket. Lucy sat, not talking much, soothed by the charming room and the gentle talk. She looked at the dogs and thought that, if she almost closed her eyes, she could fancy that they were Robinson and Friday and that Litrik was William.

The days flowed gently into a week; Lucy, getting ready for a bath and bed at the end of it, reviewed them. Each day there had been something different, and, even though Litrik had been away from home for a good deal of the day, Francesca had thought of something to do.

They had gone to Utrecht, inspected the great tower, poked around the shops, had coffee at the Café de Paris, decided against climbing the hundreds of steps of the Dom Tower, and returned home to take the children for a walk, accompanied by the dogs, until Litrik came home and friends came in for drinks. They had gone one evening to Litrik's parents' home and dined there with their other guests, and the next day Litrik had gone early to the hospital and come home again in time to drive them all up to Friesland to visit his great aunts, two formidable ladies who would never see eighty again, but who had lost none of their powers of command. Lucy had been taken on a tour of the house, which was old and furnished with heavy tables and chairs which looked as though they had taken root. They had ended up in the red salon, which had quite overpowered her.

'Frightful, isn't it?' Fran had said. 'I'd hate to live

here, though I like Friesland. We visit from time to time. Litrik has a large family.' It had still been light when he'd left, and they had driven back across the Afsluitdijk, into Alkmaar, so that Lucy might see something of that town, to skirt Amsterdam and take the road through Hilversum and so home.

On another day they had driven along the narrow quiet road beside the River Vecht, admiring the lovely old houses with their grounds bordering the water, built by the rich merchants of the eighteenth century. And one evening there had been people to dinner, and all this interspersed with the gentle day's routine and hours spent with the children.

'You must go and see Keukenhof next week,' Fran had said. 'It's a glorious sight now, you couldn't have come at a better time.'

Lucy had been tired then, but, although her head was full of all the sights she had seen, there was still room to think of William.

'Out with Fiona, I suppose,' she mumbled as she dropped off.

Litrik had Sunday free, he had said on the previous evening, and, sitting up in bed, drinking her morning tea, Lucy wondered what pleasures were in store for her. The maid had pulled the curtains back and the sky was blue, the sun was shining and there didn't seem to be too much wind. Lucy hopped out of bed, flung up the window and hung out to enjoy the expanse of velvety lawn and the flower-beds filled with tulips and hyacinths. The birds were singing too, and the sun held warmth.

'Come gentle spring, ethereal Mildness, come,' carolled Lucy from her window, just as the peace of the garden was broken. Litrik was coming round the corner of his house, the dogs with him, and, strolling beside him, his hands in his pockets, looking very much at home, was William.

She stared down at him, unable to believe her eyes, her mouth open while happiness almost choked her. The two men looked up then, and Litrik said pleasantly, 'Oh, good morning, Lucy. I think you know William? He's an old friend, come to spend a few days with us. Come on down and meet him.'

Lucy went on staring with nothing to say, and then a wide smile curved her mouth. 'Good morning,' she said in a wispy voice. 'I'll be down—' It struck her suddenly that she was hardly suitably dressed for a chat, and she withdrew her person smartly, only to poke her head out again, her hair in a tangle round her shoulders. 'Is Fiona with you?' she asked.

If Dr Thurloe was surprised, nothing of it showed on his placid face as he looked up at her. 'No, I'm alone.'

She nodded, still smiling, and shut the window, to dance across the room to the bathroom. While she showered she thought about what she would wear. It was still cool, although the sun shone and it was April. It had better be the jersey dress. She dressed rapidly, brushed her hair to shining smoothness, applied lipstick and raced downstairs.

The two men were coming out of Litrik's study

as she reached the hall, and she went to meet them, quite unaware of the delight on her face. Indeed, she might have uttered a good deal which she would have regretted later if it hadn't been for Fran running down the staircase after her, calling out as she came, 'William—how delightful! Of course, you'll stay? And it won't be just babies and us...' She gave a well-simulated start of surprise. 'Oh, do you two know each other?'

She leaned up to give William a kiss and he said gravely, 'We have met—at the clinic and various dinner parties.'

'Oh, isn't it a small world?' Fran declared and both men agreed with a blandness which belied the gleam in their eyes.

But Lucy hadn't noticed, and she said now, rather shyly, 'It does seem strange meeting here. Are you on holiday?' And, in case he should think that she was prying, 'I am, I've been here a week already. I knew Fran at school.'

'There's nothing like old friends,' observed Dr Thurloe easily. 'How are you liking Holland?'

They went in to breakfast and Lucy, the seething of her feelings settling down under his casual friendliness, joined in the light-hearted talk.

Fran, pouring coffee, asked half laughingly, 'And how is that handsome lady of thirty-odd years—the comfortably situated widow with the social graces? You were going to take her out...?'

The doctor's eyes were on Lucy's face. 'Fiona

Seymour? As handsome as ever. You must meet her next time that you come over, and see for yourself.'

Lucy buttered a roll and didn't look up. She said evenly, 'She dresses beautifully, Fran, and always in the right clothes, if you know what I mean.'

She looked up then, straight at William, and smiled at him. It was the kind of smile Boadicea might have had on her face as she led the Iceni into battle. He stared back at her; she was in a temper despite the smile, and her eyes sparkled like emeralds.

He said mildly, 'I suppose that matters to women; I don't think men notice such things.' He smiled gently. 'At least, only upon occasion.'

Lucy went slowly a very pretty pink, remembering that there had been far too much of her hanging out of her bedroom window. Just for the moment she could think of nothing crushing to say; when she did, she would say it.

Chapter 6

Since it was Sunday, they all went to church and Lucy, sitting with Fran on one side of her making sure she could follow the service, was very conscious of William's bulk on her other side. She stood up and sat down just as she should, but she didn't understand a word thundered at her from the pulpit and, although she opened her hymn book obediently at Fran's direction, she had no idea of what they were singing. She was wondering how it was that Fran had heard about Fiona; William must have said something, but when? She sat there frowning until she was gently prodded to her feet for the final hymn.

They stayed talking to the *dominee* for quite a while after the service and then Litrik and William walked on ahead, leaving her and Fran to follow. They had a lot to talk about, and William wasn't mentioned.

Nanny was in the garden playing ball with little Litrik while the baby slept in her pram.

'Go and have your coffee, Nanny,' said Fran, 'and will you ask someone to bring ours out here? We'll stay with the children.'

The two men began a gentle game of ball with the little boy staggering happily between them, and Fran and Lucy went to sit by the pram. The baby was charming, pink and white and fair-haired. Lucy bent over her and murmured, 'She's beautiful, Fran, and she has such a pretty name.'

'Lisa—I asked Litrik if I could tell you about that and he said that he'd like you to know. You see, when I first met him he had a ward, a little girl with spina bifida. Her father had died—he was a friend of Litrik's—and her mother left her. So he became her guardian until she died soon after we married. She was a darling and we still miss her.'

She smiled rather mistily at Lucy, who thought, looking at her friend's expressive face, that there was a lot more to the story than that, but all she said was, 'Thank you for telling me, Fran. Little Lisa will fill her place...'

Trugg had put the coffee-tray on the garden table and they sat around drinking and making vague plans for the week ahead.

'You two girls can do what you like tomorrow,' said Litrik. 'William will come with me to Utrecht; we shan't be back until the early evening. There's the party on Wednesday, isn't there, darling? And on Thursday I've arranged to be free and we might all go to Keukenhof.'

Sunday lunch was a leisurely affair, and afterwards—she wasn't quite sure how it happened—Lucy found herself walking briskly out of the gate beside William.

'A good walk, just what we need after that magnificent meal,' he observed.

'I don't remember saying that I wanted to come.'

'My dear girl, where is your tact? I'm sure that Litrik and Fran would like an hour or two on their own—he's a busy man, you know, and he doesn't see as much of her or the children as he would wish.'

'Oh, well—I hadn't thought of that...'

'He loves his work, you know.'

They were walking along a narrow lane leading, as far as Lucy could see, nowhere at all. 'Do you love your work too?'

'Yes, and even when I marry it will still be a large part of my life,' he looked down at her, 'however much I love my wife and children.'

'You have children round you every day for hours—in the clinics and the wards, and I suppose at your consulting rooms. And then you'll go home to them?' She frowned a little thinking that Fiona, if she had children, would keep them out of the way with a nanny—they'd be in bed by the time he got home. There would be guests for dinner and Fiona waiting for him in some exquisite outfit...

'Now what are you dreaming up?' asked William. 'I suspect you have far too much imagination. If you are worried as to my future, don't be—I have it all nicely planned.'

Lucy stopped to admire the view, a gentle rise and fall of endless fields with a farmhouse here and there and cows in abundance. There was a farm cart coming towards them too, drawn by a great horse, plodding patiently. They stood aside to allow it to pass and William exchanged unintelligible greetings with the driver. Only when it had gone did she speak.

'I am not in the least worried about your future,' she told him coldly. 'Why should I be? Nor do I need to draw on my imagination about it, for it is a foregone conclusion, isn't it?'

He looked interested. 'Oh, is it? May I know?'

She said, still coldly, 'Why should I tell you something you already know?'

He said blandly, 'I believe we are at cross purposes. Never mind, time enough for that... I saw in the *Daily Telegraph* that Imogen has become engaged. Does she plan to marry before Pauline? And when do your parents return?'

The rest of their walk was taken up with what Lucy considered to be pointless chat. She returned to the house in quite a nasty temper, although she was too well brought up to show it. But she couldn't conceal the vivid green of her eyes. The doctor was quick to see that and smiled to himself.

The men left early the next morning, and after an hour or more in the nursery Fran got into her car and, with Lucy beside her, drove to Arnhem, where they spent the rest of the morning wandering round the open air museum with its replicas of old cottages, windmills and farms from a bygone age. 'You see,' explained Fran, 'there's not time to take you all over Holland, and here you get an idea of the history of each province. I wish you could stay another week, Lucy.'

'So do I, but I have to be back because one of the other helpers is going on holiday. There are never enough of us anyway.'

They had their coffee at the Rijzenburg Restaurant, a few miles out of Arnhem and, since it was almost lunchtime, ordered omelettes and salads at the same time. 'Though I must be back by two o'clock to feed the baby,' said Fran. 'Do you think I should spend more time with the children? Of course, when there's no one visiting, I'm with them almost all day.'

'I think you're a marvellous mother,' declared Lucy, 'and I think you must be a jolly good wife too.'

'Oh, good. I'm very happy, you know—I hope you find the right man, Lucy; being married is such fun.' She looked across the table at her friend. 'But there is someone, isn't there?'

Lucy went pink. 'Yes. But he doesn't know and I don't suppose he ever will, for I won't tell him.'

Fran said gently, 'Think about it, often things have a way of turning out well. Don't ever give up hope, Lucy.' She glanced at her watch. 'Heavens, we'd better go.'

Later that afternoon they took the children for a walk, with Lisa in her pram and little Litrik on his reins, and after that it was nursery tea and the fun of bathtime. The men came home then, and Nanny went away to have her supper while the four of them saw the little ones into their cots. There was a good deal of laughter and squeals of delight from the little boy, but presently he sat on his father's knee while his evening quota of nursery rhymes were recited and baby Lisa went to sleep at once.

With Nanny back, they went to tidy themselves for the evening and presently met again in the drawing-room to discuss the day's events. The two men had been busy, although they only touched lightly on their work. Lucy had the impression that if she hadn't been there Litrik would have gone into details, for it was obvious that Fran knew exactly what he was talking about and was interested too. She allowed her thoughts to wander presently, trying to picture Fiona listening to William when he got home with just such a look of rapt attention on her face as Fran had. But the picture refused to take shape; Fiona wouldn't want to know, she would give him a drink and tell him who was coming to dinner.

She stole a quick look at him, sitting at his ease, a glass in his hand, content after his day. And that was how it should be every evening, she reflected, and how it would be if only she could marry him. It would be so helpful if Fiona could meet a very rich man who liked her lifestyle. She looked up and found the doctor's eyes on her, and just for a moment she couldn't look away, unaware that her dreams were in her face.

He smiled slowly. 'Will you come to Amsterdam with me tomorrow, Lucy?'

She nodded. 'I'd like that very much, thank you. I expect you've been there before?'

He nodded. 'But it's a place where you can go

back time and again and each time find something
new. We shan't be able to see everything, but we'll
pack in as much as we can.' He looked across the
room to Fran. 'Will it be all right if we go directly
after breakfast, Fran?'

'Of course, and come back here when you like.
If you decide to stay out to dinner, just give us a
ring. Are you going to the hospital again before you
go back?'

'Wednesday...'

'But don't forget the party. About a dozen for dinner, and hordes coming afterwards.' She got up and
went to sit by Lucy. 'What are you going to wear?'

It was a doubtful kind of morning when Lucy
woke, and her suit seemed the most suitable thing
to wear; if it rained it would afford some protection,
and if it turned fine it would be just right for the time
of year. She dressed with care, pinned up her hair
into a french pleat, got into low-heeled shoes—for
there was no knowing where William might take it
into his head to go—and went down to breakfast.

They left directly that meal was over, and since
Amsterdam was a mere twenty-five or so miles away
they were there in just over half an hour. The inner
city appeared to be jammed with cars, parked on
either side of the numerous canals and wherever
there was an inch of room on the narrow streets. But
William drove straight on and presently turned into
the forecourt of a hospital. 'I know the *Directeur*,'
he said casually. 'We can park here for as long as
we like.'

Which he did with a minimum of fuss before taking Lucy's arm and walking her out into the busy street. 'Coffee first,' he suggested, and crossed the road and plunged down a narrow alleyway which brought them out into a tree-lined street, teeming with people and traffic and lined with cafés and smart boutiques. They sat at a table on the pavement and drank their coffee, watching the passers-by while the doctor explained the layout of the city. 'Think of a spider's web,' he observed. 'The circular threads are the canals intersected by streets and alleys. Shall we walk first before we go on the canals?'

He knew his way very well, and they wandered in and out of narrow streets, across small, arched bridges, alongside the canals, admiring the patrician houses with their great front doors reached by double steps, their high windows and their gables, each one slightly different from its neighbours.

'What are they like inside?' wondered Lucy aloud.

'Delightful. Amazingly well modernised without spoiling their original charm. I've been in several—Litrik is old friends with some of the professors at the hospitals in the city. Two of them are married to English girls, I believe there are more than that number. Fran could tell you; she visits them from time to time.'

He led her into a narrow cobbled street lined with little antique shops and waited patiently while she peered into their windows. Before walking back to the Dam Square, they went along Damrak and so to where the canal tours started. The boat they took wasn't very full, and the guide's voice was easy to follow because everything was repeated in English and French. When it was over and they were back on dry land Lucy said, 'That was marvellous; I must try and remember it all...'

'Well, you can always refresh your memory—it is only a couple of hours from home, you know.'

He beckoned a taxi and popped her into it. 'Lunch,' he said.

He took her to Dikker and Thijs in which elegant restaurant they ate a delicious lunch; onion tarts, grilled sole with tiny new potatoes and green peas, and, for Lucy, an enormous ice-cream smothered in whipped cream and chocolate sauce, while the doctor enjoyed a selection from the cheese board, and since they had the afternoon before them they drank sparingly from the hock he had ordered. Over coffee he made his suggestions for the afternoon.

The Rijksmuseum for a start, because when she got home everyone would expect her to have been there. 'The Begijnhof,' he went on. 'It's just off Spui, not too far from here. A circle of charming little houses where nuns once lived; the church in the centre is used for English Services. Then Rembrandt's house, and that, I think, is about all we can manage this time.'

'Oh, yes—it's very kind of you to take me round. I should never have seen all this on my own, and even if I never come again...'

He opened his eyes wide and their blue stare sent

her heart thudding. 'But of course you will come again.'

He sounded so sure of that she didn't like to argue about it.

The afternoon was a kaleidoscope of old houses, famous paintings and exquisite silver and porcelain, all delightfully jumbled in Lucy's head so that sorting them out was going to take her quite a time.

'What a heavenly day,' she sighed happily, pouring tea. He had taken her to the Amstel Hotel, a fitting end to the day, for it was overlooking the Amstel with the barges going to and fro and an ever-changing scene. She found it a delightful place, old-fashioned and solid and very elegant.

They took a taxi back to the hospital, got into the car and drove away from the city through solid traffic which at times hardly moved. But once on the motorway, William allowed the car to rush ahead, and it was still not yet seven o'clock as he stopped in front of the house.

Trugg admitted them with the hope that they had had a nice day, and begged them to go up to the nursery as Mevrouw was putting the children to bed. They left their outdoor things in the hall and went upstairs, to find Fran and Nanny bathing the children, a leisurely business entailing a good deal of splashing and childish shouting. They were joined within minutes by Litrik, and it was another half-hour before the children were tucked up for the night. The four of them dispersed to make themselves presentable for the evening, and presently foregathered in the drawing-room for drinks and to exchange news of their days. After dinner the two men went off to Litrik's study and the two girls spent the next hour or so checking the plans for the party.

'Do you plan to do anything in the morning?' asked Fran.

'No, I'd like to help you, if you need help.'

'Oh, good. The flowers—this is such a big house it takes all day just to do the downstairs rooms. Old Jan will bring in the pot-plants from the greenhouse, so if you could dot them around... He'll leave them in the garden-room beside the kitchen. The men will be out all day, which means we will be able to get on with everything. All Litrik's family will be coming, and his friends from the hospital and from Leiden too—there'll be about fifty of us, but only a dozen for dinner.'

Lucy said thoughtfully, 'You know, Fran, you haven't changed a bit—not you, that is, but you've taken to all this—' she waved expressively with her arms '—like a duck to water. Was it very difficult?'

Fran shook her head. 'No, you see, Litrik helped me, and Trugg and all the people who work here are quite marvellous, and I've a wonderful mother-in-law.' She went on casually, 'Has William got a mother and father?'

'I haven't an idea. We—we have only met occasionally. I had lunch at his home once—one Sunday with some of his friends. In fact, I only know that he has two dogs and a devoted housekeeper.'

'Well, he'd certainly need that; Litrik says he

works a great deal harder than he should.' Fran smiled to herself. 'Litrik works too hard as well, but I nag him before it gets too bad.'

The next day passed pleasantly. In the morning Lucy was busy arranging the flowers here and there, and making herself useful running to and fro with Nanny, giving a helping hand with the children, and in the afternoon she washed her hair, did her nails and experimented with make-up. The men came home soon after tea, and the next hour was spent in the nursery before they went downstairs for a drink before going to dress.

Lucy, studying her image in the pier-glass in her room, hoped that William would find her worth a second glance, and, indeed, she looked charming. She had put on a new dress, amber silk with a long, full skirt, long tight sleeves and a ruched chiffon bodice and, excepting a thick gold chain, she wore no jewellery. She had allowed her hair to curl around her neck and, on second thoughts, hadn't used more make-up than usual. Nothing out of the ordinary, she decided, surveying her person with an eagle eye, and if Fiona Seymour were to have been among the guests Lucy would have stood no chance at all. She went downstairs and found Fran, very stylish in blue velvet, and Litrik correct in his black tie, sitting in the drawing-room, holding hands.

Litrik got up as she went in and said cheerfully, 'Drinks all round, I think, to get us in the mood.'

A moment later William joined them, the epitome of the well-dressed man at a party. He admired Fran and went to stand in front of Lucy. 'Charming,' he said, then added wickedly, 'Did it take all day?'

'Certainly not!' she retorted. 'I've been busy doing the flowers and playing with the children and running errands.' She gave an indignant snort. 'A good deal busier than you, I dare say.'

He smiled. 'Probably.' If he had been about to say more, there was no chance, for the first of the guests were arriving.

Lucy, after hopping into bed at two o'clock in the morning, lay wide awake just long enough to go over the evening. It had been tremendous fun; dinner had been a formal affair, the table appointments splendid, the food superb, and there had been no lack of enlivening conversation. She had sat between two cousins of Litrik's, both of whom had flirted with her in the nicest possible way; she had responded, hoping that William had noticed, but if he had his face remained blandly friendly and nothing more.

Presently, when the rest of the guests had arrived and they had all gone into the drawing-room, which had been cleared for dancing and with its double doors opening on to the covered veranda, she had been swept away to dance without a break. It was just as Trugg had announced that a buffet supper was being served in the dining-room that the doctor had appeared beside her.

'You're enjoying yourself.' It wasn't a question but a statement of fact. 'Let me get you something to eat before you disappear on to the dance-floor again.'

Lucy had made some casual answer, discomfited by the thought that he hadn't made any effort to dance with her. Not that she could blame him—there had been any number of pretty girls there, and he had danced with almost all of them. And, to make matters worse, they had joined a party at one of the bigger tables and, although he sat next to her, he'd made no effort to talk to her other than in the general conversation all around them. It had pleased her enormously when one of her dance partners had got up finally and came to bend over her chair. 'Tear yourself away from that ice and come and dance, Lucy. It's a waltz and I'm feeling romantic.'

She had got to her feet at once, smiling at him, allowing William the tail-end of a smile before she had gone back to the drawing-room. And she had danced every dance after that, with the *burgermeester*, the *dominee*, a selection of young men whose names she couldn't remember, and Litrik. It wasn't until the band had been striking up for the last dance that William had appeared beside her once more, swept her into his arms and danced her away. It had been a waltz and he'd danced well, and just for a moment she'd forgotten that he had ignored her for most of the evening, that he would probably marry Fiona, that when they got back to England she might not see him again for several weeks; she had been happy, floating round the vast room, her cheek pressed to his shirt-front, his arm around her. She could have gone on forever, but of course she hadn't. The music had ended in a final flourish and the party had been over. Perhaps, she thought sleepily, she could change her style, tint her hair, buy clothes in the forefront of fashion and not just those which suited her, do something really clever so that he would notice her—even accompany her father on his next excavation. She just had time to reject this last plan before she fell asleep.

She was awake again by eight o'clock and out of bed to see what kind of a morning it was. They were to go to Keukenhof and if only it were a fine day she would be able to wear the deceptively simple Jaeger outfit she had been saving for just such an occasion.

The garden was bathed in early morning sunshine and looked beautiful, and as she looked she was aware of Litrik and William with the dogs. They were striding across the paddock beyond the grounds. She showered and dressed and went downstairs, just in time to see their broad backs disappearing through the front door, and Fran, her head peering round the door of the small room where they had breakfast, said, 'Aren't they gluttons for work? But they've promised faithfully to be back here by eleven o'clock to take us to Keukenhof.' She eyed Lucy. 'I say, you do look smart, and just right for this kind of a day.' She opened the door wider. 'Come and have breakfast, and then help me bath the children; it's Nanny's morning off.'

Over breakfast Lucy asked, 'If it's Nanny's off-duty how can we go to Keukenhof?'

'She's coming with us. Twice a week she is free from half-past eight until half-past ten, so she takes the small car into Utrecht, has her hair done or shops, and so on. She likes it that way and it suits us very well.'

So the first part of the morning was spent in the nursery until Nanny came back and presently the men came home.

The party set off in two cars, Litrik with Fran, Nanny and the children, and William with Lucy— an arrangement which pleased her very well. Not easily disheartened, she was well aware that each time she spent with him gave her another chance to get him interested in her; so far she hadn't had much success, but she was a strong believer in kindly fate, although whether fate was going to be strong enough to overcome Fiona Seymour was a moot point.

They took the main road, circumventing Utrecht and, as they neared Amsterdam, turning south to Lisse. The Keukenhof gardens were just outside the town and, since it was a fine day, there were plenty of people strolling up and down the paths. They parked the cars, fastened little Litrik into his push-chair, tucked Lisa into her folding pram and set off. The flowers were a magnificent sight; huge beds of tulips, daffodils, hyacinths and still more tulips stretched as far as the eye could see. They wandered along for an hour or more and presently went to the restaurant, which was elegantly set among the background of trees and more flowers. They drank coffee and ate *broodjes* and little Litrik sat on his father's knee, eating his roll and gabbling away in a mixture of Dutch and English. And as for Lisa, good baby that she was, she slept peacefully in her pram.

There was still a great deal to see, and since Fran had said that they must go round the giant greenhouses so that she could order some plants for later on in the year they made their way there. 'I'll be ages making up my mind,' said Fran. 'William, you take Lucy with you and go at your own pace. We'll meet here at the entrance in half an hour or so, shall we? And if you're not ready by then we'll see you at the cars.'

The doctor proved to be a knowledgeable gardener, and, what was more, he ordered several boxes of bulbs for his own garden and then did the same for Lucy when she admired a particularly fine hyacinth. 'They send them over later,' he told her, and when she thanked him, 'Something to remind you of your stay in Holland.'

They were standing admiring a display of hothouse lilac when he observed placidly, 'Of course, you'll come back with me. So much easier in the car. I'll see about your ticket. I have to be home on Sunday, unfortunately—a dinner engagement I can't miss.' He glanced down at her, smiling a little. 'An important one I don't want to miss.'

She said stiffly, 'It's very kind of you to offer me a lift, but I can just as easily go by plane. I have my ticket...'

'Don't be tiresome, Lucy,' he said blandly. 'If you travel back with me there will be no need for Litrik to take you to Schiphol, and if we leave after breakfast on Saturday we'll be home for tea. I came by hovercraft.'

There was no point in arguing further; he was offering her a lift home out of consideration to his friends, and not because he wanted her company.

She said snappily, 'Very well, since it is convenient. Shall we go and find the others?'

'Tired of my company?' he asked silkily. And, before she could think of a suitable answer, 'That is an unfair question. You will either tell the truth or tell a pack of lies.'

'I am not in the habit of lying,' said Lucy haughtily.

'The truth wouldn't do either, would it?' he answered cheerfully.

At the cars he suggested that he might drive back to the house another way. 'So that Lucy can see a little more of Holland...' he explained, and Litrik agreed with him. 'A good idea. Take the road through Alphen aan de Rijn and Bodegraven. You can get a side-road from there which will take you north of Utrecht—you know the one I mean?—it weaves past the lakes and you can get to Bilthoven and Zeist. A peaceful, pleasant little run. You can get tea at Breukelen—there's a good hotel by the river, but come back to us if you don't feel like stopping.'

He smiled kindly at Lucy. 'You'll be quite safe with William; he knows this part of Holland almost as well as I do.'

He stowed his family carefully into his car, waved nonchalantly, and drove off.

Lucy got into William's car and sat silently until

it occurred to her that he might think that she was sulking. Conversation, polite conversation, that was, was imperative. 'You come to Holland quite often?' she wanted to know.

'Off and on. I'm an honorary consultant at Utrecht and Leiden, which means that I come over to lecture from time to time and also act as an examiner.' He gave her a quick sideways glance. 'Will you be sorry to go back home?'

'Yes, I think I shall. I've been happy here.' She could hardly add that that was because he had been there too. 'Fran is such a dear, and the babies are delightful. I like Litrik too.'

'A sound man. Fran is exactly right for him. I envy him—a wife, children and a lovely house that Fran has turned into a home…'

'You have a lovely house…'

'Indeed, yes. I really must add a wife and children as soon as possible.'

Lucy looked out of the window at the serene countryside. There was a potential wife waiting for him, wasn't there? Someone who would grace his table and manage his home to perfection. The children were another matter, but perhaps Fiona might change her mind… She said in a wooden voice, 'I hope you'll be very happy.'

He said placidly, 'I'm thirty-five and I've waited a long time for the right girl to come along. I know I—we shall be very happy.'

There seemed to be no answer to that. Lucy pointed out the sails of a boat apparently in the middle of a meadow and remarked on how interesting that was. He agreed gravely, 'The lakes are there—we shall turn off presently and you will have a better view. I think we might take Litrik's advice and have tea, don't you?'

A cup of tea was a panacea for all ills, she reminded herself, and agreed politely.

They stopped presently at a small, picturesque hotel by the water and sat watching the yachts gliding by in the quite stiff breeze while they drank their tea. Lucy, who had discovered that, contrary to the general idea, unrequited love had made no difference to her appetite, ate a mountainous cream cake with unselfconscious pleasure, watched, if only she had looked, by the doctor with amused tenderness.

They arrived back in good time to change for the evening and join Fran and Litrik for drinks before dinner. But before they went across the hall to the dining-room Fran said that she would just make sure the children were all right and Lucy went with her. They were both asleep, the baby's pale hair shining in the light of the small lamp near her cot, the little boy upside-down in his cot, clutching a teddy bear.

'Oh, Fran, you are lucky,' said Lucy softly, and in such a sad little voice that Fran looked at her.

'You'll be lucky too,' she said gently. 'I wonder what's round the corner for you.'

'The orphanage,' said Lucy bleakly. Nanny came from the day nursery then, and Fran stopped to speak to her, which Lucy thought was a good thing or she might have wallowed in self-pity.

She was very bright and chatty for the rest of the evening, something which puzzled all three of her companions, for she wasn't either bright or chatty by nature.

If she had been harbouring a secret hope that William might have plans to take her out on her last day, she was doomed to disappointment; at break-fast the two men were engrossed in their plans for the day—hospital rounds, an afternoon clinic, a visit to a retired professor and a meeting of consultants. There wasn't a minute to spare for anything or any-one else. They went off presently with the air of men well content with their world, and Fran took another slice of toast and poured more coffee for herself and Lucy. 'I thought we might go to Utrecht for a last look round,' she suggested. 'The men will be back soon after tea, so if you pack this afternoon we'll have a nice long evening with nothing to do. I shall miss you, Lucy.'

'I've loved being here, Fran. I'll remember these two weeks forever. And if I don't write often it's because I'm really quite busy...'

'I know, I shall phone you. Do you plan to stay at the orphanage?'

'I think so. I'm too old to train for anything, and besides, I'm not clever at exams and things like that. I took the job because I wanted to prove to Mother and Father that I could do something, and I really like my work.'

'You must come again, and I mean that.'

The pair of them spent the morning shopping,

buying last-minute presents to take home and sweets for the orphans, and in the afternoon Lucy packed and put everything ready for going away in the morning. If she felt sad, nothing of that showed when the men came home. They sat round talking after dinner until late, and when she at last got into her bed Lucy was too tired to do more than give a long sigh before she slept.

They left after breakfast the next morning, with everyone standing on the steps to see them off. Amid cries of, 'See you again very soon,' and 'Have a good journey,' William drove out of the drive and into the lane on their journey back to England.

Chapter 7

The journey back to London was accomplished without a hitch and in comfort. The doctor drew up before Lucy's home at mid-afternoon, got out to unload her luggage, opened her door and then rang the doorbell. Alice welcomed them warmly, ushered them inside, suggested tea, and offered the news that neither Imogen or Pauline would be home until Sunday evening.

Anxious that William shouldn't feel obliged to offer her entertainment, Lucy said hastily, 'Oh, good, I could do with a day to sort things out on my own.' She added, rather belatedly, her invitation to have some tea before he went on to his own house, and, when he refused smilingly, she thanked him for her lift back, saying politely, 'I hope you have a nice evening.'

He didn't answer that, only smiled a little. 'I dare say we shall see each other from time to time,' he observed in a non-committal manner. 'Miranda will still need to visit me and you will probably be with her.'

She nodded and managed a smile, engulfed in

a bitter disappointment that he had no plans to see her again unless it was at the clinic. And when he wished her goodbye a few moments later she made some inane remark about their holiday which, upon reflection, made no sense at all, but at least bridged the awkward gap between his goodbyes and departure. She stood on the doorstep and waved gaily as he drove away, and then went indoors and burst into tears.

'Things are never as bad as they seem,' said Alice, and gave her a motherly hug. 'You sit down and drink your tea and have a good cry if you want to, and then tell me all about your holiday.'

So Lucy sat down at the kitchen table with Mrs Simpkins on her lap and presently mopped her eyes, drank her tea and launched into an account of her two weeks in Holland. If there was a singular lack of information about the doctor, Alice didn't comment upon it. Instead she said briskly, 'You've 'ad two lovely weeks, Miss Lucy, and just you remember that. And now go and wash your face and telephone that nice Miss Fran and let her know you're back 'ome. And there's a note for you in the drawing-room from your sisters.'

'Is there a letter from Mother?'

Alice shook her head. 'I dare say she'll phone now you're back home.'

Lucy went upstairs taking her sisters' note with her. It bore out Alice's message that they wouldn't be at home until the following evening, and, beyond a vague hope that she had enjoyed herself, it was entirely taken up with their own doings.

Lucy read it twice and then went to look at her blotched face in the looking-glass. 'I should dearly love to wallow in self-pity,' she told her reflection, 'but a lot of good that would do. I shall plan a campaign.'

Alice had made a chicken casserole and followed it with one of her apple tarts, and over their meal Lucy discussed the forthcoming weddings, speculated over the dresses she would be expected to wear as bridesmaid, and observed that she was quite looking forward to going back to the orphanage. When she had helped Alice with the washing up, she declared herself tired after her journey and said goodnight. 'And I'll phone Fran before I go upstairs,' she told her old friend.

'Did you have a good trip?' Fran wanted to know. 'I hope William gave you a meal, you left so early.'

'We stopped on the way—just before we went on the hovercraft—and had an early lunch. We were back here in good time for tea.'

'Did you go out to dinner?'

'Well, no—William had a dinner engagement and I'm really quite tired.'

They gossiped for a few minutes more before Lucy rang off with the promise of a phone call later in the week.

Fran put the receiver down at her end and went back to sit by Litrik. 'I thought that there was something between William and Lucy,' she told her husband. 'He took her home, but he had a dinner engagement—I mean, if he was keen he would have asked her out... Do you suppose I've made a mistake, darling?'

Litrik lowered his newspaper. 'No, my love, but these things can't be hurried, you know. Lucy has a bee in her bonnet about this woman Fiona, and William, unless I am much mistaken, is holding back for a number of reasons. Give them time.'

'But they never see each other,' almost wailed Fran.

'My dearest, if William wants to see Lucy, he'll contrive to do so, be assured of that.'

Lucy spent Sunday sorting out her clothes, washing her hair, doing her nails and then going for a brisk walk along the Embankment, and if she was lonely after the cheerful company she had been in, she didn't admit it.

Everyone was glad to see her back on Monday morning, not least Miranda, who was much improved but still given to bouts of peevishness and screaming fits. Lucy, plunging into the day's work, found the hours too short; two of the girls who came in part time were off sick, and the rest of them were hard put to it to get through the ever-recurring chores. She went home late to find her sisters waiting for her.

'You must give up that job,' declared Imogen. 'It's ridiculous to work yourself to the bone like this. There's no need—'

'But I like my work, and it's useful, even if it isn't important.'

Imogen went red. 'You know Mother would love to have you at home, especially now Pauline and I will be getting married.'

'Well, I am at home each evening, and Mother and Father are often out or away.' She smiled suddenly. 'Don't let's talk about me—tell me if there are any more plans for the weddings.'

Her mother telephoned that evening too; they had discovered more iron pots and tools and now her father intended to travel some miles into the desert to investigate local tales of more finds. 'So we shan't be home for another few weeks, darling. Did you have a good holiday?'

She didn't wait for Lucy to reply. 'Ask Imogen to come to the phone, will you, Lucy? I want to know the exact date of her wedding...'

Both weddings were going to be rather grand affairs, Imogen's first, in July, and Pauline's in September, but the girls were already making lists of guests and wedding presents, and weighing the merits of oyster satin against white crêpe. Lucy, as keen as any girl to wear white satin and orange blossom, began to alter her ideas. Just to slip into a small church and get married without guests or bridesmaids seemed preferable. Perhaps, she thought wistfully, if ever she should marry, she would change her mind. Other girls' weddings weren't the same as one's own.

It was almost the end of the week when she saw

William, but not to speak to. She had just stepped off the bus on her way home when the Rolls slid past. Fiona was sitting beside him, and as her eye caught Lucy's she smiled; it wasn't a nice smile, and she made no effort to draw William's notice to Lucy standing there on the pavement. Lucy would have been very surprised if she had. Somehow the little episode made her resolve to marry William quite hopeless, so that when she got home and found Pauline waiting for her with an invitation to join a party of friends for dinner and dancing on the following evening she accepted at once. It was to be quite a grand affair, Pauline told her—a celebration of Cyril's promotion. His sister and brother-in-law would be there, a couple of old friends, and Cyril's unmarried brother. A daunting thought if he was anything like Cyril, reflected Lucy, but an evening out would distract her thoughts from William.

It was a pity that the orphans had been particularly trying all day, so that when she got home an evening out was the last thing she wanted. But a hot bath and a pot of Alice's tea improved her outlook; she dressed with care in the grey dress she had hoped William would have admired, did her hair in a top knot fastened with a glittering bow, eased her feet into her sandals and went downstairs to join Pauline.

'That's nice even if it isn't new,' said Pauline kindly. 'It's a pity Imogen couldn't make it. Cyril will be here in a moment.' She studied Lucy's quiet face. 'Are you working too hard? You're thinner, aren't you, and a bit pale? Never mind, you'll be all the better for an evening out.'

Cyril came then, more self-important than ever, taking Lucy's congratulations as his rightful due before driving them off to the Savoy. 'Bertram will meet us there with the others,' he told them. 'His days are very full now that he has taken silk—he should go far.'

'I'm sure you'll go further,' murmured Pauline dutifully. 'This promotion is marvellous.'

Lucy, sitting in the back seat, watched the smug little nod he gave in answer. She hoped that Bertram would prove to be a different kettle of fish.

He was the counterpart of Cyril—she saw that the moment the party gathered in the foyer, and her heart sank. There was no hope to be got from the old friends either, as they were middle-aged and devoid of conversation, and Cyril's sister was a disheartened doormat, hardly speaking and, when she did, looking around her apologetically as though requesting permission to speak. Lucy, sitting next to Bertram and with the old friend on the other side of her, listened to the one deploring the young people of today and the other giving her a blow by blow account of some dreary lawsuit in which he had apparently shone. She murmured at intervals and ate the food on her plate with pleasure. There hadn't been much time for lunch at the orphanage, and she was hungry, but that proved to be a problem too, for everyone else was pecking at his or her food in a polite way and the old friend began a stern lecture on the evils of rich food and drink. Lucy wondered why he had come since he felt so strongly about it, and would have had a second helping of the delicious chicken à la King only Bertram pushed back his chair and invited her to dance in what she imagined might be his barrister's voice. She got up obediently and everyone else at the table looked up from their discussion about Fine Art and smiled kindly at her. Cyril's smile was particularly benevolent; she was having a treat and he was the donor.

Bertram was an appalling dancer; her feet, already a little painful from the too-tight sandals, became a problem which emptied her head of every thought other than evading his clumsy steps. They lumbered round the dance floor while he described just how astute he had been in the case of Biggins versus Potts. Lucy, concentrating on her feet, consigned the pair of them to the bottom of the sea and Bertram with them while she nodded and smiled and said, 'Did you really? You must be clever—of course, I don't know a thing about law...' A mistake, for he began to explain it to her. She pinned a smile on her face and winced as he trod rather more heavily on her toes, and just at that moment Dr William Thurloe danced past, Fiona Seymour in his arms. He looked straight at Lucy, half smiling, and she widened her smile for Bertram's benefit and gave William a small, cool nod. A really tremendous urge to evade Bertram's clutches, push Fiona out of the way and dance off with the doctor filled her person with a fierce wave of rage at meeting the pair of them when she least expected to, and when her feet were killing her too. Mercifully the music stopped, and they went back to the table, where she accepted dessert with relief and slid her poor feet out of the sandals.

She had barely had a mouthful of the caramel mousse when there was a general uprising of the men in the party and she looked up to see Fiona and William standing by the table.

'Pauline,' gushed Mrs Seymour, 'I have not yet wished you happy, and I must congratulate Cyril. When is the wedding to be? And I see that Imogen is to marry too. How exciting.' She gave a trill of laughter and looked across at Lucy. 'Don't get left behind, Lucy.'

Lucy smiled sweetly, her eyes glittering greenly. 'There's a proverb about the hare and the tortoise,' she said gently. 'Better still, do you know a writing of John Burroughs? It's called "Waiting".' She recited clearly, '"Serene I fold my hands and wait, Nor care for wind or tide nor sea; I rave no more 'gainst time or fate, For lo! my own shall come to me."'

There was a small outburst of clapping and laughter, and Pauline said, 'Darling, how very apt, and fancy remembering it—you were always quoting poetry when we were at school. I just hope it comes true for you.'

Fiona had been looking uncertain; she had been quite out of her depth, as she had never bothered with poetry and thought it rather silly and a waste

of time. She said charmingly, 'Oh, of course it will.
I dare say Lucy will surprise us all.'

She smiled around the table and Bertram said
quickly, 'I say, would you care to dance? The band
is splendid...'

It was the signal for the general movement towards the dance floor, save for Lucy, searching feverishly under the table with her feet, hunting for
her discarded sandals.

'I won't ask you to dance,' said William in her
ear. 'Although nothing would give me greater pleasure, I suspect that you have taken your shoes off.
Would it not be a better idea to buy sandals which
fitted your feet? And stop poking around like that—
I'll get them and we can sit here comfortably while
you cram your feet back in.'

He's so nice and ordinary, reflected Lucy, watching him bend his great height to forage under the
table and put her shoes where her feet could reach
them. He had done it without fuss and quickly, waving away a waiter anxious to be of help, and then he
pulled out the chair beside her and sat down.

'And are you settling down after your holiday?'
he asked.

'Yes, no—I don't know. It's been busy at the orphanage.'

'All the more reason to enjoy this pleasant little
evening party,' his voice was silky, 'but I suspect
that you are not doing so.' He lifted a finger and
spoke to a waiter, then turned to look at her. 'I like
that dress—I liked it last time too...'

Lucy blushed. 'Oh, do you? I thought—' She stopped, and started again. 'That is, I thought…' She gave up and sat looking at him for a long moment, watching the slow smile etch his firm mouth. The arrival of the waiter with champagne in an ice-bucket broke the spell.

William said pleasantly, 'I feel that, since we have joined your party for the moment, the least we can do is to drink to our—er—further acquaintance.'

'How nice,' said Lucy inanely. She hoped the band would go on playing for a long time yet.

William crossed one long leg over the other. 'You read poetry? Do you enjoy John Donne?'

'Very much, though sometimes I'm not sure if I understand all his poems, but some lines—they stick in one's head.' She added almost humbly, 'I'm not clever.'

'If by that you mean you can't add up two columns of figures at the same time or use a computer or understand the Stock Market, then no, you're not clever in the accepted terms of the word. On the other hand, you have an understanding of babies and children and animals, and that is a gift beyond mere cleverness. Also you have the gift of holding your tongue when others might regrettably allow theirs to run away with them.'

She said with something of a snap, 'You make me sound like a saint!'

'Heaven forbid! You're a girl with green eyes.' He smiled at her with a certain touch of mockery and got up as the rest of the party returned to the table.

Fiona tucked her arm in his at once. 'William, why didn't you ask Lucy to dance? Have you just been sitting there talking?'

He didn't answer her, only smiled a little and beckoned the waiter to uncork the champagne, and a moment later everyone was talking at once and happily toasting Pauline and Cyril. Presently William and Fiona went back to their table, and Lucy, glancing round with what she hoped was a casual air, saw them dancing again.

Bertram saw her watching them and said enthusiastically, 'I say, what a splendid woman Fiona Seymour is, and a marvellous dancer. She was very interested in the law—a most intelligent woman and a good listener.'

From which remark Lucy deduced that she was neither.

The party broke up soon afterwards, Lucy said goodbye to Cyril's sister and her husband, the old friends and Bertram and got into the car with Cyril and Pauline. She had eased sore feet into her sandals but they still hurt, which made the evening seem even worse than she'd thought it had been. By the time they arrived at the house she was sunk in gloom, for Cyril and Pauline had been discussing Fiona and William, taking it for granted that their engagement would be announced any day now. Lucy retired to bed in a dark mood and cried herself to sleep.

Pauline spent the day with Cyril on Sunday, and Lucy spent the day in the quite nice garden at the

back of the house, weeding and digging and hoe-
ing, and in the evening she had a long talk with Fran
on the phone. Fran didn't mention William, which
was a good thing, for Lucy was not in the mood to
unburden herself to anyone who would listen. Indeed, when Alice questioned her about the dinner
party she told her that it had been quite nice, but that
Cyril's brother was just as prosey as he was. She described the food, the other guests and the splendours
of the Savoy Hotel, but she didn't breathe a word
about Dr Thurloe, although she longed to do so, and
Alice was wise enough not to mention him either.

Lucy went to work on Monday morning cheered
by the thought of a hard day's work ahead of her.
One of the nurses was on holiday and Sister had
days off. While Lucy had been in Holland a few of
the older children had been taken to Madame Tus-
saud's and the trip seemed to have unsettled them,
so that Sister had had her hands full for the rest of
the week and had put off her free time. Before she
had gone off duty on Saturday she had confided in
Lucy that she thought she had a heavy cold coming on. 'I must have caught it during that outing, although that was ten days ago now, but it's since then
that I've been feeling a bit under the weather. I feel
a bit mean taking days off as we're short-staffed,
but I really do need a break,' she'd said.

Lucy had assured her that they would manage,
and reminded her that the nurse on holiday would
be back in a few days' time and everything would

be normal again. 'And until then,' she said cheerfully, 'I'm sure we'll cope. You have a good rest.'

Sister, knowing Lucy to be a sensible girl and
not given to panicking in an emergency, presently
went home.

The orphanage was already well into its day when
Lucy got into her white overall, reported to the senior nurse and went to see Miranda. The child was
making progress, slow but steady. Lucy fed, bathed
and dressed her, gave her some toys to play with
and started on the next toddler. There were only six
children between one and two years at that time—
there were a great many babies, and the vast ma-
jority were five- and six-year-olds, who went to the
infant school close by. One or two of the toddlers
appeared to have colds, Lucy noted, and at lunchtime one of the older ones was brought home from
the school feeling poorly.

'Just when we're short-staffed,' said Matron worriedly. 'Thank heaven Sister will be back tomorrow.'

But Sister wasn't back in the morning. When
Lucy got to the orphanage the next morning it was
to find a harassed Matron; several of the older children were feeling poorly and the nurse who was due
back from her holiday that day was still in Greece
because of an airline strike. Matron was a level-
headed woman, not easily put out. 'If it's flu,' she
observed, 'we shall have our hands full.'

'If it would help, I could sleep here until Nurse
Swift gets back,' suggested Lucy diffidently. 'And
I don't mind working different hours '

'Bless you, it would be such a help. I'll make up your hours when we are fully staffed again and all the children are better. Sister hopes to be back within a few days—some kind of cold, she thought, or flu.'

'Then if I may I'll go home at lunchtime and fetch a few things,' said Lucy, 'and let our house-keeper know.'

Alice didn't approve when she was told. 'I don't know what your ma would say, Miss Lucy—that nasty flu—you don't want to catch it.'

'Well, I dare say I shan't, Alice. You know I never catch anything. Dr Watts is coming this afternoon to take a look at the children. Will you tell Pauline and Imogen, and if Mother phones tell her I'm quite all right? I dare say I'll be home in a couple of days—it's only until this nurse can get back from Greece and Sister is better. There's a part-time nurse off sick too, and when she's back we shall be back to normal.' With that little bit of information Alice had to be content.

Dr Watts came late that afternoon, examined the sick children and then spent half an hour closeted with Matron and came out of her office looking serious. Lucy, passing the open door, heard him say, 'I'll be in first thing in the morning. We shall have to check every single child and baby, and all the staff. You must warn your staff—you say there's Nurse Swift on holiday? She mustn't come here. And get hold of Sister at once. I may be wrong—I shall be able to tell you if I'm right in the morning.'

Lucy had paused and unashamedly listened. Something serious, she guessed. Measles? Mumps? Just flu? Whatever it was, Dr Watts, the most phlegmatic of men, sounded concerned. She went on her way with a load of small garments for the washing machine, and when she got back to the nursery where the babies were she said nothing to the nurse who was there. Matron would tell them, and until then there was plenty of work to keep her busy. More than enough.

Normally one nurse did night duty, knowing that she could call upon Sister or Matron should things get too much for her. Normally the children slept well, and once the babies had been fed and tucked down for the night they slept too until their early morning feed. The nurses who lived in worked in shifts so that there was one on duty at six o'clock each morning to help the nurse on night duty, but it was obvious as evening approached that more than one nurse would be needed for the night.

'Do you suppose,' suggested Matron to Lucy, 'that you could stay up just for tonight? You should be able to get some sleep, only I don't want to leave Nurse on her own. I'll get up if necessary, but with so many children poorly she won't have much time to see to the babies. And there's Miranda...'

Miranda was being difficult; Lucy hadn't been able to spend as much time as usual with her, and she was working herself into a state.

Lucy was tired and her feet ached; she had been

padding to and fro all day, but then so had everyone else and she had just come back from holiday.

'Of course I'll stay up, Matron. If I can get Miranda to go to sleep I'll be free for the rest of the night to help out.'

'Good girl. I must confess I shall be glad when Dr Watts comes in the morning. I shall be in the office until midnight and be up to help with the feeds in the morning. As soon as the children are seen to for the day you must go off duty.'

Miranda took a long while to settle and the rest of the children were unusually restless and wakeful. Only the babies, once they were fed, slept peacefully. Lucy went in search of Nurse Stokes and found her taking a six-year-old boy's temperature. 'It's very high,' she whispered. She looked at the chart Matron had hung up at the end of his bed. 'It's gone up too.' And by the morning, several of the other children were feverish too. Matron, up and about by six o'clock, studied each ill child in turn and then telephoned Dr Watts.

He came so quickly that Lucy wondered if he had been expecting Matron to call him, and after examining the most poorly of the children he went to the telephone. Twenty minutes later Lucy looked up from trying to get one of the small girls to drink and saw Dr Thurloe, in thin sweater and corduroys, standing in the doorway talking to Dr Watts. His eyes swept over her without any sign of seeing her; he needed a shave and his face was lined with fatigue. She wanted very much to go to him and put her arms around him and tell him not to worry. That was about the silliest thing she could do, she told herself, and applied herself once more to coaxing the little girl on her lap to drink.

Dr Thurloe was there for a long time, meticulously examining each child in turn and then going into Matron's office to talk to Dr Watts and Matron. On his way out he met Lucy, her arms full of clean baby clothes. He stopped and gave her a tired smile. 'Matron will be talking to you all presently,' he told her. 'I'm afraid we have an outbreak of legionnaires' disease on our hands. Some of the children must have picked it up when they had their outing while we were in Holland. They'll have to be sent to hospital and there are quite a few suspects. Matron tells me you're living in for the moment.'

Lucy nodded. 'Have you been up all night?'

He rubbed a hand over his unshaven chin. 'Yes. Why do you ask?'

'Well—I just thought it would be nice if you could go home and have a good sleep—'

He gave a shout of laughter. 'Don't waste your pity on me, Lucy!' He stopped abruptly when he saw the look in her face. 'I'm sorry, my dear, but sleep is the last thing I'm thinking of at the moment.' His eyes searched hers. 'You're going to be busy, do you know that? If you would rather go home, say so now. You aren't trained; you are under no professional obligation to stay.' He added, 'I believe that your parents might not like you to remain.'

'Pooh!' said Lucy forcefully. 'They're not here

anyway, and I'm quite able to decide these things for myself, thank you. Of course I'm staying. I may not be trained, but I'm another pair of hands.'

He ran a hand through his hair. 'I'm sorry, I've said it all wrong, haven't I? And you must be asleep on your feet.' He bent suddenly and kissed her gently. 'Off you go, and do whatever it was you were doing, and then for heaven's sake go to bed. You look like a small dozy doormouse.'

She was sent to bed presently after a meal and awakened again at teatime, much refreshed, to plunge back into the never-ending round of feeding and cleaning up and bed making. Soon after five o'clock Dr Thurloe came again, this time the image of an eminent specialist in his sober grey suit and snow-white shirt, and he stayed for some time, checking the progress of several suspect cases and then examining the well ones as well. All the suspected cases were together now, and the babies had been moved to the floor above. That evening an agency nurse was to come to look after them during the night, and a second nurse would take her place in the morning, which left everyone else free to look after the toddlers and the older children— no easy task since so many of them were isolated.

Lucy was to go on night duty with another nurse, and, since her nursing skills were basic, she was given the well children to look after with strict instructions to warn someone at once if any of them showed any signs of the illness. The night shouldn't be too busy, a tired Matron had told her. 'Eight children are in hospital,' she'd added. 'Two of them are very ill, and there are another nine suspected cases here. Hopefully they are only suspected, but we shan't know that for a day or two. Nurse Swift will be back tomorrow afternoon, she refuses to stay away, and there is another agency nurse coming part time.'

The toddlers and older children slept in dormitories of six or eight beds, and they normally slept through the night, but their day had been disrupted and they were inclined to be querulous. Miranda, aware that something was wrong, was indulging in screaming fits. It was almost midnight by the time Lucy had the children quiet and settled and was able to sit down under the shaded lamp and con the instructions she had been given. She was interrupted by the soft-footed entry of Dr Thurloe. He looked fresh and well fed and immaculate, which only served to remind her that she was hardly looking her best. She was still tired, and it had seemed a waste of time to do more than brush her hair severely into a french pleat and leave her face unmadeup. All the same, she looked very pretty in the dim light of the shaded lamp.

He said, 'Hello,' softly and went on to ask a string of questions. 'Any trouble with Miranda?' he wanted to know finally.

'Well, she took ages to drop off—things have been a bit different, moving cots and children and so on, and she didn't like that.'

'You slept?'

'Yes, thank you. How are the children who went to hospital?'

'Holding their own, although there are two very ill little girls. Litrik phoned today—he and Fran send you their love.'

'Oh, that's nice. It seems such a long time ago...'

'But still very much alive in my thoughts. Yours too?' He stood looking down at her, smiling a little.

'Well, yes. Do you want to look at the children?'

'A quick round if I may, although I'm pretty sure this lot you've got here are going to be all right.'

'Are there any more cases—outside the orphanage?'

'Several. Don't get up, I'll just stroll round and cast an eye.'

He wandered off, in and out of the dormitories, and then back to where she was sitting. 'Everything quiet. Are you on permanent night duty?'

'I don't know. Nurse Swift will be back tomorrow and there's another agency nurse coming.'

He nodded. 'Matron is a most capable woman. Good-night, Lucy.'

He had gone as silently as he had come, leaving her to dream. But not for long—a small demanding voice wanting a drink of water brought her back to reality.

As for Dr Thurloe, he left the orphanage, got into his car and drove to Lucy's home. Late though it was, there were lights shining from several downstairs windows. He rang the bell and Imogen opened the door.

She gave him a look of smiling surprise. 'Oh, hello—do come in. Is this a social call? Would you like some coffee? Alice is getting ready for bed, but Pauline and I have been out and are only just back.'

He followed her into the drawing-room and Pauline looked up with a smile. There were fashion magazines all over the floor and a number of pattern books on the table. 'Hello, how nice to see you. As you see, we're busy planning our weddings. Do sit down—have some coffee?'

'Thank you, no. I can't stop. I thought you might like to know that I've seen Lucy at the orphanage. She's doing night duty and coping very well.'

'She's such a sensible girl,' said Imogen. 'Pigheaded about this job of hers, but she really likes it. Alice said there's flu there.'

'Legionnaires' disease, which is a rather more serious matter.'

'It's not catching?' Pauline looked up sharply. 'Lucy isn't ill?'

'No. It isn't transmitted from person to person, only through the air.'

'Oh, good. Seemingly she left a message to say she would stay at the orphanage for a few days. I dare say she'll phone when she wants to come home.'

The doctor said in an expressionless voice, 'Oh, I'm sure she will. It was kind of you to see me at this late hour. Goodnight, I'll see myself out.'

They chorused a goodnight and added vague

wishes that they might meet at some future date. Alice was waiting by the door when he reached it.

'Miss Lucy—she's all right, Doctor? She's not working too hard? She won't catch anything?'

He smiled kindly at her. 'She's fine, Alice, working hard, but perfectly all right. I'll keep an eye on her.'

'She's such a dear girl, Doctor.'

'Yes, she is, Alice. Don't worry about her. Has her mother phoned?'

Alice shook her head. 'No. What shall I say?'

'Why, that she is living at the orphanage for a few days because some of the children are ill and they are short-staffed. Mrs Lockitt has no cause to worry.'

Alice stared up at him. 'She never worries about Miss Lucy—only that she doesn't get married.'

'Well, we shall have to do something about that. Goodnight, Alice.'

Alice went back to the kitchen and began to lock up for the night. 'Well, I never did,' she muttered to Mrs Simpkins. 'I wonder if 'e meant what I think 'e did! And 'er sweet on 'im too. And would 'e know that?'

Mrs Simpkins blinked yellow eyes and curled herself into a tidy ball preparatory to a good night's sleep, so that Alice was obliged to answer her own question. ''Course 'e knows,' she told herself, and nodded her head in a satisfied manner.

Lucy, happily unaware of the interest being taken in her future, had no time to speculate about it during the next few days. Even with Nurse Swift and the part-time helpers there was an endless round of chores, and the news that Sister was laid low with legionnaires' disease had cast a gloom over everybody. Dr Thurloe came and went, sometimes with Dr Watts, sometimes alone; one of the suspected cases had turned out to be positive and had been taken to the hospital, and there were still several suspected cases among the older children.

Lucy worked through the nights and sometimes for part of the day too, and she didn't sleep well and began to look rather pale and wan. She had formed the habit of getting up long before she needed to and taking herself for a brisk walk through the dreary streets around the orphanage. It was on her return from one of these unsatisfactory outings that she came face to face with the doctor.

He took her by the shoulders and studied her face. 'Not sleeping? Feel all right? Suffering from a surfeit of orphans?' He didn't wait for her answer. 'Time that you had a day off.'

She said stiffly, 'Thank you, but I don't want one. None of us is having one and we can manage very well.'

He nodded. 'I am sure you can. Fiona asked me to invite you to her birthday party on Saturday...'

A little colour crept into her cheeks. 'How kind. Especially as she doesn't know me very well, but I can't accept. Please thank her from me when you see her. I hope that she has a happy birthday.' She added waspishly, 'They're fun, even when you're getting on a bit…' She gasped. 'Oh, I'm sorry I said that. I—I didn't mean it, she's quite lovely and striking even if she is—' She stopped herself just in time. 'What I mean is you must be very proud of her.'

She fled then, darting past him and down the passage, leaving him smiling and presently laughing.

Chapter 8

The days slipped by, and two more children were taken to hospital, but the other suspected cases remained well and the first little patients who had been in hospital for a week or more were responding well to erythromycin. All the same, everyone on the staff went round on the alert for shivering fits, coughs and high temperatures. Dr Thurloe came and went, and on one occasion Lucy was summoned to hold Miranda while he checked her shunt, during which he had little to say other than to ask a few questions and give some simple instructions.

'Miranda's doing well,' he told Lucy. 'What is needed shortly is a loving foster parent.' He spoke with pleasant aloofness, so that Lucy felt very aware of her humble status and burned with what was misplaced resentment. She didn't answer him and he looked at her briefly. 'Largely due to you, Lucy,' he added kindly. 'Now, I wonder if I might talk to Matron for a few minutes.'

The signal for her to carry Miranda back to her cot and tuck her up for her usual afternoon nap. The moppet had no wish to do anything of the sort.

Kindly, Lucy sat with Miranda on her lap, carrying on the quiet gossipy talk which she liked and which soothed her, while Lucy allowed a small part of her mind to dwell on William. That she loved him she had no doubt; that she didn't understand him was very clear to her. One moment he was a friend, almost more than that, the next he was a kind, rather distant consultant who spoke to her with great civility and not a trace of friendliness.

She soothed Miranda to sleep at last and went away to feed the smallest of the babies.

The doctor found her ten minutes later. 'Alice asked me to give you these letters,' he observed.

'Alice?' She forgot she was annoyed with him in her surprise.

'I called to let her know how you were. She worries about you.' He smiled faintly. 'So do I.'

'Well, there's no need,' said Lucy tartly. 'I'm not a young girl, you know...'

He put the letters on the cot beside her. 'No, you're not,' he agreed, quite unruffled. 'You're a very pretty young woman, and at the moment, I suspect, a cross one.'

He went away before she could do more than goggle at him.

Two days later, just as things were beginning to quieten down, Miranda began to shiver and cough and run a high temperature.

'But she didn't go with the other children,' cried Lucy, cuddling the unhappy toddler on her lap.

'No, but while you were in Holland—the day

you came back, in fact—she was taken out in her pushchair and, as far as I can make out, it was to the same area,' Matron sighed. 'There's no end to it. Dr Thurloe is on his way—she will have to be X-rayed, as she's chesty.'

The doctor, presenting an unshakeable air of confidence, confirmed Matron's fears. 'I'll have her in—she will need an X-ray and careful nursing.' His thoughtful eye studied Lucy, holding the child. 'If you can spare her, Lucy had better come too; Miranda must be kept content and as quiet as possible.' He turned away. 'Fix up an ambulance, will you, Matron? I'll just check those two suspects while I'm here.'

He went away, and so did Matron, leaving Lucy soothing Miranda. She could have done with some soothing herself. No one had asked her if she minded going to the hospital—not that she had the slightest objection, but it would have been nice to have been asked. 'I might just as well have been a chair,' she said indignantly to the moppet grizzling on her lap.

'Nothing—absolutely nothing would convince me that you look like a chair,' said William from the door. 'And if I have taken advantage of your good nature it is because I have a good deal to worry about just at this moment.'

Lucy twisted her head round to look at him. 'Oh, William, I'm sorry, I truly am. And you're tired too. Do you get enough sleep?'

His mouth twitched. 'Why, thank you, Lucy, just about enough. The worst seems to be over—they've traced the source to the water-cooling plant on one of the stores and it's being dealt with. There haven't been any fresh cases for three days. It is unfortunate that our Miranda should fall sick—you'll come to the hospital with her?'

'Yes, of course. Is she very bad?'

'No worse than several others, but we have the added complication of the shunt. Provided we can keep her happy and as comfortable as possible, she should do. I'll start the antibiotic course at once.' He turned to go. 'I'll see you at the City Royal.'

He might be a busy man, but he had found time to arrange for Miranda's admission. At the hospital, Lucy tucked her up in her cot in a glass-walled cubicle in one of the children's wards, and was led away to be shown where she was to sleep. It was a small room adjoining the ward, one of several set apart for mothers of ill children. 'And you can be free from one o'clock until teatime each day,' said the ward sister, a fierce, elderly dragon with a beaky nose and old-fashioned spectacles. 'I shall expect you to look after Miranda during the rest of the day and, if necessary, until she settles for the night. Have you an overall?'

Lucy said yes meekly, and presently unpacked her overnight bag and put away the few essentials she had stuffed it with, then went back to Miranda, who was lying back in her cot. She looked very ill and she was in a furious childish rage. Lucy took down the cot sides and sat her on her lap and talked to her.

She was still murmuring the tale of the Three

Bears when Dr Thurloe and Sister came in. 'The child should be in bed,' Sister spoke sharply and Miranda let out an outraged yell.

'You are quite right, Sister,' said William suavely, 'but perhaps in this case it might be best if Miranda were pandered to; you know her case history, do you not? I am anxious that she is kept as quiet as possible until her chest clears. I'd like her X-rayed as soon as you can arrange it.'

He held out a hand and the house doctor, who had slipped in behind him, handed him a form. He filled it in and handed it to Sister. 'There is some consolidation in the lungs.' He spoke to the young doctor. 'Keep a sharp eye open, Charles, and let me know if you are worried. Miss Lockitt understands how the shunt works, but check it if you please.'

He smiled at the young man and turned to Sister. 'I know Miranda is in your very good hands, Sister.' He smiled again with great charm and that lady bridled and allowed her severe features to relax.

He turned to go. 'Take a look at the X-rays and let me know, Charles. I'll be at my rooms until six o'clock. Good day to you, Lucy.'

She was tempted to say, 'Good day to you, William,' but instead she allowed a respectful murmur to escape her lips, which caused Sister to cast her a look of limited approval. At least the young woman knew her place.

Miranda gave Lucy no peace for the rest of the day, and twice in the night she was called because Miranda's screams of rage were keeping the other children awake, so that by one o'clock the next day Lucy was more than ready for a few hours' freedom. A quick lunch, she thought, and then bed. Sister had told her sharply that she should take some exercise during the afternoon, but to curl up on her bed and sleep was all she wanted.

She went down the corridor to the lifts. The dining-room was in the basement, three floors down; she would have a hurried snack, she decided, her finger on the button. The lift door opened and William stepped out.

'There you are,' he remarked pleasantly. 'Get that overall off, I'll be outside in five minutes.'

'Why? I'm going to bed...'

'No, you're not. Just get out of that thing, never mind how you look. You're coming back with me for lunch and then you can lie in the garden and sleep.'

Her mind fastened on the one important thing in this speech. He didn't care how she looked, which was even further proof of his indifference to her. She said pettishly, 'I don't want to.'

There was no one to see them, and William started to unbutton the nylon garment she was wearing. She had a strong feeling that even if the corridor had been knee-deep in people he would have done the same. He finished the buttons and said, 'Well, take it off, dear, we shall be here all day and I'm hungry.'

The pettishness was giving way to a pleasantly vague feeling that she need not bother about a thing because William would see to everything. She took off the garment, folded it carefully and hung it over her arm. 'My hair,' she said. 'And I want to wash and do my face.'

'And so you shall.' His voice was soothing. He pressed the button, and, when the lift opened its door, pushed her gently into it. The lifts were in a row at the back of the entrance hall, and he walked across to the door, nodding affably to the hall porter as they went, and outside, stowed her tidily into the Rolls, got in beside her and drove away.

'I'm on duty at five o'clock,' said Lucy making a last attempt to be sensible.

'Yes, I know. I'll get you back in good time.' He didn't say any more and she sat back, her head pleasantly empty. If their journey had been any longer she would undoubtedly have gone to sleep, but even with the midday traffic it was brief enough. Urged to alight, she sat up as he got out and opened her door, scooped her out and marched her briskly up to the front door where Trump was already standing.

He greeted her with subdued pleasure, listening gravely while the doctor asked him to fetch Mrs Trump, and returned with that lady with commendable speed.

'One of the bedrooms, I think, Mrs Trump,' advised the doctor. 'You'll see that Miss Lockitt has all she needs?'

'Indeed I will, sir. You come with me, miss, there's ten minutes before lunch and you can take all the time you want.' With which contradictory remark Mrs Trump trotted up the stairs with Lucy behind her, swept open a door in a long, narrow passage facing the stairhead and bustled into the room beyond, where she pointed out soap, towels, powders, creams and hairbrushes in the adjoining bathroom, and then bustled away again, murmuring that she had just the meal for them both. 'Tired to your deaths,' she declared. 'Our dear doctor on the go all the time, and you too, I dare say, miss. Now you just put yourself to rights and then come downstairs.'

It was surprising what a wash, followed by the making up of her face and a fierce brushing of her hair, did to ward off Lucy's tiredness. She gave an appreciative sniff at the several bottles of toilet water standing on the dressing-table, cast a quick eye round the charming room, and went downstairs, wondering as she went if Fiona used that room. Not to stay in, she told herself hastily; the doctor, she felt sure, was a man to guard his reputation sternly. He behaved in a high-handed fashion, it was true, but she fancied that he had strict ideas…

He came into the hall as she reached it. 'Just time for a drink, in here.'

The room welcomed her, as did Friday and Robinson, Thomas and the ginger kitten, curled up in a bright patch of sunlight by the open french doors. She sat in one of the comfortable chairs and the sherry went straight to her head, so that she wished that she could sit there forever. Not that she was given the chance; ten minutes later, during which time William had carried on a mild conversation about nothing at all, she was invited to have her lunch and crossed the hall to the dining-room. Last time she had been there had been with the other guests sitting round the oval mahogany table; now there were just two places laid, side by side at one end. The table was covered by a damask cloth and there was a vase of lilies of the valley and forget-me-nots at its centre. The heavy silver gleamed and the crystal glasses shone and she wondered if William, even when alone, ate his meals in such splendour.

They had potato soup, its humble name concealing a flavour out of this world, followed by fillets of sole, mangetout peas and little new potatoes, and they finished their lunch with a magnificent apple pie with accompanying clotted cream. 'We'll have coffee here,' said William, 'then you can go into the garden and doze. I've a pile of work to do.'

A remark which brought her down to earth with a rush.

She slept, curled up on a soft mattressed lounger, and would have gone on sleeping for untold hours if the doctor hadn't wakened her a couple of hours later. 'Tea?' he wanted to know. 'There's half an hour or so before you need to go back.'

They had tea in the garden too, at a white-painted table under the copper beech in one corner. It was amazing, she thought, how such a small garden had been made to appear spacious with its small velvet lawn, its flower-beds, full of colour, and the high screen of trees. She accepted another of Mrs Trump's feather-light scones and observed that she could stay just where she was forever. A remark she wished to recall the moment she had uttered it, but since that was impossible she mumbled, 'Well, you know what I mean—it's so very pleasant after the City Royal.'

William agreed lazily and watched the quick colour fade again from her cheeks. 'You will have to stay there for some days,' he pointed out, 'and while you are there I just hope you will come here each afternoon. There's nowhere to go around the hospital, and it would take you too long to go home to Chelsea by bus. I'm free for a couple of hours on most afternoons. The car will be outside at one o'clock and I shall expect you.'

Lucy sat up straight. 'Really? How extremely kind of you, but won't it be inconvenient for you? I mean, don't you want to do things when you're free?'

He said carelessly, 'It will make no difference to me, Lucy. Either I dictate letters or catch up on reports and so on, and you are more than welcome to spend an hour or two in the garden.'

His reply chilled her and she thought about refusing his offer. But he had been quite right, there was nowhere to go around the hospital, and to get home and back by bus would take too long. She said meekly, 'Well, thank you, William, if you're quite sure I'm not being a nuisance.'

He took her back presently, leaving her at the entrance with a brief nod and a laconic, 'One o'clock, tomorrow.'

So each afternoon, she was driven to his home,

given lunch and installed in a lounger and told to sleep, to be wakened by the pleasant clatter of tea-cups, with the doctor sitting nearby, reading a news-paper. She began to depend on these quiet hours; Miranda, while not desperately ill, was proving to be a bad patient, not wanting Lucy out of her sight and waking at night, screaming for her. There was little actual work for Lucy, but the days dragged while she did her best to keep the child happy and quiet.

It was almost a week later, after a splendid lunch at the doctor's house, that she was wakened by a tinkling laugh and, before she opened her eyes, she knew whose laugh it was. There was no sign of the doctor, although Trump was arranging the teatray just so, but a moment later, as she sat up, he came out of the house with Fiona.

Lucy got up and went and sat in a chair, aware that she was untidy and crumpled from her nap, a fact which Fiona turned to her advantage at once. She came across the grass, cool and beautifully turned out and oozing charm. 'Lucy—William has been telling me what a Trojan you have been, you must be exhausted. How I do admire you strong young women, I'm hopeless at illness—too sensi-tive.' She ran an eye over Lucy's flushed face. 'You poor dear, let us hope that they let you have a holi-day when you're free of this child—you certainly need it.'

The doctor stood beside her, listening with an impassive face. He observed quietly, 'It's because Lucy is sensitive that she is so successful at caring for Miranda.' He smiled at Lucy, who didn't smile back; she had no reason to.

He hid a smile. 'Will you stay for tea, Fiona? I shall be taking Lucy back very shortly.'

'In that case I'll wait here for you, William; we can have a nice quiet hour or so here—it is such glorious weather.'

'I'm not coming back,' he told her blandly. 'I shall be at the hospital for the rest of the day, and then at a consultants' meeting.'

Fiona frowned. To sit and gobble her tea with William's eye on his watch was pointless. 'I might as well go.' She sighed wistfully. 'I see so little of you, William...' She frowned again, because that sounded as though they were little more than casual acquaintances, not at all the impression she wanted the silly, untidy girl sitting there to have. She gave one of her tinkling laughs. 'Oh, well, perhaps one evening.' She gave him a smiling, questioning look which wasn't noticed, so that her abrupt, 'Well, goodbye, Lucy. I hope you'll be looking better when we next meet,' was uttered in a snappy voice.

She went back into the house; Lucy could hear her voice, high and plaintive, gradually fading away, and presently William came back and sat down, and she poured their tea and embarked on a pointless conversation until he interrupted her without warning. 'You and Fiona don't like each other.'

She answered carefully, anxious not to upset him, since she thought he was so enamoured of the woman, while her loving heart longed to tell him what a frightful mistake he was making. 'Well, we haven't much in common. She's very attractive, and I should think she would be a most amusing companion and a splendid hostess. She dresses beautifully too.' She stopped then because he was looking at her so strangely. He wasn't smiling, and yet she had the impression that he was amused.

'That's very generous of you, Lucy.'

He smiled with such charm and gentleness that she spoke before she had time to stop herself. 'I'd like you to be happy, William.'

'And you think that Fiona Seymour will give me that happiness?' He got up, took her cup and saucer and pulled her gently to her feet. 'Listen to me carefully. She means nothing to me, never has—just someone to take out to dinner or invite to lunch. As you say, amusing and well dressed,' he paused, 'and empty of all feeling. She never asks me about my work either. It satisfies her that I am successful with sufficient money to live in comfort, and know all the right people. If I were to die tomorrow she would feel regret only because she would be forced to find another man to provide her with the kind of life she considers necessary for her happiness.'

'So why do you take her out?' asked Lucy tartly.

He sighed. 'I have been lonely. I love my work, I have friends enough, but that isn't all. I want a wife and children to come home to.' He bent his head and kissed her gently. 'You, Lucy.'

She stared up at him speechless. 'Me?' A great wave of delight swept over her, so that her breath caught in her throat. 'But would I do? I'm not at all clever, I told you that.'

'You are so anxious to be clever, my dear. You cannot see that a string of letters after your name and a highly paid job are of no consequence at all compared with kindness and patience and being able to listen—so many people have lost the art of listening... So would you consider marrying me, Lucy?'

She wished to throw her arms round his neck, but she forbore from that; he had asked her to be his wife, but he hadn't said that he loved her. Even making allowances for his reserved nature, she reflected, that was something that she thought he could have mentioned.

'I should like to think about it,' she told him in a cool little voice which disguised her bubbling excitement. She added, 'If you don't mind.' Anxious to make things clear, she added, 'You see, I thought you were in love with Fiona.' She frowned. 'Won't she mind?'

He looked all at once remote. 'I cannot see why she should mind—I have never at any time even hinted that I wish to marry her.'

'Oh, well, that's all right, then. All the same, I'd like to think about it.'

Of course she would marry him; her heart had told her that, but she had no intention of allowing him to think she would fall into his lap like an over-ripe apple. Besides, a little voice at the back of her head reiterated, he hadn't said that he loved her.

'I think I should go back,' she said, and without a word the doctor got up.

'We mustn't allow Sister to wait for you,' he said pleasantly, and swept her back into the house and thence into the car, and drove her back to the City Royal.

There was a message for her on the following day. He had gone to Northern Ireland for a consultation and would be away for two days. And when he came back he pronounced Miranda was out of danger and able to return to the orphanage, so that Lucy didn't see him to speak to. She left the hospital with mixed feelings; had William had a change of heart while he was away, or was he annoyed because she had asked him to wait for an answer? And at least, she told herself indignantly, he could have smiled at her.

She settled Miranda back in her own cot and was summoned to Matron's office. Almost all the children were back at the orphanage, although two of the older ones were still in hospital. Sister was back too, and two new assistants had joined the staff.

'You've earned a few days off,' said Matron kindly. 'Let me see, it is Tuesday—supposing you report for duty next Monday morning? I'm sure you must be anxious to go home for a few days.' She added a few words of thanks and Lucy, immensely cheered at the prospect of the best part of a week at home, stuffed her few odds and ends into her overnight bag and caught a bus for home.

Alice was delighted to see her, and over a pot of tea she told Lucy the news. 'Your ma and pa are on their way 'ome,' she declared. 'I 'ad a phone call from someone saying they were expected back very shortly, though 'e couldn't say when exactly. I've got in extra groceries and told the butcher… Miss Imogen and Miss Pauline will be 'ome for supper, they'll be ever so pleased.' She eyed Lucy narrowly. 'You look peaky, love. What you need is a nice quiet day at 'ome! Just you go and put your things away and I'll get you a nice bite of tea.'

It was nice to be fussed over by the kindly Alice. Lucy ate a splendid tea and then went away to wash her hair and do her nails and attend to her neglected make-up. 'Oh, Alice,' she said, 'it's so nice to be home again.' She smiled at her old friend and then surprised the pair of them by bursting into tears. 'I'm just tired,' said Lucy, between great heaving sobs.

''Course you are, ducks. You'll be right as rain in a couple of days. Worked you too 'ard, they 'ave, at that 'ospital. You just go and 'ave that bath and I'll find a nice drop of sherry for you when you come down.'

The dear soul gave Lucy an encouraging push towards the stairs and went in search of Mr Lockitt's best sherry.

As for Lucy, she lay in a blissfully hot and foamy bath and tried to sort out the niggling thoughts whirling around inside her head; none of them amounted to much, but she knew that she wasn't happy and she should have been. William had asked her to marry him, hadn't he? But without any of the romantic trimmings such an occasion surely warranted. She frowned heavily and got out of the too-hot bath, and presently wandered down to the kitchen to drink the sherry Alice had poured for her. She would have to wait until she saw William again, she decided; there was no use getting worked up about it. Fortified by the sherry, she went back to her room, dressed and did her hair and face, and presented her normal self to her sisters when they came home.

They were pleased to see her, enquiring with vague kindness as to whether she had had a boring time in the hospital and not waiting for an answer. But they were glad that she would be free for a few days.

'I had a cable from Father,' Imogen told her. 'It was sent to the office. He and Mother will be home the day after tomorrow. They want me to get a drinks party together so that they can say hello to everyone at one go. It was all very successful, and they'll probably be going back later in the year. So lucky you're here, Lucy. Will you get drinks and food organised for Saturday? I'll phone everyone— it's short notice, but I'm sure they will all come.'

The evening was spent in making plans for the party, and then, inevitably, more plans, this time for the weddings.

Lucy, who had been looking forward to doing nothing for a few days, found herself immersed in preparing for Saturday evening so that she really had no time to think about William. Of course, he was always at the back of her mind; she thought of him with love and longing and a good deal of doubt. Surely if he loved her enough to want to marry her he would have found the time to phone or scribble a note? But he hadn't said that he loved her, had he? The thought recurred at intervals during the next couple of days, and was never wholly absent even during the bustle and excitement of her parents' return.

Professor and Mrs Lockitt, although glad to be home again, were full of their expedition. It had been a tremendous success and every aspect of it had to be discussed and commented on. It fell to Lucy's lot to help with the unpacking, take loads of clothes to the cleaners, make appointments and make sure that everything was in train for the Saturday evening. Not that she minded—she was glad to be kept busy, and, as her mother pointed out, it made a nice change for her after her little job at the orphanage. Lucy agreed, placidly; no one in the family had understood about her work there, and she had long ago given up talking about it. Alice was the only one she confided in and the only one who really understood. But now there was too much to do to think about the orphanage. Caterers were supplying the food—tiny vol-au-vents filled with salmon mousse, creamed chicken, shrimps chopped with scrambled egg, minute sandwiches and *petit-fours*—but glass and china had to be got from the cupboards, flowers had to be arranged and furniture moved.

On Saturday evening Lucy went to her room to

dress, satisfied that everything that needed to be done had been attended to. Two of Alice's nieces were coming in to wait, and Alice would be stationed in the kitchen, dealing with the refilling of plates and making sure that there was plenty of coffee should anyone want it, although that wasn't likely. Lucy showered, and, for no other reason than the fact that William had liked the grey dress, got into it.

Her mother frowned when she saw her in it. 'Darling, surely you've got something else than that grey dress? It's quite pretty, but haven't you worn it rather a lot?' She didn't wait for Lucy to answer, but hurried away to greet the first of the guests.

The big drawing-room and the conservatory beyond were soon full. The Lockitts had a great many friends and several distinguished members of the Archaeological Society had turned up, bent on hearing about the professor's finds. Imogen and Pauline had formed their own circle, leaving Lucy to circulate on her own. She was good at that, even though she was shy with people she didn't know very well, but she put people at their ease, moving from one group to the next, making sure that no one was left on their own. She knew everyone there and stopped to chat from time to time, and it was as she was turning away from old Mrs Winchell that she found Fiona Seymour at her elbow. She had known that she was to be invited, but had been at pains to avoid her. It was silly to feel guilty; William had said that he had no interest in Fiona other than that of an occasional companion for an evening out, and she had believed him, but Fiona didn't know that…

She said, 'Hello, Fiona. I'm glad you could come. It's lovely for Mother and Father to have all their friends here.'

'Well,' drawled Fiona, 'they aren't quite my age-group, but I've always enjoyed a party. A pity William couldn't make it.' She watched the colour creep into Lucy's cheeks. She went on smoothly, 'He's always so busy, bless him—he's been away for a couple of days. Northern Ireland again, you know. Of course, he hates to talk about it.' She watched the look of hurt puzzlement on Lucy's face and at once decided to risk passing on some news of her own invention. 'He's at my place now, but don't tell anyone.' She gave Lucy a conspiratorial smile. 'I'm going back and we'll have a cosy little supper together. The weekend together will do him good. He needs peace and quiet and someone who understands him.'

She watched the effect of her words and was satisfied. For good measure, she added, 'He always comes back to me.' She took a glass of wine from a waitress's tray. 'Will you be a darling and make my excuses to your parents? It's been lovely seeing you again. Still at the orphanage?' And when Lucy nodded dumbly, added lightly, 'William says you're one of the Marthas of this world, and I'm sure you are.'

She patted Lucy's arm and smiled her sweet smile and slid away.

'I can't stand that woman,' declared old Mrs

Winchell, tapping Lucy sharply on the shoulder. 'What was she saying to you? You look as though you've just been stabbed in the back.'

Lucy looked at the elderly face staring at her with such shrewd eyes. 'Oh, nothing, Mrs Winchell, nothing that matters at all. Let me get you something to eat...'

Everyone went home presently, and Lucy, with the excuse that she should make sure that everything was cleared away ready for the massive washing up which would have to be done soon, kept herself busy until they sat down to a belated dinner. And, since the talk was all of the expedition and its success, and various discussions about their guests and, once again, the weddings, no one noticed that she was rather quiet.

'Tired, dear?' asked her father eventually. 'You look as though you could do with another holiday. Back to work on Monday?'

He smiled broadly; after four years he still regarded her job as something of a joke.

Lucy wasn't tired, she was numb, and a good thing too for she was unable to think. She replied suitably to her father's gentle teasing and listened to everyone's plans for Sunday. Her sisters would be with their fiancés, and her parents were lunching with friends who lived at Henley.

'I dare say you could come too, darling,' said her mother. 'They would never mind an extra guest.'

If William was back, Lucy's tired brain reminded her, there was just the unlikely chance that he might come to see her, even if it were only to explain… 'I promised I'd have lunch with Joe Walter.'

Her mother looked pleased. 'Oh, good, dear. He's such a nice boy too and the only young man you know well, really, as I was saying to that elegant Mrs Seymour earlier. We shall be back quite late, I expect; they're sure to ask us to stay for the evening.' She looked at Imogen and Pauline. 'And you two? Will you be back for supper—I must tell Alice…' They told her no and she went on comfortably, 'Oh, well, Alice will give you a meal when you get back, Lucy. You'll be all right, dear?'

Lucy said that yes, of course she would, and when presently she lay in bed she planned her day. Joe was invention, of course. She cast around in her muddled head as to where she might go; there were various aunts and uncles and cousins, but they all lived too far away, and besides, if she went out there was a chance that she might meet William and possibly Fiona with him—something to be avoided at all costs. She decided to stay at home. She could garden and lie in the sun, and Alice could go off to her sister's for the afternoon—no one would know and Alice would never tell. She closed her eyes resolutely, determined not to think about William, but it was almost morning before she slept.

The family dispersed by mid-morning and Lucy went to the kitchen to explain to Alice. 'And, darling Alice, if—just if Dr Thurloe arrives before you leave—but he won't—tell him that I'm having lunch with Joe Walter.'

'If you say so, Miss Lucy, though why you have to tell a parcel of lies to such a nice gentleman is more than I can understand.'

'Thank you, Alice. There's—there's a good reason; perhaps one day I'll tell you. I'm going to stay in the garden, it will be super in the sun with nothing to do. I'll get my lunch, so do go to your sister's as soon as you like. Don't come back until after tea— no one but I shall be here.'

Alice agreed reluctantly and presently the house was quiet. Lucy, in an old cotton dress, made coffee and took it out into the garden with the Sunday papers. There was a lot of day ahead of her, but if she read all of the papers properly it would take her until it was time for her to get her lunch. She had been reading for half an hour when the front door knocker was thumped. She shot out of her chair and went quietly into the house, and even more quietly upstairs, to peep out of a bedroom window which faced the street. William's car was outside. He didn't go away for several minutes, and she watched him with longing eyes as he got into the car. He drove away without looking about him, and she went back into the garden. The phone rang twice after that, but she let it ring, sitting with her hands clenched together and her feet boring into the ground to stop her from going to answer it.

The day dragged. She made a sandwich for her lunch, and welcomed four o'clock when she could have a pot of tea. And soon after that Alice came back, fussing because Lucy hadn't had a proper meal. She set about getting one as soon as she had taken off her hat and coat, and Lucy, tired of her own unhappy company, sat at the kitchen table with Mrs Simpkins on her knee and listened to Alice's soothing voice telling of her day. The thump of the knocker took them both by surprise. Lucy got up and went to the door. 'I'm going upstairs. Alice, if it's him tell him I went to lunch with young Mr Walter and I'm not back yet. Quick, Alice, and then perhaps he'll go away.'

She whisked herself upstairs, and Alice went to the door to confront a grim-faced doctor. He heard her out in silence. 'Thank you, Alice,' was all he said, and he went back to his car and drove away.

'What did he say?' asked Lucy, back in the kitchen.

'Just, thank you, Alice. He looked as though he was in a fine temper.'

Which he was. He had returned home very early that morning intent on seeing Lucy. Even Fiona, phoning to see if he was back and with some story about Lucy and young Walter tripping off her tongue, hadn't stopped him. He had been puzzled and then angry when he'd found no one at home, and when at last Alice had answered the door his rage, seldom in evidence, had threatened to choke him. Fiona would have been delighted if she had known the havoc her tissue of lies had wrought.

Chapter 9

Monday morning began badly. Lucy overslept because she had lain awake for a good part of the night, unhappy thoughts running round her woolly head and none of them making sense. She missed her usual bus too, so that she arrived late at the orphanage, with almost no breakfast inside her and a headache. Worse was to follow. As she sat with Miranda on her knee, patiently spooning porridge into the small, unwilling mouth, Matron joined her. Lucy wished her good morning and wondered why that lady looked ill at ease. Because she herself had been ten minutes late? It seemed unlikely, especially as she had explained to Sister about missing the bus. Matron sat down on the only other chair. 'We must have a talk,' she began briskly. 'The Board of Governors have been looking into the administration of the orphanage and have decided to make one or two changes. In short, one full-time member of the staff or two part-time members must be made redundant. I'm more than sorry that it must be you, Lucy—you have been such a good worker here and done so much, but, you see, the two part-time both need the money and, if you will forgive me for saying so, you don't. One has an invalid mother and the other is quite on her own and lives on her wages.'

She paused. Lucy inserted another spoonful of porridge with a gentle cluck of encouragement. 'I quite understand, Matron. I shall be awfully sorry to go, as I've loved working here, but it's quite true, I don't need the money.' She kept her voice quiet and steady with an effort. 'I would be glad to work here as a voluntary worker...'

'Yes, I'm sure you would, and I would have been so glad to agree to that, but the board emphasised that only a certain number may work here, paid or unpaid.' Matron frowned. 'I can't see why—something to do with reorganisation, I believe. I can promise you that if this can be altered I will let you know at once.'

She got up, looking relieved. 'If you would just work this week out? And I promise you a splendid reference. Believe me, I did my best to persuade the governors, but they were adamant.'

On her way to the door she stopped and came back again. 'I almost forgot to tell you a splendid piece of news. Miranda is to be adopted, by a charming young couple—he's a curate here in London, and they are unable to have children of their own. They have had Miranda for odd days—while you were in Holland—and now she is well again they will come each day so that she gets used to them. She's very happy with them, and she will be with them as much as possible until she actually goes to live with them.'

'Oh, I'm so glad. She'll be happy to have a mum and dad, and she's so much better.' Lucy meant every word of it.

'Largely thanks to you, Lucy.'

It was fortunate that there was precious little time to sit around and mope; it wasn't until she got home that evening that Lucy allowed her thoughts to turn to the future. And even then she was thwarted, since both Imogen and Pauline were at home for the evening and, as was to be expected, they and her mother plunged into talk of the weddings, her father having prudently retired to his study. Lucy, agreeing with her usual calm to everything which was asked of her, consigned her future and William to the back of her head and shut the door on them. Time enough to think things over calmly when the shock of it had died down.

But it didn't; if anything, it got worse. She carried the hurt of it around with her and no one knew except Alice, who, quick to see that Lucy was worrying about something, winkled it out of her one evening when there was no one else at home. Even to her Lucy couldn't bring herself to talk about William, and at the moment she had no idea what she was going to do about him. She supposed that he had been feeling lonely without Fiona and got carried away, and she had hardly discouraged him, and, after all, there was nothing definite, for Lucy hadn't said that she would marry him. All the same, it seemed strange to her that he hadn't written or asked to see her and explain. True, he had called on the Sunday, but even from the glimpse she had had of him from the window he had looked to be in a towering rage. He probably felt a fool. The one thought that consoled her was that she had never even hinted that she loved him. And as for him, well, everyone, she told herself, could have a change of heart. He might, just for a moment, have thought she would make a good wife for him, and for all she knew he might have been unhappy about Fiona...

The week dragged to a close and she went to the orphanage for the last time, and at the end of the day bade Miranda and her small companions goodbye in a cheerful way, and in the same cheerful fashion took her farewell of the rest of the staff there, and, last of all, Matron. Not once did she complain at leaving, but assured everyone who asked that she intended taking a holiday and then looking for a similar job. 'But this time I think I'll go further afield,' she told them. 'I rather like the idea of Scotland.'

Matron looked at her with relief because she hadn't made a fuss. 'Well, remember that I will give you a splendid reference, Lucy.' They clustered round the entrance and she turned and waved when she got to the corner of the street.

It was a Friday evening and the bus queues were long, so she got home later than usual. Since everyone was in the drawing-room, it seemed as good a time as any to tell them. She hadn't expected sympathy, for none of them had ever taken her job seriously, and they offered none.

'Hard luck, darling!' her mother exclaimed. 'But

how providential, now you will be at home to help
me with the wedding arrangements.'

Pauline chimed in, 'It wasn't worth much, anyway, Lucy—one of those dead-end jobs that get you
nowhere."

Imogen added, 'You'll be far more useful at
home.'

Lucy bit back an answer to that; to stay home and
do the flowers and write her mother's letters inviting friends and accepting their invitations seemed
unimportant compared to caring for the daily needs
of small orphans, but there was no point in arguing
the matter. With a heavy heart and a docile manner
she set herself to the trivial tasks her mother handed
over to her. That she became a little pale and quiet
over the next week or two went unnoticed, except
by the faithful Alice, who went around her kitchen
muttering to herself and breathing down fire upon
the heads of those who had made Lucy unhappy.
She even remarked upon Lucy's quietness to Mrs
Lockitt, who looked surprised.

'Oh, I hadn't noticed, Alice. She's always been
the quiet one, you know that. Anyway, she will be
going to the reception in honour of her father next
week; that should cheer her up.'

The reception was at Claridge's Hotel, a rather
grand affair, and Mrs Lockitt had spent a good deal
of time and thought on her dress. So had Imogen and
Pauline, and they in their turn persuaded Lucy to
get herself a new dress for the occasion. 'Something
really striking,' they begged her, and sighed loudly

when she showed them the soft grey chiffon dress she intended to wear. It was, in fact, quite charming and suited her, but it had no pretensions to high fashion, and they pointed out that no one was going to look twice at her if she wore it. Lucy forbore from telling them that she had no wish for anyone to look even once at her, and only filial duty was the reason for her going to the reception anyway.

All the same, they had to admit that when she joined them, ready to leave the house, she looked charming in a gentle sort of way.

An opinion echoed by Dr Thurloe, catching sight of her standing with a group of acquaintances before the speeches began. He excused himself from the friends he was talking to and edged his way towards her. Despite his size and bulk, he was a quiet man; she had no notion that he was there beside her until he spoke quietly into her ear.

'You and I have to talk, Lucy.' His voice was pleasant, but there was a hint of steel in it which she was quick to hear.

'Why?' she asked baldly.

'Don't waste time being silly.' He smiled down at her and her heart turned over. 'How very nice you look, like a very beautiful grey mouse.'

'I don't think we have anything to say to each other.' She smiled brilliantly at an acquaintance and waved to him. A third party might be a good idea. William was being charming and it was going to her head. The acquaintance waved back and started to inch towards them, then caught William's eye and inched away again.

'Now, before we have to listen to the speeches— where have you been? On holiday? Ill?'

She said quite fiercely, 'You know quite well that I've been given the sack. They call it being made redundant, and, since you're on the Board of Governors and agreed to it, it's silly to pretend you know nothing about it.'

He said calmly, 'Well, I don't. I wasn't at the last meeting, I gave my vote to someone else to deal with. How did you know I was a governor?'

'I had a letter saying how sorry they were.' Lucy smouldered. 'Bah— they couldn't care less…and there was your name with all the other VIPs who run the orphanage.' She added thoughtfully, 'You do have an awful lot of letters after your name.'

'Yes, well, that's beside the point. We have to talk—can't we leave here and go somewhere quiet?'

She had become dangerously close to forgetting Fiona. 'There's nothing to talk about,' she said in a cold voice.

He stared at her downbent head. 'Perhaps not now.' He took her hand in his and looked at it. 'No ring?' he asked blandly.

Her green eyes flashed. 'I'm not getting married yet,' she told him sweetly, and turned tail and lost herself in the fashionable crowd around them.

She had made the remark for no reason at all other than to annoy him; it was a pity that it did nothing to clear up their misunderstanding. For the rest of that evening William made no attempt to seek her out again, although he took care to know just where she was and who she was with. It puzzled him that young Joe Walter wasn't there at her elbow, and, for her part, Lucy, chatting with her parents' friends and some younger ones of her own, was puzzled too. Where, she wondered, was Fiona? She cast any number of casual glances around the elegant reception, but there was no sign of her. It seemed strange that she was absent, for she was to be met at almost all the local social gatherings. Perhaps she was ill...

She had in fact, not been invited, and had done her best to persuade William not to go without her, but since she had been unable to see him her arguments on the telephone had fallen very flat. As she had put down the phone she had reflected that he had sounded both cool and casual. Perhaps it was time she gave up her efforts to attract him and looked around for someone else. There had been that American she had met a couple of weeks ago—a poor second to William when it came to looks, but certainly wealthier. William, she had to admit, had been singularly hard to captivate.

It was a pity that Lucy knew none of that, circulating in a very proper fashion, listening to what was said to her and not really hearing a word, although she looked deeply interested and said 'Really?' and 'Oh?' and 'How interesting!' just when she should, so that people told each other afterwards that she was by far the nicest of the Lockitt girls, even if the other two were outstandingly clever.

William, watching her without appearing to do so, found her enchanting, and was quite unable to believe that she and Joe Walter were intending to marry. He was prepared to wager every penny he possessed that she was the last girl in the world to behave as she was behaving now. It was a pity that he was engaged to give a series of lectures in Leiden at the medical school and would be going there early the next day, but he was a patient man and he could wait for someone he wanted more at the moment than anything else in the world. That there was something wrong somewhere was obvious, and possibly ten minutes' talk would have put it right, only Lucy, usually so malleable and gentle, was in no mood to talk, and matters would only be made worse. He waited until Professor Lockitt, as the guest of honour, had made his farewells and left with his family before he went home himself.

He didn't go to bed at once, but went to his study and wrote a note to Lucy, addressed the envelope and sealed it, and on his way to bed asked Trump to post it in the morning.

He left the house early the next morning, driving himself down to Dover to take the hovercraft.

Fiona Seymour rang his doorbell several hours later. She thought it unlikely that he would be at home, but she would have one more try before she gave him up for the American, and, being a determined woman, she intended tracking him down and giving him a last chance to fall for her. Being also a conceited woman, it didn't enter her head that his interest in her had been both passing and very superficial. She intended to weep a little to arouse his pity... Trump opened the door and bade her a polite but guarded good morning. He didn't like her, but no feelings showed upon his face. He listened gravely to her request to see the doctor and informed her with inward glee that he was away from home.

'Where?' she asked, and added, 'I dare say he told me, but I must have forgotten.'

'Abroad, madam, but I have no forwarding address. He will be travelling.'

She pushed past him. 'Then I'll leave a note.' She waited while he shut the door, her eyes taking in with regret the delightful furnishings in the hall which could have been hers... The envelope on the console-table caught her eye and she edged nearer so that she could see the address. And what, she wondered, would he have to say to Lucy Lockitt? She had been sure that he had believed her when she had told him that the wretched girl and Joe Walter were on the point of getting engaged. She went past Trump into the drawing-room, where he provided her with paper and pen and drew up a chair to the davenport in one corner of the room, and she composed a letter she had no intention of leaving for William and pondered the best way to take the envelope as she left the house.

It was easy enough as it turned out; telling Trump that she would take her letter with her in the hope of hearing of the doctor's whereabouts from one of his friends, she went back into the hall and, as he turned to open the door, slipped the envelope down the front of her dress. Once outside, she hurried away as fast as she dared just in case he should notice that it had gone. Providentially a bus drew up at a stop a few yards from the end of Strand on the Green and, although she did dislike public transport, Fiona jumped on and was borne rapidly away. Fortunately for her, because Trump, closing the door behind her, had swept a sharp eye round the hall just to make sure that everything was as it should be, and had seen at once that the letter had gone. There was no one in sight when he opened the door, so he closed it without haste and went thoughtfully to the kitchen where he conferred with Mrs Trump.

Fiona got off the bus within a few minutes, walked the short distance to her flat and, once there, opened William's letter. Fury at its contents turned her face ugly, but when she had read it a second time a look of cunning triumph took its place. Even if she had lost all hope of charming William into marriage, she could make sure that Lucy Lockitt didn't get him. But she had to have an excuse... She thought for a moment, and then put the letter in her handbag and went out on to the street and took a taxi to the end of the road where Lucy lived. She knew exactly what she was going to say and rang the bell with confidence.

Alice answered the door.

'Oh, good morning—Alice, isn't it? Is Miss Lucy

in? Could I see her for a few minutes—just something I have to return.'

Alice admitted her. Lucy was at home, although no one else was, and the good soul, even though she disliked Mrs Seymour, had no reason not to let her in. She showed her into the drawing-room and went in search of Lucy, who was turning out an attic cupboard.

'Oh, bother,' said Lucy, well aware that she was dusty and a bit untidy. All the same, she went downstairs and into the drawing-room to bid Fiona good morning and ask her to sit down. 'Perhaps you would like coffee?' she asked politely.

Fiona shook her head. 'Sweet of you, but I'm on my way to my dressmaker—I shall need lots of new clothes…' She looked arch and Lucy wondered why. She opened her bag and took out something wrapped in tissue paper. 'William found this at the reception yesterday; he felt sure it was yours and he asked me to let you have it. He's gone abroad for a few days.'

Lucy took the packet and unwrapped it slowly. There was a brooch inside, but it wasn't hers. 'He's mistaken, it isn't mine. Perhaps you should take it to the police.'

'Oh, my dear—I'm so sorry to bother you, I wonder why he thought it was yours?' She gave her tinkling laugh. 'We had so much to talk about that it never entered my head to make sure he was right. And now actually I'm so happy and thrilled that I'm scarcely able to hold a sensible thought in my head. You would never know that he was such a romantic man, would you? But this morning I found such a charming letter when I opened my post.' She gave an angelic smile. 'I'm so excited that I must tell someone...' She opened her handbag and took out the letter. 'Poetry, my dear, can you beat that? He writes, "My dear, darling, do you know your Wordsworth? The bit that goes, 'The past unsighed for, and the future sure'? That's how I feel about you, and I believe you feel it too. When I return we will talk."'

'I don't think you should be telling me this,' said Lucy in a steady, expressionless voice, 'and I'd rather not hear it. I hope you will both be very happy.'

'What a sweet creature you are,' said Fiona gushingly. 'So understanding, especially as you were growing rather fond of him yourself.'

'William is a very nice person; I think there are a great many people who are fond of him.' Lucy got up. 'Do find the owner of that brooch, she must be so worried.' She went to the door and stood by it, smiling although it was an effort to do so. 'I hope you won't be late for your dressmaker.'

She shut the street door on Mrs Seymour and stood leaning against it, the tears pouring down her cheeks. Things had gone wrong between her and William, but she had still nurtured the hope that they would be put right. Now there was no hope of that. She had been a fool—she should have said yes when he had first suggested marrying her, but since she hadn't, and it didn't seem to have worried him overmuch, she had to conclude that it had been the spur of the moment—just an impulse. Perhaps Fiona had quarrelled with him and he'd wanted to annoy her.

Alice came from the kitchen, offered a large handkerchief and led her back to sit by the kitchen table. 'Now, you just tell me all about it, Miss Lucy. That woman—making mischief, I'll be bound…'

So Lucy told her, and it was a great relief to talk to someone about it, for she felt Alice was the only person who would understand—William would have understood, but telling him, even if she were able, would have made no sense at all.

She drank two cups of tea, listening to kind Alice's comforting clucks and wondering what she should do. Pack a bag and go away on a long visit to one or other of her aunts and uncles living in a variety of rural retreats around the country? Stay and pretend nothing had happened? Do something really drastic like joining the ATS? A notion nipped in the bud by an urgent peal on the door bell.

'Who's that?' she asked. 'Don't let them in, Alice; say there's no one here.'

Alice opened the door to a dignified but agitated Mr Trump. 'I've some urgent news for Miss Lucy, Alice. It's most important.'

'She said not to let anyone in.'

'Tell her it concerns herself and Dr Thurloe.'

Alice opened the door wide. 'Never mind me asking, you come on in.'

He followed her into the kitchen and Lucy, seeing who it was, frowned and then said, 'Trump, good morning. Is something the matter? Can we help?'

'Well, yes and no, miss. There's something I must tell you...'

He related the morning's happenings, not leaving out a single detail. 'So you see, miss, Mrs Seymour has the letter which was addressed to you, though I'm sure I don't know why she took it.'

Lucy's face, puffy and red with weeping, had taken on an instant prettiness. 'For me? That letter? She pretended it was for her—she read me some of it.' She smiled at the memory of it. 'Oh, Trump, I can never thank you enough for being so prompt. I know exactly what I must do.' She beamed at him. 'Do sit down and have a glass of beer and tell me where the doctor is.'

He accepted a chair and the beer with a grave inclination of his head. 'As to that, miss, I cannot say exactly. But I was told that he would be in Leiden in Holland for the rest of this week. I believe he is to give a series of lectures there. Presumably the authorities there would know.'

Lucy nodded slowly. 'Better still, those friends I stayed with; they know him well. I'll go there first and then I'll go to Leiden.'

'All that way, Miss Lucy, and supposing you don't find him?'

Lucy smiled radiantly at them both. 'Oh, but I shall,' she assured them. 'Thank you very much for coming, Trump. You have no idea what this means.'

Trump, who had a very good idea, smiled at her in a fatherly fashion. 'I'll be off, then, miss.' He paused. 'How will you go to Holland?'

'Catch a plane.' She glanced at the clock. 'I'll try and get a flight this afternoon.'

'In which case, miss, I'm sure the doctor would wish me to drive you to the airport. If you would be good enough to telephone me when you have made your arrangements I will return here with the car.'

'Not the Rolls?'

'We have a second car, miss, a small Daimler.'

'Well, thank you, Trump, that would be lovely. I'll ring you as soon as I know when I can go.'

On the afternoon flight to Schiphol, crammed between a stout lady who couldn't keep still and a gentleman who coughed a great deal and swallowed pills every ten minutes or so, Lucy took time to reflect upon her extraordinary behaviour. She had booked a seat on the plane, packed an overnight bag, changed into a thin jersey dress and jacket, primed Alice and left a note for her parents. They would possibly be quite bewildered, but not unduly worried; they travelled so extensively themselves that her unexpected trip to Holland would leave them only mildly surprised. Schiphol lay beneath her and she still had no idea what she would do. It had seemed vital to see William at once, but now she was actually in Holland she wasn't quite sure how to set about it. Fran might be able to help. She took the airport bus into Amsterdam and then a taxi to the station and caught a train to Utrecht. There she found a taxi to drive her out to Litrik's home. It was early evening by then, and the house, tranquil in the midst of its lovely gardens, seemed to welcome her. She rang the bell, suddenly feeling foolish.

Trugg opened the door and, to her everlasting relief, welcomed her with a smile and a total lack of surprise. 'A pleasure to see you again, Miss Lockitt. I'll fetch mevrouw...'

Fran was already running down the staircase. 'Lucy, how lovely! You've come to stay? I do hope so.' She tucked her arm in Lucy's. 'Come into the drawing-room, and, Trugg, please ask Mrs Trugg to make sure that the room Miss Lockitt had when she was here is quite ready for her.'

She opened the drawing-room door and urged Lucy into the room. 'Litrik, look who is here. Isn't it great?'

Litrik was on the floor, building a brick castle for his firstborn. He got to his feet, and Lucy, looking anxiously at his face, could see nothing but pleasure at the sight of her.

'I feel awful coming like this,' she began, 'but I—I must see William, and Trump doesn't know where he is. At least, he said he was in Leiden, but he doesn't know just where.'

'Then you've come to the right place, and very sensible of you,' said Litrik kindly. 'William is staying with us, only unfortunately he went to Groningen this morning and won't be back until tomorrow afternoon or evening.'

'That's in the north, isn't it? I could catch a train...'

'Not this evening, my dear. It's quite a long

journey—a hundred and thirty miles, two and a half hours' run—and what would you do when you got there?' He caught Fran's eye and smiled faintly. 'Fran has a Mini; I'm sure she won't mind if you borrow it and drive up in the morning.'

'Oh, that would be simply marvellous. You wouldn't mind really?'

'Not in the least, but upon reflection I think it might be a better idea if Trugg were to drive you, then he can bring the Mini back. You will, of course, come back with William.'

Lucy's eyes glowed like emeralds. 'Oh, will I? You won't tell him I'm here? He might not want—'

'Not a word shall be said. Darling, take Lucy up to her room and then we'll have a drink and hear all her news.'

They didn't ask her to explain why she had come. They talked about her parents and her sisters and the children, and listened with sympathy when she told them that she had left the orphanage, never betraying the fact that they had heard it all already from William. Presently they had dinner and, after another hour or so of undemanding talk, Lucy went to bed. She had had every intention of rehearsing exactly what she would say to William when she saw him, but she went to sleep instead.

Driven by a dignified Trugg, she left very soon after breakfast. 'Trugg will bring the Mini back,' said Fran, 'because of course, William will bring you back with him. I'm not sure, but I think he said that he had a lecture in the morning and then in-

tended coming back here. Trugg will take you to
the university buildings and see you safely inside.
William is lecturing there in the big hall.' She embraced her friend with the remark that she would
expect them back for dinner that evening, but earlier if they could manage it. Her matter-of-fact acceptance of Lucy's sudden appearance did much to
steady the latter's nerves, which by now were jan-
gling. The drive up to Groningen with the staid but
friendly Trugg did much to steady her, and when
they reached the university buildings she bade him
goodbye and got out of the car without hesitation,
although the sight of him driving away considerably
lessened her resolution. All the same, she walked
boldly through the great doors into the entrance hall,
a dark, forbidding expanse of marble floor and dim
walls, hung with portraits which looked even darker,
and ringed around by busts of long-dead and learned
men, each atop his pedestal. A little daunted, she
looked around her and saw William at the bottom
of the great stone staircase, talking to two elderly
men. He looked stern and remote and, as always,
faultlessly dressed, but she had no intention of letting any of these intimidate her and started across
the marble space between them. She was a third of
the way when he saw her, said something to his companions and came to meet her. If he was surprised
or pleased there was nothing on his face to show it,
but she was past caring about that. She fetched up
in front of him and all her well rehearsed speeches
flew out of her head. 'I had to come,' she told him

breathlessly. 'It was that bit from Wordsworth, you know—"The past unsighed for, and the future sure," When she read it, I knew I'd have to tell you.'

William took her two hands in his; he saw that his long-held patience would have to be held for a little longer.

'Tell me about it, my darling,' he said, in the quiet soothing voice in which he spoke to his small, scared patients.

Lucy lifted her face, glowing with love and trust, to his. 'She came to see me yesterday morning—she said you asked her to, that you had found a brooch at the reception and that it was mine and you had asked her to return it. It wasn't until later that I knew that that was an excuse.' She frowned. 'I never wear brooches…'

She paused long enough for the doctor to ask gently, 'Fiona?'

She nodded. 'She saw your letter to me at your house—the one with the Wordsworth in it.' She smiled radiantly for a moment. 'She took it while Trump wasn't looking and then came to see me. She said it was from you to her…' She stared up at his calm face and a tear trickled down her cheek. 'I wanted to die.'

The doctor took a very white handkerchief from his pocket and wiped away the tear, and she went on, 'Then Trump came and told me, so I knew.' She drew a long gulping breath and said uncertainly, 'I came as quickly as I could.'

The hall had filled quite a lot as they had been

standing there; students in their variety of coloured caps, learned professors with bald heads, a sprinkling of ordinary looking people, looking rather out of place, all milling around the pair of them just as though they weren't there.

Lucy hadn't even seen them, and the doctor ignored them. 'One small point, my darling—this nonsense about you and Joe Walter...'

She remembered his remark about her ringless hand. 'Oh, did she tell you...? She wanted you to think that Joe and I...so, she could marry you.'

'Er—perhaps I might point out that I have never at any time wished to marry her.' He was still holding her hands tightly. 'The only person I want to marry is you, my dear heart, and I knew that the moment I saw you at the clinic.'

'So did I, only I didn't know it till later on,' said Lucy obscurely.

He let go of her hands, put his hand under her arm and started making his way through the throng.

'Where are we going?'

He didn't answer her, but turned into a narrow dark passage and opened a door. The room was even darker than the entrance hall, a gloomy mixture of dark green curtains and heavy leather furniture.

He pushed her in in front of him and closed the door. 'The consultants' room,' he told her, 'but, as you can imagine, no one comes here unless there's a meeting.'

He grinned suddenly, and she saw with satisfaction that he was going to be fun to live with; under that sombre grey suit was a man who would be a delightful husband. She asked, knowing the answer, 'Why have we come here?'

He took her in his arms and drew her close. 'Because I want to tell you that I love you more than anything or anyone in this world, and, when I've made that quite clear, I'm going to kiss you, both of which I prefer to do in privacy.'

She held him off for a mere moment. 'William, do you think we could be married before Pauline and Imogen? Would you mind?'

He kissed her thoroughly before he answered. 'My dearest love, not only do I not mind, but I insist upon it. A special licence and a quiet wedding within the next week or two.'

An entirely satisfactory answer, reflected Lucy. She said meekly, 'Just as you say, William,' and lifted her face to his.

* * * * *

THE MOON FOR LAVINIA

Chapter 1

It was quiet now that the day's lists were over; the operating theatre, gleaming with near-sterile cleanliness and no longer lighted by its great shadowless lamp, looked a very different place from the hive of ordered activity it had been since early morning, for now the surgeons and anaesthetists had gone, as well as Theatre Sister and most of her staff; indeed, the department held but one occupant, a nurse sitting on a stool in front of one of the trolleys, sorting instruments with swift precision.

She was a small, neat person, a little plump, and with a face which was neither plain nor pretty, although when she laughed her hazel eyes widened and twinkled and her too large mouth curved charmingly. It was a pity that she laughed all too seldom, and now, deep in thought as she worked, she looked rather on the plain side and sad with it. She finished her task, tidied everything away neatly and began a final inspection of the theatre before she went off duty. It was a Sunday evening, and for some reason one staff nurse was considered sufficient to be on duty after six o'clock; presumably on the principle that it being a Sunday, people would be less prone to require emergency surgery, and for once this had been proved right; the evening hours, spent in doing the necessary chores had been too quiet, so that Lavinia Hawkins had had time to think, which was a pity, for she had nothing pleasant to think about.

She went along to take off her gown, threw it into the laundry bin, and then sat down again, this time on the only chair the changing room possessed. The June sun, still warm and bright, streamed in through the window, and she could hear, very faintly, the subdued hum of the London evening traffic, most of it returning from an outing to the sea. It would have been a perfect day for them, thought Lavinia without envy, although she wasn't very happy herself; it was a good thing that she was going to Aunt Gwyneth's in two days' time and would have the chance to talk to Peta, her young sister—perhaps they would be able to plan something. Quite forgetful of the time, she took Peta's letter from her pocket and read it once more.

Peta was dreadfully unhappy; when their mother had died, more than a year ago now, and Aunt Gwyneth had offered her a home, Lavinia had been grateful for her help. There was no money, the annuity her mother had lived upon died with her; her father had died a number of years earlier, and although she herself had been self-supporting and had even been able to help out with Peta's school fees, her sister's education had been at a stage when to make changes in it would have been nothing short of criminal. For one thing, Peta was clever and working for her O levels, and for another, Lavinia was only too well aware that a sound education for her sister was essential if she was to be self-supporting too, so that when her mother died Lavinia accepted her aunt's offer with an eager gratitude which she had since come to regret.

It hadn't worked out at all. Aunt Gwyneth was a widow and comfortably off, living in a large house on the outskirts of Cuckfield which was run by a highly efficient housekeeper, leaving her free to indulge her passion for bridge and committee meetings. Lavinia had honestly thought that she would be glad to have Peta to live with her; she had no children of her own and Peta was a darling, pretty and sweet-tempered and anxious to please. It was after she had been at Cuckfield for several months that Lavinia began to sense that something was wrong, but it had taken her a long time to persuade Peta to tell her what was amiss and when, at last, she had got her to talk about it it was to discover that it wasn't just the natural unhappiness she felt at the loss of her mother—life wasn't fun, she confided to Lavinia; her aunt had discovered that having a teenager in the house had its drawbacks. True, Peta was at school all day, but at the week-ends and during the holidays she was made to feel a nuisance, and whenever she suggested that she might spend a few days with Lavinia, there were always good reasons why she shouldn't...

Lavinia, her arm round her sister's slim shoulders, had frowned. 'Darling, you should have told me,' she had said. 'I could have spoken to Aunt Gwyneth,' but even as she uttered the words she had known that it wasn't going to be as easy as all that. Peta was due to take her O levels in a week or two's time, and the plan had been for her to stay on at school and try for her A levels in a couple of years. Even if Lavinia had had a flat of her own, which she hadn't, it would still be difficult, for there would still be the question of where Peta should go to school and how would she ever afford the fees? 'Look,' she had advised, 'could you hang on for another year or two, love—just until you've got those A levels? I'm to have Sister Drew's job when she retires, and that's less than a year now; I'll save every penny I can and find a flat.'

And Peta had agreed. That had been barely a week ago, and now here was her letter, begging Lavinia to take her away from Aunt Gwyneth, promising incoherently to stay until the exam results were out, if only she would take her away... Lavinia folded the letter up once more and put it in her pocket. She had a headache from worrying about what was to be done, for whatever it was, it would have to be done quickly, and at the moment she had no ideas at all. She went down to supper, turning over in her mind a variety of ideas, none of which, unfortunately, stood up to close scrutiny.

Most of her friends were already in the canteen, queueing for baked beans on toast and cups of tea. They shared a table, making the beans last as long

as possible while they discussed the day's work.
It was as they lingered over the last dregs of their
tea that Shirley Thompson from Women's Surgical
declared herself to be completely fed up with that
ward, its Sister, the patients, and indeed the whole
hospital. 'I'm sick of Jerrold's,' she declared. 'I'm
going to look for another job. I've got the *Nursing
Mirror* in my room, let's go and make a pot of tea
and find me a new job.'

No one quite believed her; for one thing, she was
going steady with one of the house surgeons; and for
another, she made this same announcement every
few months, but it was too soon for bed and there
wasn't much else to do; they trooped from the canteen and across to the Nurses' Home, where they
crowded into the Sisters' lift, strictly forbidden, but
no one was likely to see them on a Sunday evening,
anyway, and besides, everyone did it and hoped not
to be caught, and once on the top floor they disposed
themselves around Shirley's room, ready to drink
more tea and give her their not very serious advice.

They were debating, in a lighthearted manner, the
advantages of nursing an octogenarian recovering
from a fractured femur in Belgravia, as opposed to
a post as school nurse in a boarding establishment
in Cumberland, when the *Nursing Mirror* came into
Lavinia's hands. She glanced through it idly and
turning a page had her eye instantly caught by a
large advertisement headed simply 'Amsterdam'.
She read it carelessly, and then, struck by a blindingly super idea, very carefully.

Registered nurses wanted, said the advertisement, with theatre experience and at a salary which was quite fabulous. Knowledge of Dutch was unnecessary; lessons could be arranged, and provided the applicant proved suitable and wished to remain for a period of not less than six months, outside accommodation would be found for her. Lavinia, never very good at her sums, got out her pen and did some basic arithmetic on the underside of her uniform skirt. Supposing, just supposing that the job was all it said it was, if she could get somewhere to live, Peta could live with her, for they could manage on that salary if they were careful. Of course, the plan was completely crazy; Peta's education would come to a halt, but then, Lavinia feared, it would do that if Peta stayed at Cuckfield; her sister's vehemence was clear enough in her letter, it would be awful if she were to run away... Lavinia shuddered just thinking about it—and wouldn't it be better to have her sister under her eye and once she had settled down, devise some plan whereby she might finish her education? She calculated quickly; Peta was only a week or two under sixteen when she could leave school quite legitimately, so there would be no trouble there, and although she knew nothing about education in Holland there would surely be some way of completing her studies.

When the gathering broke up, she begged the journal from Shirley and before she went to bed that night, applied for the job.

She went down to Cuckfield two days later and

found Peta alone in the house, waiting for her, and when she saw her sister's face any doubts which she had been secretly harbouring about a plan which common sense told her was a little short of hare-brained were put at rest. Peta was dreadfully unhappy and Lavinia, ten years her senior, felt a motherly urge to set things right as quickly as possible.

Aunt Gwyneth was out and would be back for lunch, and, the housekeeper told Lavinia, Mrs Turner was looking forward to a nice chat before her niece went back that evening.

Lavinia sighed. The nice chats were really nothing but questions and answers—her aunt asked the questions; rather rude ones usually, and she answered them with a polite vagueness which invariably annoyed her elderly relation, for her aunt, while professing a fondness for Peta, had never liked her. Even as a small girl she had refused to be browbeaten by her father's elder sister and her hectoring manner had left her quite unimpressed; it had never worried her father either, who had brushed it aside like a troublesome swarm of flies, but her mother, a gentle creature like Peta, had often wilted under her sister-in-law's tongue. Lavinia, made of sterner stuff, had refused to be intimidated, and Aunt Gwyneth, annoyed at this, took her petty revenge by never inviting her to stay at her home, either for her holidays or her free days. She was too clever to do this openly, of course, but somehow, when holidays came round, the bedrooms were being decorated, or her aunt was going away herself or felt too poorly to have visitors, and as for her days off, invariably at teatime Lavinia would be asked which train she intended to catch and some reference would be made as to her eagerness to get back to Jerrold's, in order, presumably, to plunge into a hectic round of gaiety with every doctor in the place.

This veiled assumption of her popularity with the men was something which amused Lavinia very much; her aunt knew well enough that she had no men friends; she got on very well with the doctors and students she worked with, but none of them had shown her any decided preference and she doubted if they ever would; she had no looks to speak of and a quiet manner which, while encouraging young men to confide in her, did nothing to catch their fancy.

They were sitting together in the sitting room having their morning coffee when Peta burst out: 'Lavinia, I can't stay here—I simply can't! Aunt Gwyneth keeps telling me how good she's been to me—and you, though I can't think how—she makes me feel like a—a pauper. I know we haven't any money, but she is our aunt and our only relation, and do you know what she said? That in a year or two, when I've finished school and am earning my living, you'll have to leave your job in hospital and be her companion, because she'll need someone by then and it's only natural that you should be the one because she's given me a home.' She added unhappily: 'Lavinia, what are we going to do?'

Lavinia refilled their coffee cups. 'I'll tell you, darling.'

She outlined her plan simply, making light of its obvious drawbacks, glad that Peta hadn't spotted them in her excitement. 'So you see, Peta, everything will be super, only you must promise to stay here and take your O levels and say nothing about our plan to anyone. I haven't heard from these people yet, but I think I've got a good chance of getting a job. I'll have to give a month's notice at Jerrold's—give me a couple of weeks to find my way about, and I'll come for you. Could you stick it for just a little longer?'

Peta nodded. 'Darling Lavinia, of course I can. You're sure we can live on what you'll earn in Amsterdam? I could get a job...'

'Yes, love, I know, but I think we'll be able to manage. I'd rather you went on with your studies—perhaps if you could learn Dutch, enough to help you get a job later on? UNO and all that,' she added vaguely, and looked at the clock. 'Aunt Gwyneth will be here very soon, let's talk about something else so that we're just as usual when she comes. Tell me about school.'

Their aunt found them poring over school books, arguing cheerfully about applied physics although Lavinia knew almost nothing about the subject. She got up to greet her aunt and received a chilly peck on her cheek while the lady studied her. 'You must be twenty-six,' she observed. 'Such a pity you have no looks, Lavinia. How fortunate that you took up nursing as a career, although waiting until you were twenty-two seems to me to have been a needless waste of time—you could have been a ward Sister by now.'

Lavinia thought of several answers to this unfortunate remark, but none of them were very polite; they went in to lunch in a little flurry of polite and meaningless remarks.

Lunch was excellent; Aunt Gwyneth enjoyed her comforts and made sure that she had them, although she pointed out during dessert that her nieces were lucky girls indeed to enjoy the benefits of her generosity. Lavinia, still peevish about her aunt's remark about her lack of looks, felt an urge to throw her trifle across the table at her. No wonder poor little Peta was fed up; anything would be better than putting up with the succession of snide remarks which tripped off her relation's tongue. For once she answered with relief when she was asked at what time she was returning to hospital.

'I daresay you have plans for the evening,' said Aunt Gwyneth, 'and I'm not so selfish as to delay you in any way. After tea, you say? That is admirable, for I have a small bridge party this evening, and Peta has a great deal of studying to do in preparation for her exams.' Her two listeners expected her to add a rider to the effect that if it hadn't been for her, there would have been no possibility of exams, but she contented herself with a smug smile.

So Lavinia went back after tea, not liking to leave Peta, but seeing no alternative, but at least she was heartened to see how much more cheerful her sister was. They parted under their aunt's eye, so that all

Lavinia could say was: 'See you next week, Peta—
if I may come down, Aunt?' she added politely, and
received a gracious nod of assent.

There was a letter for her on Monday morning,
asking her to go for an interview, either that afternoon or on the following morning, and as luck
would have it she had been given a split duty because Sister wanted the evening, and the morning's
list was too heavy for them both to be off duty at the
same time. She changed into a plain coffee-coloured
linen dress, coiled her long hair with care, made up
her face, and caught a bus; only as she was going
through the open door of the hotel where the inter-
views were to be held did she pause to think what
she was doing, and by then it was too late. There
were a dozen or more girls waiting, some of them
younger than she, and most of them prettier; there
was a possibility of her not getting a job after all;
she hadn't expected quite so many applicants.

She was brooding over this when her turn came,
and she found herself on the other side of the door,
invited to sit down by a middle-aged lady sitting at
a table, and stared at by the two people on either side
of her. A man, a large comfortable-looking man in
his fifties, and another woman, young this time—
not much older than herself and very fair with a
wholesome out-of-doors look about her.

The lady in the middle opened the interview with
a pleasant: 'Miss Hawkins? We are pleased that
you could come and see us. My name is Platsma—
Mevrouw Platsma, and this is Juffrouw Smid and

also Professor van Leek, who is the Medical Director of our hospital in Amsterdam. Miss Smid is the Sister-in-Charge of the theatre unit.' She paused to smile. 'What are your qualifications, Miss Hawkins?'

Lavinia gave them without trying to make more of them than they were.

'And your reasons for wishing to work with us?'

She told them the truth, fined down to the facts and without enlarging upon Aunt Gwyneth. 'I think I could live on the salary you offer and have my sister to live with me, something we both would like very much—I can't do that here because I can't afford a flat—I live in at Jerrold's. I should like to live in Amsterdam too; I've never been out of England.'

'You like your work?'

'Very much.'

'You are accustomed to scrub?'

'Yes. There are four theatres in our unit, I work in General Surgery and take most of the cases when Sister is off duty.'

'You have no objection to us referring to your superiors at the hospital?'

'No, none at all. If I should be considered for the job, I should have to give a month's notice.'

They all three smiled at her and Mevrouw Platsma said: 'Thank you, Miss Hawkins, we will let you know at the earliest opportunity.'

She went back to Jerrold's feeling uncertain; her qualifications were good, she would be given excellent references she felt sure, but then so might the other girls who had been there. She told herself sensibly to forget about it, something easily done, as it turned out, for there was an emergency perforation that evening, followed by a ruptured appendix. She went off duty too tired to do more than eat a sketchy supper, have a bath, and go to bed.

There was a letter by the first post in the morning. She had got the job. She did an excited little jig in the scrubbing-up room, begged permission to go to the office at once, and presented herself, rather breathless still, before the Principal Nursing Officer's desk.

Miss Mint heard her out, expressed regret that she should want to leave, but added in the same breath that it was a splendid thing to broaden one's mind when young and that should Lavinia wish to return to Jerrold's at some future date, she could be sure of a post—if there was one vacant—at any time. She finished this encouraging speech by observing that probably she had some holidays due to her, in which case she should be able to leave sooner.

Lavinia becamed at her. 'Oh, Miss Mint, I have— a week. I knew you would understand about me wanting to go somewhere where I could have Peta with me... I only hope I'll make a success of it.'

Miss Mint smiled. 'I can think of no reason why you shouldn't,' she said encouragingly. 'Come and see me before you go, Staff Nurse. I shall of course supply references when they are required.'

Lavinia went through the rest of the day in a daze, doing her work with her usual efficiency while she thought about her new job. She spent a good deal of her lunch hour writing to accept the post, and only restrained herself by a great effort from writing to Peta too, but there was always the danger that their aunt would read the letter, and telephoning would be just as chancy; she should have thought of that sooner and arranged for her sister to telephone her on her way home from school. Now the news would have to wait until she paid her weekly visit on Saturday.

The days flashed by; she received particulars of her job, how she was to travel, and the day on which she was expected, as well as the gratifying news that her references were entirely satisfactory. She had a few pounds saved; the temptation to spend some of them on new clothes was very strong, so on her morning off she went along to Oxford Street.

It was a splendid day and the gay summer clothes in the shop windows exactly matched her mood; discarding all sensible ideas about practical rainwear, hard-wearing shoes and colours which wouldn't show the dirt, she plunged recklessly, returning to the Nurses' Home laden with parcels; new sandals—pretty pink ones to match the pink cotton dress and jacket she hadn't been able to resist, a pale green linen skirt with a darling little linen blouse to go with it, and as well as these, a long cardigan which happily matched them both. There was a dress too, pale green silk jersey, and as a sop to her conscience, a raincoat, coffee-coloured and lightweight. She laid everything out on her bed and admired them and tried not to think of all the money she had spent, cheering herself with the thought that she still had something tucked away and enough besides to get her through the first month in Amsterdam before she would be paid. And when Peta joined her, she would buy her some pretty dresses too; Aunt Gwyneth's ideas ran to the serviceable and dull for her niece; the two of them would scour Amsterdam for the sort of clothes girls of Peta's age liked to wear.

Her sister was waiting for her when she got to Cuckfield on Saturday morning and so was their aunt. There was no chance to talk at all until after lunch, and then only for a few minutes while Aunt Gwyneth was telephoning. 'It's OK,' said Lavinia softly. 'I've got the job—I'm going two weeks today. I'll tell Aunt when I come next week, but only that I'm going —nothing about you yet—and don't say anything, love, whatever you do.' She smiled at Peta. 'Try not to look so happy, darling. Tell me about your exams—do you think you did well?'

She didn't stay as long as usual; her aunt had a bridge date directly after tea and was anxious for her to be gone, and a tentative suggestion that she might take Peta out for the evening was met with a number of perfectly feasible reasons why she shouldn't. That was the trouble with Aunt Gwyneth, thought Lavinia crossly, she never flatly refused anything, which made it very hard to argue with her. She wondered, as she went back to London, how her aunt would take the news of her new job.

She thought about it several times during the ensuing week, but theatre was busy and there really wasn't much time to worry about anything else. Saturday, when it came, was another cloudless day. Lavinia, in a rather old cotton dress because she was starting on the business of packing her things, felt cheerful as she walked the short distance from the station to her aunt's house. And her aunt seemed in a good mood too, so that without giving herself time to get nervous, Lavinia broke her news.

It was received with surprising calm. 'Let us hope,' said her aunt ponderously, 'that this new venture will improve your status sufficiently for you to obtain a more senior post later on—it is the greatest pity that you did not take up nursing immediately you left school, for you must be a good deal older than the average staff nurse.'

Lavinia let this pass. It was partly true in any case, though it need not have been mentioned in such unkind terms. Everyone knew quite well why she had stayed at home when she had left school; her mother was alone and Peta was still a small girl, and over and above that, her mother hadn't been strong. She said now, schooling her voice to politeness: 'I don't know about that, Aunt, but the change will be nice and the pay's good.'

'As long as you don't squander it,' replied Aunt Gwyneth tartly. 'But it is a good opportunity for you to see something of the world, I suppose; the time will come when I shall need a companion, as you well know. Peta will be far too young and lively for me, and I shall expect you, Lavinia, to give up your nursing and look after me. It is the least you can do for me after the sacrifices I have made for you both.'

Lavinia forbore from commenting that she had had nothing done for her at all; even holidays and days off had been denied her, and though she was a fair-minded girl, the worthy stockings, edifying books and writing paper she had received so regularly at Christmas and birthdays could hardly be classed as sacrifices. And her aunt could quite well afford to pay for a companion; someone she could bully if she wanted to and who would be able to answer back without the chain of family ties to hold her back. She sighed with deep contentment, thinking of her new job, and her aunt mistaking her reason for sighing, remarked that she was, and always had been, an ungrateful girl.

Lavinia wasn't going to see Peta again before she left England, although she had arranged to telephone her at a friend's house before she went. She spent the week in making final arrangements, aided, and hindered too, by her many friends. They had a party for her on her last night, with one bottle of sherry between a dozen or more of them, a great many pots of tea and a miscellany of food. There was a great deal of laughing and talking too, and when someone suggested that Lavinia should find herself a husband while she was in Holland, a chorus of voices elaborated the idea. 'Someone rich -good-looking— both—with an enormous house so that they could all come and stay...' The party broke up in peals of laughter. Lavinia was very popular, but no one really believed that she was likely to find herself such a delightful future, and she believed it least of all.

She left the next morning, after a guarded telephone talk with Peta and a noisy send-off from her friends at Jerrold's. She was to go by plane, and the novelty of that was sufficient to keep her interested until the flat coast of Holland appeared beneath them and drove home the fact that she had finally left her safe, rather dull life behind, and for one she didn't know much about. They began to circle Schiphol airport, and she sat rigid. Supposing that after all, no one spoke English? Dutch, someone had told her, was a fearful language until you got the hang of it. Supposing that there had been some mistake and when she arrived no one expected her? Supposing the theatre technique was different, even though they had said it wasn't…? She followed the other passengers from the plane, went through Customs and boarded the bus waiting to take her to Amsterdam.

The drive was just long enough to give her time to pull herself together and even laugh a little at her silly ideas. It was a bit late to get cold feet now, anyway, and she had the sudden hopeful feeling that she was going to like her new job very much. She looked about her eagerly as the bus churned its way through the morning traffic in the narrow streets and at the terminal she did as she had been instructed: showed the hospital's address to a hovering taxi-driver, and when he had loaded her luggage into his cab, got in beside it. The new life had begun.

Chapter 2

The hospital was on the fringe of the city's centre; a large, old-fashioned building, patched here and there with modern additions which its three-hundred-year-old core had easily absorbed. It was tucked away behind the busy main streets, with narrow alleys, lined with tiny, slightly shabby houses, round three sides of it. On the fourth side there was a great covered gateway, left over from a bygone age, which was still wide enough to accommodate the comings and goings of ambulances and other motor traffic.

Lavinia paused to look about her as she got out of the taxi. The driver got out too and set her luggage on the pavement, said something she couldn't understand, and then humped it up the steps of the hospital and left it in the vast porch. Only when he had done this did he tell her how much she needed to pay him. As she painstakingly sorted out the *guldens* he asked: 'You are nurse?' and when she nodded, refused the tip she offered him. London taxi drivers seldom took tips from a nurse either, sometimes they wouldn't even accept a fare—perhaps it

was a worldwide custom. She thanked him when
he wished her good luck and waited until his broad
friendly back had disappeared inside his cab before
going through the big glass doors, feeling as though
she had lost a friend.

But she need not have felt nervous; no sooner
had she peered cautiously through the porter's lodge
window than he was there, asking her what she
wanted, and when he discovered that she was the
expected English nurse, he summoned another porter, gave him incomprehensible instructions, said,
just as the taxi driver had said: 'Good luck,' and
waved her into line behind her guide. She turned
back at the last moment, remembering her luggage,
and was reassured by his cheerful: 'Baggage is OK.'

The porter was tall and thin and walked fast;
Lavinia, almost trotting to keep up with him, had
scant time in which to look around her. She had
an impression of dark walls, a tiled floor and endless doors on either side of the passages they were
traversing so rapidly. Presently they merged into a
wider one which in its turn ended at a splendid arch-
way opening on to a vestibule, full of doors. The
porter knocked on one of these, opened it and stood
on one side of it for her to enter.

The room was small, and seemed smaller because
of the woman standing by the window, for she was
very large—in her forties, perhaps, with a straight
back, a billowing bosom and a long, strong-featured
face. Her eyes were pale blue and her hair, drawn
back severely from her face, was iron grey. When

she smiled, Lavinia thought she was one of the nicest persons she had ever seen.

'Miss Hawkins?' Her voice was as nice as her smile. 'We are glad to welcome you to St Jorus and we hope that you will be happy here.' She nodded towards a small hard chair. 'Will you sit, please?'

Lavinia sat, listening carefully while the Directrice outlined her duties, mentioned off-duty, touched lightly on uniforms, salary and the advisability of taking Dutch lessons and went on: 'You will find that the medical staff speak English and also some of the nurses too—the domestic staff, they will not, but there will be someone to help you for a little while. You will soon pick up a few necessary words, I feel sure.'

She smiled confidently at Lavinia, who smiled back, not feeling confident at all. Certainly she would make a point of starting lessons as soon as possible; she hadn't heard more than a few sentences of Dutch so far, but they had sounded like gibberish.

'You wish to live out, I understand,' went on the Directrice, 'and that will be possible within a week or so, but first you must be quite certain that you want to remain with us, although we should not stand in your way if before then you should decide to return to England.'

'I was thinking of staying for a year,' ventured Lavinia, 'but I'd rather not decide until I've been here a few days, but I do want to make a home for my young sister.'

Her companion looked curious but forbore from

pressing for further information, instead she rang the bell on her desk and when a young woman in nurse's uniform but without a cap answered it, she said kindly:

'This is Juffrouw Fiske, my secretary. She will take you over to the Nurses' Home and show you your room. You would like to unpack, and perhaps it would be as well if you went on duty directly after the midday meal. Theatre B, major surgery. There is a short list this afternoon and you will have a chance to find your feet.'

Lavinia thanked her and set off with Juffrouw Fiske through more passages and across a couple of small courtyards, enclosed by high grey walls until they finally came to a door set in one of them—the back door, she was told, to the Home. It gave directly on to a short passage with a door at its end opening on to a wide hall in which was a flight of stairs which they climbed.

'There is a lift,' explained her companion, 'but you are on the first floor, therefore there is no need.'

She opened a door only a few yards from the head of the stairs and invited Lavinia to go in. It was a pleasant room, tolerably large and very well furnished, and what was more, her luggage was there as well as a pile of uniforms on the bed.

'We hope that everything fits,' said Juffrouw Fiske. 'You are small, are you not?' She smiled widely. 'We are quite often big girls. Someone will come and take you to your dinner at twelve o'clock,

Miss Hawkins, and I hope that you will be happy with us.'

Nice people, decided Lavinia, busily unpacking. She had already decided that she was going to like the new job—she would like it even better when she had a home of her own and Peta with her. Of course, she still had to meet the people she was to work with, but if they were half as nice as those she had met already, she felt she need have no fears about getting on with them.

The uniform fitted very well. She perched the stiff little cap on top of her tidy topknot and sat down to wait for whoever was to fetch her.

It was a big, well-built girl, with ash blonde hair and a merry face. She shook hands with enthusiasm and said: 'Neeltje Haagsma.'

For a moment Lavinia wondered if she was being asked how she did in Dutch, but the girl put her right at once. 'My name—we shake hands and say our names when we meet—that is simple, is it not?'

Lavinia nodded. 'Lavinia Hawkins. Do I call you *juffrouw*?'

Neeltje pealed with laughter. 'No, no—you will call me Neeltje and I will call you Lavinia, only you must call the Hoofd Zuster, Zuster Smid.'

'And the doctors?' They were making for the stairs.

'Doctor—easy, is it not? and *chirurgen*—surgeon, is it not?—you will call them Mister this or Mister that.'

Not so foreign after all, Lavinia concluded happily, and then was forced to change her mind when they entered an enormous room, packed with nurses sitting at large tables eating their dinner and all talking at the tops of their voices in Dutch.

But it wasn't too bad after all. Neeltje sat her down, introduced her rapidly and left her to shake hands all round, while she went to get their meal; meat balls, a variety of vegetables and a great many potatoes. Lavinia, who was hungry, ate the lot, followed it with a bowl of custard, and then, over coffee, did her best to answer the questions being put to her. It was an agreeable surprise to find that most of her companions spoke such good English and were so friendly.

'Are there any other English nurses here?' she wanted to know.

Neeltje shook her head. 'You are the first—there are to be more, but not for some weeks. And now we must go to our work.'

The hospital might be old, but the theatre block was magnificently modern. Lavinia, whisked along by her friendly companion, peered about her and wished that she could tell Peta all about it; she would have to write a letter as soon as possible. But soon, caught up in the familiar routine, she had no time to think about anything or anyone other than her work. It was, as the Directrice had told her, a short list, and the technique was almost exactly the same as it had been in her own hospital, although now and again she was reminded that it wasn't quite the same—the murmur of voices, speaking a strange language, even though everyone there addressed her in English.

Before the list had started, Zuster Smid had introduced her to the surgeon who was taking the list, his registrar and his houseman, as well as the three nurses who were on duty. She had forgotten their names, which was awkward, but at least she knew what she was doing around theatre. Zuster Smid had watched her closely for quite a while and then had relaxed. Lavinia, while not much to look at, was competent at her job; it would take more than working in strange surroundings to make her less than that.

The afternoon came to an end, the theatre was readied once more for the morning's work or any emergency which might be sent up during the night, and shepherded by the other girls, she went down to her supper and after that she was swept along to Neeltje's room with half a dozen other girls, to drink coffee and gossip—she might have been back at Jerrold's. She stifled a sudden pang of homesickness, telling herself that she was tired—as indeed she was, for no sooner had she put her head on her pillow than she was asleep.

It was on her third day, at the end of a busy morning's list, that she was asked to go up to the next floor with a specimen for section. The Path. Lab. usually sent an assistant down to collect these, but this morning, for some reason, there was no one to send and Lavinia, not scrubbed, and nearest to take the receiver with the offending object to be inves-

tigated, slid out of the theatre with it, divested herself of her gown and over-shoes and made her way
swiftly up the stairs outside the theatre unit.

The Path. Lab. was large—owing, she had been
told, to the fact that Professor ter Bavinck, who
was the head of it, was justly famed for his brilliant work. Other, smaller hospitals sent a constant
stream of work and he was frequently invited to
other countries in order to give his learned opinion
on some pathological problem. Neeltje had related
this in a reverent voice tinged with awe, and Lavinia had concluded that the professor was an object of veneration in the hospital; possibly he had
a white beard.

She pushed open the heavy glass doors in front
of her and found herself in a vast room, brightly
lighted and full of equipment which she knew of,
but never quite understood. There were a number
of men sitting at their benches, far too busy to take
any notice of her, so she walked past them to the end
of the room where there was a door with the professor's name on it; presumably this was where one
went. But when she knocked, no one answered, so
she turned her back on it and looked round the room.

One man drew her attention at once, and he was
sitting with his back to her, looking through a mi-
croscope. It was the breadth of his shoulders which
had caught her eye, and his pale as flax hair, heavily
silvered. She wondered who he might be, but now
wasn't the time to indulge her interest.

She addressed the room in general in a quite loud

voice. 'Professor ter Bavinck? I've been sent from Theatre B with a specimen.'

The shoulders which had caught her eye gave an impatient shrug; without turning round a deep voice told her: 'Put it down here, beside me, please, and then go away.'

Lavinia's charming bosom swelled with indignation. What a way to talk, and who did he think he was, anyway? She advanced to his desk and laid the kidney dish silently at his elbow. 'There you are, sir,' she said with a decided snap, 'and why on earth should you imagine I should want to stay?'

He lifted his head then to stare at her, and she found herself staring back at a remarkably handsome face; a high-bridged nose dominated it and the mouth beneath it was very firm, while the blue eyes studying her so intently were heavy-lidded and heavily browed. She was quite unprepared for his friendly smile and for the great size of him as he pushed back his chair and stood up, towering over her five feet four inches.

'Ah, the English nurse—Miss Hawkins, is it not? In fact, I am sure,' his smile was still friendly, 'no nurse in the hospital would speak to me like that.'

Lavinia went a splendid pink and sought for something suitable to say to this. After a moment's thought she decided that it was best to say nothing at all, so she closed her mouth firmly and met his eyes squarely. Perhaps she had been rude, but after all, he had asked for it. Her uneasy thoughts were interrupted by his voice, quite brisk now. 'This specimen—a snap check, I presume—Mevrouw Vliet, the query mastectomy, isn't it?'

'Yes, sir.'

'I'll telephone down.' He nodded at her in a kindly, uncle-ish way, said: 'Run along,' and turned away, the kidney dish on his hand. She heard him giving what she supposed to be instructions to one of his assistants as she went through the door.

She found herself thinking about him while they all waited for his report; the surgeon, his sterile gloved hands clasped before him, the rest of them ready to do exactly what he wanted when he said so. The message came very quickly. Lavinia wondered what the professor had thought when his sharp eyes had detected the cancer cells in the specimen, but possibly Mevrouw Vliet, lying unconscious on the table and happily unaware of what was happening, was just another case to him. He might not know— nor care—if she were young, old, pretty or plain, married or unmarried, and yet he had looked as though he might—given the right circumstances— be rather super.

It was much later, at supper time, that Neeltje wanted to know what she had thought of him.

'Well,' said Lavinia cautiously, 'I hardly spoke to him—he just took the kidney dish and told me to go away.'

'And that was all?'

'He did remark that I was the English nurse. He's...he's rather large, isn't he?'

'From Friesland,' explained Neeltje, who was

from Friesland herself. 'We are a big people. He is of course old.'

Lavinia paused in the conveyance of soup to her mouth. 'Old?' she frowned. 'I didn't think he looked old.'

'He is past forty,' said a small brown-haired girl from across the table. 'Also he has been married; his daughter is fourteen.'

There were a dozen questions on Lavinia's tongue, but it wasn't really her business. All the same, she did want to know what had happened to his wife. The brown-haired girl must have read her thoughts, for she went on: 'His wife died ten years ago, more than that perhaps, she was, how do you say? not a good wife. She was not liked, but the professor, now he is much liked, although he talks to no one, that is to say, he talks but he tells nothing, you understand? Perhaps he is unhappy, but he would not allow anyone to see that and never has he spoken of his wife.' She shrugged. 'Perhaps he loved her, who knows? His daughter is very nice, her name is Sibendina.'

'That's pretty,' said Lavinia, still thinking about the professor. 'Is that a Friesian name?'

'Yes, although it is unusual.' Neeltje swallowed the last of her coffee. 'Let us go to the sitting-room and watch the *televisie*.'

Lavinia met the professor two days later. She had been to her first Dutch lesson in her off duty, arranged for her by someone on the administrative staff and whom probably she would never meet but who had nonetheless given her careful instruction as to her ten-minute walk to reach her teacher's flat. This lady turned out to be a retired schoolmistress with stern features and a command of the English language which quite deflated Lavinia. However, at the end of an hour, Juffrouw de Waal was kind enough to say that her pupil, provided she applied herself to her work, should prove to be a satisfactory pupil, worthy of her teaching powers.

Lavinia wandered back in the warmth of the summer afternoon, and with time on her hands, turned off the main street she had been instructed to follow, to stroll down a narrow alley lined with charming little houses. It opened on to a square, lined with trees and old, thin houses leaning against each other for support. They were three or four stories high, with a variety of roofs, and here and there they had been crowded out by much larger double-fronted town mansions, with steps leading up to their imposing doors. She inspected them all, liking their unassuming façades and trying to guess what they would be like on the other side of their sober fronts. Probably quite splendid and magnificently furnished; the curtains, from what she could see from the pavement, were lavishly draped and of brocade or velvet. She had completed her walk around three sides of the square when she was addressed from behind.

'I hardly expected to find you here, Miss Hawkins—not lost, I hope?'

She turned round to confront Professor ter Bavinck. 'No—at least...' She paused to look around her; she wasn't exactly lost, but now she had no idea which lane she had come from. 'I've been for an English lesson,' she explained defensively, 'and I had some time to spare, and it looked so delightful...' She gave another quick look around her. 'I only have to walk along that little lane,' she assured him.

He laughed gently. 'No, not that one—the people who live in this square have their garages there and it's a cul-de-sac. I'm going to the hospital, you had better come along with me.'

'Oh, no—that is, it's quite all right.' She had answered very fast, anxious not to be a nuisance and at the same time aware that this large quiet man had a strange effect upon her.

'You don't like me, Miss Hawkins?'

She gave him a shocked look, and it was on the tip of her tongue to assure him that she was quite sure, if she allowed herself to think about it, that she liked him very much, but all she said was: 'I don't know you, Professor, do I? But I've no reason not to like you. I only said that because you might not want my company.'

'Don't beg the question; we both have our work to do there this afternoon, and that is surely a good enough reason to bear each other company.' He didn't wait to hear her answer. 'We go this way.'

He started to walk back the way she had come, past the tall houses squeezed even narrower and taller by the great house in their centre—it took up at least half of that side of the square, and moreover there was a handsome Bentley convertible standing before its door.

Lavinia slowed down to look at it. 'A Bentley!' she exclaimed, rather superfluously. 'I thought everybody who could afford to do so drove Mercedes on the continent. I wonder whose it is—it must take a good deal of cunning to get through that lane I walked down.'

'This one's wider,' her companion remarked carelessly, and turned into a short, quite broad street leading away from the square. It ran into another main street she didn't recognize, crowded with traffic, but beyond advising her to keep her eyes and ears open the professor had no conversation. True, when they had to cross the street, he took her arm and saw her safely to the other side, but with very much the tolerant air of someone giving a helping hand to an old lady or a small child. It was quite a relief when he plunged down a narrow passage between high brick walls which ended unexpectedly at the very gates of the hospital.

'Don't try and come that way by yourself,' he cautioned her, lifted a hand in salute and strode away across the forecourt. Lavinia went to her room to change, feeling somehow disappointed, although she wasn't sure why. Perhaps, she told herself, it was because she had been wearing a rather plain dress; adequate enough for Juffrouw de Waal, but lacking in eye-catching qualities. Not that it would have mattered; the professor hadn't bothered to look at her once—and why should he? Rather plain girls were just as likely two a penny in Holland as they were in England. She screwed her hair into a shining bun, jammed her cap on top of it, and went on duty, pretending to herself that she didn't care in the least whether she saw him again or not.

She saw him just one hour later. There had been an emergency appendix just after she had got back to theatre, and she had been sent back to the ward with the patient. She and one of the ward nurses were tucking the patient into her bed, when she glanced up and saw him, sitting on a nearby bed, listening attentively to its occupant. The ward nurse leaned across the bed. 'Professor ter Bavinck,' she breathed, 'so good a man and so kind—he visits...' she frowned, seeking words. 'Mevrouw Vliet, the mastectomy—you were at the operation and you know what was discovered? When that is so, he visits the patient and explains and listens and helps if he can.' She paused to smile. 'My English—it is not so bad, I hope?'

'It's jolly good. I wish I knew even a few words of Dutch.' Lavinia meant that; it would be nice to understand what the professor was saying—not that she was likely to get much chance of that.

She handed over the patient's notes, and without looking at the professor, went back to theatre. Zuster Smid had gone off duty, taking most of her staff with her, there were only Neeltje and herself working until nine o'clock. She had been sorting instruments while her companion saw to the theatre linen, when the door opened and Professor ter Bavinck walked

in. He walked over to say something to Neeltje before he came across the theatre to Lavinia.

'Off at nine o'clock?' he asked.

'Yes, sir.'

His mouth twitched faintly. 'Could you stop calling me sir? Just long enough for me to invite you
out to supper.'

'Me? Supper?' Her eyes were round with surprise. 'Oh, but I…'

'Scared of being chatted up? Forget it, dear girl;
think of me as a Dutch uncle anxious to make you
feel at home in Amsterdam.'

She found herself smiling. 'I don't know what a
Dutch uncle is.'

'I'm vague about it myself, but it sounds respectable enough to establish a respectable relationship,
don't you agree?'

A warning, perhaps? Letting her know in the nicest way that he was merely taking pity on a stranger
who might be feeling lonely?

'Somewhere quiet,' he went on, just as if she had
already said that she would go with him, 'where we
can get a quick snack—I'll be at the front entrance.'

'I haven't said that I'll go yet,' she reminded him
coldly, and wished that she hadn't said it, for the
look he bent on her was surprised and baffled too,
so that she rushed on: 'I didn't mean that—of course
I'll come, I'd like to.'

He didn't smile although his eyes twinkled reassuringly. 'We don't need to be anything but honest with each other,' a remark which left her, in her

turn, surprised and baffled. He had gone while she was still thinking it over, and any vague and foolish ideas which it might have nurtured were at once dispelled by Neeltje's, 'You go to supper with the Prof. Did I not tell you how good and kind a man he is? He helps always the lame dog...'

Just for a moment the shine went out of the evening, but Lavinia was blessed with a sense of humour; she giggled and said cheerfully: 'Well, let's hope I get a good supper, because I'm hungry.'

She changed rapidly, not quite sure what she should wear or how much time she had in which to put it on. It was a warm evening and still light; still damp from a shower, she looked over her sketchy wardrobe and decided that the pink cotton with its jacket would look right wherever they went. As she did her face and hair she tried to remember if there were any snack bars or cafés close to the hospital, but with the exception of Jan's Eethuisje just across the road and much frequented by the hospital staff who had had to miss a meal for some reason or other, she could think of none. She thrust her feet into the pink sandals, checked her handbag's contents and made her way to the entrance.

The professor was there; it wasn't until she saw him, leaning against the wall, his hands in his pockets, that she realized that she hadn't been quite sure that he would be. He came across the hall to meet her and she noticed that his clothes were good; elegant and beautifully cut if a little conservative—but then he wasn't a very young man.

He said hullo in a casual way and opened the door for her and they went out to the forecourt together. It was fairly empty, but even if it hadn't been, any cars which might have been there would have been cast into the shade by the car outside the door.

'Oh, it's the Bentley!' cried Lavinia as her companion ushered her into its luxury.

'You like it? I need a large car, you see.' He got in beside her. 'One of the problems of being large.'

She sat back, sniffing the faint scent of leather, enjoying the drive, however short, in such a fabulous car. And the drive was short; the professor slid in and out of the traffic while she was still trying to discover which way they were going, and pulled up after only a few minutes, parking the car on the cobbles at the side of the narrow canal beside an even narrower street, and inviting her to get out. It seemed that their snack was to be taken at what appeared to be an expensive restaurant, its name displayed so discreetly that it could have passed for a town house in a row of similar houses. Lavinia allowed herself to be shepherded inside to a quiet luxury which took her breath and sitting at a table which had obviously been reserved for them, thanked heaven silently that the pink, while not anything out of the ordinary, at least passed muster.

It was equally obvious within a very few moments that the professor's notion of a quick snack wasn't hers. She ran her eyes over the large menu card, looking in vain for hamburgers or baked beans on toast, although she doubted if such an establishment served such homely dishes.

'Smoked eel?' invited her companion. 'I think you must try that, and then perhaps coq au vin to follow?' He dismissed the waiter and turned to confer with the wine waiter, asking as he did so: 'Sherry for you? Do you prefer it sweet?'

She guessed quite rightly that it wasn't likely to be the same sort of sherry they drank at hospital parties. 'Well...' she smiled at him, 'I don't know much about it—would you choose?'

The sherry, when it came, was faintly dry and as soft as velvet. Lavinia took a cautious second sip, aware, that she hadn't had much to eat for some time, aware, too, that conversationally she wasn't giving very good value. Her host was sitting back in his chair, completely at his ease, his eyes on her face, so that she found it difficult to think of something to talk about. She was on the point of falling back on the weather when he said: 'Tell me about yourself—why did you take this job? Did not your family dislike the idea of you coming here? There are surely jobs enough in England for someone as efficient as you.' He saw the look on her face and added: 'Dear me, I did put that badly, didn't I? It just shows you that a lack of female society makes a man very clumsy with his words.'

She took another sip of sherry. 'I haven't a family—at least, only a sister. She's fifteen, almost sixteen, and lives with an aunt. She hasn't been happy with her and when I saw this job advertised I thought I'd try for it—I shall be able to live out, you see, and Peta will be able to come here and live with me. I couldn't do that in England—not in London at any rate, because flats there are very expensive and nurses don't earn an awful lot.'

She finished the sherry. It had loosened her tongue; she hadn't told anyone her plans, and here she was pouring out her heart to a stranger—almost a stranger, then, though he had never seemed to be that, rather someone whom she had known for a very long time.

'You are prepared to take that responsibility? You should marry.' There was the faintest question in his voice.

'Well, that would be awfully convenient, but no one's asked me, and anyway I can't imagine anyone wanting to make a home for Peta as well as me.'

She couldn't see his eyes very well; the heavy lids almost covered them, probably he was half asleep with boredom. 'I think you may be wrong there,' he said quietly, and then: 'And what do you think of our hospital?'

It was easy after that; he led her from one topic to the next while they ate the smoked eel and then the chicken, washed down with the wine which had been the subject of such serious discussion with the wine waiter. Lavinia had no idea what it was, but it tasted delicious, as did the chocolate mousse which followed the chicken. She ate and drank with the simple pleasure of someone who doesn't go out very often, and when she had finished it, she said shyly:

'That was quite super; I don't go out a great deal—
hardly ever, in fact. I thought you meant it when you
said a quick snack.'

He laughed gently. 'It's quite some time since I
took a girl out to supper. I haven't enjoyed myself
so much for a long while.' He added deliberately:
'We must do it again.'

'Yes, well…that would be…' She found herself
short of both breath and words. 'I expect I should
be getting back.'

He lifted a finger to the hovering waiter. 'Of
course—a heavy day tomorrow, isn't it?'

He spoke very little on their way back to the hospital, and Lavinia, trying to remember it all later,
couldn't be sure of what she had replied. He wished
her good night at the hospital entrance and got back
into his car and drove off without looking back. He
was nice, she admitted to herself as she went to
her room; the kind of man she felt at ease with—
he would be a wonderful friend; perhaps, later on,
he might be. She went to sleep thinking about him.

There was the usual chatter at breakfast and several of her table companions asked her if she had
had a good supper. Evidently someone had told
them. Neeltje probably; she was a positive fount of
information about everything and everyone. She
informed everyone now: 'The Prof's going to a con-
ference in Vienna; he won't be here for a few days,
for I heard him telling Doctor van Teyl about it. We
shall have that grumpy old van Vorst snapping our
heads off if we have to go to the Path. Lab.' She

smiled at Lavinia. 'And he is not likely to ask you to go out with him.'

Everyone laughed and Lavinia laughed too, although in fact she felt quite gloomy. Somehow she had imagined that she would see Professor ter Bavinck again that morning, and the knowledge that she wouldn't seemed to have taken a good deal of the sparkle out of the day.

She settled down during the next few days into her new way of life, writing to Peta every day or so, studying her Dutch lessons hard so that she might wring a reluctant word of praise from Juffrouw de Waal, and when she was on duty, working very hard indeed. She had scrubbed for several cases by now and had managed very well, refusing to allow herself to be distracted or worried by the steady flow of Dutch conversation which went on between the surgeons as they worked, and after all, the instruments were the same, the technique was almost the same, even if they were called by different names. She coped with whatever came her way with her usual unhurried calm.

Only that calm was a little shattered one morning. They were doing a gastro-entreostomy, when the surgeon cast doubts on his findings and sent someone to telephone the Path. Lab. A minute or two later Professor ter Bavinck came in, exchanged a few words with his colleagues, collected the offending piece of tissue which was the cause of the doubt, cast a lightning look at Lavinia, standing behind her trolleys, and went away again.

So he was back. She counted a fresh batch of swabs, feeling the tide of pleasure the sight of him had engendered inside her. The day had suddenly become splendid and full of exciting possibilities. She only just stopped herself in time from bursting into song.

Chapter 3

But the day wasn't splendid at all; she was in theatre for hours as it turned out, with an emergency; some poor soul who had fallen from a fourth floor balcony. The surgeons laboured over her for patient hours and no one thought of going to dinner, although two or three of the nurses managed to get a cup of coffee. But Lavinia, being scrubbed and taking the morning's list, went stoically on until at length, about three o'clock in the afternoon, she had a few minutes in which to bolt a sandwich and drink some coffee, and because the morning's list had been held up it ended hours late; in consequence the afternoon list was late too, and even though she didn't have to scrub, she was still on duty. When she finally got off duty it was well past seven o'clock. There was no reason why she should look for the professor on her way to supper; he was unlikely to be lurking on the stairs or round a corner of any of the maze of passages, so her disappointment at not meeting him was quite absurd. She ate her supper, pleaded tiredness after her long day, and retired to the fastness of her room.

A good night's sleep worked wonders. She felt quite light-hearted as she dressed the next morning; she would be off at four o'clock and the lists weren't heavy; perhaps she would see Professor ter Bavinck and he would suggest another quick snack... She bounced down to breakfast, not stopping to examine her happiness, only knowing that it was another day and there was the chance of something super happening.

Nothing happened at all. Work, of course—there was always plenty of that; it was a busy hospital and the surgeons who worked there were known for their skill. The morning wore on into the afternoon until it was time for her to go off duty. Neeltje was off too—they were going out with some of the other nurses; a trip round the city's canals was a must for every visitor to Amsterdam and they would take her that very evening. She got ready for the outing, determined to enjoy herself. She had been silly and made too much of the professor's kindness—it was because she went out so seldom with a man that she had attached so much importance to seeing him again. Heaven forbid that she should appear over-eager, indeed, if he were to ask her out again she would take care to have an excuse ready, she told herself stoutly. She stared at her reflection in the looking glass—he wasn't likely to ask her again, anyway. He was in the hospital each day, she had heard someone say so, and there had been plenty of opportunities...

She left her room and took the short cut to the

hospital entrance where she was to meet the others. The last few yards of it gave her an excellent view of the forecourt so that she couldn't fail to see the professor standing in it, talking earnestly to a young woman. It was too far off to see if she was pretty, but even at that distance Lavinia could see that she was beautifully dressed. She slowed her steps the better to look and then stopped altogether as he took the girl's arm and walked away with her, across the tarmac to where his motorcar was standing. She didn't move until they had both got into it and it had disappeared through the gates, and when she did she walked very briskly, with her determined little chin rather higher than usual and two bright spots of colour on her cheeks.

When they all got back a couple of hours later, the professor was standing in the entrance, talking to two of the consultants, and all three men wished the girls *Goeden avond*. Lavinia, joining in the polite chorus of replies, took care not to look at him.

She wakened the next morning to remember that it was her day off. The fine weather still held and she had a formidable list of museums to visit. She was up and out soon after nine o'clock, clad in a cool cotton dress and sandals on her bare feet and just enough money in her handbag to pay for her lunch.

She went first to the Bijenkorf, however, that mecca of the Amsterdam shopper, and spent an hour browsing round its departments, wishing she had the money to buy the pretty things on display, cheering herself with the thought that before very

long, she might be able to do so. But it was already
ten o'clock and the museums had been open half an
hour already, so she started to walk across the Dam
Square, with its palace on one side and the stark war
memorial facing it on the other, down Kalverstraat,
not stopping to look in the tempting shop windows,
and into Leidsestraat. It was here that she noticed
that the blue sky had dimmed to grey, it was going to
rain—but the museum was only a few minutes' brisk
walk away now, she could actually see the imposing
frontage of her goal. The first few drops began to
fall seconds later, however, and then without warning, turned into a downpour. Lavinia began to run,
feeling the rain soaking her thin dress.

The Bentley pulled into the curb a little ahead
of her, so that by the time she was level with it the
professor was on the pavement, standing in the rain
too. He didn't speak at all, merely plucked her neatly
from the pavement, bustled her round the elegant
bonnet of the car, and popped her into the front seat.
When he got in beside her, all he said was: 'You're
very wet,' as he drove on.

Lavinia got her breath. 'I was going to the museum,' she began. 'It's only just across the road,'
she added helpfully, in case he wanted an excuse to
drop her off somewhere quickly.

'Unmistakable, isn't it?' he observed dryly, and
drove past it to join the stream of traffic going back
into the city's heart.

Her voice came out small. 'Are you taking me
back to St Jorus?'

'Good lord, no—on your day off? We're going to get you dry, you can't possibly drip all over the Rijksmuseum.'

He was threading the big car up and down narrow streets which held very little traffic, and she had no idea where she was; she didn't really care, it was nice just to sit there without question. But presently she recognized her surroundings—this was the square she had visited that afternoon, and she made haste to tell him so. 'I remember the houses,' she told him, 'they've got such plain faces, but I'm sure they must be beautiful inside. If you want to set me down here, I know my way—I expect you're going to the hospital.'

'No, I'm not.' He circled the square and on its third side stopped before the large house in the middle of the row of tall, narrower ones, and when she gave him a questioning look, said blandly: 'I live here. My housekeeper will dry that dress of yours for you—and anything else that's wet.' He spoke with friendly casualness. 'We can have our coffee while she's doing it.'

'Very kind,' she said, breathless, 'but your work—I've delayed you already.'

He leaned across her and opened the door before getting out of the car. 'I have an occasional day off myself.' He came round the car and stood by the door while she got out too, and then led her across the narrow cobbled street to his front door.

She had no idea that a house could be so beautiful; true, she had seen pictures of such places in magazines, and she was aware that there were such places, but looking at them in a magazine and actually standing in the real thing were two quite different things. She breathed an ecstatic sigh as she gazed around her; this was better than anything pictured—a large, light hall with an Anatolian carpet in rich reds and blues almost covering its black and white marble floor, with a staircase rising from its end wall, richly carved, its oak treads uncarpeted and a chandelier of vast proportions hanging from a ceiling so high that she had to stretch her neck to see it properly.

'You don't live here?' she wanted to know of her companion, and he gave a short laugh. 'Oh, but I do—have done all my life. Come along, we'll find Mevrouw Pette.'

He urged her across the floor to a door at the back of the hall, beside the staircase and opened it for her, shouting down the short flight of stairs on the other side as they began to descend them. At the bottom there was a narrow door, so low that he was forced to bow his head to go through. It gave on to a surprisingly large and cheerful room, obviously the kitchen, decided Lavinia, trying not to look too curiously at everything around her. Nice and old-fashioned, but with all the modern gadgets any woman could wish for. There were cheerful yellow curtains at the windows, which looked out on to a narrow strip of garden at the back of the house, and the furniture was solid; an enormous wooden dresser against one wall, a scrubbed table, equally enormous, in the centre of the brick floor and tall Windsor chairs on either side of the Aga cooker. There were cheerful rugs too, and rows of copper pots and pans on the walls. It was all very cosy and one hardly noticed the fridge, the rotisserie and the up-to-date electric oven tucked away so discreetly. Out of sight, she felt sure, there would be a washing-up machine and a deep-freeze and anything else which would make life easier. The professor must have a very good job indeed to be able to live so splendidly—and there were no fewer than three persons working in the kitchen, too. The elderly woman coming to meet them would be the housekeeper and as well as her there was a young girl cleaning vegetables at the sink, while another girl stood at the table clearing away some cooking utensils.

The professor spoke to them as he went in and they looked up and smiled and then went on with what they were doing while he talked to Mevrouw Pette at some length. She was a thin woman, of middle height, with a sharp nose and a rosy complexion, her hair, still a nice brown, drawn back severely from her face. But she had a kind smile; she smiled at Lavinia now and beckoned to her, and encouraged by the professor's: 'Yes, go along, Lavinia—Mevrouw Pette will take your dress and lend you a dressing gown and bring you down again for coffee,' Lavinia followed.

So she went back up the little stair once more and across the hall to the much grander staircase and mounted it in Mevrouw Pette's wake, to be ushered into a dear little room, all chintz and dark oak, where she took off her dress and put on the dressing gown the housekeeper produced. It was blue satin, quilted and expensive; she wondered whose it was—surely not Mevrouw Pette's? It fitted tolerably well, though she was just a little plump for it. She smoothed back her damp hair, frowned at herself in the great mirror over the oak dower chest against one wall, and was escorted downstairs once more, this time to a room on the right of the hall—a very handsome room, although having seen a little of the house, she wasn't surprised at that. All the same, she had to admit that its rich comfort, allied with beautiful furniture and hangings of a deep sapphire blue, was quite breathtaking.

The professor was standing with his back to the door looking out of a window, but when he turned round she plunged at once into talk, feeling shy. 'You're very kind, and I am sorry to give you so much trouble.'

He waved her to an outsize chair which swallowed her in its vast comfort and sat down himself opposite her. 'I'm a selfish man,' he observed blandly. 'If I hadn't wished to trouble myself, I shouldn't have done so.' He crossed one long leg over the other, very much at his ease. 'You didn't look at me yesterday evening,' he observed. 'You were annoyed, I think—I hope…and that pleased me, because it meant that you were a little interested in me.'

He smiled at her look of outrage. 'No, don't be

cross—did I not say that we could be nothing but
honest with each other, as friends should be? I have
been back for three days and I had made up my mind
not to see you for a little while, and then yesterday
I changed my mind, but I met an old friend who
needed advice, so I was hindered from asking you
to come out with me.'

She had no idea why he was telling her all this,
but she had to match his frankness. 'I saw her with
you.'

He smiled again. 'Ah, so you were hoping that I
would come?'

The conversation was getting out of hand; she
said with dignity and a sad lack of truth: 'I didn't
hope anything of the sort, Professor,' and was saved
from further fibbing by Mevrouw Pette's entrance
with the coffee tray, but once the coffee was poured,
her relief was short-lived.

'You probably think that I am a conceited middle-
aged man who should know better,' said the professor suavely.

She nibbled at a spicy biscuit before she replied.
'No. You're not middle-aged or conceited. And I did
hope you'd ask me out again, though I can't think
why, me being me. If I were a raving beauty I don't
suppose I'd be in the least surprised...'

He laughed then, suddenly years younger. 'Is
your young sister like you?' he wanted to know.

'To look at? No; she's pretty, but we like the same
things and we get on well together—but then she's
easy to get on with.'

'And you are not?'

'I don't know. My aunt says I'm not, but then she doesn't like me, but she has given Peta a home for a year now and sent her to school...'

'But not loved her?'

'No.'

He passed his cup for more coffee. 'You think your sister will like Amsterdam?'

'I'm sure she will. She takes her O levels this week and then she'll leave school—just as soon as I can get somewhere to live here she can come. I thought she could have Dutch lessons...'

'And you plan to stay here for the foreseeable future?'

Lavinia nodded cheerfully, happy to be talking to him. 'I like it, living here. I feel quite at home and I earn so much more, you see, and if I stay here for a year or two I could save some money, enough to go back to England if Peta wanted to, and start her on whatever she decides to do.'

'No plans for yourself?'

She said a little stiffly: 'I'm quite happy, Professor.'

His thick eyebrows arched. 'Yes? I ask too many questions, don't I?' He got up and went to open the french window and a small hairy dog, all tail and large paws, came romping in, followed by an Irish setter, walking with dignity. 'You don't object to dogs?' asked the professor. 'Dong and Pobble like to be with me as much as possible when I'm home.'

Lavinia was on her knees making friends. 'Nonsense Songs!' she cried happily. 'Which one's Dong?'

'The setter. My daughter named them—most people look at me as though I'm mad when I mention their names, but then the Nonsense Songs aren't read very widely.'

'No—my father used to read them to me when I was a little girl.' She got to her feet. 'I'm sure my dress must be dry by now—you've been very kind, but I'm wasting your morning; I'll go and find your housekeeper if I may.'

For answer he tugged the beautifully embroidered bell-pull beside his chair, and when Mevrouw Pette came said something or other which caused her to smile and nod and beckon to Lavinia, who got up obediently and followed her out of the room.

Her dress was dry once more and moreover pressed by an expert hand. She did her face and hair, laid the dressing gown lovingly on the thick silk bed quilt, and went downstairs. The professor was in the hall, and she stifled a pang of disappointment that he appeared so anxious to speed her on her way, even as she achieved a bright, friendly smile and hurried to the door. He opened it as she reached his side and she thrust out a hand, searching frantically for something suitable to say by way of farewell. But there was no need to say anything; he took her hand, but instead of shaking it, he gripped it firmly, whistled piercingly to the dogs, and went out of the door with her. At the car she halted. 'Thank you,' she tried again, in what she hoped was a final sort of

voice. 'There's really no need… I know where I am.'
She glanced up at the sky, the greyness had changed
back to blue once more. 'I shall enjoy walking.'

'Fiddle,' declared her companion, and opened the
car door. 'I'm going to show you the Rijksmuseum,
and we'll have to take the car because these two like
to sit in the back and guard it when I'm not there.'

He opened the other door as he spoke and the two
astute animals rushed past him and took up position
with a determination which brooked no interference
on Lavinia's part; she got in too, at a loss for words.

Her companion didn't appear to notice her silence
but drove off with the air of a well-contented man,
and only when they were almost at the museum did
he remark: 'Everyone comes to see the Nachwacht,
of course —it's a wonderful painting, but there are
several which I like much better. I'd like to show
them to you.' He paused and added gently: 'And
if you say how kind just once more, I shall wring
your neck!'

Lavinia jumped and gave him a startled look; he
wasn't behaving like a professor at all, nor, for that
matter, like a man who would never see forty again.
'I can't think why you should speak to me like that,'
she reproved him austerely, and was reduced to silence by his: 'Am I cutting the corners too fine for
you? It seemed to me that since we liked each other
on sight, it would be a little silly to go through all the
preliminaries, but if you would prefer that, I'll call
you Miss Hawkins for a week or two, erase from my

mind the sight of you in Sibendina's dressing gown, and drop you off at the next bus stop.'

She had cried: 'Oh, don't do that,' before she could stop herself, and went on a little wildly: 'You see, I'm not used to—to…well, I don't get asked out much and so none of this seems quite real—more like a dream.'

'But dreams are true while they last—your Tennyson said so, what's more doesn't he go on to say: "And do we not live in dreams?" So no more nonsense, Lavinia.'

He swept the car into the great forecourt of the museum, gave the dogs a quiet command and opened her door. He took her arm as they went in together and it seemed the most natural thing in the world that he should do so. She smiled up at him as they paused before the first picture.

There was no hurry. They strolled from one room to the next, to come finally to the enormous Nachtwacht and sit before it for a little while, picking out the figures which peopled the vast canvas, until the professor said: 'Now come and see my favourites.' Two small portraits, an old man and an old woman, wrinkled and blue-eyed and dignified, and so alive that Lavinia felt that she could have held a conversation with them.

'Nice, aren't they?' observed her companion. 'Come and look at the Lelys.'

She liked these even better; she went from one exquisitely painted portrait to the next and back again. 'Look at those pearls,' she begged him. 'They look absolutely real…'

'Well, most likely they were,' he pointed out reasonably. 'Do you like pearls?'

'Me? Yes, of course I do, though I'm not sure that I've ever seen any real ones. The Queen has some, but I don't suppose there are many women who possess any.'

He smiled and she wondered why he looked amused. 'Probably not. Will you have lunch with me, Lavinia?'

She hesitated. 'How k…' She caught the gleam in his eye then and chuckled delightfully. 'I've never fancied having my neck wrung in public, so I'll say yes, thank you.'

'Wise girl.' He tucked an arm in hers and began to walk to the exit, then stopped to look at her. 'How old are you?' he wanted to know.

She breathed an indignant: 'Well…' then told him: 'Twenty-six,' adding with an engaging twinkle: 'How rude of you to ask!'

'But you didn't mind telling me. I'm getting on for forty-one.'

'Yes, I know.' And at his sharp glance of inquiry: 'One of the nurses told me—not gossiping.'

He said very evenly: 'And you were also told that I am a widower, and that I have a daughter.'

'Oh, yes. You see, they all like you very much—they're a bit scared of you too, I think, but they like it that way—you're a bit larger than life, you know.'

He didn't answer at once, in fact he didn't speak

at all during their short drive back to the house, only as he drew up before his door he said in a quiet voice: 'I don't care for flattery, Lavinia.'

Her pleasant face went slowly pink; a quite un-accountable rage shook her. She said on a heaving breath: 'You think that's what I'm doing? Toadying to you? Just because you're smashing to look at and a professor and—and took me out to supper…and so now I'm angling for another meal, am I?'

She choked on temper while she made furious efforts to get the car door open. Without success at first and when she did manage it, his hand came down on hers and held it fast. His voice was still quiet, but now it held warmth. 'I don't know why I said that, Lavinia, unless it was because I wanted to hear you say that I was wrong—and you have. No, leave the door alone. I'm sorry—will you forgive me?' And when she didn't answer: 'Lavinia?'

She said stiffly: 'Very well,' and forgot to be stiff. 'Oh, of course I will; I fly off the handle myself sometimes—only you sounded horrid.'

'I am quite often horrid—ask my daughter.' His hand was still on hers, but now he took it away and opened the door for her, and when she looked at him he smiled and said: 'Mevrouw Pette has promised us one of her special lunches, shall we go in?'

She smiled back; it was all right, they were back where they had been; a pleasant, easy-going friendship which made her forget that she wasn't a raving beauty, and allowed her to be her own uncomplicated self.

'Super, I'm famished, though I keep meaning not to eat, you know—only I get hungry.'

He was letting the dogs out and turned round to ask: 'Not eating? A self-imposed penance?'

'No—I'm trying to get really slim.'

Dong and Pobble were prancing round her and she bent to rub their ears and then jumped at his sudden roar. 'You just go on eating,' he said forcefully. 'I like to be able to tell the front of a woman from her back, these skeletal types teetering round on four-inch soles don't appeal to me.'

She laughed. 'It would take months of dieting to get me to that state, but I promise you I'll eat a good lunch, just to please you.'

They went into the house then, the dogs racing ahead once they were inside so that they could sit as near the professor as possible, while Lavinia went upstairs to do things to her face and hair, and when she came down again they had drinks, talking companionably, before going into lunch, laid in what the professor called the little sitting-room, which turned out to be almost as large as the room they had just come from.

'The dining-room is so vast that we feel lost in it,' he explained, and then as a door banged: 'Ah, here is Sibendina.'

Lavinia had only just noticed that there were places laid for three on the table and she wasn't sure if she was pleased or not; she was curious to meet the professor's daughter, but on the other hand she had been looking forward to being alone with him. She turned to look over her shoulder as the girl came into the room, at the same time advising herself not to become too interested in the professor and his family; he had befriended her out of kindness and she must remember that.

Sibendina was like her father, tall and big and fair, with his blue eyes but fortunately with someone else's nose, for his, while exactly right on his own handsome face, would have looked quite overpowering on her pretty one. She came across the room at a run, embraced her father with pleasure and then looked at Lavinia, and when he had introduced them with easy good manners, she shook hands, exclaiming: 'I've heard about you—may I call you Lavinia? I've been looking forward to meeting you.'

She sat down opposite her father and grinned engagingly. 'Now I can practise my English,' she declared.

'Why not, Sibby? Although Lavinia might like to practise her Dutch—she's already having lessons.'

'And hours of homework,' said Lavinia, 'which I feel compelled to do, otherwise Juffrouw de Waal makes me feel utterly worthless.'

They all laughed as Mevrouw Pette brought in lunch, and presently the talk was of everything under the sun, with Sibendina asking a great many questions about England and Peta's school. 'She isn't much older than I am,' she observed, 'but she sounds very clever—what is she going to study next?'

'Well, I don't really know; if she comes here to live with me I thought she might have Dutch lessons, then if she's passed her eight O levels, she might be able to take a secretarial course—the Common Market,' Lavinia finished a little vaguely.

'Not nursing?' the professor wanted to know.

Lavinia shook her head. 'Peta's too gentle—she can't stand people being angry or bad-tempered, and there's quite a bit of that when you start training.'

Sibendina was peeling a peach. 'She sounds nice, I should like very much to meet her. When does she come?'

'I don't know if the hospital will keep me yet—if it's OK I'll find somewhere to live and then go and fetch her.'

'And this aunt she lives with—will she not mind?'

Lavinia smiled at the girl. 'I think perhaps she will mind very much—I'm rather dreading it, but I promised Peta.'

'But if you did not go what would your sister do?'

'I think she might run away,' said Lavinia soberly. 'You see, she's not very happy.'

Sibendina looked at the professor, sitting quietly and saying almost nothing. 'Papa, you must do something.' She looked at the Friesian wall clock. 'I have to go; I shall be late for class—you will excuse me, please.' She went round the table and kissed her father. 'Papa,' she said persuasively, 'you will do something, please. I like Lavinia very much and I think that I shall like Peta too.'

He spoke to her but he looked at Lavinia. 'Well, that's a good thing,' he observed blandly, 'for I'm

going to ask Lavinia to marry me—not at once, I
shall have to wait for her to get used to the idea.'

Lavinia felt the colour leave her face and then
come rushing back into it. She hardly heard Sibendina's crow of delighted laughter as she ran out of
the room, calling something in Dutch as she went.
She was looking at the professor who, in his turn,
was watching her closely. 'Don't look like that,' he
said in a matter-of-fact voice. 'I shan't do anything
earth-shattering like dropping on one knee and begging for your hand; just let the idea filter through,
and we'll bring the matter up again in a few days. In
the meantime what about a brisk walk to the Dam
Palace? It's open for inspection and worth a visit.'

She spoke in a voice which was almost a whisper.
'Yes, that would be very nice—I've always wanted
to see inside a palace. Is it far?'

'No, but we'll go the long way round; the nicest part of Amsterdam is tucked away behind the
main streets.'

She could see that he had meant what he had said;
he wasn't going to do anything earth-shattering. With
an effort she forced herself back on to the friendly
footing they had been on before he had made his
amazing remark, and even discussed with some degree of intelligence the architecture of the old houses
they passed, and once they had reached the palace,
her interest in it and its contents became almost feverish in her efforts to forget what he had said.

They had tea at Dikker and Thijs and then walked
slowly down Kalverstraat while she looked in the

shop windows; a pleasant, normal occupation which soothed her jumping nerves, as did her companion's gentle flow of nothings, none of which needed much in the way of replies on her part. They turned away from the shops at last and the professor led her through the narrow streets without telling her where they were going, so that when they rounded a corner and there was the hospital a stone's throw away, Lavinia almost choked with disappointment. He was going to say good-bye; he had decided to deliver her back safely after a pleasant day, foisted on him by the accident of the rain. He had been joking, she told herself savagely—he and Sibendina, and she had actually been taken in. She swallowed the great unmanageable lump in her throat and said politely: 'Well, good-bye—it's been lovely...'

His surprise was genuine. 'What on earth are you talking about? I've only brought you back so that you can change your dress—we're going out to dinner.'

She didn't stop the flood of delight which must have shown in her face. 'Oh, are we? I didn't know.'

He shepherded her across the street and in through the hospital gates. 'I'll be here at seven o'clock, Lavinia—and don't try and do any deep thinking—just make yourself pretty and be ready for me.'

Her, 'Yes, all right,' was very meek.

Chapter 4

Lavinia hadn't brought many clothes with her; she hadn't much of a wardrobe anyway. She searched through her cupboard now and came to the conclusion that it would have to be the green silk jersey, with its tucked bodice gathered into a wide band which emphasized her small waist and its full sleeves, deeply cuffed; it wasn't exactly spectacular, but it would pass muster. All the same, as she put it on, she wished fervently that it had been a Gina Franati model; something quite super to match the professor's faultlessly tailored clothes.

Anxious not to be late, she hurried down to the entrance to find him already there, deep in conversation with one of the doctors, and at the sight of his elegance she regretted, once again, the paucity of her wardrobe. But there was no point in brooding over that now. She hitched her coat over one arm and when he turned and saw her, went to meet him, and the pleased look he gave her quite compensated her for having to wear the green jersey. It was flattering too, the way he took her arm and included her in the conversation he was having for a few minutes. She liked him for that; his manners were beautiful, even if he did startle her sometimes with the things he said.

As they got into the Bentley he said: 'I thought we might drive over to den Haag, it's only thirty miles or so. We'll go on the motorway; it's dull, I'm afraid, but I've booked a table for eight o'clock.'

She had expected to feel a little awkward with him, but she didn't. They talked about all manner of things, but not about themselves; she still wasn't sure if he had been joking with Sibendina, and there was no way of finding out, only by asking him, and that she would never do. She would have to wait and see; in the meantime she was going to enjoy herself.

And she did. They dined at the Saur restaurant in the heart of den Haag—upstairs, in a formal, almost Edwardian room, and the food was delicious. She wanted the evening to go on for ever; she knew by now that she liked the professor very much, although she wasn't going to admit to any deeper feelings, not until she knew the truth about his astonishing remark about marrying her. She didn't know much about falling in love, but she suspected that this was what was happening to her, but presumably it was something one could check or even smother before it became too strong.

They walked about the town after they had dined, and the professor pointed out the Ridderzaal, the Mauritshuis museum, some of the more interesting statues, an ancient prison gate and the old City Hall, and then strolled goodnaturedly beside her while she took a brief peep at the tempting displays in the shop windows.

On the way back to Amsterdam, tearing along the motorway, they didn't talk a great deal and then only of trifling things, but as they neared the hospital the professor said: 'I have to work tomorrow—a pity, I should have enjoyed taking you for a run in the car. We could have had a swim.'

Lavinia made a mental note to buy a swimsuit first thing in the morning. 'I've a whole lot of museums to see,' she told him brightly.

'Yes? May I pick you up tomorrow evening? Seven o'clock?'

She watched his large capable hands on the wheel and felt her heart tumbling around inside her. 'I'd like that very much,' she said in a sedate voice.

At the hospital entrance he got out to open her door and walk with her across the forecourt to the farther side where a covered way led to the nurses' home. His good night was pleasant and formal.

Lavinia went to bed, her head filled with a muddle of thoughts; the pleasant and the not so pleasant jostling each other for a place until she fell into an uneasy sleep.

She was pottering along the corridor to make herself some tea the next morning when she met Neeltje and several other nurses going down to breakfast. They were almost late, but that didn't prevent them from stopping to greet her and then break into a babble of questions. It was Neeltje who said in her own peculiar brand of English: 'We hear all—Becke

Groeneveld sees you with Professor ter Bavinck as you return—that is for the second time that you go out with him. We are all most curious and excited.'

The ring of cheerful faces around her wore pleased smiles, rather as though their owners had engineered her outing amongst themselves. She was touched by their interest and their complete lack of envy; the least she could do was to tell them about her day—well, at least parts of it. 'Well, you see,' she began, 'I got caught in the rain and the professor happened to be passing in his car, so he took me to his house and his housekeeper dried my dress.'

Her listeners regarded her with motherly expressions. 'Well?' they chorused.

'We went to the Rijksmuseum after lunch—oh, and I met his daughter, she's a sweet girl.' The memory of the professor's conversation with Sibendina was suddenly vivid in her mind and she went rather pink. 'I—we, that is, went to dinner in the Hague.'

'You and the Prof?'

She nodded.

'And you go again?' asked Neeltje.

'Well, as a matter of fact, yes.'

'We are glad,' declared Neeltje, 'we have pleasure in this, you understand. But now we must hurry or we do not eat.'

They cried their *tot ziens* and tumbled down the stairs, laughing and talking, and Lavinia made her tea and got dressed slowly, trying not to think about the professor. But it wasn't easy, and later in the morning, even in the most interesting museums, his face kept getting between her and the exhibits she examined so carefully. She had her coffee and then, satisfied with her morning's sightseeing, went to the Bijenkorf and had a snack lunch, then went to look in the shop windows again, making a mental and ever-lengthening list of things she would buy when she had some money. And always at the back of her mind was the professor. By five o'clock she decided that she might well return to the hospital and get ready for her evening, and it was only with the greatest difficulty that she stopped herself from tearing back as though she had a train to catch. She told herself to stop behaving like a fool and forced her feet to a slow pace, so that she was in a fine state of nervous tension by the time she reached the hospital. She went at once to the home and looked at the letter board; there might be a letter from Peta. There was. There was another one, too, in a scrawled handwriting which she knew at once was the professor's. She tore it open and read the one line written on the back of a Path. Lab. form. It stated simply: 'Sorry, can't make it this evening,' and was signed M. ter B. She folded it carefully and put it back in its envelope, then took it out again and re-read it with the air of someone who hoped for a miracle, but there it was, in black and white.

She went slowly to her room, put the note in her handbag and kicked off her sandals. Her disappointment was engulfing her in great waves, but she refused to give way to it; she sat down and opened Peta's letter and started to read it. It was lengthy and unhappy too; Aunt Gwyneth, it seemed, was taking every opportunity to remind Peta that she depended entirely upon her charity and had made veiled hints as to what might happen should Peta fail to get her O levels. Ungrateful girls who didn't work hard enough for exams could not be expected to live in the lap of luxury for ever; there were jobs for them, simple jobs which required no advanced education costing a great deal of money, her aunt had said—a great girl of sixteen would do very well as a companion to some elderly lady...

Lavinia, noting the carefully wiped away tear stains, longed for just half an hour with her sister, but although that wasn't possible, a letter was. She sat down and wrote it, then and there, filling it full of heartening ideas, painting a cheerful picture of the life they would lead together, and that was not so far off now. She went out to post it and then went to supper, where she parried her new friends' anxious questions as cheerfully as she could. It was when Neeltje joined them that she discovered where the professor had gone: Utrecht, to some urgent consultation or other. The news cheered her a little. It wasn't until that moment that she admitted to herself that she had been imagining him spending the evening with some fascinating and exquisitely dressed beauty.

Theatre was busy the following day and Lavinia scrubbed for the afternoon list. They were half way through a splenectomy when the professor came in; he was in theatre kit, and after a nod in the general direction of those scattered around, took his place by the surgeon who was operating. He stayed for five minutes or so, peering down at the work being done while he and his colleague muttered together. Finally, he took the offending organ away with him. Lavinia had the impression that he hadn't seen her.

She felt even more certain of this by the time she went off duty at five o'clock, for she had seen him with her own eyes, leaving the forecourt; she had glanced idly out of an upstairs window and then stayed to watch him drive the Bentley out of the gates—out of sight.

Some of the nurses had asked her to go to the cinema with them, but she had pleaded letters to write, aware that if the professor should ask her to go out with him the letters would get short shrift, but now it looked as though that was the way she was going to spend her evening. She showered and changed into slacks and a cotton blouse and made herself some coffee, having no wish for her supper, and then started on her writing; it wasn't very successful, probably because her mind wasn't on it; she gave up after the second letter and went down to the post, thinking, as she went through the hospital, that she would ask to see the Directrice in the morning about living out; perhaps if her future plans were settled she might feel more settled herself. She was turning away from the post box in the front hall when she came face to face with the professor. Her first reaction was sheer delight at seeing him, the second one of annoyance because she must surely look a fright, consequently her 'Good evening, Professor,' was distant, but he ignored that.

'I was on my way over to see you,' he said cheerfully. 'I thought we might spend the evening together.'

A medley of strong feelings left her speechless. Presently she managed: 'I hadn't planned to go out this evening.'

His answer infuriated her. 'Well, I didn't expect you would have—just in case I came...' He gave her an interested look. 'Are you sulking?'

'I have no reason to sulk.'

'Oh? I thought you might because I had to cancel our date yesterday.' He grinned. 'I did think of mentioning it in theatre this afternoon, but I didn't think you would like that.'

She drew a deep breath. 'Professor...' she began, and was cut short by his bland: 'My dear girl, how is our relationship going to progress if you insist on calling me professor at every other breath? My name's Radmer.'

'Oh, is it? I've never heard it before.'

'Naturally not; it's a Friesian name, and you're English.' He smiled with great charm. 'Shall we go?'

'Like this? I'm not dressed for going out.'

He studied her deliberately. 'You're decently covered,' he observed at length. 'I like your hair hanging down your back. If it will make you happier, we're only going home for dinner—just two friends sharing a meal,' he added matter-of-factly.

'Well, all right.' She gave in with a composure

which quite concealed her indignation. No girl, however inadequately dressed, likes to be told that she's decently covered—not in that casual, don't care voice. She got into the Bentley with an hauteur which brought a little smile to her companion's mouth, although he said nothing. But he did set himself out to entertain her over dinner, and his apologies for breaking their date the previous evening were all that any girl could wish for; her good nature reasserted itself and she felt happier than she had felt all day. His undemanding small talk, allied to the smoked salmon, duckling with orange sauce, and fresh fruit salad with its accompanying whipped cream and served on exquisite china, all combined to act on her stretched nerves like balm. She found herself telling him about Peta's letter and what she intended doing about it.

He listened gravely, watching her across the table. When she had finished he observed: 'I see— well, Lavinia, I said that you should have time, did I not, but now I think that we must settle the matter here and now.' He smiled at her with faint mockery. 'Any maidenly ideas you may have been cherishing about being courted, wooed and won must go by the board.'

She sat up very straight in her chair. 'You're not serious?'

'Indeed I am. If you have finished, shall we go to the sitting-room for coffee? Sibby is out with friends and we shall be undisturbed.'

Coffee seemed a good idea, if only to clear her

head and dispel the somewhat reckless mood the excellent wine they had had engendered.

She poured it from a charming little silver coffee pot into delicate Sèvres china and wished that her companion wouldn't stare quite so hard at her; she concluded that it was because he was waiting for her to say something, so she asked composedly: 'Would you mind explaining?'

'It's very simple, Lavinia. I have no wife, and a daughter who badly needs female company—to designate you as stepmother would be absurd, but a kind of elder sister? And there is Peta, just a little older than Sibby and an ideal companion for her...'

'They might hate each other.'

He shook his head. 'No, Sibby is likely to take to her on sight; remember that she already likes you very much. And then there is me; I need someone to entertain for me, buy Sibby's clothes, run my home, and I hope, be my companion.' He was silent for a moment. 'I am sometimes lonely, Lavinia.'

He got up and came and stood in front of her and pulled her to her feet, and put his hands on her shoulders. 'There is no question of falling in love, my dear. I think I may never do that again—once bitten, twice shy—as you say in English. Ours would be a marriage of friends, you understand, no more than that. But I promise you that I will take care of you and Peta, just as I shall take care of Sibby.'

Lavinia swallowed. 'Why me?' she asked in a small voice.

He smiled a little. 'You're sensible, your feet are

firmly planted on the ground and you haven't been too happy, have you? You will never be tempted to reach for the moon, my dear.'

She was speechless once more. So that was what he thought of her—a rather dreary spinster type with no ambition to set the world on fire. How wrong he was, and yet in a way, how right. If she chose to refuse his strange offer, the future didn't hold very much for her, she knew that. Several more years of getting Peta on to her own feet and then, when her sister married, as she most certainly would, she herself would be left to a bachelor girl's existence. But to marry this man who was so certain that his idea was a good one? She was old-fashioned enough— and perhaps sentimental enough too—to believe in falling in love and marrying for that reason.

'Would it be honest—I mean, marrying you? I've very little to offer. Sibendina might grow to dislike me, you know, and I'm not much good at entertaining or running a large house.'

'If I tell you that I'm quite sure that it will be a success, will you consider it?'

It was a crazy conversation; she said so and he laughed in genuine amusement. 'Will you think about it, Lavinia?'

'Well—yes.' Even as she said it, she marvelled at herself; her usually sensible head was filled with a mass of nonsense which, once she was alone, she would have to reduce to proper proportions. Indeed, it had suddenly become an urgent matter to get away from this large man who so disquieted her, and think coolly about everything, without his eyes watching her face as though he could read every thought. She said abruptly: 'Would you mind very much if I went back now? I have to think.'

He made no attempt to dissuade her; in no time at all she found herself running up the Home stairs, his brief, friendly good night echoing in her ears.

Being alone didn't help at all, she found herself wishing that he was there so that she might ask his advice, which, on the face of it, was just too absurd. Not only that, her thoughts didn't make sense. Probably she was too tired to think clearly, she would go to bed and sleep, and in the morning she would be able to come to a rational decision.

Amazingly, she slept almost as soon as her head touched the pillow, to waken in time to hear the carillons from Amsterdam's many churches ringing out three o'clock. She buried her head in the pillow, willing herself to go to sleep again. There was a busy day ahead of her in theatre, and in another three hours or so she would have to get up. But her mind, nicely refreshed, refused to do her bidding. 'Radmer,' she said aloud to the dark room. 'It's a strange name, but it suits him.' She turned over in bed and thumped her pillows; somehow it helped to talk to herself about him. 'I wish I knew more about his wife. Perhaps he loved her very much, even if no one else seems to have liked her.'

What was it he had said? Once bitten, twice shy. Anyway, he had made it very plain that he wasn't marrying her because he loved her, only because he liked her.

Lavinia gave up the idea of sleep, and sat up in bed, hugging her knees. She didn't know him at all, really, and it was preposterous that after such a short acquaintance, he should wish to marry her. Primarily for his own convenience, of course, he had made no bones about that; someone to look after Sibby and order his household and entertain for him, he had said; just as though she had no feelings in the matter. She was suddenly indignant and just as suddenly sleepy. When she woke, the sun was up and she could hear the maid coming along the passage, knocking on the doors.

By the time she had dressed she had made up her mind not to marry him, although this decision depressed her dreadfully, and that very day she would see the Directrice and arrange about living out; that would make an end of the matter. She sat silently through breakfast so that Neeltje wanted to know if she felt ill. She made some remark about seeing too many museums all at once and everyone laughed as they dispersed to their various wards, and Neeltje, who had taken her remark seriously, took her arm, and began to warn her of the dangers of too much sightseeing all at once. They were close to the theatre unit doors when they were flung wide with a good deal of force and Professor ter Bavinck came through them. He was in theatre kit again, his mask dangling under his unshaven chin. He looked tired, cross and even with these drawbacks, very handsome.

Lavinia, watching him coming towards them, was aware of a peculiar sensation, rather as though she had been filled with bubbles and wasn't on firm ground any more, and at the same time she knew exactly what she was going to do. She gently disengaged her arm from Neeltje and walked briskly forward to meet the professor. She wasted no time over good mornings or hullos; she planted her small person before his large one so that he was forced to stop, staring at her with tired eyes. She said, not caring if Neeltje heard or not: 'I was very silly last night. Of course I'll marry you.'

She didn't wait for his reply but slid through the theatre doors with a bewildered Neeltje hard on her heels. 'Whatever did you say?' asked her friend. 'I didn't hear.'

'I said I would,' Lavinia told her, hardly aware of what she was saying, her mind completely taken up with the sudden wonder of finding herself in love. She would have liked to have gone somewhere quiet to think about it, instead she found herself laying up for the first case. It wasn't until she was having her coffee, the first case dealt with, the second laid up for and Sister scrubbing, that she had a few minutes in which to think. The delightful, excited elation was still there, although it was marred just a little by the realization that the professor neither expected nor wished her to love him—it really was enough to put any girl off, she thought with a touch of peevishness, but now that she had discovered that she loved him, to marry him would be perfectly all right, or so it seemed to her.

Her feverish thoughts were interrupted by the two nurses having coffee with her. 'There was a patient in the night,' one of them told her, 'a girl with stab wounds, and a laparotomy must be done, you understand. The surgeon is not happy when he looks inside—there is a question of CA—so he calls for Professor ter Bavinck at three o'clock in the morning and they are here for a long time and he finds that it is CA. Is it not sad?'

'Very,' agreed Lavinia. So that was why he had looked so tired... The other nurse spoke. 'And it is not nice for the Prof, for he goes to Brussels this morning—I heard Zuster Smid say so.'

'Oh,' said Lavinia; disappointment was like a physical pain. She added nonchalantly: 'How long for?'

The nurse shrugged. 'Two-three days, perhaps longer, I do not know. There is a seminar... You wish more coffee?'

'No, thanks.' Lavinia felt exactly like a pricked balloon, and it was entirely her own fault for being so stupidly impetuous. As though the professor had been in a hurry to know her answer; he had thought of it as a sensible arrangement between friends with no need to get excited about it. She shuddered with shame at her childish behaviour; quite likely he had been appalled at it. She went back to theatre with the other two girls, and presently, at Zuster Smid's command, scrubbed to take a minor case. It kept her well occupied until dinner time, and because there was a heavy afternoon list, she stayed behind with Neeltje to get the theatre ready. They had just finished when the professor walked in. He was freshly shaven now, his face wore the look of a man who had had a sound night's sleep, he wore a black and white dogtooth checked suit, cut to perfection, and he looked superbly elegant.

He said something softly to Neeltje as he crossed the floor and she smiled widely as she went into the anaesthetic room—which left Lavinia alone behind her draped trolley, thankful that she was masked and gowned and capped so that almost nothing of her showed. He came to a halt a few yards from her so that there was no chance of him sullying the spotlessness around her.

'That was just what I needed,' he declared, and when she looked bewildered: 'This morning. I stayed up half the night wondering if I had been too precipitate—hurrying you along relentlessly, not giving you time to think. I was no nearer a conclusion when I was called in for that poor girl.'

'Oh,' said Lavinia, 'and I've been worrying all the morning, thinking that you might have found me very silly.' And when he smiled and shook his head: 'I thought you were going to Brussels—one of the nurses told me.'

'I'm on my way, I shall be gone two days. When I come back we'll tell Sibby and the rest of them. When are your days off?'

She told him and he nodded. 'Good. I'll take you to see my mother and father.'

This was something she hadn't known about, and the look she gave him was so apprehensive that he burst out laughing. 'Regretting your decision, Lavinia?'

'No, of course not, it's just that I don't know anything about you…'

'We'll have plenty of time to talk, my dear. I must go. *Tot ziens*!'

She was left staring at the gently swinging door. He had been very businesslike; she doubted if many girls had their marriage plans laid before them with such cool efficiency. Come to think of it, he hadn't shown any gratifying signs of satisfaction concerning his—their future. But then why should he? It was, after all, a sensible arrangement between friends.

She was going off duty on the evening before her days off when the hall porter on duty called to her as she crossed the hall. His English was as sparse as her Dutch, but she was able to make out that she was to be at the hospital entrance by nine o'clock the next morning. She thanked him with the impeccable accent Juffrouw de Waal insisted upon, and sped to her room. There was a lot to do; her hair would have to be washed, and since she had nothing else suitable, it would have to be the pink again and that would need pressing. She set about these tasks, daydreaming a little, wondering if Radmer would be glad to see her.

The fine weather held, the morning sun was shining gloriously as she dressed, ate a hurried breakfast
and went down to the hospital entrance. The professor was waiting, in slacks and a thin sweater this
time. His greeting was cheerful enough although
quite lacking in any sentiment.

'Hullo,' he said. 'We'll go back to the house, shall
we—we have to talk, you and I.' He got into the car
beside her and turned to smile at her. 'We can do that
better sitting comfortably and undisturbed. Sibby
will be home for lunch. I thought, if you agree, that
we might tell her today; she should be the first to
know—she and your sister.'

He was a man for getting to the point without any
small talk to lead up to it, she perceived. 'Yes, of
course I agree,' she told him with composure, 'but
I don't think I'd better tell Peta—she might get so
excited that she would tell Aunt Gwyneth, and that
wouldn't do at all.'

'Well, we'll have to think about that. I should
like you to meet my mother and father today, and as
soon as I can get away I'll take you up to Friesland.'

'Friesland? But that's in the north, isn't it? Have
you family there?'

'No—a house, left to me by my grandfather. I
should like you to see it. I have a sister, by the way,
married and living in Bergen-op-Zoom.'

They had reached the house and went inside. The
gentle gloom of the hall was cool after the bright
sunshine outside; its beauty struck her afresh as
they crossed it and entered the sitting-room. Here

the doors were open on to the small garden and the room was alight with sunshine and they went to sit by one of the open windows as Mevrouw Pette followed them in with the coffee tray. It wasn't until she had gone and Lavinia had poured the coffee that the professor spoke, and very much to the point.

'It takes a week or two to arrange a marriage in Holland,' he explained, 'so I think we might get started with the formalities today, then we can marry at the first opportunity—there is no point in waiting, is there?' He glanced briefly at her. 'The sooner the better, then we can go over to England and fetch Peta together; that might make things easier for you both.'

She tried to keep her voice as casual as his, just as though getting married was an everyday occurrence in her life. 'That's awfully kind of you—I'm sure it would. Do—do I have to do anything about our wedding?'

'Not today—you will need your passport later. Church, I take it?'

'Yes, please.'

'We shall have to be married by civil law first, otherwise we shan't be legally man and wife. Shall we keep it as quiet as possible?'

It cost her an effort to agree to this cheerfully. Was he ashamed of her, or did he suppose they would be the subject of gossip? Perhaps she wasn't good enough for his friends—in that case why was he marrying her? There must surely be girls more suitable amongst his acquaintances.

His voice jolted her gently back to her surround-

ings. 'None of the reasons you are so feverishly examining are the right ones. When I married Helga
we had an enormous wedding, hundreds of guests,
a reception, wedding bells, presents by the score,
but it was only a wedding, not a marriage. Do you
understand? This time it will be just us two, marrying each other for sound and sensible reasons, and
no phoney promises of love.' His voice was bitter.

He must have been very unhappy for him to
sound like that after all those years. She managed
a tranquil: 'I understand perfectly. That's what I
should like too, and if you don't want to talk about
your—your first wife, you don't have to. I daresay if we were marrying for all the usual reasons,
I might feel differently about that, but as you say,
this is a sensible arrangement between friends. I
shall do my very best to help Sibby in every way,
you can depend on that, and I'll learn to run your
home as you wish it to be run. I'm not much good
at parties, but I expect I'll learn. You're quite sure
it's what you want? Peta will be an extra mouth to
feed, you know, and I should very much like her to
have another year at least of schooling—would you
mind paying for that?'

He looked amused. 'Not in the least. I should tell
you that I'm a wealthy man—money doesn't have to
come into it.' He gave her a thoughtful look. 'And
you, my dear—you are content? Perhaps it is an odd
state of affairs for a girl—to marry and yet not be
a wife; I'm being selfish.'

She answered him steadily. 'No, not really, for I

am getting a great deal out of it, too. I—I have no prospects; no one has ever asked me to marry him, and if I didn't marry you, I should be hard put to it to get Peta educated. I'm not much of a catch,' she added frankly. 'I hope Sibendina will like the idea.'

He said on a laugh: 'She was the first one to suggest it, if you remember.' He got up, and the dogs, lying at his feet, got up too. 'Shall we go to the Town Hall and get the preliminaries over?' he asked.

She didn't understand all of what was said when they got there, but it really didn't matter. She stood watching the professor talking to the rather pompous man who asked so many questions, and wished with all her heart that he could love her, even just a little, even though she felt sure that she had enough love for both of them. Of one thing she was sure already; he thought of her as a friend, to be trusted and talked to and confided in, that at least was something. And if he had decided to marry her for Sibby's sake, it was surely better that he should marry her, who loved him so much, rather than some other girl who didn't.

He turned to speak to her and she smiled at him. He had said that she would never be tempted to reach for the moon, but wasn't that exactly what she had done?

Chapter 5

They got back to the house with just enough time to have a drink before lunch and the return of Sibendina from school, and Lavinia, although outwardly calm, was glad of the sherry to stop the quaking going on inside her. Her companion, she noticed, was sitting back in his chair looking the picture of ease while he drank his gin, just as though the prospect of getting married in a couple of weeks' time had no worries for him at all. She envied him his cool while she kept up a rather feverish chat about nothing in particular, until he interrupted her with a gentle: 'Don't worry, Lavinia—Sibby will be delighted.'

She did her best to believe him while she wished secretly that he might have felt a little more sympathy for her nerves. After all, not every girl found herself in the kind of situation she was in at the moment. And he could have shown some warmth in his feelings towards her...she corrected the thought hastily, for it had made him seem heartless and cold, and he was neither, only most dreadfully business-like and matter-of-fact about the whole thing. But then she had herself to blame for that. Perhaps she appeared as businesslike to him as he did to her, even though she loved him, but of course he didn't know that, and never would. She moved restlessly and caught his eye and managed a smile as the door opened and Sibendina came in.

There had been no need to be nervous after all; Sibby paused in the doorway, looking from one to the other of them, then swooped on her father while a flow of excited words poured from her lips. She had turned and engulfed Lavinia, still chattering madly, before the professor said on a shout of laughter: 'And here is poor Lavinia worrying herself sick in case you don't approve!'

His daughter gave Lavinia a quick kiss and a bearlike hug. 'That is absurd—I am so pleased I do not know what I must say.'

'But how did you know?' asked Lavinia.

'But I see your face, of course—and Papa, sitting there looking just as he looks when his work has gone well and he does not need to worry any more.' She sat down on the sofa between their chairs. 'When will you marry? Shall I be a bridesmaid? And Peta, of course—What shall we wear?'

Her father answered her. 'We shall marry just as soon as it can be arranged—it will be very quiet, *liefje*, I think Lavinia doesn't want bridesmaids.' He smiled at Lavinia, who smiled back. Of course she wanted bridesmaids and white silk and a veil and flowers—all girls did, but since he had made it clear that he didn't, she would have to forget all that. She said now: 'I really would like a small wedding, but it would be lovely if you and Peta could have pretty dresses.'

Sibby became enrapt. 'Blue,' she murmured, 'long, you understand, with little sleeves and large floppy hats for us both. Peta and I will go shopping together.' She beamed at Lavinia. 'It is very good to have a stepmother; Papa is a dear, but he is a man—now I shall be able to talk about all the things girls talk about.' She sighed blissfully. 'We shall be most happy. When do we go to fetch Peta?'

'That will have to wait until a day or so before the wedding,' interpolated the professor, 'and Lavinia and I will go—you won't mind that, will you, Sibby? You can make sure that everything is ready for our return.'

His daughter eyed him rebelliously and then giggled. 'Of course, I am stupid—people who are to be married do not like to have companions, do they, so I will not mind at all. I will buy flowers and make the house beautiful and order splendid meals.' She was struck with a sudden idea. 'I will also invite guests—a great many.'

'Oh, no, you don't,' said her father firmly. 'Your grandmother will do that; I daresay there will be a big party at her house.'

'She does not know about you and Lavinia, Papa?'

'Not yet. We're going to see her and Grandfather when we've had lunch.' He heaved himself out of his chair. 'Shall we go and have it now?'

He took an arm of each of them and they all went
into the dining-room where they had a hilarious
meal, largely due to Sibendina's high spirits.

The drive to Noordwijk was short, a bare twenty-
five miles, a distance which the Bentley swallowed
in well-bred, silent speed. Lavinia was surprised to
see that the town appeared to be little more than a
row of rather grand hotels facing the sea, but presently they turned away a little and drove through the
small town and took a tree-lined road leading away
from its centre. Large villas lined it at intervals and
she supposed that Radmer's parents lived in one of
them, but he didn't stop, leaving them behind to
cross the heath, slowing down to drive over a sandy
lane which presently led through open gates into the
well laid out grounds of a low solidly built house
facing the sea. He stopped before its open front door
and giving Lavinia no time to get nervous, whisked
her out of the car and into the house, and still holding her arm, walked her across the wide hall and
through a pair of doors at the back. The room they
entered ran across the width of the house so that it
had a great many windows overlooking a delightful
garden. There were doors too, flung open on to a verandah, its striped awning casting a pleasant shade
on to the chairs scattered along its length. The professor wasted no time on the room, but strode rapidly across it and through to the verandah, to stop
by the two people sitting there.

Lavinia had no difficulty in recognizing them;
the professor's father might be white-haired and a

little gaunt, but in his younger days he must have had his son's good looks—even now he was quite something. And his mother, although she was sitting, was a big, tall woman, considerably younger than her husband, with quite ordinary features redeemed by a pair of sparkling blue eyes, as heavy-lidded as her son's. She looked up now and smiled with pleased surprise, and her 'Radmer!' was full of delight as she said something in Dutch in a soft, girlish voice. He bent to kiss her, still with a hand tucked firmly in Lavinia's arm, shook his father by the hand and spoke in English.

'I want you to meet Lavinia—Lavinia Hawkins. She came from England to work at St Jorus a short while ago.' He paused and they greeted her kindly, speaking English as effortlessly as their own tongue, then embarked on small talk with a total lack of curiosity as to who she was and why she was there. Perhaps presently they would ask questions, but now they sat her down between them, plied her with iced lemonade and discussed the summer weather, the garden, and the delights of living close to the sea. Lavinia had pretty manners. She took her share of the conversation while she wondered why Radmer hadn't dropped at least a hint about their approaching marriage. Surely he wasn't going to keep his parents in the dark about it? She couldn't believe it of him, and her sigh of relief when he at last spoke was loud enough for him to hear and glance at her with a smile of understanding.

There had been a pause in the conversation and

old Mijnheer ter Bavinck had suggested that his son might like to accompany him to his study, so that they might discuss some interesting article or other. Radmer got to his feet, pulled Lavinia gently to hers too and turned to face his parents.

'My dears,' he said quietly, 'I think you will have guessed that Lavinia is someone special; we hope to be married within a very short time.'

There was no doubt of their pleasure. There were congratulations and kisses and handshakes, and Mevrouw ter Bavinck picked up a handbell in order to summon a rather staid, middle-aged woman and give her some low-voiced instructions, at the same time telling her the news. She turned to Lavinia as the woman went to wring Radmer's hand and then did the same for Lavinia. 'This is Berthe,' she explained. 'She has been with us since Radmer was a very small boy, so of course she must hear the news too. Joop, her husband, who also works for us, is going to bring up a bottle of champagne.'

She beamed down at Lavinia and touched her lightly on the arm. 'We will allow the men to go away and discuss their dull business; you and I will talk—for now that you are to be our daughter, I may ask you questions, may I not?'

'Of course, Mevrouw ter Bavinck.' Lavinia warmed to the older woman's charm. 'I hope I haven't been too much of a surprise. It—it happened rather suddenly, I'm still surprised myself.'

They were sitting opposite each other now, and her hostess gave her a thoughtful look. 'It has been my dearest wish that Radmer should marry again. Has he told you about Helga—his first wife?'

'Not a great deal, and I told him that if he didn't want to talk to me about her, I wouldn't mind. Should I know?'

Mevrouw ter Bavinck looked doubtful. 'I think you should, but that is something which you will decide between you. But there is one thing, my dear, and you must forgive an old woman's impertinence in asking such a question, but it is important to me—after Helga. Do you love Radmer?'

Lavinia met the blue gaze squarely. 'With all my heart.'

Her companion sighed contentedly. 'That is good—and you will need all that love, Lavinia; he has been a solitary man for more than ten years, he is not young, and he has lived for his work— Now he will live for you, of course, but perhaps he may not realize that just yet.'

Her future mother-in-law was a wise woman who perhaps saw more than she was expected to see. Lavinia said gently: 'He loves Sibendina.'

'Very much, and she, thank God, is wholly his daughter.' The blue eyes twinkled. 'You will be a very young mother for her, but just what she needs. And now tell me, my dear, have you family of your own?'

Lavinia told her about Peta and her parents and Aunt Gwyneth; she found it easy to do this because her listener had the gift of listening as well as putting others at their ease; by the time the two men, followed by the champagne, returned, the two ladies were firm friends, and as Radmer sat himself down close to Lavinia, his mother remarked: 'You are both right for each other, Radmer—I believe you will be very happy. Is the wedding to be a quiet one?'

They drank their champagne and talked in a pleasant desultory way about the marriage, and presently they went into the sitting-room and had tea and small crisp biscuits, and this time Lavinia found herself sitting with Radmer's father, answering his questions, warmed by his kindness.

They got up to go shortly after, with a promise to come again very soon, so that the details of the wedding might be finalized, and when they were once more in the Bentley, driving slowly this time, the professor asked:

'Well, Lavinia, do you think you will like my parents?'

She felt a little tired after the day's excitement, but content too. The answer she gave him must have satisfied him, for he said: 'Good girl, they like you too—I knew they would.'

Which, she supposed with faint bitterness, was, from him, a compliment.

They went out to dine later, but not before he had taken her to a small room at the back of the hall she hadn't previously been into, and opened a drawer in a charming medallion cabinet set against one of its silk-hung walls. The box he took from it was small and leather-covered and when he opened it she saw that it held a ring; a diamond cluster in a cup setting, the gold heavily engraved. He put the box down and came towards her with the ring in the palm of his hand and they looked at it together for a few moments. 'It has been in my mother's family for years,' he said at length. 'I should like you to have it. It hasn't been worn for a long time, for Helga refused to wear it, she considered it old-fashioned.'

Lavinia held up a small, capable hand. It was a pity that Helga had to be dragged into it, but she supposed she was being given the ring for appearances' sake, and anyway, he would have no idea that she was already fiercely jealous of his first wife— indeed, if he found that out, he might cry off, appalled at the very idea of her feeling anything at all but a comfortable, uncomplicated friendship for him. She thanked him nicely, admired the ring, remarked upon its excellent fit, and when he bent and kissed her cheek, received the salute with what she hoped was a warm but not too warm manner. Apparently it was satisfactory, for Radmer took her arm as they went back into the hall, and remarked with some satisfaction that he had no doubt that they would be excellent friends. He even halted halfway to the staircase to say: 'You see, if no emotions are involved, my dear, the success of our marriage is assured; we shall have no bouts of jealousy or imagined feelings of neglect, and no wish to interfere with each other's lives.' He smiled down at her and kissed her for a second time, still on her cheek. 'You do understand that I am deeply engrossed in my work?' he wanted to know.

She said that yes, she quite understood that, and wondered for the first time, deep in her heart, if she would be able to endure living with him in such a manner, but it was a little late to think of that now, and at least she would make him happier than a girl who didn't love him. The thought consoled her as she went upstairs to tidy herself for their evening out.

Time telescoped itself after that evening; some days she didn't see Radmer at all, some days she spent an hour or so at his house or snatched a brief meal with him somewhere, and several times they drove to see his parents.

She had found that, without bothering her with details, he had smoothed the way for her to leave the hospital. All the tiresome formalities had been taken care of, and when she received her salary he had told her to spend it on herself as he had arranged for her to have an allowance which would be paid into the bank on their wedding day. And he had been of the greatest help in writing to Peta, who, they had decided, wasn't to be told anything until they actually arrived at Aunt Gwyneth's house. Lavinia had composed a careful letter, full of optimism about the future, and had told Peta that if she didn't write again for a little while it was because she was going to be busy. She read it out to Radmer on one of their rare evenings together and looked at him anxiously when she had done so. 'Does it sound all right?' she wanted to know. 'And are you sure we're doing the right thing?'

He had reassured her with a patience which soothed her edginess, and when Sibendina had joined them later, he had taken care to keep the conversation light and cheerful, so that she had gone back to hospital and slept like a contented child.

She was still working, of course. Radmer had asked her if she wished to leave St Jorus and she had no doubt that if she had said yes, he would have arranged it for her without fuss or bother, just as he had arranged everything else, but she had chosen to stay on until a few days before they were to marry, going on duty each day, an object of excited attention from her new friends in the hospital.

It was a few days before she was due to leave that Radmer had driven her up to Friesland. They had left very early in the morning, before breakfast, and done the eighty odd miles in under two hours, to eat that meal upon their arrival. Lavinia had been a little overawed at the sight of the large square house set in its small estate to the north of Leeuwwarden. The grounds around it were beautifully laid out with banks of flowers screened by a variety of shrubs and trees, and a freshly raked gravel drive leading from the great iron gateway at the roadside.

The housekeeper had come to welcome them— Juffrouw Hengsma, a tall, homely woman who said little but smiled her pleasure at seeing them before serving the breakfast they didn't hurry over. Lavinia sat listening to Radmer's history of the house and then spent the remainder of the morning going over it with him, lingering over its treasures of silver and

glass and porcelain, and admiring the splendid hangings at the windows and the well-polished furniture.
But it was a very comfortable house too, for all its
age and size. There were easy chairs and sofas and
pretty table lamps scattered around the rooms, thick
carpets on the floors, and even though each apart-
ment had an enormous chandelier hanging from the
centre of its high ceiling, there was an abundance
of wall lighting so that even on the gloomiest day,
the rooms would glow with soft light.

'You like it?' asked Radmer, and smiled warmly
at her when she declared that she had never seen
anything as beautiful. 'Except for your house in Amsterdam,' she added. 'I love it.'

'So do I. We come up here quite often, though.
Come and see the garden.'

It was a happy day for her, at any rate, and she
thought Radmer had been happy too; she had wanted
to be reassured about that quite badly and it had
been a good test, spending the whole day together
like that, with nothing much to do and only each
other to depend upon for company. Looking back,
she was as sure as she could be that he had enjoyed
being with her—they had found a great deal to talk
about and they had discovered similar tastes and
ideas. She had gone to bed that night full of hope.

She left the hospital two days later, early in the
morning, so that they could catch a Hovercraft at
Calais and be at Cuckfield by the afternoon, and
although it wasn't yet eight o'clock, she had a tremendous send-off when Radmer came to collect

her with the Bentley. He had laughed and waved good-naturedly at the small crowd of nurses, then glanced sideways at her. 'That's a new outfit,' he remarked. 'I like it.'

The sun, already shining, seemed to shine a little brighter; it was a good beginning to a day of which Lavinia felt a little uncertain. 'I'm glad,' she said happily. 'I went to Metz and Metz yesterday and bought some clothes...'

'A wedding dress?' he asked lightly.

'Well, yes.' It had been more expensive than she had expected, but the simplicity of the rich cream crêpe had seemed just right, and she had bought a hat too, covered in cream silk roses. She only hoped that it wouldn't seem too bridal for his taste. She looked down at the blue and white coat dress she was wearing, satisfied for once that she was in the forefront of fashion. She had bought blue sandals too and a leather handbag, and now she had very little money left.

It occurred to her at that moment that Radmer had said nothing at all about a honeymoon; perhaps the Dutch didn't have them, possibly he felt it would be a waste of time. Honeymoons were for people in love, although surely two friends could go on holiday together, and if anyone else wanted to call it a honeymoon, they were at liberty to do so.

They were already out of Amsterdam and as though he had read her thoughts, he asked: 'Would you mind very much if we go straight home after the wedding? I'm up to my ears in work and there's a lecture…'

Her pride wouldn't allow him to finish, to seek more excuses. 'Of course I don't mind—I'll have Peta and Sibby and that lovely house to explore and I shall go shopping.'

He nodded and they didn't talk about themselves or the wedding again. It was much later, when they were leaving Dover behind them, that she asked: 'I expect you know where Cuckfield is? It's not far.'

'I've driven through it, I believe.' He took the Bentley neatly past a great juggernaut and started down the hill towards Folkestone.

'You know England?'

He smiled. 'I was at Cambridge.'

'Oh, were you?' She added with faint bewilderment: 'I don't know anything about you.'

He laughed. 'It will all come out in good time. Shall we stop for an early lunch? I'm going along the coast road, we could have a meal at the Mermaid in Rye.'

It was during that meal that she asked: 'Which church are we being married at? I did ask you, but if you remember you had to go somewhere or other in a hurry before you could tell me.'

He looked rueful. 'What you mean is, I forgot all about it. I'm sorry—I'm not proving very informative, am I? You wanted somewhere quiet, didn't you, so I've arranged it at the English church in the Begijnsteeg—I hope you'll like that.'

Her face showed that she did. 'An English service? How nice, now I can wear my ring on my left hand...'

He laughed again, very softly. 'If it makes you feel more securely married, why not? I thought we might go straight there after we've had the civil wedding. Mama is giving a small reception for us afterwards at Noordwijk and the two girls are going to stay there for a couple of days. We can be back home again in the early evening.' She could almost hear relief in his voice at the thought of getting it all over and done with as speedily as possible. It surprised her when he leaned across the table and took her hand in his. 'Have you ever thought how appropriately you are named, my dear?'

She shook her head, conscious of his hand, wishing very much to clasp it with her own.

'Lavinia was the second wife of Aeneas.'

'Oh—Greek mythology.' She furrowed her forehead in thought. 'But my name isn't appropriate at all—I've just remembered, wasn't there someone called Thompson who quoted something about the lovely young Lavinia, and I'm not lovely; I remember my father telling me about it and laughing...'

He said very gently: 'Kind laughter, I'm sure, and there are a great many variations on that word, you know—amiable, sweet, angelic...'

If he had loved her—been in love with her, he wouldn't have needed to say that; she winced at the pain his words had given her and smiled back at him. 'I hope you don't suppose me to be angelic? I can be as cross as two sticks sometimes.'

'I know. The first time you spoke to me you were just that. It intrigued me even before I turned round to look at you. I knew you would be different from other girls.'

Her voice was unconsciously wistful. 'I'm just the same inside,' but she smiled widely as she spoke, just to let him see that she wasn't taking their conversation seriously.

They drove on presently and the nearer they got to Cuckfield, the more nervous Lavinia became, twisting her lovely ring round and round her finger, opening and shutting her handbag for no reason at all, and Radmer, who had shown no sign of nerves, smiled a little to himself, ignoring her small fidgets until on the outskirts of the little town he slowed the car and stopped in a layby, and when she looked at him inquiringly, said mildly: 'Look, Lavinia, I know how you feel, but will you stop worrying and leave it all to me?'

She nodded wordlessly. He would, without doubt, sail through the awkward situation without any outward sign of ill-humour, whatever Aunt Gwyneth said to him. Indeed, he looked capable of moving a mountain if he had a mind to; he also looked very handsome and impeccably turned out. He was wearing the dog-tooth check again with a silk shirt and a tie of sombre magnificence. She had no doubt that he would get his own way without difficulty, whatever obstacle was put in his path.

And she was right. Aunt Gwyneth was at home, having just finished lunch, and was taken com-

pletely by surprise. They listened to her bluster-
ing efforts to prevent Peta going with them until
Radmer settled the matter with a suave confidence
which left her shaken.

'There can be no objection,' he pointed out
firmly. 'You are not Peta's guardian, and now that
Lavinia and I are to be married and can offer her
a good home, I can see no reason for your objection. You have yourself just said that she has cost
you a great deal and forced you to make sacrifices.
I imagine that you have no plans for Peta's future?'

Aunt Gwyneth eyed him angrily. Her plans, such
as they were, would have been torn to shreds by
this quiet, dreadfully self-possessed man. She made
an exasperated sound and turned her spite on Lavinia, sitting as quiet as a mouse, feeling sick. 'Well,
it didn't take you long to find yourself a husband,
did it?' she demanded. 'And now I suppose all my
kindness and money will have been wasted on the
pair of you.'

'I can't remember you spending any money on
me, Aunt,' Lavinia said with spirit, 'and Peta's
school fees can't have been all that much—Father
said you had more money than you knew what to
do with.' She added bitterly: 'And I can't remember
you being kind.'

'Then we can take the matter as settled,' the professor interrupted quietly. 'You will be glad to be
rid of your burden, Mrs Turner, and if you have in-
curred expense beyond your means, I shall be glad
to reimburse you.'

Aunt Gwyneth sniffed angrily. 'Indeed I shall…' she began, and got no further as the door opened and Peta came into the room. 'There's a gorgeous Bentley outside—Lavinia!' She flung herself into her sister's arms. 'Lavinia, you said you'd come and I knew you would—oh, dear, I'm going to howl. You will take me with you…?'

Lavinia gave her sister a hug and turned her round. 'Yes, darling—we have just been talking to Aunt Gwyneth—and this is Radmer, we're going to be married in two days' time and you're coming to live with us.'

Peta crossed the room and gazed into his imperturbable face. 'Of course, the Bentley. However did Lavinia find you? You're super!'

He took her hand and said gravely: 'Hullo, Peta, and thank you. Lavinia didn't find me, I found her.'

She was still staring at him. 'What shall I call you?'

'Won't Radmer do? I've a daughter, you know, she's fourteen, and she calls your sister Lavinia, so that makes it right, doesn't it?'

She nodded and smiled then. 'I like you,' she told him shyly. 'Can we go now?'

He looked over her head and smiled faintly, but it was to Mrs Turner, sitting ignored, to whom he spoke. 'Perhaps if Lavinia might pack Peta's things? We don't wish to take up too much of your time.' He spoke with the utmost politeness, quite sure that he would have his way. Apparently Aunt Gwyneth thought so too, for she said angrily: 'Lavinia can do what she likes; she's always an ungrateful, sullen girl. I'm surprised you're going to marry her—she's plain enough, and I can't think what you can see in her.'

The politeness was still there, tinged with arrogance now. 'Probably not, Mrs Turner, but I must remind you that you are speaking of my future wife.' He looked at Lavinia and smiled, warmly this time. 'Perhaps if Peta goes with you?' he suggested. 'She need only bring the things she treasures—we'll buy anything she needs.'

It took ten minutes. Peta had few possessions and a small wardrobe, the two girls packed a case, talking in excited snatches, and went back to the drawing-room where they found their aunt angrily firing questions at Radmer, who was answering them with a patience and ease of manner which Lavinia couldn't help but admire. He got up as they entered the room, took the case from her, stood silently while they wished their aunt good-bye and then offered his own farewells, but all Aunt Gwyneth said was: 'Don't come running back to me, either of you—you would have had a secure home here, Lavinia, as my companion, but if you're fool enough to marry a foreigner...'

Lavinia rounded on her 'Aunt Gwyneth, don't you dare speak of Radmer in that fashion! He's a good, kind man and we shall be very happy.'

She went through the door Radmer was holding open for her, her cheeks fiery, her head high, and allowed him to settle her in the car without looking at him. Only when he got in beside her did she whisper: 'Oh, I'm so ashamed—she had no right...'

His hand covered hers for a brief moment. 'Thank you, dear girl,' then he took it away and turned to look at Peta, bouncing with impatience on the back seat. 'We're going to spend the night in London. I thought we might go to a theatre this evening, and if we don't stop on the way for tea I think there might just be time for you girls to do some shopping.'

It was Peta who answered him. 'I say, you are super. What sort of shopping?'

'Well, a dress for this evening, perhaps. How about Harrods?'

Peta made a small ecstatic sound and Lavinia murmured: 'But we shan't have time. I thought we were going to spend the night at Dover—I haven't anything with me, only night things.'

'Then you must have a new dress too.'

'Oh, Lavinia, yes!' Peta had leaned forward to poke her pretty face between them. 'Oh, isn't this marvellous? I simply can't believe it! And now tell me about the wedding and where you live and your daughter's name, and am I to go to school...?'

He laughed. 'Lavinia, I leave it to you. See how much you can get into the next half hour.'

Almost everything; enough to satisfy Peta and make her sigh happily. By the time they reached Knightsbridge and Harrods, she was starry-eyed.

It was surprising how much shopping could be done in a short space of time when one didn't need to look too closely at the price tags, and there was someone waiting with a cheque book to pay. They had begun by looking at the less expensive dresses; it was Radmer who had got up from the chair he had taken in the middle of the salon, caught Lavinia by the hand, and pointed out several models which had taken his fancy. She had tried them on, not daring to ask their price, and when she had been unable to decide which of them she preferred—the apricot silk jersey or the grass green patterned crêpe, he had told her to have them both. She went and stood close to him, so that no one should hear, and murmured: 'Radmer, they're frightfully expensive…'

His blue eyes twinkled kindly. 'But you look nice in them,' he pointed out, 'so please do as I ask,' and when she thanked him shyly he only smiled again and then said briskly: 'Now where is Peta—for heaven's sake don't let her buy black with frills.'

But Peta, though young, had as good a taste as Lavinia. She had picked out a cotton voile dress in a soft blue, a Laura Ashley model, and came hurrying to display it. 'Only I don't know how much it is,' she said in a loud whisper, 'and I don't like to ask.'

Radmer settled himself in his chair. 'Try it on,' he suggested. 'I'm sure it's well within my pocket.'

She looked sweet in it, and when he suggested that they might as well buy shoes while they were there, Lavinia gave in, but only because Peta would have been disappointed if she had refused. They were going through the shop when he whispered in her ear: 'It's quite proper, you know, a man may give his future wife anything he chooses. You mustn't forget that we are to be married in two days' time.'

As though she could forget! She smiled and thanked him and turned to admire the sandals Peta had set her heart on.

She had no idea where they were to stay the night. It was Peta who recognized the hotel. 'Claridges!' she breathed. 'I say, how absolutely super. Are you a millionaire, Radmer?'

He chuckled. 'Not quite. Out you get.'

They had a belated tea before they went to their rooms. Lavinia gasped when she saw the luxury of her room, with its bathroom, and Peta's room on the other side. She changed, constantly interrupted by visits from her excited sister, who was full of questions, when Radmer came across from his room on the other side of the corridor to take them down to dinner—a merry meal, but how could it be otherwise, with Peta chattering so happily? They were enjoying their sorbets when she leaned across the table to say: 'Radmer, what a lucky man you are— you've got everything you want, and now you've got Lavinia too, you must be wildly happy.'

Lavinia found herself listening anxiously for his reply. 'Isn't it apparent?' he asked lightly. Which was a most unsatisfactory answer.

They went to a musical show, an unsophisticated entertainment which Lavinia suspected must have bored Radmer for most of the time, but it was entirely suitable for Peta's youthful ears and eyes, and she thanked him warmly when they got back to the hotel, and when she had gone to bed, Lavinia thanked him once more for taking Peta under his wing. 'It's like a dream,' she told him, 'and everything has happened so quickly, it doesn't seem quite real.'

He touched her cheek with a gentle finger. 'It's real, my dear.' He spoke so softly that she exclaimed: 'Oh, Radmer, are you sorry that…? Do you want to change your mind…? It would be all right, truly it would. I can't think why you chose me in the first place.'

He took her hands in his, there in the empty corridor outside her room. 'Don't be a goose! I'm not sorry and I don't want to change my mind, although, like you, I'm not quite sure why I chose you.'

He bent to kiss her and wished her good night and she slipped into her room, glad that Peta was already asleep. It was silly to cry about nothing, and that was what she was doing. She told herself that over and over again before she at last fell asleep.

Chapter 6

Lavinia was curled up in a corner of one of the great sofas in the drawing-room of the Amsterdam house, leafing through a pile of magazines, and opposite her, sitting in his great wing chair, was Radmer, reading his post. They had been married that morning, and as she stole a quick glance at him, the wry thought that anyone coming into the room might have mistaken them for an old married couple crossed her mind. She dismissed it at once as being unworthy. No one could have been kinder than Radmer during the last two days, and at least he liked her, she thought bleakly. He had considered her every wish and his generosity had been never-ending. She turned a page and bent her head, pretending to read while she reflected on the past forty-eight hours or so. She was bound to admit that everything had gone splendidly. They had arrived back with Peta to find Sibby waiting for them, and the liking between the two girls had been instantaneous and genuine; she had felt almost sick with relief, and Radmer, who had been watching her, had flung an arm around her shoulders and observed easily: 'Exactly as I anticipated; they're just right for each other—give them six months and they'll be as close as sisters.'

Lavinia had been grateful for his quick understanding, but when she had tried to thank him he had stopped her with a careless word and gone on to talk about something quite trivial. And that night, after the hilarious dinner they had shared with the girls, he had taken her to spend the night with an aunt of his—a nice old lady living on the other side of Amsterdam in a massive house furnished in the heavy style of Biedermeier. She had been surprised at being whisked off in that fashion; quite under the impression that she would stay in Radmer's house. It was only after he had left her with Mevrouw Fokkema that that lady had remarked in her slow, careful English: 'It is correct that you stay here until your marriage, my dear—we are an old-fashioned family, but we all know, and dear Radmer too, what is due to a ter Bavinck bride.'

Lavinia, somewhat taken aback, had smiled and agreed, and wished that her betrothed had taken leave of her with a little more warmth; his casual: 'See you tomorrow, Lavinia,' had sounded positively brotherly.

But the next day had been all right. He had fetched her after breakfast and although he had been at the hospital most of the day, she and the two girls had gone shopping together and come home laden with parcels and talking excitedly about the wedding; at least Peta and Sibby had; Lavinia had been

wholly occupied in overcoming a severe attack of
cold feet... She thought that she had concealed her
apprehension rather well, but that evening, when
the girls had gone to Sibby's room to try on their
new dresses and she had found herself alone with
Radmer, he had asked quietly: 'Wanting to cry off,
Lavinia?'

She had put down the letters she had been reading, and because she was an honest girl, had given
him a straight look and said at once: 'No, not that—I
think I'm a little scared of all this...' She waved an
arm at the splendid room they were in. 'I'm afraid
I shall let you down, Radmer.'

'Never!' He was emphatic about it. 'And it isn't as
though I have quantities of friends, you know—I've
friends enough, but most of them are sober doctors
and their wives, and I don't entertain much.' For a
moment he looked bleak. 'Helga entertained a great
deal—she liked that kind of life; the house always
full of people—and such people!' He blinked and
smiled. 'Mind you, we shall have to do our best for
Sibby and Peta in a year or two, but I think you like
a quiet life, too, don't you?'

She imagined herself as he must think of her—a
home body, content to slip into middle-age, running
his house with perfection and never getting between
him and his work. The hot resentment had been bitter in her mouth even while she knew that she had
no right to feel resentful.

Her rather unhappy musings were interrupted by
his quiet: 'You haven't turned a page in five min-

utes, Lavinia,' so that she made haste to throw him a warm smile and a cheerful: 'I was thinking about today; trying to remember your family—it was all so exciting.' She thought she had convinced him, for he smiled a little and commented: 'The kind of wedding I like,' before he picked up the next letter and became absorbed in it.

Lavinia put down her magazine, picked up her letters again, and re-read them before casting them down once more and choosing another magazine. She must remember to turn the pages this time, while she let her thoughts wander. If I were a raving beauty, she pondered sadly, we wouldn't be here; he wouldn't be reading his letters—we'd be out dancing, or going for a trip round the world, or buying me lashings of diamonds and clothes, just because he loved me. She jumped when he spoke with sudden urgency: 'Good lord, I quite forgot!' and went out of the room, to return almost at once with a jeweller's velvet case in his hand. 'A wedding present,' he explained, and opened it to take out a pearl necklace and stoop to clasp it round her neck. She put a surprised hand up to feel its silky smoothness and then looked up at him. His face was very close; she kissed him on a hard cheek and said in a wondering voice: 'Oh, Radmer, for me? Thank you—they're beautiful!' She managed a smile. 'Now I feel like the Queen...and you've given me so much!'

She was thinking of the new cheque book in her handbag and the abundance of flowers in her beautiful bedroom, the accounts he had opened for her at several of the fashionable shops, and last but not least, the gold wedding ring he had put on her finger that morning.

He stood up, said to surprise her: 'You're a very nice girl, Lavinia,' and went to sit down again and pick up the *Haagsche Post*, which left her with nothing to do but sit and think once more.

Their wedding had been a happier and gayer affair than she had anticipated; she hadn't expected quite as many people, but then she hadn't known that Radmer had such a large family or so many old friends. She had dressed at his aunt's house and he had come to fetch her with his offering of flowers—roses and orchids and orange blossom in creamy shades to match her gown—and they had driven together, first to the civil wedding and then to the little church in the peaceful Beguinehof, where they had been married again, this time by the English chaplain. It wasn't until they had stood together in the old church that she had felt really married.

They had driven to Noordwijk after that, to the reception Radmer's mother had arranged for them, and where she had met aunts and uncles and cousins and watched Peta and Sibby flitting amongst the guests, having the time of their lives. At least the two girls were blissfully happy. Sibby had hugged and kissed her and declared that she looked super and would make a marvellous mother, and Peta had kissed her and whispered: 'Oh, Lavinia, I'm so happy! Who could have dreamt that this would happen—aren't you crazy with joy?'

Lavinia assured her that she was, and it was true—she was; life wasn't going to be quite the wonder-world it might have been, but at least she could do her best to be a good wife. She turned a page, mindful of his watchful eye. If this was what he wanted then she would do her best to give it to him; peace and quiet at home and a self-effacing companionship. It sounded dull, but it wouldn't be; they got on well together, she knew that for certain; the drive back from Noordwijk had been relaxed and pleasant, even amusing. Dinner had been fun too, with champagne and Lobster Thermidor and an elaborate dessert in her honour.

She turned another unread page and glanced at the clock—a magnificent enamel and ormolu example of French art. It was barely ten o'clock, but probably Radmer was longing to go to his study and work on the pile of papers which never seemed to diminish on his desk. Lavinia said good night without fuss, thanked him again for the pearls, and walked to the door.

He reached it before she did, to open it for her, and then, just as she was passing through, caught her by the shoulder. 'I enjoyed my wedding,' he told her soberly, 'and I hope you did too. Anyone else but you would have felt hard done by, coming back on your wedding day to sit like a mouse, pretending to read...' His eyes searched her face. 'I've not been fair to you, Lavinia.'

'Of course you have.' She was glad to hear her voice so matter-of-fact. 'You explained exactly how it would be when you asked me to marry you.' She drew a sharp breath. 'It's what I want too,' she told him steadily.

He bent and kissed her. 'You understand, don't you? You're the only girl I felt I wanted for a wife without getting involved—I've known that since the moment we met. I've built a good life, Lavinia, and a busy one, my work is important to me, you know that, and now we will share that life, but only up to a point, you know that too, don't you?'

'Oh, yes. I don't know much about it, but I can guess that losing your—your first wife made you so unhappy that you've shut the door on that side of your life—there—the loving part. I'll not open that door, Radmer.' She smiled and asked lightly: 'May I have breakfast with you? I'm used to getting up early—besides, I've an English lesson tomorrow morning with Juffrouw de Waal—she was annoyed because I've missed several just lately.' She nodded brightly at him, crossed the hall and started up the stairs. At the top she turned to lift a hand. The smile she had pinned on her face was still there, and he was too far away to see the tears in her eyes.

She didn't sleep much, but she was up early to bathe her puffy eyelids and rub the colour back into her cheeks, and when she went downstairs she looked just as usual; a little pale perhaps, but that was all. She was wearing the blue and white dress and sandals on her bare feet, and when Radmer saw her as he came in from the garden with the dogs, he wished her a cheerful good morning and said how nice she looked. 'It's going to be a hot day,' he remarked, 'and you look delightfully cool.' They walked together to the small room at the back of the house where they were to have breakfast, his arm flung round her shoulders. 'I've a busy day,' he told her as they sat down. 'Don't expect me back for lunch, but with luck I'll be home about four o'clock, and if you feel like it, we might go out for dinner.'

She poured their coffee carefully. 'That would be delightful—but can you spare the time?'

He looked up from the letters he was examining, his eyes narrowed, but she had been innocent of the sarcasm he had suspected. He said blandly: 'My dear, you had the shabbiest treatment yesterday evening, and we aren't going away for a holiday; the least I can do is to take you out and about—besides, I should like very much to do that. We'll go to the Amstel and dine on the terrace overlooking the canal—you'll enjoy that, and tomorrow evening I've booked a table at the Hooge Vuursche Hotel. It's near Baarn—we might dance as well as dine there.'

Her eyes sparkled. 'It sounds fun. Are they very smart places?'

He took his cup from her. 'Yes, I suppose so. Why not go out after your session with Juffrouw de Waal and buy a couple of pretty dresses? I like you in pink.' He picked up the first of his letters. 'You looked pretty in that cream silk dress, too.'

She said thank you in a contained little voice; a triumph, albeit a small one—he had noticed what she was wearing and liked it. 'I'll go along to the

Leidsestraat, there's a boutique—oh, and Kraus en Vogelzang in Kalverstraat…' She saw that he wasn't listening any more, but frowning over a sheaf of typewritten pages. Someone had placed a *Daily Telegraph* by her place. She poured herself some fresh coffee and began on its headlines.

Juffrouw de Waal received her sternly, only relaxing sufficiently to congratulate her on her marriage, observe that the professor was a fine man and deserved a good wife, and point out that now Lavinia was that wife, it behoved her to learn Dutch in the quickest possible time.

'And not only conversation, Mevrouw ter Bavinck,' she pointed out soberly. 'It is necessary that you read, and understand what you read, so that you may take part in talk of a serious nature—politics, for instance, as well as the day-to-day events in our country—the world too. You must also learn about our prices and the keeping of accounts as well as how to order household requirements. I suggest that you read a small portion of a daily newspaper to me, which you will translate and discuss in Dutch, and I hope that you will use every opportunity to speak our language.'

Thus admonished, Lavinia applied herself to her lesson with more enthusiasm than ever before; how pleased Radmer would be when she could discuss the meals with Mevrouw Pette without the aid of dictionary or sign language; lift the receiver off the hook and order the groceries in Dutch; ask him—in his own language, how his day had gone… Fired with this praiseworthy desire, she accepted a great deal of homework from her teacher, promised that she would see her in two days' time, and made her way to the Leidsestraat.

It was exciting to examine the elegant clothes in the shop windows and know that she could buy any of them if she wished. Finally, she found just what she was looking for in a boutique; a pink organza dress with a brief tucked bodice, a deep square neckline, and elbow sleeves, very full and caught into satin bands which matched the narrow band below the bodice. The skirt was wide, the darker pink roses of the pattern rambling over it. It was a beautiful dress and very expensive, but she bought it; she bought a peach-coloured chiffon which caught her eyes, too—after all, Radmer had told her to get two dresses and she couldn't wear the same dress twice running. She shopped for matching slippers and a white velvet shoulder wrap which would go nicely with both dresses, and then, very happy with her purchases, went back to the house in the square.

She had her lunch, held a long telephone conversation with Peta and Sibby, took the dogs for a walk and then settled down to wait for Radmer. It had gone four o'clock when he telephoned; he would be late—something had turned up, but would she go ahead and dress? He would be home as soon after six o'clock as he could.

But it was almost two hours until then; she took the delighted dogs for another walk, made herself work at her Dutch lesson, and then at last permitted herself to go to her room and dress. She took a long time about it, trying not to look at the little gilt clock ticking away the minutes so slowly, until finally, complete to the last dab of powder on her ordinary little nose, she went downstairs.

She was half-way down the staircase when Radmer came in, flung his case into the nearest chair and paused to look at her. 'Oh, very nice,' he said, 'very nice indeed. I can see that coming home is going to be a real pleasure now that I have a wife. I like the dress.' He was crossing the hall to meet her as he spoke and took her hands and held her arms wide while he studied her person. She stood quietly, her heart capering around beneath her ribs, making it difficult for her to breathe calmly; all the same she managed a very creditable, 'I'm glad you like it,' and then lost her breath altogether when he suddenly pulled her close and kissed her; not a gentle kiss at all, but fierce and hard.

'I like you too,' he told her, and then: 'I'll be fifteen minutes—pour me a drink while I'm changing, will you? Whisky.'

Lavinia waited for him in the sitting-room, the whisky ready, and with nothing better to do but wonder why he had kissed her in that fashion, it augured well for their evening—it might even augur well for their future. The memory of the look on his face when he had come home stirred her pulse, and the tiny flame of hope which flickered so faintly, and which she had promised herself she would keep alive at all costs, glowed more strongly, so that when she heard his step in the hall, she turned a smiling face to the door.

He had changed into a dinner jacket and he looked good in it—she saw that with her first glance. The second showed her that whatever feeling had prompted him to kiss her in that fashion had been cast off with his other clothes, without him uttering a word she could see that. So she said hullo with a lightness she didn't feel and added: 'I've poured your drink—it's over there, on the drum table,' and as he went to fetch it: 'Have you had a busy day?'

He went and sat down. 'Yes, there was a heavy list in both theatres—and Mevrouw van Vliet— you remember her?' He began to tell her about the case. 'We did another frozen section, you know— I'm afraid there's nothing much to be done. We had several positives today, too.'

'I'm sorry,' said Lavinia, and meant it. 'It clouds the day, doesn't it?'

He gave her an appreciative glance. 'Yes—but I shouldn't bring my work home with me, I'm afraid it's rather a temptation to talk about it with you— you see I never could…and with Sibby, it's been out of the question, of course.' He smiled a little. 'What have you been doing with yourself? And did the girls telephone?'

She related the peaceful happenings of her own day and passed on the messages Sibby and Peta had sent him, adding: 'They're having a lovely time. Peta says she's never been so happy before in her life, and that's true, you know—when she was a little girl, there was never much money and besides that, Mother wasn't very strong…!'

'And you, Lavinia—were you happy?'

She considered his question. 'For most of the time, I think; at least until Father died.' She got up and straightened a few cushions, wishful to change the conversation. 'I went to the kitchen today,' she told him, 'and Mevrouw Pette and I had a long talk—I had my dictionary, and we got on quite well.'

She succeeded in making him laugh. 'I should have enjoyed the conversation. How is the Dutch coming along?'

'I know a great many words,' she told him hopefully, 'and a few sentences.'

He put down his glass. 'When you know a few more, we will give a dinner party.' He grinned at her look of horror. 'Don't worry, we'll invite only those who speak English—all the same, you must try and speak Dutch as often as possible.'

She promised him that she would as they walked to the door together and she had the satisfaction of seeing that he was not on his guard with her. The kiss had been a reaction after a bad day, she decided, and he had been afraid that she would take advantage of it, despite what she had told him. She got into the car beside him, determined to be a pleasant, undemanding companion for the rest of the evening.

It was perfect weather and warm. They had a table in the window, where they could watch the barges chugging steadily up and down the canal, and they talked of a great many things while they ate. Radmer, once more his usual friendly, faintly impersonal self, took pains to please her. She had looked at the vast menu in some perplexity until he had suggested that she might like him to choose for her: hors d'oeuvres, Poulet Poule mon Coeur and syllabub, and when he asked her what she would like to drink, she left that to him too and drank the chilled Amontillado and then the white Burgundy with enjoyment, pronouncing the latter to be very pleasant, an innocent remark which caused her husband's mobile mouth to twitch very slightly; the bottle of Corton Charlemagne which he had ordered had been treated with due reverence by the wine waiter, being a wine to be taken seriously, but he only agreed with her and refilled her glass, remarking at the same time that wine was an interesting subject for anyone who cared to learn about it.

Lavinia took a sip and eyed him thoughtfully. 'I expect this is a very good one, isn't it? I don't know one from the other, but I'll have to learn, won't I?' She frowned. 'Would Mevrouw Pette…?'

A smile tugged at the corner of his mouth. 'Well, I daresay she's an authority on cooking sherry and so forth—I'm by no means that myself, but I daresay I could put you on the right track remind me to do so when we have a quiet evening together.'

They sat over their meal, and as the evening darkened slowly, Lavinia, sitting in the soft glow of the pink-shaded table lamp, her ordinary face brought to life by excitement and the wine, became positively pretty.

'Do you come here often, Radmer?' she asked.

'Occasionally, with friends. I don't—didn't go out a great deal. It must be months since I was here.'

She poured their coffee. 'But the head waiter knew you.'

He chuckled. 'That's his job. Shall we bring the girls here one evening? When is Peta's birthday?'

She told him, smiling with pleasure. 'She'd love it—she hasn't had much fun…' She looked away quickly because of the expression on his face; she didn't quite know what it was, but it might have been pity—it disappeared so quickly that afterwards she told herself that she had imagined it.

They drove back in a companionable silence and when they reached the house she wished him good night at once and went upstairs to bed; probably he had had enough of her company for one evening; she would have to give him time to get used to having her around. He made no effort to detain her and when she had thanked him he had replied that he had enjoyed himself too and looked forward to the following evening.

She knew better than to be chatty at breakfast; she poured his coffee, replied quietly to his query as to whether she had slept well, and sat down to her own meal and the *Daily Telegraph*. Her good-bye was cheerful as he got up to leave her, and she added a: 'And I hope it's a better day for you all,' for good measure as he left the room. She was heartily ashamed of the forlorn tears which dripped down on to her uneaten toast. She wiped them away fiercely, telling herself that she was becoming a regular cry-baby, and then took the dogs for a walk in the park before telephoning Peta and Sibby, who were coming home again on the following day. The pair of them sounded very pleased with life, taking it in turns to talk so that there was very little need for her to say more than a word or two. She put the receiver down at length and went along to find Mevrouw Pette, who had suggested that she might like to go through the linen cupboard with her.

Radmer came home earlier than she had expected him to. She was on her knees in the middle of the sitting-room carpet, the dogs sprawled on either side of her, learning Dutch verbs, when he walked in. The dogs rushed to greet him and she would have got to her feet if he hadn't said at once: 'No, don't move—I'll join you. What on earth are you doing?'

He glanced through the dry-as-dust grammar and shut the book. 'My poor dear,' he observed. 'I had quite forgotten how difficult our language is. Is Juffrouw de Waal a tyrant?'

She giggled. 'Well, yes, a bit. She gave me quite a lecture yesterday, though it was a useful one too... she told me that it was even more necessary that I should master Dutch quickly now that I was married to you. I have to read the papers each day, and translate what I read, so that I can discuss politics with you.'

He shouted with laughter. 'My dear girl, I almost never talk politics, and I should find it boring if you did. I'd rather come home to a wife in a pink dress who listens sympathetically to my grumbles about work and makes sensible comments afterwards.'

She sat back on her heels. 'Did you have a good day?'

He had stretched out beside her, lying full length with his hands behind his head, looking up at her. 'Yes, it was a good day. Have we had tea?'

'No, not yet. I'll ask for it right away. Do you want it here or in your study?'

His eyes were closed, but he opened them to stare at her. When he spoke it was so softly that she almost didn't hear him. 'I like your company, Lavinia—it grows on me—don't ever doubt that; even when I'm irritable or tired or worried—you have the gift of serenity.' He closed his eyes again and added: 'I'm hungry; somehow or other I missed lunch.'

It would have been very satisfying to have asked him what he had meant, instead she whisked down to the kitchen, made herself understood by the co-operative Mevrouw Pette and hurried back to assure Radmer that a sustaining tea was on the way. It gave her deep satisfaction presently, to watch him make short work of the sandwiches, anchovy toast and wholesome homemade cake Bep brought in a few minutes later, and when he had finished and closed his eyes in a nap, she sat, as still as a mouse, until he opened them again, wide awake at once, to look at the clock and suggest that they should change. 'I've booked a table for half past seven,' he told her, 'it's only half an hour's drive, but I thought it would be nice to sit over our drinks.'

The peach chiffon looked stunning; she did her face with care, brushed her hair until it shone and went downstairs to find him already waiting and any last lingering qualms she might have entertained about the extravagance of purchasing two dresses and expensive ones at that, at the same time, were successfully extinguished by his surprised admiration. 'Very nice,' he commented. 'I liked the pink, but this one is charming.'

'Well, it is a kind of pink,' she told him seriously. 'I didn't really need it, but it looked so pretty and fitted so well...'

He studied her carefully. 'Very well.' He took the wrap from her and put it round her shoulders. 'Remind me to buy you a fur wrap.'

She turned round slowly to face him. 'I wouldn't dream of doing that,' she assured him earnestly. 'Wives don't remind their husbands to buy them things like furs,' and then she giggled when he took his handkerchief out of his pocket to tie a knot in a corner of it. 'Don't be absurd!'

'Ah, but you don't understand, Lavinia. I'm a little out of touch when it comes to remembering what husbands do and don't do—it's been a long time.'

And what, in heaven's name, was a second wife's answer to a remark like that? She decided to ignore it and said instead: 'Shall we go? I'm looking forward to seeing this hotel. I told Sibby that we were going there and she said it was super.'

Sibby had been right; it was a splendid place, a castle once, but now a famous hotel standing in its own grounds, and as the evening was, for once, windless and warm still, they strolled about the terraces and then sat down by one of the fountains for their drinks, and presently, seated at a table by the window so that they had a splendid view of that same fountain, they dined off kipper paté, entrecote sauté Cussy, and crêpes soufflés aux pêches, and as the steak had been cooked with port wine, and the soufflé was flavoured with kirsch and they, in their turn, had been washed down with the excellent claret Radmer had chosen, Lavinia began to enjoy herself, and when he suggested that they might dance, she got up with all the will in the world, determined not to miss anything of her treat. She danced delightfully, and Radmer, after the first few seconds, realized it. He was a good dancer himself—they went on and on, not talking much, sitting down for a drink from time to time and then, by common consent, taking to the floor again. She had been surprised to find that he was as good at the modern dances as the more conservative waltz and foxtrot, and at the end of one particularly energetic session he had said almost apologetically: 'Sibby taught me; I find them rather peculiar, but they're fun sometimes—you're very good yourself.'

'But I prefer waltzing,' said Lavinia, as indeed she did; she could have danced all night and the evening was going so fast—probably once the girls were back home, he wouldn't ask her out again; not just the two of them. Their outings would more than likely be family ones from now on.

They danced a last, dreamy waltz and she went to fetch her wrap. As they got into the car she said: 'That was wonderful, Radmer, thank you for a lovely evening.'

'We'll do it again,' he promised her as he manoeuvred the car on to the road, and Lavinia stifled disappointment because he hadn't said that he had enjoyed it too. She smoothed the soft stuff of her gown, and sat quietly, thinking about the evening, until he broke into her reverie. 'It's a splendid night,' he observed casually. 'We'll go back down the country roads, shall we? There'll be no traffic—we can miss Hilversum completely and work our way round the Loosdrechtsche Plassen, go through Loenen and back on to the motorway below Amstelveen—almost as quick, and far nicer.'

She agreed happily. She wasn't in the least tired, on the contrary, the dancing had left her glowing and wide awake. They talked with idle contentment about nothing in particular as Radmer drove across the golf course, under the motorway and on to the narrow roads which bordered the lakes. They were already two-thirds of the way to Loenen; indeed, Lavinia could make out a few lights, still well ahead of them across the water when, looking idly around her at the quiet, moonlit countryside, she exclaimed suddenly: 'Radmer—that light, over there, on the right...'

'I've seen it, dear girl—a fire, unless I'm mistaken. There's a lane somewhere—here it is.' He swept the big car into a rough, unmade road, a mere

cart track. 'This will take us somewhere close, I
fancy.'

The fire could be seen more plainly now; a dull
glow brightening and fading, almost dimmed by the
brilliant moonlight. And it was further away than
Lavinia had thought—it must be an isolated farmhouse set well back from the road, in the rough heath
bordering the lakes. She fancied she could smell
smoke now and hear the faint crackling of fire in the
quiet of the night, and presently they had their first
real view of the house. A farmhouse, right enough,
standing amongst trees and rough grass; the lane
they were driving along ended in its yard. Radmer
came to a halt well away from the farm buildings,
said 'Stay here,' and got out, to disappear quickly
through a side door which he had had no compunc-
tion in breaking down with a great shoulder. Lavinia could hear him calling and someone answering
faintly. She heard other sounds too, now—horses,
snorting in fright, and cows bellowing; they would
be in the great barn at the back of the house. The
fire wasn't visible from where she sat, only a faint
flickering at the windows; it might not be too bad at
the moment, but by the time Radmer had roused the
family, it might be too late to save the animals. She
got out of the car and looked about her; she could see
no one. She put her handbag and wrap carefully on
the car seat, shut the door, and ran towards the barn.

Chapter 7

It was easy enough to find the door in its vast side; the moonlight showed Lavinia that—it crept in after her, too, showing her the enormous lofty place, with cow stalls down each side of a wide cobbled path, two horses, giants to her shrinking eyes, stamping and snorting in the partitioned-off stables at the further end. There were a medley of farm carts in another corner, and bales of hay... She wasted no more time in looking, but shaking with fright, went to unbar the great doors opening on to the yard and the fields beyond, and then, uttering loud, encouraging cries, more for her own benefit than those of the beasts, went to untie the horses, relieved to find that despite their fear, they had no intention of kicking her to pieces, merely snorting violently as they backed out of their stable and trotted ponderously out into the yard. She wasn't too keen on cows, either, but she went from one spotless stall to the next, taking down the bars and trusting to their readiness to respond to her pleas that they should bestir themselves. And they did, to her great relief; they hurried, as well as cows will hurry, jostling each other in their common wish to get away from the smell of smoke.

She saw them on their way and then made a cautious round of the vast place to make sure that there was nothing left alive in it. A bull, she thought despairingly—if there's a bull I'll not dare go near it, but there was no bull, only a cow dog, growling at her from his fenced-off pen in a dark corner. Lavinia remembered now that she had heard him barking when she had been seeing to the horses. She went to him at once and started to untie the rope attached to his collar, talking hearteningly the while, so anxious to set him free that she hardly noticed his curled lip. 'Good dog,' she encouraged him as she let him go, still happily unaware of his fierceness, 'run along and look after those cows.' And he rolled a yellow eye at her and went.

The smell of smoke was strong now and wisps of it were oozing through the end wall of the barn. When Lavinia found another small door, obviously leading to the house, and went through it, she was instantly enveloped in a thick smoke which set her coughing and made her eyes smart and water, but there was no going back; she wasn't sure where she was, but Radmer must be somewhere close by and he might be needing help. The thought sent her blundering ahead, out of the worst of the smoke into a comparatively clear space which she took to be a lobby between the kitchen and the front of the house. She could see the fire now and hear it as well; and although the stairs were still intact she saw flames licking the stair head above. There seemed to be no one downstairs. Lavinia started to climb, just as Radmer came carefully down, a child in his arms.

'I told you to stay in the car,' he said calmly, 'but since you're here, will you take this infant? Not injured, just terrified.'

She received the small, shaking form. 'Who else is there?'

'The mother—had a baby yesterday—I'll have to carry them down. The man of the house got up to see what was the matter and was overcome by smoke. I dragged him on to the doorstep.' He grinned at her and went back upstairs.

The farmer was lying outside his front door, recovering slowly, not really aware of her, all the same she told him in a bracing tone as she stepped carefully over him, 'Don't worry, you'll be all right. I'll be back in a minute.'

Lavinia put the child in the back of the car and closed the door on its frightened bawling; she would have liked to have stayed to comfort it, but she had to go back into the house again. Radmer couldn't manage the mother and baby all at once and the fire might get fiercer.

There had been more smoke than flames, but now, looking up the narrow stairs, she could see that the landing was well alight and filled with a thick smoke. She ran through to the kitchen, snatched up a tea towel, wrung it out with furious speed under the sink tap and swathed it round her nose and mouth and then ran upstairs, where she was far more frightened by Radmer's furious look than the fire. 'Get out of here!' he told her furiously. 'You little fool, do you want to be killed?'

'No!' She had to shout because of the tea towel. 'But now I am here, I'll take the baby.'

She snatched the small scrap from the bed and raced downstairs and out to the car, saying 'Excuse me,' politely to the farmer as she stepped over him once more. The baby was whimpering; she laid it on the car's floor, begged the toddler not to cry and went back to the man. He was feeling better, although his colour was bad. '*Mijn vrouw—die kinderen*,' he muttered urgently, and tried to get up. Lavinia didn't know the word for safe, so she smiled, nodded reassuringly and said OK, a useful phrase which she had found of the greatest help since she had arrived in Holland. But he had lapsed into semi-consciousness again and could offer no help as she began to heave him to one side—and only just in time, for a moment later Radmer came through the door with the woman in his arms. Lavinia got to the car ahead of him, flung open the door, whisked up the baby and toddler and hugged them to her while he deposited his burden on the back seat, then handed them over to be tucked in with their mother.

Radmer spoke in a reassuring voice, shut the door again and said briefly:

'See if you can get the man to come round a bit while I get the animals out of the barn.'

'I have.'

He looked at her in astonishment. 'All of them? Cows—horses?'

She nodded. 'And a dog. There's nothing left there, I looked to see.'

He said on a laugh: 'You brave girl—were you frightened?'

'Terrified. The man...?' As he turned away: 'Is there anywhere I can go for help?'

He paused. 'I imagine someone will have seen the fire by now even in this remote area; thank heaven it took its time before it got a hold. If I could get the man on his feet we might save quite a lot of furniture, but we can't put the fire out, I'm afraid.' He gave her a thoughtful look.

'Lavinia, can you drive?'

'Yes. I took lessons and passed my test—ages ago—I haven't driven more than a couple of times since.'

'Think you can handle the Bentley? I'll reverse her for you—take her back to the road and stop at the nearest house.' He saw the look on her face and went on: 'I know you're scared to do it, my dear, but the woman needs to go to hospital as soon as possible.' He smiled suddenly. 'Do you suppose you could make yourself understood?'

'I'll do my best.'

'Good girl—now let's get the car turned.' He left her for a moment and went to bend over the farmer; when he came back he said: 'I think he'll be all right—I'll get to work on him when you've gone.'

She waited while he turned the Bentley and then

got into the driver's seat. He had left the engine running, she only had to drive away… She turned a white face to his as he put his head through the open window.

'Off with you,' he said cheerfully, and kissed her.

She went very slowly at first; the car seemed huge, and although she hadn't forgotten how to drive, she was decidedly slow. But there was nothing to hinder her and the moon was still bright, lighting up the countryside around her. She gained the main road, turned clumsily into it and put her foot down gingerly on the accelerator; there must be something within a mile or so, and at the worst, Loenen was only a short drive away.

The road wound along, close to the water and there were no houses at all, but presently, as she slowed down to take a bend in the road, she saw a massive pair of gates opened on to a drive. The house might be close by; it was worth trying anyway. She edged the Bentley between the posts and sent the car up the tree-shadowed drive, to slither to a halt before a sizeable house, shrouded in darkness. She got out, murmuring reassuringly to the occupants of the back seat, and then turned back to look at the clock on the dashboard. Two o'clock in the morning—whatever would the occupants say? She rang the bell, not waiting to give herself an answer.

The elderly man who came to the door after what seemed a very long time, stood and stared at her in astonishment; as well he might, she conceded. Callers in grubby evening dress didn't usually ring door bells at that hour of night. She wished him good evening, and not wanting to get involved in a conversation she surely wouldn't understand, asked urgently: 'Telephone?' She added helpfully: '*Politie*,' and waved towards the car.

The man gave her a sharp look and spoke at some length until she interrupted him with another urgent 'Telephone?' but he still hesitated, and she was marshalling her Dutch to try again when there were steps behind him and a voice demanded: '*Wat is er aan de hand*?'

'Oh, if only someone could speak English,' cried Lavinia, very much frustrated, and found herself looking over the man's shoulder at a woman's face that smiled at her and asked: 'What is it that you want? You are in trouble?'

'Yes,' said Lavinia, and drew a relieved breath before explaining briefly what had happened. 'And my husband says that the woman must be got to hospital as soon as possible,' she finished. 'Could an ambulance be called?'

The woman smiled again. 'Of course, but first we bring the mother and children in here. Does your husband know where you are?'

Lavinia shook her head. 'No, he told me to go to the first house I saw.'

Her questioner turned to the elderly man and spoke quietly and he went away; Lavinia could hear his voice somewhere inside, presumably telephoning. 'And now the children...' The lady held out a hand, obviously meaning it to be shaken. 'Mevrouw van der Platte.'

It seemed funny to stop for introductions at such a time, but Lavinia shook the hand and murmured: 'Mevrouw ter Bavinck.'

Her hostess's smile broadened. 'The wife of Radmer? We know him slightly.' She nodded her head in a satisfied fashion, pulled her dressing gown more closely round herself and followed Lavinia to the car, and in a moment the elderly man joined them.

Between them they bore the woman and children indoors, into a large hall, comfortably furnished, where the three unfortunates were made comfortable on a large sofa and the elderly man was dispatched to warm some milk.

'My husband is away from home,' explained Mevrouw van der Platte. 'Henk is our houseman, he lives here with his wife, who is the cook, but I think there is no reason to call her. Can I do anything to help you, Mevrouw ter Bavinck?'

Lavinia was bending over her patient, who looked ill and very pale. The toddler was asleep now, and the baby tucked up with his mother.

'I don't think so, thank you. I don't think they have burns, but the smoke was very bad. Will the ambulance and fire engine take long?'

As if in answer to her question she heard the sing-song wail coming towards them along the road, followed by a second. 'Fire engine, police,' said Mevrouw van de Platte unnecessarily, and handed her a glass of warm milk. 'You will want this for your patient. When you have done, there is coffee for you.'

She watched while Lavinia gave the woman the milk. 'Tell me, you saw the fire?'

'We were coming home from Baarn—Radmer thought it would be pleasant to drive through the country roads.'

'And he is there now? At the fire?'

'Yes. If he could get the farmer on to his feet, he thought they might be able to save some of the furniture.'

'The animals?'

'I let them out of the barn—I do hope they won't stray. The dog was with them.'

The companion eyed her with respect. 'You are a sensible girl—your husband must be proud of you.'

Lavinia wiped her patient's mouth and said nothing to that, only: 'I hope he knows where to find me.'

'He will. Henk told the police where you were and they will tell your husband. The ambulance should be here very soon now.'

Radmer got there first, though. Lavinia heard his voice when Mevrouw van der Platte went to answer the door bell. He came in quickly and went at once to her and took her hands. 'You're all right?' he wanted to know, wasting no time in greeting her.

Her heart had given a joyful skip at the sight of him although she answered him calmly enough. 'Yes, thanks—I'm fine, but will you take a look at Mum? I've given her some milk, but she doesn't look too good.'

They were bending over the woman when their hostess came back with a tray of coffee. Radmer straightened himself as she set the tray down. 'She needs treatment—there's an ambulance on the way?'

'Yes—are the babies to go with her?'

'Yes. The father went straight to hospital in one of the police cars—he's all right, but he'll need a check-up. They'll keep him there until they've had a look at this dear soul and the children.'

'Do you want me to go with them?' Lavinia was sipping coffee and looking quite deplorable, with her pretty dress covered in soot and bits of straw and a great tear in its skirt. Her hair had tumbled down too, giving her the look of a lost waif.

Radmer shook his head. 'There'll be a nurse with the ambulance, once we've seen them safely on their way, I'll take you home.'

She smoothed back a wisp of hair in an absent-minded fashion. 'You're coming home too?'

'I shall go over to the hospital when I've seen you indoors.'

Lavinia put her cup down. 'I'd like to come with you—that's if you don't mind. Just to be sure she's all right—and the babies.'

He raised his eyebrows. 'My dear girl, it's getting on for three o'clock in the morning.' He smiled at her kindly. 'Besides, what could you do? And I'll probably be there some time.'

She stooped to pick up the toddler who had wakened suddenly and burst into outraged tears. 'Yes, of course,' she answered in a colourless voice, 'how silly of me not to think of that.' She began wandering about the hall, the moppet against her shoulder, murmuring to it, not looking at Radmer at all.

The ambulance came almost immediately after that and she went and stood out of the way, in a corner with Mevrouw van de Platte, watching the mother and her children being expertly removed by two ambulance men and a pretty nurse, with Radmer quietly in charge of the whole undertaking, and presently, when he had bidden their kind hostess good-bye, she added her own thanks to his, wished the older lady good-bye in her turn, and went out to the car with him.

'You must be tired,' Radmer observed as they went down the drive and into the road. 'Did you find the car difficult to handle?'

'Yes,' said Lavinia baldly, 'I did. At least, it wasn't the car, it was me—I've only ever driven an Austin 1100, and that was years ago.'

He grunted noncommittally and didn't speak again for quite some time, and then it was to make some remark about Peta and Sibby's return; it was very obvious that he didn't want to talk about the fire; which was a pity, for she longed, like a little girl, to be praised for her help. She swallowed tears and stared resolutely out of the window at the dark streets of Amstelveen. They would soon be home.

At the house he got out with her, opened the massive front door and followed her in, and when she said in a surprised voice: 'Oh, I thought you were going to the hospital,' he said with the faint-

est hint of impatience: 'I can hardly go like this—
I'll change.'

Lavinia looked him over carefully. His clothes,
at first glance, appeared to be ruined; filthy with
stains of heaven knew what and grimy with soot and
smoke, and there was a jagged tear in one trouser
leg. She asked suddenly: 'You're not hurt?'

'Not in the least. We look a pretty pair, don't we?'
He smiled briefly. 'Go to bed, Lavinia.'

She went towards the staircase, her bedraggled
wrap trailing from one arm. At their foot she turned
to encounter his hard stare. 'Good night, my dear,
you were splendid.'

She didn't answer; she wanted to be hugged and
fussed over and told she was the most wonderful
and bravest girl in the world. She summoned up a
smile and went slowly up the stairs, dragging her
feet, sliding her hand along the polished balustrade.
She was almost at the top when he spoke again, so
quietly that she almost didn't hear him. His voice
sounded as though the words had been dragged out
of him. 'These last few hours have been the worst
I have ever known—and I've only just realized it.'

She supposed him to be talking about the fire and
the efforts he had made to rescue the farmer and his
family; he must be tired... She said in a motherly
little voice, meant to soothe: 'Yes—I was scared too,
and I wasn't even in danger...'

Radmer had started towards the staircase, now
he stopped to laugh so that Lavinia looked at him in
bewilderment. She was on the point of asking him

what was so funny when Mevrouw Pette, swathed in a dressing-gown and with her hair severely plaited, appeared on the landing above and leaned over the head of the stairs to stare down at them both, burst into speech and bear down upon Lavinia, whom she swept under a motherly wing and led towards her room, exchanging a rapid fire of question and answer with the professor as she did so.

Lavinia was tired and dispirited; it was pleasant to be fussed over, to have a bath run for her, to have her ruined gown removed with sympathetic tuts, and after a quick bath, to be tucked up in her vast bed like a small child. She drank the hot milk Mevrouw Pette insisted upon and went to sleep at once despite the kaleidoscope of events, nicely muddled with her tiredness, going on inside her head.

She woke to find Bep standing by her bed with a tray in her hands, and when she looked at the little bedside clock she saw to her astonishment that it was almost ten o'clock. She sat up, struggling to assemble her Dutch, and came out with: 'Late—I must get up.'

Bep smiled and shook her head, put the tray on Lavinia's lap and indicated the folded note propped against the coffee pot. It was a scrawl from Radmer, telling her simply that he would go straight from the hospital after he had finished his work there, to fetch Sibby and Peta; she could expect them all home for dinner, he hoped she would enjoy a quiet day, he was hers, R.

Lavinia had been looking forward to the drive to

Noordwijk, for she had quickly gathered that Radmer had no intention of allowing her to infringe upon his work, and somehow he seemed to have very little leisure. It was obvious to her now that their two evenings out together had been in the nature of a sop to her acceptance without fuss of his plans for their wedding, and yet she had thought on the previous evening, while they had been dancing, that he was enjoying her company.

Wishful thinking, she told herself, drank the rest of her coffee, fed the toast to the birds on the balcony so that Mevrouw Pette would think that she had made a good breakfast, and got up. She would have to do something to take her mind off her problems, just for a little while. She didn't know how to handle the situation and panicking about it wouldn't help. One thing was certain; the quicker she got herself used to the manner of living Radmer expected of her, the better; she would have to learn to fill her days for herself and never take the sharing of his leisure for granted. She had the two girls, of course, and naturally there would be evenings out with his friends and family and some entertaining at home as well, when they would be together, but any vague hope which she had cherished that they might sometimes slip off together just for the sheer pleasure of each other's company could be scotched.

She dressed rapidly, snatched up her handbag and her lesson books, and after a short conversation with Mevrouw Pette, left the house. Her Dutch lesson would take care of the next hour and after that, she told herself, with a touch of defiance, she would go shopping.

Juffrouw de Waal was sharp with her; not only did she not know her lessons, she was decidedly distraite. She was sent on her way at the end of the hour, with a stern recommendation to apply herself to her Dutch verbs, and by way of penance, write a short essay on any subject she wished—in Dutch, of course. She agreed meekly to her teacher's views on her shortcomings, rather to that lady's surprise, and went out into the sunny streets. Five minutes' walk brought her to the shops and here she slowed her pace until her eye was caught by the sight of an extremely exclusive hair dressing salon. She went inside on an impulse and luckily for her the exquisite damsel at the reception desk felt sure that someone could be found to attend to her immediately and when she was asked to give her name, the damsel murmured: 'Oh, Mevrouw ter Bavinck,' rather as though she had introduced herself as the Queen of the Netherlands, and before she knew where she was, she had been whisked away to be attended by the proprietor himself, Monsieur Henri, who talked a great deal about the ter Bavinck family in a tone of reverence which greatly astonished her.

She emerged an hour later, considerably poorer, with her hair transformed from its usual simple style to an artless coiffure which looked simple but wasn't. Such a transformation deserved a new outfit; she spent a delightful half hour in La Bonneterie, emerging presently with a splendid collection of boxes and parcels, so that she was forced to get a taxi back to the house. Besides, she was very late for lunch, for it was long past one o'clock and she had told Mevrouw Pette that she would be back well before half past twelve.

The taxi driver was so kind as to carry her packages up to the door; Lavinia gathered them up in both arms, opened it with some difficulty and went inside.

Radmer was standing at his open study door, and at the expression on his face she faltered a little on her way across the hall. He looked tired; he looked furiously angry as well. She made for one of the marble-topped console tables in order to shed her purchases and he came to meet her, taking them from her and laying them down carefully, and when she stole another look at him, he didn't look angry at all, only tired.

He said blandly: 'I had expected you to be still in bed, sleeping off last night's exertions.' He smiled faintly. 'Have you had lunch?'

She flushed. 'No. I—I was shopping and I didn't notice the time.' They entered the dining-room together and Bep, by some well-managed miracle, was already there, waiting to serve the soup. 'I didn't expect you to come home,' she went on coldly. 'From your note...'

He stared at her across the table. After a pause he said merely: 'I hope you had a good morning's shopping?'

She took a good drink of wine and felt it warm

her cold inside. 'Yes, thank you. I spent a great deal of money.'

He was still staring at her and there was a gleam of amusement in his eyes now, although she didn't see it. Surely he would say something about her hair? It had looked quite different at the hairdressers, but all he said was: 'I'm sure you will have spent it to advantage. I'm sorry that pretty dress was ruined.'

'Oh, it's not ruined,' she told him earnestly. 'I'll have it cleaned and I can mend the tear quite easily. I'll send your dinner jacket to the cleaners too and see if they'll repair that tear in the leg...'

He answered her seriously although the gleam was decidedly more pronounced. 'Oh, I don't think I should bother about that—I've more than one suit, I believe, and why not buy another dress instead of—er—patching up the torn one?' He leaned over to re-fill her glass. 'If you need any more money, just say so.'

Was he annoyed because she had spent so much that morning? She went rather pink and said gruffly: 'I've a great deal of money left, thank you.'

He nodded rather vaguely and she asked him how the farmer and his wife were, and then, desperate for a nice neutral subject, enlarged on the weather. It was almost a relief when he said that he would have to be getting back to the hospital.

'I'll bring the girls back in good time,' he told her, and was gone before she had time to frame a careful request to go with him. Left alone, she reflected

that perhaps it was a good thing that she had had
no chance to say anything, for if he had wanted her
to go with him, surely he would have said so. She
wandered out of the dining-room and upstairs to her
room, where her shopping had been laid out for her.
It should have been great fun trying on the pretty
things she had bought, but it wasn't; if Radmer was
indifferent enough not to notice that her waist-length
hair, instead of being pinned in a neat topknot, had
been swathed round her head and the strands twisted
and crossed high in front and pinned by a handsome tortoiseshell comb, he certainly wouldn't notice what clothes she wore. She took a close look at
her reflection now and wondered if she would ever
be able to dress her hair herself—probably not, but
at least she would leave it as it was until Sibendina
and Peta came home to admire it; she would wear
one of her new dresses too. She decided on a silver
grey silk jersey smock with an important colour
and very full sleeves caught into deep cuffs. It was
floor-length and she considered that it was exactly
the sort of garment a stepmother might be expected
to wear. Studying it in the mirror, she came to the
erroneous conclusion that it added dignity to her appearance and made her look much older. In fact, it
did nothing of the sort—indeed, she looked younger
if anything, and positively pretty.

She got back into a cotton dress finally and took
the dogs out into the park. The lovely summer day
had become a little overcast and as she turned for
home with Dong and Pobble at her heels, she could

see black clouds massing over the rooftops. There was going to be a storm, and she hated them; it wouldn't be quite so bad if she were back home with Mevrouw Pette and Bep in the kitchen. She put the dogs on their leads and hurried. They gained the porch, very out of breath as the first slow drops of rain fell.

Lavinia had her solitary tea sitting with her back to the enormous windows, and tried not to flinch at each flash of lightning, and the dogs, quite as cowardly as she, pressed themselves close to her. But presently the storm blew over, leaving a downpour of rain, and she got out her lesson books and applied herself to her homework until it was time to go and change her dress. She took a long time over this; even so, there was still plenty of time before Radmer and the girls would arrive. She filled it in by inspecting the table in the dining-room. While she was there Mevrouw Pette came in, and together they admired the stiffly starched linen, the polished silver and sparkling glass. Between them they had concocted a festive menu too, and Lavinia, glad to have something to do, accompanied the housekeeper back to the kitchen to sample the delicacies prepared in honour of the girls' homecoming.

It was pleasant in the kitchen, warm and fragrant with the smell of cooking, and the copper pans on the wall glowed cosily and it was nice when its occupants complimented her upon her appearance, even Ton, who came in each day to help, a good hard-working girl but hardly talkative, managed to tell her that she looked pretty. Lavinia went back upstairs sparkling with their praise, and the sparkle was still there a few minutes later when the front door was flung open and hurrying feet across the hall heralded the family's return. The girls came in together, calling 'Lavinia!' at the tops of their voices, to stop and stare at her waiting for them in the centre of the drawing-room. 'Gosh, you look absolutely gorgeous!' cried Peta. 'You've done something to your hair, and look at that wizard dress…'

'Why, you're pretty,' declared Sibby with the candour of youth. 'You always are,' she added hastily, 'but you know what I mean.'

The pair of them fell upon her, hugging and kissing her in a fashion to warm her heart although she cried laughingly: 'Oh, darlings, do take care of my hair!'

They let her go then, still holding her hands, turning and twisting her from side to side, admiring every aspect of her person, talking and giggling until Sibby cried: 'Papa, doesn't Lavinia look absolutely super? No wonder you wanted to marry her—and don't you just love the way her hair is done?'

Lavinia hadn't known that he was in the room. She said too quickly: 'Dinner's all ready—hadn't you two better go upstairs and wash your hands?' She smiled rather blindly at them and then turned round to face him. 'I do hope you had a pleasant drive and that your parents are well,' she observed cheerfully; she sounded like a hostess, anxious to please, and the two girls exchanged puzzled glances as they went from the room.

He poured their drinks with a brief: 'Yes, thanks,' but when he brought her glass over, he remarked ruefully: 'I should have said something about the hair, shouldn't I? I'm sorry, I did notice it, you know. I told you that I had become clumsy with women, didn't I? Please forgive me. And your dress is very pretty.'

Lavinia thanked him quietly and took a heartening sip of her sherry; she felt that she needed it. Perhaps when the girls had gone to bed, she should have a talk with him; try and get back on to the old friendly footing which somehow they had lost. On the other hand, he was probably tired and the awkwardness she felt between them was due to that. She finished her sherry and asked for another, and when he handed it to her he said with a twinkle: 'Dutchman's courage, Lavinia?'

Of course he thought that she was nervous because the girls had come back; quite likely he imagined that she had dressed up and had her hair done with the same reason in mind. She smiled at him and lied cheerfully: 'Yes, I think I need it—I'm nervous, isn't it silly? though I'll get over it. It's lovely to have them here, isn't it?'

Radmer's voice was bland. 'Delightful,' he agreed, and added lightly: 'And such a weight off my shoulders, I shall be able to catch up on my reading without feeling guilty of leaving Sibendina alone.' He put down his glass. 'How do you like the idea of

Peta having Dutch lessons with Juffrouw de Waal?
Not with you, of course, and I thought it might be
a good idea if she had lessons in Dutch history and
geography, and as soon as she has a smattering of
Dutch, she could go to Sibby's school—I'm sure
they will take her. Do you suppose she would like
that?'

Lavinia lifted a grateful face to him. 'Oh, Radmer, how kind you are—I'm sure she'll love it. Have
you asked her?'

He looked surprised. 'Well, no—I hadn't spoken
to you about it, my dear.'

She wished most fervently that she was his dear.
'Is there anything I can do to save your time?' she
asked, and when he shook his head, she repeated:
'You've been more than kind,' and then before she
could stop herself because the sherry was doing its
work: 'Why didn't you want me to go with you to
Noordwijk?'

He was standing close to her, watching her. Now
he frowned. 'I'm not sure,' he told her. 'I...' Whatever he had been about to say was cut short by the
entry of the two girls and they all went in to dinner.

The meal was a gay one, with a great deal of
laughing and talking, and if Lavinia was a little quieter than the others, no one seemed to notice. They
made plans later, sitting in the drawing-room while
Lavinia poured the coffee, and Peta immediately
professed the greatest satisfaction with the plan for
her to have lessons with Juffrouw de Waal; she was
to join Sibby's tennis club too, and go swimming

whenever she wished, and when Radmer disclosed his plans for sending her to Sibby's school just as soon as she had mastered a little Dutch, she was in transports of delight.

'And now what about going to bed?' he wanted to know, cutting her thanks short. 'Sibby has to go to school in the morning and I suggest that you go with Lavinia, Peta, and meet Juffrouw de Waal.'

They said good night, embracing Lavinia first and then going to kiss Radmer. It was Peta who observed bracingly: 'You mustn't be shy about kissing Lavinia, you know, while we're here—we shan't mind at all.' She continued reflectively: 'You didn't when we came home this evening.'

It was Sibendina who unconsciously saved the situation by remarking: 'Well, they're only just married, you know, I expect they like to be alone. Don't you, Papa?'

'Oh, decidedly,' agreed the professor mildly. 'And now bed, my dears.'

They went, giggling and talking still, up the stairs, and when their voices could no longer be heard, Lavinia got up too. 'Well, I think I'll go to bed as well,' she told him. 'I daresay you want the house quiet so that you can read in peace.'

'Good lord, did I say that?' he asked her, and when she laughed, 'You're a very nice girl, Lavinia.' He walked to the door with her and opened it, but when she made to pass him, he put out a sudden hand and caught her by the shoulder.

'We're quite alone,' he said lightly. 'We'd better do as Sibby suggested.'

He bent to kiss her, a brief salute on one cheek, and then to her utter surprise, a quite rough kiss on her mouth. He let her go at once and she flew away, up the staircase and into her room before she really knew what she was doing. Undressing, she told herself that she had behaved in the stupidest fashion; like a silly schoolgirl. She should have made a graceful little joke about it, instead of tearing off in that way. He must think her a complete fool. She got into bed, determined that it wouldn't happen again; she would be careful to keep such incidents as light-hearted as possible, if ever they should occur again. She closed her eyes resolutely upon this resolve, although her last thought before she slept was that being kissed in that fashion was decidedly interesting, even if he had intended it as a joke.

Chapter 8

It was a simple matter to slip into the well-ordered way of living which Radmer's household enjoyed. Lavinia, aided by the kindly Mevrouw Pette, took upon herself those household tasks which the housekeeper considered were suitable for the lady of the house, although in actual fact they took up very little of her time, but she worked for hours over her Dutch lessons and she was always home when the girls got back at lunchtime, and never failed to be sitting by the tea tray when they came home in the afternoon. Of Radmer she saw very little. True, they breakfasted together, but then so did the girls, and conversation, such as it was, was general. He was always the first to leave the table, and perhaps because of what Peta had said, he never neglected to come round the table and bend to kiss her cheek, and if Sibby and Peta were with her when he got back in the evenings, he repeated this, while she, for her part, greeted him with a welcoming smile and a few wifely inquiries as to how his day had gone. Very rarely he came home for lunch, although he never went out in the evenings, retiring after a decent interval to his study, so that before very long Lavinia was forced to the conclusion that he was avoiding her as often as he could.

On one or two occasions they had dined out with friends and they all paid regular visits to Noordwijk, but the opportunity to talk to him, even get to know him better, was non-existent. And yet, on the rare occasions when they were together, he appeared to take pleasure in her being with him, and from every other aspect she supposed that their marriage was a success, for Sibby was deeply fond of her already and even though she regarded her more as an elder sister than a stepmother, she confided in her to an extent which proved how much in need she had been for an older and wiser head with which to share her youthful problems.

Peta was happy too. Lavinia had never seen her so carefree and content, treating Radmer like a big brother and yet quite obviously regarding him as the head of the household to be obeyed, as well as the one to go to when in trouble.

The house had taken on a new air, too. It had always been beautifully managed by Mevrouw Pette, but now Lavinia was slowly setting her own mark upon it; arranging great bowls of flowers in every room, bearing home baskets of plants from the flower market and bedding them in great masses of colour in the small garden. She had taken over the conservatory too, buying new lounge chairs and a hammock seat which was the delight of the girls, and attending with loving care to a vine she had

planted there. She did these things gradually and
by the end of a month she had made a niche for herself, so that, while not absolutely essential to the life
of the house, she certainly contributed to its well-
being. Her Dutch was making strides too, and now
that Peta was having many more lessons than she
herself was, it was an incentive to work even harder
at her books. And as for Radmer, he seemed content
enough and at week-ends at least, quite prepared to
take them out and about, but there had been no more
tête-à-tête dinners, and as the days slipped by, Lavinia resigned herself to the fact that there probably
never would be again.

They were to go to Friesland for a short holiday
in August; the professor had a yacht which he kept
at Sneek and they would go sailing for a good deal of
the time, as well as touring Friesland. Lavinia, col-
lecting a suitable wardrobe with the help of Sibby,
who knew all about life on board a boat, hoped that
she would quickly pick up all the salient points about
sailing. She had mentioned, rather diffidently, that
she didn't know one end of a boat from the other,
but Radmer had only laughed and told her that she
would soon learn.

They set off one Saturday, in a brilliant morning
which promised to become hot later in the day, and
drove straight to the ter Bavinck estate, where Juffrouw Hengsma was waiting for them, and this time
Lavinia was able to address her in Dutch, which
pleased her mightily and made Radmer laugh.

'You are making progress, Lavinia,' he observed.

'Now you must learn the Friesian language, because Juffrouw Hengsma prefers to speak that.' He had spoken to her in Dutch too, to her secret delight, and she answered him haltingly in that tongue, feeling that sharing his language was a small link between them.

They had coffee together before they went to their rooms to unpack and then meet again to wander round the house and grounds. Radmer ran a small stable and naturally enough they spent a good deal of time there, and when he offered to teach Peta to ride, she flung her arms round his neck. 'You really are a darling!' she declared. 'I do hope there'll be someone like you for me when I grow up.'

He laughed gently at her and tweaked her ear. 'I'll make a point of finding just the right one,' he assured her. 'Sibby has already told me whom she intends marrying, so I'll only have you to worry about.'

He flung an arm round Sibby's shoulders. 'Sibby has made a very wise choice, too,' he added, and she grinned widely.

'I don't mind Lavinia and Peta knowing,' she told him, and tucked an arm into Lavinia's. 'He's a student at St Jorus, but I've known him for years, ever since I was a baby. Peta, who do you want to marry?'

'I've just said—someone like Radmer, and we'll have dozens of babies and they'll grow up very clever and be doctors...' She looked at Lavinia. 'Are you going to have some babies, Lavinia?'

Lavinia felt her cheeks redden, although she said

airily enough: 'There's certainly heaps of room for them, isn't there? And wouldn't this be a gorgeous place for their holidays? Did you like coming here when you were a little girl, Sibby?'

She only half listened to Sibby's reply. She was dreaming, just for a few delightful moments, of a carload of little boys, blue-eyed and flaxen-haired like their father, and a sprinkling of little girls, much prettier than their mother, tumbling around, laughing and shouting. She blinked the dream away and asked Radmer when he intended to go sailing.

The marvellous weather held. They spent long, lazy days swimming in the pool in one corner of the grounds, playing tennis on the court behind the house, or just sitting and doing nothing. Lavinia felt herself unwinding slowly so that she was able to think of the future, if not through rose-coloured spectacles, at least with a degree of optimism.

'I shall get fat,' she worried out loud as they lounged on the terrace after breakfast. 'I don't do anything...'

Radmer looked up from his newspaper and allowed his gaze to sweep over her. 'Never fat—curvaceous is the word, I believe. It suits you—besides, you're hardly idle; you swim and play tennis, and now you're not frightened any more on Juno, we shall have you galloping in all directions before we go back to Amsterdam.' He stood up slowly. 'I've some telephoning to do, then we'll drive over to Sneek and take a look at the yacht.'

She watched him go, her heart in her eyes, and in

turn she was watched by Peta and Sibby. When he had rounded the corner of the house Sibby spoke: 'You are happy, aren't you, Lavinia?' She sounded anxious, so that Lavinia said at once and warmly: 'Oh, my dear—yes. Why do you ask?'

It was Peta who joined in. 'We've noticed—you never kiss each other or—or hold hands, do you? Oh, I know Radmer pecks your cheek twice a day—I don't mean that—I mean...' she hesitated. 'Well, we expected you'd be... You act like good friends.'

'We are good friends, my dears,' said Lavinia steadily. 'There are lots of ways of loving people, you know, and perhaps you forget that your papa—Radmer—is a busy man. He comes home tired. Besides, his work is more important to him than anything else.' She looked across at Sibendina and smiled. 'That doesn't mean you, Sibby.'

And because the girls looked so unhappy still, she went on gaily: 'How about getting ready?' She looked down at her nicely tanned person. 'Ought I to wear slacks?'

They decided that she should and they all went upstairs, laughing together, so that Lavinia was quite reassured that Sibby's little outburst had been quite forgotten.

She was the last down, and she hadn't known that they would all be waiting for her in the hall. She had put on the pale blue denim slacks and an Indian cotton shirt which matched them exactly, and her hair she had brushed back, plaited into a waist-long rope and tied with a blue ribbon. She looked, she had considered, exactly right for a day's sailing.

It was therefore a little disconcerting to hear Sibby's cry of: 'Oh, smashing, Lavinia, and very sexy too—isn't she, Peta?'

'Oh, rather,' echoed Peta. 'Hey, Radmer, what do you think…?'

But Lavinia interrupted her, studying herself worriedly. 'But I thought it was exactly right…'

Radmer had been bending over the straps of the picnic basket, but he had straightened up to watch Lavinia come down the stairs. His blue eyes, very bright under their heavy lids, met hers. 'It's exactly right,' he told her, and his placid voice set her doubts at rest at once, so that, quite happy again, she skipped down the last stair or two, declaring that she must just have a word with Juffrouw Hengsma before they went. She was pleased that Radmer found her appearance quite normal, although a small, sneaking wish that he could have found her sexy too persisted at the back of her mind. She dispelled it sternly; of course he wouldn't, and come to think of it, she wasn't.

She felt that she had further proof of this when they got into the car, for Radmer suggested in the nicest possible way that Sibby might like to sit in front with him, which meant that Lavinia shared the back seat with Peta and the dogs. She listened to Sibby's happy chatter, and told herself it was foolish of her to feel hurt; Sibby had as much right to sit beside Radmer as she had—besides, it had seemed to her just lately that he had become somehow remote, retreating behind a friendly front which while pleasant enough, kept her at arms' length. Was he regretting their marriage already, and if he were, what had she done or not done to make him feel that way?

She made up her mind to discover what it was. Perhaps she had been spending too much? There had been clothes, more than she needed, she thought guiltily, and although Radmer invariably complimented her when she appeared in something new, he might be annoyed at her extravagance, and then there had been clothes for the girls, the new furniture for the conservatory, the flowers she delighted in buying, her lessons, Peta's lessons... He had told her not to worry about money, but she had no idea how much of it he had. She had better ask him at the first opportunity and have a sensible talk at the same time before the constraint between them had built itself up into an insurmountable barrier.

Having come to this decision, she sensibly decided to forget about it for the time being, and applied herself to the pleasant task of answering the girls' excited babble. An opportunity would present itself sooner or later, she felt sure.

Sooner, as it turned out. They had boarded the *Mimi* at Sneek, and Lavinia had been quite overcome by the size and comfort of her. Sibby had taken her and Peta on a tour of inspection while Radmer got the yacht ready to sail, and she had admired the cabins and the galley and all the mod cons which she had never expected to find. It was all simply lovely. She went back on deck and told him so, a little breathless with the excitement of it all, that the *Mimi* was the most marvellous boat she had ever thought to see, and he had thanked her gravely. 'And later on,' he had added, 'when we've had lunch, the girls can sunbathe and I'll give you your first lesson in sailing her.'

They had set sail then, using the *Mimi*'s engine to travel down the canal which took them to Sneckemeer, and once there, they had bowled along before a stiff breeze until the girls clamoured for their lunch, when they tied up to a small, broken-down jetty on the further bank of the lake and eaten their sandwiches and fruit. The younger members of the party had packed up afterwards while Lavinia was shown how to sail the yacht out into the lake again. She managed rather well; almost stammering with pleased surprise at herself, she cried: 'I did it—isn't it a marvellous feeling? May I carry on for a while?' She looked around her; there were plenty of other boats about, but none very near. 'I shan't bump into anything, shall I?'

Radmer was lounging beside her, apparently content to let her take the yacht where she wished. 'Not at the moment. Set a course for that clump of trees at the end of the lake; there's a canal close by which leads to a charming stretch of water.'

Peta and Sibby had stretched themselves out in the bows, lying on their stomachs, half asleep. There was only the gentle splash of water around them and the faint sounds from the shore mingling in with the bird cries. Very peaceful, thought Lavinia, and closed her eyes to enjoy it all better. But only for a second; she felt Radmer's hand clamp down on hers and his voice, half laughing, said: 'Hey, you can't sail a boat with your eyes shut!' His blue eyes surveyed hers. 'Would you like to sunbathe too?'

She was very conscious of his hand, still holding hers fast. 'No—no, I'd like to talk, if you don't mind.'

He was lighting his pipe, but he paused to look at her. 'Of course we can talk, dear girl. What about?'

She met his gaze bravely. 'You and me—us. It's a little awkward and I daresay I'll get a bit muddled, only if we don't talk about it now it'll only get worse.' She paused, but he said nothing, looking at her now with the faintest of smiles. 'You see, we were friends, weren't we? I mean before we married, and afterwards too, and I thought it was going to be all right—we both knew what it was going to be like, didn't we? Only it's not turning out… I thought we were getting on rather well; I tried to keep out of your way as much as I could—I still do, for you did tell me that your work was more important to you than anything else and I—I can understand that, and I can understand you not wanting to talk about your wife—you must have loved her very much, even if…so it's natural for you to…' She came to a stop, finding it much harder to explain than she had imagined it would be. 'I told you it would be muddled,' she said crabbily.

He had taken his hand away. Now he put it back

again in an absent-minded manner, but he said nothing, so that after a moment she felt forced to go on. 'I wondered if I'd been spending too much money...' and stopped at his laugh.

'Lavinia, did I not tell you not to worry about money? You could buy a dozen dresses at a time if you had a mind to do so. I think you have been very careful in your spending—and there is not the least need of that.'

She looked ahead of her. 'Are you very rich?' she asked.

'Very. You see, I have money of my own—I inherited it from my grandparents—a great deal of money, Lavinia, and besides that, I make a good living at my work.'

'Oh, well, it isn't that, is it?' She smiled at him with relief. 'That's one thing settled. So it must be your wife...'

He gave her a long searching look from under his heavy lids. 'Are you not my wife, my dear?'

She frowned at him. 'Yes, of course I am, but you know very well what I mean.' She rushed on, anxious to say what she intended as quickly as possible. 'You see, now we're married, perhaps you feel that I'm trying...that is, I do want you to understand that I'll never come between you and her.' Her voice became rather high and very earnest. 'I wouldn't want to anyway.'

'Shall we be quite blunt?' His voice was bland. 'What you are trying to say, in carefully muffled-up ladylike phrases, is that you have no wish to—er—

form a deeper relationship with me and that any fears I had on that score may be safely put at rest and we can be friends again. Is that not the gist of the matter? Well, Lavinia,' he spoke with deliberation, 'let me set your mind at rest; you could never come between me and Helga.'

Lavinia heard these words with a sinking heart. She had said what she had wanted to say, true enough, but his answer, which should have satisfied her, had only served to make her wish to burst into tears. But she did know where she stood now—any faint hopes she might have been cherishing that he might fall in love with her could be killed off once and for all. She let out a long sigh, quite unconscious of doing so, and slamming a mental lid down on the conversation exclaimed: 'Oh, look, we're almost at the end of the lake. Shall I hand over to you now?'

She was looking away from him as she spoke, studying the scenery with eyes which really saw none of it, so that she failed to see the expression on her companion's face.

Peta came to take her place soon afterwards and she went and lay down close to Sibendina, letting the sun warm her, although she felt that the coldness inside her would never go away again.

They had another few days of sailing before they returned to Amsterdam, and although Radmer treated her with an easy-going friendliness and consideration, Lavinia couldn't help but notice that he avoided being alone with her, so although she was sorry to leave the lovely old house and the simple pleasures of their holiday, she was relieved to be involved once more in the routine of their Amsterdam home. Sibendina was still on holiday, and although Peta went each day to Juffrouw de Waal, she was free for a good deal of the day. The three of them went out a good deal together, exploring the city, and in the evenings Radmer, putting aside his work for the time being, took them to the Concertgebouw, the Stadsschouwburg for the opera, and on a tour of the city's canals after dark. He was an excellent escort, she discovered, for he knew the city well and took pains to tell her as much about it as possible. They went to den Haag too, to dine out and visit the Koninklijke Schouwburg. The season was over, but although the ballet was finished, there were plays—in Dutch, which Radmer pointed out were very good for Lavinia and Peta.

They went to Delft, to watch the military tattoo. Lavinia had never been out so much in her life before, nor, for that matter, had she been able to indulge her taste in clothes to such an extent. She should have been very happy, and she tried hard to present a bright face to the world while she saw Radmer becoming increasingly remote—if only he wasn't so nice, she thought desperately, if only there was a good reason to have a quarrel—it might clear the air. But he remained kind, good-natured, and despite his preoccupation with his work, careful that she should want for nothing. All the same, they were almost never alone, and on the two occasions when the two girls had gone to bed, leaving them sitting together in the drawing-room, Radmer had excused himself within a very few minutes on the grounds of work to be done, and after that second time Lavinia had taken care to follow the girls upstairs, to sit lonely in her room with her unhappy thoughts.

It was a morning shortly after this, as she faced him across the breakfast table before the girls got down, that he said casually: 'I've ordered a Mini for you, Lavinia. I thought you might like a car of your own—you've proved yourself a good driver, so I don't need to worry on that score, but I'm afraid you will have to wait several weeks for it to be delivered.'

She had picked up the coffee pot, but now she set it down again. 'For me?' she asked. 'A car for me? How very kind of you, Radmer—thank you very much—how absolutely super! I'll have to get a licence, won't I?' She smiled with delight. 'I'll be able to visit your mother...'

He was buttering toast and didn't look at her. 'You get on well with her?'

'Oh, yes, we're already the best of friends. She calls here quite often, you know—when she comes to Amsterdam to shop. She's going to take me to Bergen-op-Zoom one day soon, to visit your sister.'

He frowned. 'Something I should have done already.'

She had picked up the coffee pot once more. 'Why should you? You're at St Jorus all day and almost every day,' she answered quietly. She smiled at him as she spoke and was astonished at the expression on his face—Rage? Exasperation? She wondered which; she had always supposed him to be an even-tempered man, but now suddenly she wasn't sure. The look had gone so quickly, though, that she was left wondering if she had imagined it, and his face was as bland as his voice. 'That is so, my dear—you don't object?'

She buttered a roll. 'You said once that I was a sensible girl and that my feet were planted firmly on the ground. They still are, Radmer.'

Their eyes met and he made an impatient gesture. 'Did I really say that?' he wanted to know, and added inexplicably: 'But in another world.'

An odd remark which she would have challenged if the girls hadn't come in at that moment.

It was Sibendina who remarked, after they had exchanged good mornings: 'You look awfully pleased with yourself, Lavinia. Has Papa given you a diamond coronet?'

'Oh, much nicer than that,' said Lavinia, stifling an ungrateful wish that his gift had indeed been some extravagant trifle to adorn her commonplace person. 'A car—a Mini.'

The two of them chorused their pleasure and Sibby wanted to know when she would have one too.

'When you're eighteen, *liefje*,' her father declared firmly. 'And Peta too, of course.'

This statement was met with cries of delight and a sudden surging of the pair of them from their places at table, to hug him. He bore their onslaught with fortitude, looking at Lavinia over their heads with a faintly mocking smile which caused her to pinken deeply; the difference between the girls' rapturous thanks and her own staid gratitude was only too well marked. Should she have leapt to her feet and rushed round the table and hugged him too? She wondered what he would have done if she had. She busied herself with the coffee cups and didn't look at him again, not until she raised startled eyes to his, when, Peta and Sibby once more settled in their chairs, he remarked: 'I've ordered another car too, though we shall have to wait a long time for it. It's the new Rolls-Royce—the Camargue.'

The girls burst into excited chatter, but he took no notice of them, looking down the table at Lavinia, her mouth a little open with surprise. 'You'll like that, Lavinia?'

'Like it?' she managed. 'It'll be out of this world! But won't it be too big?'

'Not a bit of it—just right for holidays with the four of us—besides, I take up a lot of room. You'll look nice sitting in a Rolls, my dear.' He got up from the table. 'I shall be late home this evening; I have to go to Utrecht to give a lecture. I'll leave there about six o'clock, I expect, and get here half an hour later.' He kissed Sibby good-bye and then Peta, and last of all Lavinia, a brief peck on her cheek. 'Unless, of course,' he added smoothly, 'I meet any old friends who want me to spend the evening with them.'

'Old friends?' Sibby giggled. 'Lady friends, Papa?'

'That's telling,' he grinned at her, and a moment later the front door closed behind him.

Lavinia had a busy day before her; her usual lesson with Juffrouw de Waal, some shopping to do for Sibby, who was going back to school the next day, and some books to buy for Peta's lessons. Besides, her mother-in-law was coming to have coffee with her and in the afternoon she had promised to go to the hospital to Zuster Smid's tea party, given in honour of Neeltje's birthday. She bustled around, seeing the girls off for a walk with the dogs, arranging lunch with Mevrouw Pette and arranging the flowers she had bought from the nice old man who came past the door each week with his barrow. She was running downstairs after tidying herself at the conclusion of these housewifely exertions, when Mevrouw ter Bavinck was admitted, and the two ladies went at once to the sitting-room, gossiping happily about nothing in particular, pleased to be in each other's company.

It was after they had been seated for ten minutes or so and the first cups of coffee had been drunk that Mevrouw ter Bavinck inquired: 'Well, Lavinia, how do you like being married to Radmer?'

Lavinia cast her companion a startled glance, wondering why on earth she should ask such a question. 'Very much,' she said at length.

'And has he told you about Helga?'

'No—I don't think he intends to.'

Her companion blinked at her. 'No? And do you not wish to know?'

'Very much, but I wouldn't dream of asking him.'

The older woman put her cup and saucer down

on the table beside her. 'Radmer has led a solitary
life for a good many years now, and it is all a long
time ago—all the same, I find it strange that he
hasn't explained...'

Lavinia stirred uncomfortably. 'Perhaps he can't
bear to talk about her—he must have loved her very
much.' She didn't look up. 'Oh, I know—at least
I heard at the hospital that she was—was rather
frivolous...'

She was cut short abruptly. 'Loved her?' questioned her mother-in-law. 'My dear child, after the
first few months he had no feeling for her at all.
She was quite unfitted to be his—any man's wife,
but because she was expecting Sibby by then, he
looked after her and to the outside world at least,
they were happily married. Perhaps Radmer thought
that when the baby was born, they might be able to
patch things up again, but it was actually worse. She
had not wanted Sibby in the first place, and once
she was born she was left to a nurse and Helga went
back to her own way of living, and although Radmer no longer loved her, he had Sibby to consider.
When Helga was killed—and I will leave him to tell
you about the accident—he told me that he would
never allow himself to love a woman again, and at
the time he meant it. Then you came along, my dear,
and everything was changed.'

She beamed at Lavinia, who smiled back with an
effort. As far as she could see, nothing was changed.
Radmer lived in a world of his own making, content
with it, too, not needing her or her love, only a sen-

sible young woman who would mother his daughter and order his household. She said now: 'That is very sad. What does Sibby think of it?'

'It was explained to her that her mother died in an accident when she was visiting a friend, and as she cannot remember her at all, it has never mattered to her very much. She loves her father very much, you will have seen that for yourself, and he has done his best to be father and mother to her, although I believe that you will make her an excellent mother, Lavinia—she loves you already, you know. The dear child goes back to school tomorrow, does she not?'

They talked of other things after that, and presently the elder lady went off to do her shopping and Lavinia was left to do her own small chores while she mulled over what her mother-in-law had told her. She would have to get used to the idea of Radmer not loving Helga, although that fact made it clearer than ever why he had chosen to marry herself. He must have felt quite safe in marrying her, knowing that he had not a spark of love for her. The idea of falling in love with her must have been so remote to him that it would have been laughable.

She did her shopping in a sour state of mind and for the first time found Sibby and Peta's chatter at lunch almost more than she could bear, but they went off arm-in-arm to play tennis at last, and Lavinia was able to indulge her desire to be alone and think. It was only a pity that after a few fruitless minutes she discovered that her rather woolly thoughts were of no value to her at all, and she had

no idea as to how she could charm Radmer into loving her. She gave up and took the dogs out.

Six o'clock came and went and there was no sign
of Radmer, an hour later the three of them sat down
to dinner, and Lavinia did her best to check the girls'
uneasiness. She was uneasy herself, but perhaps not
for the same reasons as they; she remembered only
too clearly what he had said about spending the evening with old friends, and he hadn't really denied
it when Sibby had teased him about going out with
a lady friend. Perhaps he had already arranged to
meet her. He talked cheerfully to her two companions while her imagination ran riot, providing her
with an image of some strikingly beautiful girl, superbly dressed and loaded with charm—the type
men fell for...

The evening passed emptily and at nine o'clock
the girls, at her suggestion, went to bed.

'I'll stay up,' she told them bracingly. 'Probably
your papa has met old friends after all, Sibby.'

'Then why didn't he telephone?' demanded his
daughter.

'Oh, darling, probably there wasn't a telephone
handy.' It was a silly remark; Radmer, if he had
wanted to telephone, would have found the means
of doing so. But it contented Sibby, who gave her
an affectionate kiss and went off to bed with Peta.

The bracket clock had chimed eleven o'clock in
its small silvery voice when Lavinia went down to
the kitchen. Bep had already gone to bed, Mevrouw
Pette was sitting at the table, knitting. He looked up

as Lavinia went in and said: 'The professor is late, Mevrouw.'

Lavinia answered in her careful, slow Dutch. 'Yes, I'll stay up, Mevrouw Pette, you go to bed. Perhaps you would leave some coffee ready?' She said good night and went back upstairs into the quiet room, where she sat down on one of the enormous sofas, a dog on either side of her. The house was still now, and the square outside was silent. She sat doing nothing, not thinking, watching the hands of the clock creep round its face. It was almost two o'clock when she fell asleep, still sitting bolt upright, the dogs' heads on her lap.

She wakened from an uneasy nap to hear the gentle click of the front door lock. Radmer was home. Lavinia's eyes flew to the clock's face; its delicately wrought hands stood at twenty minutes to three in the morning. She had been sitting there for simply hours. Rage and relief and love churned together inside her as she got off the sofa and erupted into one vast surge of feelings which manifested themselves in a cross, wifely voice. 'Where have you been?' she demanded in a loud whisper as she sped across the hall, quite forgetting that she had been weeping and that her face was puffy and stained with tears.

Radmer had given her a penetrating look as she spoke, not missing the tears or the sharp anxious voice on her white, tired face. If she had been nearer to him and the light had been brighter, she might have seen the sudden gleam in his eyes, very much at variance with his calm face.

He said now, as meekly as any husband would:
'I got held up, dear girl.'

Lavinia was so angry that she didn't wait for him
to continue. 'You've been spending the evening with
your old friends, I suppose,' she declared in a wasp-
ish whisper, 'not that I can blame you; you married me because I was sensible, not because I was
good company…' She drew a deep breath and went
on, anxious only to have her say, and not bothering about the consequences. 'Was she good fun, or
shouldn't I ask that?' She paused, gave a snort of
sheer temper and went on: 'I'm being vulgar, aren't
I? and I'm quite enjoying it! Just to say what I…' She
stopped, choked a little and went on in a quite different voice: 'I beg your pardon, Radmer, you look
very tired, though I don't suppose that matters to
you if you enjoyed yourself.' She wanted to giggle
and cry at the same time, and it cost her quite an
effort to say quietly: 'There's coffee in the kitchen,
shall I fetch you some?'

He shook his head. 'No, thank you. Go to bed,
Lavinia.' He spoke quietly and she knew that he was
angry. She turned on her heel without another word
and went upstairs to her room.

Chapter 9

Lavinia was late for breakfast, for after tossing and turning until the sky was light, she had fallen into a heavy sleep and wakened only when she had heard Sibby and Peta laughing and talking their way downstairs.

Radmer was reading his newspaper when she entered the dining-room, but he got up, wishing her good morning as he did so, pulled the bell-rope for more coffee, and sat himself down again. The girls greeted her with rather more animation, and then seeing her swollen eyelids and peaky face, demanded to know if she was feeling well. 'Not that I am surprised that you look as you do,' explained Sibby, 'for you must have been greatly upset when Papa came home and told you about the accident.'

'Accident? What accident?' Lavinia looked at them in turn, their faces expressing nothing but concern and astonishment. Radmer, invisible behind his paper, had apparently not been listening.

'But, Lavinia, you must have seen Papa when he came home...?'

'I dozed off in the drawing-room, I hadn't gone to bed. Radmer?'

The newspaper was lowered and his blue eyes, very calm, met hers. His bland: 'Yes, my dear?' was all that a wife could have wished for, but she almost snapped at him: 'You didn't tell me what happened? Were you hurt?'

'You were tired, Lavinia.' He smiled kindly. 'You shouldn't have stayed up for me, my dear.'

She wished irritably that he would stop calling her his dear when she wasn't anything of the sort. 'Yes—well, now I'd like to know.'

Before he could reply, Sibendina and Peta chorused together: 'There was a pile-up on the Utrecht motorway—it was on the news this morning, we heard it while we were dressing—and Papa stopped to help.'

'What a pair of gossips you are,' Radmer interpolated mildly. 'Suppose you go and get ready to go to school?'

They went, grumbling a little. Lavinia heard them going upstairs to their rooms, and when she could no longer hear their voices, she asked crossly: 'And why didn't you tell me? You let me say all those things about—about...you could have stopped me...'

'And then you wouldn't have said them,' he pointed out reasonably, 'only thought them to yourself. At least you have been honest.'

'I wasn't—I'm not.' Her voice, despite her best efforts to remain calm, had become a good deal higher. 'Anyone would suppose that you had done it deliberately so that I should say all the...' She stopped, because he wasn't looking at her, but over her shoulder, towards the door, and when she turned her head to look, there were the two girls, standing silently, watching them. She wondered if they had been there long.

But Radmer was smiling at them and he spoke easily, just as though they had been enjoying a pleasant conversation. 'I'll give you a lift,' he told them, 'and drop you off at the end of the street; Peta can walk round to Juffrouw de Waal from there.'

He wished Lavinia a cheerful *'Tot ziens'* and a few minutes later she heard the three of them leave the house, the two girls chattering happily. Probably, she told herself uneasily, they hadn't heard anything—Radmer would have seen them the moment they reached the door.

He came home at teatime—a great pity, for Lavinia, with the whole day in which to indulge in self-pity, was spoiling for a quarrel, but as he brought the girls with him, there was nothing she could do but turn a cool cheek to his equally cool kiss, inquire as to his day, and then join in the schoolgirl high spirits of Peta and Sibendina, both of whom had a great deal to say for themselves. They looked at her curiously once or twice, for in her efforts to be bright and gay, she only succeeded in talking much too much and laughing a great deal too often.

Nobody mentioned the traffic pile-up of the previous evening. Lavinia, who had struggled with little success to read about it in the newspapers, had actually started out to enlist Juffrouw de Waal's help in the matter, but on the point of doing so, she remembered that this was one of the days when Peta would be there with the teacher until teatime. And what would the pair of them think if she were to burst in, demanding to know about something which any husband, in normal circumstances, would have told his wife the moment he opened his own front door?

Presently the girls went away to do their homework together in the small sitting-room on the first floor, and as Radmer got up in his turn and started for the door, she said humbly: 'I did try to read the papers, and I was going to get Juffrouw de Waal to help me, but Peta was there—and your parents were away from home. There is no one else I can ask about last night, so please will you…? I'm sorry about last night.'

He came back at once and sat down opposite her. 'One is apt to forget that your Dutch is fragmental,' he observed in a faintly amused voice. 'There was a multiple crash—a tanker jack-knifed and caught a car as it was passing on the fast lane. The cars behind couldn't stop in time—there were thirty or so cars damaged, I believe.'

She asked impatiently: 'But you? What about you?'

He gave her a quick, hooded glance. 'There was a fair amount of first aid to be done,' he observed mildly.

'Couldn't you have telephoned?'

He smiled faintly at some private joke. 'No. There was a great deal to do.' And before she could speak again, he was on his way to the door again. 'And now I really must get those notes written up.'

Lavinia dressed defiantly and rather grandly for dinner that evening. Mijnheer de Wit and his wife were coming, and another surgeon whom she had met briefly at their wedding, and she had taken the precaution of inviting Sibby's student friend as well as a young cousin of Radmer's, still in his first year at Leiden medical school.

She was downstairs long before anyone else, wandering restlessly from room to room in her pink-patterned organza dress, the pearls clasped round her throat, her hair carefully coiled. She was giving the dining table a quite unnecessary inspection when Radmer looked in.

'Very nice,' he commented, and she wondered if he was referring to the table, the beautiful room, or her own person. She played safe. 'White linen always looks perfect,' she assured him earnestly, 'and I thought the pink roses would be just right with the silver and glass.'

He left the door and strolled across the room to where she was standing. He was in a dinner jacket and looked somehow taller and broader than ever. A few inches from her he stopped, half smiling 'I must admit,' he said suavely, 'that considering your low— your very low opinion of me as a husband, you have excelled yourself in the management of our home, and since I am now quite beyond the pale, I might, if I may mix my metaphors, as well be hanged for a sheep as a lamb.'

She felt herself held fast and pulled close by one great arm, while his other hand lifted her chin. He kissed her fiercely, and when she opened her mouth to speak, he kissed her again, but this time gently, still holding her tightly.

'You know,' he told her, 'I've been wanting to do that, and now that I have I feel much better.'

'Oh,' said Lavinia in a very small voice. 'Why?'

His smile mocked her. 'For all the wrong reasons, my dear.'

She hadn't known what he was going to say, but she had hoped for something else without realizing it, so that sudden tears pricked her eyelids and filled her throat. His arms had slackened a little. She tore herself away from him and rushed to the door, to collide with Peta and Sibby, on the point of coming in. Lavinia caught a glimpse of their surprised faces as she ran up the staircase.

She mustn't cry, she told herself in her bedroom. She dabbed her eyes, powdered her nose and drank some water, and then, with her chin well up, went downstairs again, where she joined the others in the sitting-room, making light conversation as though her life depended upon it, and not once looking at Radmer, or for that matter, speaking to him.

The evening should have been a failure, she had felt convinced that it would be, but it was nothing of the sort; dinner was superb, the talk lighthearted and never flagging, and the party, adjourning to the drawing-room afterwards, broke up only after its members had expressed themselves enchanted with their evening. Lavinia, standing on the top step out-side the front door, waving good-byes, felt no en-chantment, however. The evening for her had been endless; all she had wanted to do was to have gone somewhere quiet and had a good cry.

The girls went to bed almost at once, and paus-ing only to make sure that the dining-room had been set to rights, and plump up a few cushions in the drawing-room, Lavinia made haste to follow them, bidding Radmer a subdued good night as she went, not waiting to see if he had anything else to say to her but his own quiet good night.

She managed to avoid Radmer during the next few days, coming down to breakfast a little earlier than anyone else, so that she excused herself almost as soon as he got to the table, on the plea of having to see Mevrouw Pette about something or other, and if he came home for tea, there were the girls to act as an unconscious barrier between them, and as for the evenings, if he didn't go to his study, she engrossed herself in letter writing or grocery lists so that she wasn't called upon to take more than a desultory part in the conversation around her. She felt rather pleased with herself on the whole; she had remained pleasant and friendly, she considered, just as she always had been. Certainly there had been one or two small lapses; she preferred not to remember them. But she didn't know how pale she had become, causing her to look positively plain as well as sad, nor did she know how false her gaiety was and how stiff she was with Radmer.

It was a week after the dinner party when she came home from her Dutch lesson at lunch time to find a worried Mevrouw Pette, and because there was no one there to help them understand each other, it took her a few minutes to get the gist of what the housekeeper was saying.

'The girls,' said Mevrouw Pette, anxiously. 'They came home not half an hour ago, *mevrouw*, and they went to Sibendina's room and talked, and then they asked me for coffee, and when I asked if they couldn't wait until you came home at lunch time they said no, they had to go out. I gave them their coffee, *mevrouw*—I hope I did right?—and a little later, I came into the hall to fetch the tray and they were going out of the house, and they each had a case with them. They didn't see me, but I heard Sibendina talking about the train and the Zuidplein and the metro.' She broke off and cast a worried look at Lavinia. 'There is a shopping centre at the Zuidplein, *mevrouw*, but that is in Rotterdam—there is also a metro there.'

Lavinia had gone rather white. She hadn't followed Mevrouw Pette's speech easily and for the moment she was totally bewildered. 'Are you sure?' she asked. 'I mean, there are masses of shops in Amsterdam, why should they go there? I'll look in their rooms, perhaps they've left a note—they must have left something. Will you look downstairs?'

There were no notes, but some clothes had gone; night clothes, toilet things, undies. Lavinia raced downstairs again and telephoned the school. It had been one of the mornings when Peta went with Sibby to join her class. Neither of them would normally come home until lunch time. While she waited to be connected she remembered unhappily that Peta had asked her only the previous evening if she were happy, and when she had assured her that she was, her sister had said forcefully: 'Well, Sibby and I don't think you are—and Radmer isn't either.' She had run away to her room then, and Lavinia had thought it wiser to say nothing more about it. Now she wished that she had.

The authoritative voice which answered her query about the girls assured her that there had been no reason why they had left school early—indeed, no one, it seemed, had been aware of their absence. The voice, speaking very concise English, wanted to know if they were ill.

'No,' said Lavinia. 'I'll telephone you later, if I may.'

She went to her room then, found her handbag, stuffed some money into it, and without bothering to see if she were tidy enough to go out, went to find Mevrouw Pette. 'I'll go after them,' she explained to that good lady. 'I'll go to Rotterdam just in case they went there. Will you get a taxi for me? Perhaps they haven't gone there.'

'I heard them,' said Mevrouw Pette. 'Shall I tell the Professor?'

Lavinia shook her head. 'I'm not quite sure where he is, and he's got that very important post-mortem today. Besides, the girls may be back long before he comes home. If they are, don't let them go out again, Mevrouw Pette, and if I don't find them, I'll telephone you later.' She added hopefully: 'It's just a joke, I expect—how did they look? Did you see them laughing?'

Mevrouw Pette shook her head. 'They were very earnest.' She frowned. 'And you, *mevrouw*, you have had no lunch—I will fetch you some coffee.'

But Lavinia shook her head; she had wasted quite enough time already and she had no idea how frequently the trains ran to Rotterdam or how long they took over the forty-five-mile journey, and even when she got there, she still had to find Zuidplein.

She sat in the taxi, fretting, and when she reached the Central Station wasted a few precious minutes finding the ticket office and the right platform. She arrived on it to see the tail end of a Rotterdam-bound train disappearing from sight.

The trains ran frequently, though; she watched the outskirts of Amsterdam slide away and reviewed the situation, but somehow, because she was tired and frightened about the girls, her brain refused to function. She stared out of the window, seeing nothing of the view from it, her head quite empty.

At Rotterdam station she wandered around for a short time, trying out her Dutch without much success, until a kindly ticket collector pointed out the way to the metro and told her to get on it and stay there until it stopped at the end of its run—that would be Zuidplein, he explained carefully.

It was easy after that. She left the metro thankfully, but dismayed that it was more than two hours since she had left home, and for all she knew, she reminded herself, she had come on a wild goose chase.

She followed everyone else hurrying off the platform and disappearing through various exits, and after several false starts, went down a flight of stairs and pushed open the heavy doors at the bottom, to find herself in a vast hall, brightly lighted and noisy with the hum of a great many people all talking at once. It was lined with shops of every sort and size, and Lavinia started to walk towards the centre, appalled at the prospect of trying to find anyone in such a crowded place.

She turned her back on the big stores of Vroom and Dreesman, which took up the whole of one end of the enormous place, and began to revolve slowly, getting her bearings. She was two thirds of the way round when she saw Radmer standing a little way off, watching her.

She didn't know how her joy at seeing him there showed on her worried face. She ran towards him without a moment's hesitation, bumping into the shoppers milling around her as she went, and when she reached him, she clutched at his jacket rather in the manner of someone half drowned hanging on to a providential tree trunk.

'Radmer!' she babbled. 'How did you know? How did you get here so quickly? They're here somewhere; Mevrouw Pette heard them talking—I don't know why they had to come so far... I got on the first train I could—they couldn't have got here much before I did…well,' she paused and added worriedly: 'It must be hours by now. Radmer…' She stopped to gulp back all the terrifying thoughts she longed to voice.

He had her hands in his, nice and firm and secure, and although he looked grave, he smiled a little at her. 'How fortunate that I should have gone home early—I wanted to talk to you. Mevrouw Pette told me what had happened and I drove down; I had just got there when I saw you. And don't worry, Lavinia, it shouldn't be too difficult to find them if they're here.' His voice was comfortably matter-of-fact as he tucked an arm in hers and went on calmly: 'I think our best plan will be to walk right round this place, not too fast, just in the hope of meeting them. If we have no luck, we'll think of what is to be done.'

It took them almost an hour, for there were lanes of shops leading from the centre hall, and these led in turn to other lanes. There was even a market, packed with shoppers, and any number of snack bars and cafés. At any other time, with nothing on her mind, Lavinia would have found it all rather fun and enjoyed exploring the shops; now, looking in all directions at once, she hardly saw them.

Back where they had started from, Radmer said easily: 'Now, supposing we go round once more, but this time we'll look in every shop.' He smiled down at her. 'We can ask in all the most likely ones if anyone has seen them—you must tell me what they were wearing. Are you tired, Lavinia?'

She was, but she shook her head. She had hardly

spoken as they had walked round, but now she said in a polite little voice: 'No, not in the least, thank you. Where shall we start?'

He took her arm again. 'What about Hema?' he asked. 'Isn't that the sort of shop they would enjoy looking round?' He started across the shopping centre, skirting the small, circular boutiques, chic confectioners and knick-knack shops which occupied its hub. They were almost across it when she felt his fingers tighten on her arm. 'There they are!' his voice was quiet, but she could hear the relief in it. 'Over there, in that teashop.'

It was another circular structure, glass and wood, with a tiny terrace built around it, its interior brilliantly lighted. Lavinia could see Sibby and Peta, their two heads close together over a table in the window, deep in conversation. Even at that distance she saw that although they were in earnest conversation, they didn't look dejected.

Radmer was walking her briskly towards the teashop. At its door he said calmly: 'Go and join them, my dear, I'll bring you a cup of tea.' His eyes met hers briefly and he smiled as she made her way through the crowded little place and sat down opposite Sibby. She was quite unprepared for her: 'Oh, good we've been praying ever so hard that you'd come,' and Peta chimed in with: 'Did Radmer come after you, Lavinia?'

She nodded, not daring to speak, for if she had done so, she would have burst into tears and spoilt her image of stepmother and elder sister for ever.

Fortunately Radmer joined them then, sitting down beside Sibby and facing her.

'I'm glad we found you,' he observed in a cheerful voice, and Sibendina said at once: 'So are we, Papa. We were just wondering what we should do next—we counted on you coming after us; at least, we guessed Lavinia would, and if you came after her…it was a gamble.'

'Why did you run away, my dears?' His voice was placid with no hint of anger.

Peta answered him. 'It seemed a good idea. We didn't do it on the spur of the moment, you know; we talked about it for days. We had a reason, didn't we, Sibby?' She paused, but he made no effort to prompt her, instead he put milk and sugar in Lavinia's cup and put it into her hands.

'Drink up, dear girl,' he urged her, and she drank obediently, swallowing her tears with the tea, still not daring to trust her voice.

'It isn't our business,' began Peta awkwardly, and looked at Radmer to see if he was going to agree with her, but all he did was to smile faintly, so that she felt encouraged to go on. 'Sibby and I—we thought that if we did something really drastic, like almost drowning, or being knocked down by a car or running away, you would both have to help each other and it would make you fond of each other, because you love Sibby and Lavinia loves me, and that would make you understand each other and share the same feelings…' She looked at him anxiously. 'Perhaps that's not very clear?'

'On the contrary, I get your point very clearly.' He had stretched out a hand and taken Lavinia's small clenched fist in his, but he hadn't looked at her.

'We decided we'd run away,' said Sibby, taking up the tale, 'because we both swim too well to drown easily, and to walk in front of a car—just like that—' she waved an expressive hand, 'we found that we were unable to do that—besides, we might have been killed instead of just a little wounded and then our idea would have been wasted. So we ran away, and if you had not come after us we would have known that you did not love each other.' She beamed at them both. 'I explain badly, but you must agree that it was a good idea.'

Lavinia found her voice then, a little gruff but quite steady. 'But, my dears, supposing we hadn't found you in this crowd of people? Whatever would I do without you both?'

Sibby said softly: 'It would have been OK. You have Papa, you belong…'

Lavinia clenched her hands tightly so that the knuckles showed white. For a few moments she forgot where she was, she forgot, too, her well-ordered upbringing which had taught her so painstakingly never to display her feelings in public and always to speak in a well-modulated voice. She said loudly and rather fast: 'You're wrong, I don't belong. It's your papa who belongs—to his work and your mother— or her memory. He—he…' She stopped, appalled at her words, to look at their faces, Sibby and Peta expectant and inquiring, Radmer, daring to lounge in his chair like that and actually smiling... She glared at him, muttering, snatched up her handbag, pushed her stool violently away and made for the kiosk's second door. She had no idea where she was going and she really didn't care. She hurried blindly ahead, quite unaware that Radmer was right behind her.

The two girls watched their progress with interest until Sibby said: 'It has worked, Peta, I do believe it has! In a few minutes they will have what you call a showdown, although I cannot think that this is a very good place.' She looked around her. 'There is no romance here.' She shrugged her shoulders and grinned at Peta. 'They will be back, but not yet—we have time for one of those delicious ices—the one with the nuts and chocolate.'

They went arm-in-arm to the counter to give their order.

Lavinia walked very fast through the throng of shoppers, colliding with one or other of them continuously and apologizing carefully in English each time she did it. She wanted to lose herself as quickly as possible, although common sense was already asking the nagging question where she should go and what would she do when she got there. And what would happen to the girls? Of Radmer she refused to think. She shut her eyes for an instant on the memory of his smile and bumped into a stout matron with a shopping basket. She was close to Vroom and Dreesman now, so she plunged into the mass of people thronging its open shop front, and allowed herself to be pushed and shoved from one counter to the other, getting lightning glimpses of watches, gloves, tights and costume jewellery. She managed to stop here, and stood staring at the bead necklaces and bangles and diamanté brooches until the salesgirl looked at her inquiringly, so that she felt she should walk on, into a corner this time where there was a circular stand with a display of scarves on it. For the moment there was no one there, so she stood forlornly, staring at the bright silky things, her mind quite empty.

'Darling,' said the professor very quietly in her ear, and clamped a hand on to her shoulder. Lavinia cried 'Oh!' so loudly that a smartly dressed woman who had paused to finger the scarves gave her a sharp look and moved away.

'I don't think that this is the ideal spot for a man to tell his wife that he loves her...'

She choked on a sob and then said woodenly, addressing the merchandise before her: 'But you don't...'

She was swivelled round in gentle hands and held fast, so that all she could see was a portion of waistcoat and the glimpse of a white silk shirt. She muttered into it: 'You told me, you know you told me—that I could never come between you and Helga.'

A finger tilted her chin so that she was forced to look into his face, and the expression on it made her catch her breath. 'Oh, yes, I said that, and it was true, you know—for how could you come between me and someone who is no longer there—has not

been there for very many years? Helga means nothing to me, my darling—nor did she for the greater
part of our life together. One day I'll tell you about
that, but not now. We have other, more important
things to talk of.'

She stared up into his calm, assured face. 'But
when we married—no, before that, when you asked
me to marry you—you told me that you didn't love
me. You said you wanted a friendly relationship,
you said...'

He kissed her to a halt. 'Quite right. What a fool
a man can be, for even then the idea of not marrying you was quite insupportable, even though I pretended to myself that I was going to marry you for
a number of very sensible reasons. And my darling,
you were so very careful to let me know as often as
possible that you wanted it that way, too. But that
night at the farm, when I saw you standing at the
bottom of the stairs, waiting for me in the smoke, I
had to admit to myself that I loved you too much to
go on as we had intended—either I would have to
tell you that or keep out of your way.'

'You made me drive the Bentley,' she reminded
him, following her own train of thought, 'and I was
terrified, and when you came to that house you were
quite beastly.'

He pulled her closer so that a young woman with
a pushchair could pass them. 'My darling, I wanted
to wring your neck and take you in my arms and
tell you how wonderful you were and how you were
driving me slowly mad.'

She said idiotically: 'I bought those dresses and had my hair done...'

'And I wanted to tell you that you were the most beautiful girl in the world, but I was afraid to in case I frightened you away.' He bent to kiss her. 'I never thought to love like this,' he told her. 'Nothing means anything any more if you aren't with me.' He paused and smiled at a massive woman in Zeeuwse costume who was edging past them. 'The other night, when I came home late and I knew that you loved me...'

'I never said a word!'

'You said a great many words. You were very cross, my darling.'

'I was angry because I was frightened.'

'I know.' He kissed her again, not minding in the least that a small boy and two girls had stopped to watch them.

Lavinia caught their fascinated eyes and went pink. 'Don't think I don't like being kissed, Radmer darling, but isn't it rather public?'

He looked around him. 'You are probably right, my love. Let us go back to Sibby and Peta, who are probably congratulating each other and making themselves sick on ice-cream.'

'Well, they did what they set out to do; I mean, running away like that, it did make us come together.'

They began to walk, not hurrying in the least, back to the teashop.

'Why do you suppose I came home early?' asked Radmer.

'I don't know—tell me.'

'Because I couldn't go on any longer as we were. I was going to ask you if you could forgive me for being so blind, and start all over again.'

She stopped to smile at him. 'Oh, yes, please, Radmer,' and she looked away quickly from his eyes. 'Oh, look, there are the girls, watching.'

They both waved, and Radmer said: 'I once said that you were a girl who would never reach for the moon, dearest Lavinia, but you will have no need to do that, for I intend to give it to you—I'll throw in the sun and the stars for good measure.'

'How nice,' said Lavinia, 'but I'd just as soon have you, my darling.'

* * * * *

Special excerpt from

⟨H⟩ HARLEQUIN® SPECIAL EDITION

Read on for a sneak preview of
The Maverick's Baby-in-Waiting
by Melissa Senate, part of the
Montana Mavericks:
The Lonelyhearts Ranch series!

"Have you picked out a name for the baby?"

Twenty-six-year-old Mikayla Brown looked from the display of baby photos on the wall of the Rust Creek Falls Clinic, where she was waiting for her ob-gyn appointment, to her friend Amy Wainwright. Names? Oh, yeah, she had names. Mikayla's life might be entirely up in the air at the moment, but names were easy. Late at night, when she lay in bed, unable at this point—seven months along—to get all that comfortable, she'd picture herself sitting in the rocking chair on the farmhouse porch with a baby in her arms and she'd try out all her name ideas on the little one.

Problem was, she had too many possibilities. "I have six if it's a girl," she told Amy. "Seven if it's a boy. And ten or so more I'm thinking of for middle names. Can I give my child four names?"

Amy laughed. "Sure, why not? You're the mama."

Mikayla shivered just slightly. The mama. Her. Mikayla Brown. She barely had her own life together these days, and soon she'd be solely responsible for another life—a tiny, helpless little one with no one to depend on but her.

Hey, you in there, she directed to her stomach. *Are you a Hazel? A George?* Mikayla loved the idea of honoring her late parents, who'd always been so loving and kind. Or her maternal grandparents, also long gone—Leigh and Clinton, who'd sent birthday and Christmas cards without fail but had moved to Florida when Mikayla was young. Then there was her dear aunt Elizabeth, her mother's sister, who went by Lizzie, and her hilarious uncle Tyler, and their one-of-a-kind son, Brent, Mikayla's cousin. Brent was the one who'd suggested Mikayla move up to Montana—to Rust Creek Falls—for a fresh start. Which was how Brent's name had ended up on the possibilities list. She owed him big.

Moving to this tiny town in the Montana wilderness had sounded crazy at first. Population five hundred something? More than a half hour's drive from the nearest hospital—when she was now seven months pregnant? No family or friends?

You'll make friends, Brent had assured her. *Sunshine Farm will feel like home.*

Brent had been right. Mikayla had been a little worried that she'd get the side eye or pity glances from the town's residents. Pregnant and alone. But from the moment she'd arrived at Sunshine Farm three weeks ago and met the owner, Brent's friend Luke Stockton, she'd been invited to Luke and his fiancée's joint bachelor and bachelorette party held that very day. Since the recent wedding, she'd become good friends with Luke's wife, Eva, and Amy, who'd also lived at Sunshine Farm at the time.

Now Amy was engaged, with a gorgeous, sparkling diamond ring on her finger. Mikayla sighed inwardly while ogling the rock. She'd fantasized like a bridezilla in training about a ring on her own finger and a fairy-tale wedding. Hell, even a city hall wedding would have been fine. But all that was before she'd caught her baby's father having sex with his paralegal in his law firm office.

A door opened, and a woman with a baby bump exited, followed by a man carrying a pamphlet. *Your Second Trimester.* Both their gold wedding rings shone in the room. Or maybe Mikayla's gaze just beelined to rings on fingers these days.

A nurse appeared at the door and smiled at Mikayla. "Mikayla Brown? Dr. Strickland is ready to see you now."

Mikayla and Amy stood and followed the nurse into the examination room. Mikayla sat on the paper-covered table and Amy on the chair in the corner. The nurse took Mikayla's vitals, handed her a paper gown to change into, then let them know Dr. Strickland would be in shortly.

"You're the absolute best, Amy," Mikayla said, her voice a little clogged with emotion, when the door closed behind the nurse. She quickly shimmied out of her maternity sundress and into the gown, Amy tying the back for her. "Thank you for coming with me today." It meant a lot not to come alone. Her ex had accompanied her to her first appointment back in Cheyenne when she'd discovered she was pregnant, but he had made it clear he didn't want a baby, wasn't ready for a baby and wasn't sure of anything. He'd added that he was a man of deep principles, a "crusading" attorney (read: litigator for a major corporation) and wouldn't leave Mikayla, "of course." Apparently he'd been cheating even before she told him she was pregnant. *I have strong feelings for you, Mik, but I am who I am, and I'm not ready for any of this. Sorry.*

Who needed a lying, cheating, no-good rat sitting in the corner chair?

"That is what friends are for, my dear," Amy said, flicking her long auburn hair behind her shoulder. "And honestly? I might have ulterior motives of finding out what goes on at these appointments. One day I hope to be sitting exactly where you are. Okay, maybe no woman loves putting her bare feet into those metal stirrups…"

Mikayla laughed. Amy would make an amazing mother.

And so would she. Mikayla had had to give herself a few too many pep talks over the past several months, that she could do this, that she *would* do this—and well.

There was a gentle knock on the door and a tall, attractive man wearing a white lab coat entered the room with her chart and a warm smile. He introduced himself as Dr. Drew Strickland, an ob-gyn on temporary assignment here from Thunder Canyon, but he let Mikayla know he would absolutely be here through her delivery.

Fifteen minutes later, assured all was progressing

as it should with the pregnancy, Mikayla sat up, appreciating the hand squeeze from Amy.

"Will the baby's father be present for the labor and delivery?" Dr. Strickland asked.

Were those tears stinging the backs of her eyes? Hadn't she cried enough over that louse? When she'd first held on to hope that Scott would come around for her and the baby, she'd pictured him in the delivery room— or tried to, anyway. Not that she'd actually been able to imagine Scott Wilton there for the muck or the glory. She and her baby would be just fine. She blinked those dopey tears away and lifted her chin.

"Nope. Just me."

"And me," Amy said with a hand on her shoulder. "Here if you need me. I'll even coach you through Lamaze, not that I'd know what I was doing."

Mikayla smiled. "Thank God for girlfriends. Thank you, Amy." Between Amy and then Eva, her landlady at Sunshine Farm, Mikayla had truly comforting support.

"You know what?" Mikayla added, nodding at the doctor. "I might be on my own, but I have great friends and a very nice doctor, and I'm going to be a great mama to my little one. That's all I need to know right now."

Dr. Strickland beamed back. "I couldn't have said it better myself."

Mikayla smiled. Why did she have a feeling the doc had been waiting for her to come to those conclusions?

"See you in two weeks for the ultrasound," the doctor said. "Call if you have any questions. Even if it's after-hours, I'll get back to you right away."

Feeling a lot better about everything than she had an hour ago, Mikayla and Amy left the exam room. Mikayla checked out, and then Amy had a really good idea.

"Of course we have to go to Daisy's Donuts," Amy said, linking her arm with Mikayla's. "A gooey treat and a fabulous icy decaf something or other. To celebrate an A-OK on the little one," she added, gently patting Mikayla's very pregnant belly.

Mikayla laughed. "Lead the way."

"Jensen Jones, you listen to me! I want you out of that two-bit Wild West blip-on-the-map town this instant! You're to fly back to Tulsa immediately. Do you hear me? Immediately! If not sooner!"

Jensen shook his head as his father ranted in his ear via cell phone. Walker Jones the Second was used to his youngest son doing as he was ordered by the big man in the corner office, both at home and at Jones Holdings Inc. But Jensen always drew the line where it needed to be. When his dad was right, great. When Walker the Second was wrong? Sorry, Dad.

"No can do," Jensen said, glancing around and wondering if he was headed in the right direction for Daisy's Donuts. Apparently, that was *the* place to get a cup of coffee in Rust Creek Falls. Maybe even the only place. "I've got some business to take care of here. I should be back in Tulsa in a few days. Maybe a week. This negotiation is going a bit slower than I thought it would be."

His father let out one of his trademark snorts. "Yeah, because you're in Rusted Falls River or whatever that town is called. Nothing goes right there."

Jensen had to laugh. "Dad, what do you have against Rust Creek Falls? The land out here is amazing." It really was. Jensen was a city guy, born and bred in Tulsa, Oklahoma, and he liked the finer things in life, but out here in the wilds of Montana, a man could think. Breathe. Figure things out. And Jensen had a lot to figure out. He hadn't expected to like this town so much; hell, he'd been as shocked as his father was that three of his four older brothers had found wives in Rust Creek Falls and weren't coming home to Tulsa.

"What do I have against Rusted Dried-Up Creek?" his father repeated. "I'll tell you what," he added in one of his famous bellows. "That town is full of Jones-stealing women! There are sirens there, Jensen. Just like in the Greek myths. You'd better watch out, boy. One is going to sink her claws into you and that'll be the last your mother and I will see of you. Jones Holdings can't operate remotely! I want my sons here in Tulsa where they belong. If not all, then you. You've always been the one I could count on to listen to reason."

His poor father. The man hated not getting what he wanted. And it was rare. His mother said the man stealing in Rust Creek Falls couldn't be helped, that there was something in the water—literally. Apparently, at a big wedding a couple years ago, some local drunk had spiked the punch with an old-timey potion or something and no man was safe from the feminine wiles of Rust Creek Falls women. Especially the millionaire Jones brothers.

"Dad, I assure you, I'm not about to fall for anyone. The last thing on my mind is marriage. You've got nothing to worry about." He wasn't exaggerating for his father's sake, either. Jensen was done with love.

"Yeah, I think that's what Autry said right before he proposed to that mother of seven."

Jensen rolled his eyes. "*Three*, Dad. Three lovely little girls. Autry is very happy with Marissa. So is Walker with Lindsay. As is Hudson with Bella."

His father made a noise that sounded like a harrumph. "They were happy running Jones Holdings right here in Tulsa until those women got to them! Just come home now."

"I'll see you in a few days, Dad," Jensen said. "Speaking of women—what are you getting Mom for your fortieth anniversary?"

"That woman will be the death of me!" Walker the Second bellowed. "I— Oh, Jensen, my assistant is signaling me. Get home quick or I'll come get you myself. And I'm not kidding."

Before Jensen could say a word, a click sounded in his ear.

Now it was Jensen's turn to harrumph. His

parents' anniversary was in two weeks and his mom and dad were barely speaking. Lately, Jensen had heard the strain in their voices, seen it on their faces, and once he'd caught his mother crying when she thought she was alone in the family mansion.

As the youngest, Jensen had always fought for his brothers' respect and his parents' attention and had barely been noticed in the big crew. But Jensen was the one who cared about family dinners and holidays and birthday celebrations, insisting, even as a teenager, that his older brothers come home for his big sports games. When he was seventeen, his parents had taken him to a therapist, insisting that Jensen be cured of "caring too much," that it would make him soft when family in the Jones world meant business.

He still cared. And his parents still didn't get it.

But there was one thing his father would get his way on. Jensen *would* be coming home in a few days—once he finally convinced the most stubborn old coot in Montana to sell a perfect hundred acres of land to him for a project very close to his heart. The man, a seventy-six-year-old named Guthrie Barnes, was holding out. But Jensen was a Jones and a skilled negotiator. He'd get that land. And then he'd go home.

Because no woman, siren or otherwise, could tempt him beyond the bedroom. Adrienne, his ex, had made sure of that. He wasn't even sure if he could count her as an ex since she'd never really been his; she'd been after his money and had racked up close to a million dollars on various credit cards she'd opened in his name, then fled when he'd confronted her. The worst part? She'd admitted she'd done her research for weeks before setting her sights on him, finding out his likes and dislikes, what made him tick. When she'd engineered their meeting, the trap had been set so well he'd fallen right into it.

The bell jangled over his head as he entered the donut shop, the smell of freshly baked pastries mingling with coffee. A large, strong blast of caffeine, some sugary fortification and he'd be good to go on his plans.

Except when he looked left, all thoughts fled from his head. His brain was operating in slow motion, his gaze on a woman sitting at a table and biting into a donut with yellow custard oozing out. She licked her lips. He licked his, mesmerized.

Was it his imagination or was she *glowing*?

She had big brown eyes and long, silky brown hair past her shoulders. There was something very... lush about her. Jensen couldn't take his eyes off her—well, the half of her that was visible above the table, covered by a red-and-white-checked tablecloth. And he was aware that he was staring. She put down the donut and picked up an iced drink, then laughed at something her companion said.

A woman behind the counter, her name tag reading Eva, smiled at him. "May I help you?"

"I'd like to send refills of whatever is making those women so happy," he said, nodding his chin toward the brunette beauty.

Eva slid a glance over and raised an eyebrow. "You sure about that?"

"I'm a man who knows what he wants."

Eva grinned. "Well, then. I'll just ring you up and then bring over their refills."

"Thank you, ma'am," he said. "You can add a café Americano and a chocolate cider donut for me."

She raised another eyebrow after the *ma'am*; she couldn't be older than midtwenties, but he was a gentleman born and bred.

After handing him his much-needed coffee and donut, Eva went over to the women's table with two more donuts and two more coffee drinks. She whispered something, then lifted her chin at him. Two sets of eyes widened, and they looked over.

He locked eyes with his brunette. The most beautiful woman he'd ever seen. The woman he planned on spending the night with. He'd show her an amazing evening, give her anything her heart desired and then they'd go their separate ways, maybe not even knowing each other's last names.

Eva waved him over, and he sidled up. The brunette was staring at him. The auburn-haired friend seemed delighted by the turn of events. "Mikayla Brown, Amy Wainwright. I don't even have to ask this man's name to know he's a Jones brother. I'm right, right?" she said, looking at him.

He smiled. "Jensen Jones." He bit into the donut on his plate. Chocolate cider, his favorite. "Mmm— this donut is so good you should charge a thousand bucks for just one."

"You'd probably pay that," Eva said, shaking her head with a smile.

"Hey, my family might have done all right in business, but we're not idiots. *Two* thousand."

The three women laughed, and then the bell jangled, so Eva went back to the counter.

"Mikayla," he said, unable to take his eyes off her. "I know this is going to sound crazy. We just met. We don't know a thing about each other. But I'm going to be in town for a few days and would love for you to show me around, show me the sights—if you're free, of course."

His fantasy woman looked positively shocked. Her mouth dropped slightly open, that sexy pink lower lip so inviting, and she glanced at her friend. Both their eyes widened again, as if his asking her out, politely couched in terms of a sightseeing guide, was so unusual. The woman was beautiful, her lush breasts in that yellow sundress so damned sexy. Surely she was hit on constantly. Maybe not by millionaires, though.

Ah, Jensen thought, disappointment socking him in the gut. That was it. That was what was so unusual about his interest. She probably wasn't used to attention from a man with so many commas in his bank account.

Another gold digger? Oh, hell, what did it matter if she was? Jensen wasn't going there—never again. His heart wasn't up for grabs. Mikayla Brown was gorgeous, not wearing a ring, and he had a few days to enjoy her company—around town and in bed. He'd wine and dine her, she'd give him her *full* attention, and then they'd both go their separate ways, maybe hooking up once or twice a year when he came to Rust Creek Falls to visit his brothers. Perfect.

"Oh, I don't think I'm your type, Mr. Jones," Mikayla said. She took another bite of her donut, a hint of pink tongue catching a flick of errant custard.

He held her gaze, able to feel his desire for her in every cell of his body. "Trust me. You are."

She took a breath, lifted her chin and stood up.

Which was when it became obvious that she was pregnant.

Don't miss The Maverick's Baby-in-Waiting
by Melissa Senate,
available August 2018 wherever
Harlequin Special Edition
books and ebooks are sold.

www.Harlequin.com

"Are you going to ask when you can meet your niece?"

Grant grimaced. "You don't know that she's my niece.
You only think she is."

"It's a pretty good hunch," Ali continued. "If you're
willing to provide a DNA sample, we could know for
sure."

His DNA wouldn't prove squat, though he had no
intention of telling her that. Particularly now that they'd
become the focus of everyone inside the bar. The town
had a whopping population of 5,000. Maybe. It was
small, but that didn't mean there wasn't a chance he'd be
recognized. And the last thing he wanted was a rabid fan
showing up on his doorstep.

He'd had too much of that already. It was one of the
reasons he'd taken refuge at the ranch that his biological
grandparents had once owned. He'd picked it up for a
song when it was auctioned off years ago, but he hadn't
seriously entertained doing much of anything with it—
especially living there himself.

At the time, he'd just taken perverse pleasure in being able to buy up the place where he'd never been welcomed while they'd been alive.

Now it was in such bad disrepair that to stay there even temporarily, he'd been forced to make it habitable.

He wondered if Karen had stayed there, unbeknownst to him. If she was responsible for any of the graffiti or the holes in the walls.

He pushed away the thought and focused on the officer. "Ali. What's it short for?"

She hesitated, obviously caught off guard. "Alicia, but nobody ever calls me that." He'd been edging closer to the door, but she'd edged right along with him. "So, about that—"

Her first name hadn't been on the business card she'd left for him. "Ali fits you better than Alicia."

She gave him a look from beneath her just-from-bed sexy bangs. "Stop changing the subject, Mr. Cooper."

"Start talking about something else, then. Better yet—" he gestured toward the bar and Marty "—start doing the job you've gotta be getting paid for since I can't imagine you slinging drinks just for the hell of it."

Her eyes narrowed and her lips thinned. "Mr. Cooper—"

"G'night, Officer Ali." He pushed open the door and headed out into the night.

Don't miss
SHOW ME A HERO by Allison Leigh,
available August 2018 wherever
Harlequin® Special Edition books and ebooks are sold.

www.Harlequin.com

HARLEQUIN®

SPECIAL EDITION

Life, Love and Family

Save **$1.00**

on the purchase of ANY

Harlequin® Special Edition book.

Available whever books are sold,
including most bookstores, supermarkets,
drugstores and discount stores.

Save $1.00

on the purchase of any Harlequin® Special Edition book.

Coupon valid until September 30, 2018.
Redeemable at participating outlets in the U.S. and Canada only.
Limit one coupon per customer.

52615825

5 65373 00076 2 (8100)0 12373

® and ™ are trademarks owned and used by the trademark owner and/or its licensee.

© 2018 Harlequin Enterprises Limited

HSEHOTRCOUP0718

Looking for inspiration in tales
of hope, faith and heartfelt romance?

Check out **Love Inspired**® and
Love Inspired® Suspense books!

New books available every month!

CONNECT WITH US AT:

Harlequin.com/Community

 Facebook.com/HarlequinBooks

Twitter.com/HarlequinBooks

 Instagram.com/HarlequinBooks

 Pinterest.com/HarlequinBooks

ReaderService.com

LIGENRE2018

Love Harlequin romance?

DISCOVER.

Be the first to find out about promotions, news and exclusive content!

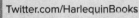

f Facebook.com/HarlequinBooks

Twitter.com/HarlequinBooks

Instagram.com/HarlequinBooks

Pinterest.com/HarlequinBooks

ReaderService.com

EXPLORE.

Sign up for the Harlequin e-newsletter and download a free book from any series at **TryHarlequin.com.**

CONNECT.

Join our Harlequin community to share your thoughts and connect with other romance readers!
Facebook.com/groups/HarlequinConnection

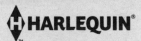

HARLEQUIN®

**ROMANCE WHEN
YOU NEED IT**

HSOCIAL2018

lover in you!

Earn points on your purchase of new Harlequin books from participating retailers.

Turn your points into **FREE BOOKS** of your choice!

Join for FREE today at **www.HarlequinMyRewards.com.**

Harlequin My Rewards is a free program (no fees) without any commitments or obligations.

MYR18